HUCKLEBERRY HILL

SADDLES & SPURS BOOK 1

EMMA SLATE

Tabula Rasa Publishing

For the Seven Brides for Seven Brothers girlies.

I can't give you a Pontipee brother, but I can give you all the vibes.

P.S. Team Benjamin

And yes, I know he can't dance.

CHAPTER ONE

THE RANCH

"Oh, shit!"

I fumbled with my keys as the grizzly bear ambled from the tree line twenty yards from the cabin's porch.

The waxing moon bathed the four-hundred-pound predator in a bright glow, yet there wasn't enough light to help me get the key into the lock.

"Come on," I muttered when the key refused to go in.

The grizzly stood on its hind legs for a moment and sniffed the air, and then charged.

"Shit, shit, shit!"

Just as the key slid into the lock, lights flicked on inside the cabin. The door opened, and before I could react, someone grabbed me by the shirt collar and yanked me inside. The door slammed behind me but the force of being pulled inside propelled me into a warm, bare chest, and we both tumbled to the ground in a blaze of tangled limbs and curses.

A grunt of pain, followed by a breath of air in my face told me I'd knocked the wind from his lungs as I lay atop him.

The scrape of claws on the wooden porch made terror churn in my stomach. There was a huff and a loud sniff.

I looked over my shoulder to make sure the door was really closed.

Bear paws thudded across the porch steps and all sound disappeared. No doubt the grizzly went back to the woods, in search of an easier midnight snack.

"I usually buy a woman a drink before winding up in this position," wheezed the man.

"Sorry," I cried, scrambling to get off him. But in my haste, I accidentally kneed him in the ribs. At least it wasn't his—

He grunted again.

"Woman, are you trying to kill me?" he rasped.

I leaned my back against the door and raised my knees to my chest.

"No," I replied. "Wait, is that a rhetorical question?"

He arched a dark brow at me.

Awareness flooded my stomach when I finally realized the man I'd fallen on wasn't wearing a shirt. And his gray sweatpants were riding ridiculously low. Low enough that I could see the V of his stomach . . . and the smattering of dark hair the same color that was on his head trailing down even farther out of sight.

He sat up and ran a hand across scruff covering his angular jaw.

"Who are you?" I demanded. "And what are you doing in my family's guest cabin?"

"Your family?" He cocked his head to the side and peered at me with blue eyes the color of a North Idaho sky before a storm. "Ah, you must be one of Connor's daughters."

"Hadley Powell," I confirmed. "And you are?"

"Declan Brewer." He flashed a pleasant grin. "The new wrangler."

"New? How new?"

I had talked to my father and grandmother recently. They hadn't mentioned a new wrangler.

"Got to Elk Ridge about a month ago." He bent his legs and stood. Declan held out a hand to me.

I took it, hating the betrayal of warmth that curled through my belly at his touch.

"Connor didn't say anything about his daughter coming home for a visit," he said.

"My trip was unexpected. I texted Dad and Muddy, but they must've already been asleep."

"Muddy?"

"Grandmother," I clarified absently. "When I was a baby and I tried to say grandmother, it came out Muddy."

"Cute."

I looked at the door. "My suitcase is outside. And my keys are still in the lock."

"Both will be there tomorrow morning," Declan remarked. "I might like a bit of danger in my life, but I'm not opening that door so a grizzly can make a spring snack out of both of us."

"Fair point," I drawled. I twisted my long, chestnut-colored hair into a messy top bun and secured it.

"Why didn't you head to the main house?"

"I didn't want to wake them up."

If I'd woken them up, then I would've had to explain why I'd come home in the middle of the night without warning. And I wasn't ready to explain it.

"Ah. And since you didn't know about me, you figured you'd crash in the cabin and head to the main house in the morning."

I nodded, my gaze dropping to his naked, sculpted chest. He had a tattoo wrapped around his upper arm like a cuff and another on his left pectoral.

"Do you have a shirt?" I asked pointedly.

"Several." He grinned. "I can lend you one to sleep in."

"Oh, that's not what I—"

"You can have the bed."

"I'm not taking the bed."

"The sheets are clean," he promised.

I sighed in exasperation. "I meant, I'm not kicking you out of your bed. I intruded on your space. I'll take the couch."

"And then I'll have to tell Connor that I let his daughter sleep on the couch? No way. Take the bed. I don't mind. Really."

I nibbled my lip and inclined my head. "That's very . . . chivalrous of you."

"Aww shucks, ma'am," he drawled with a teasing grin.

Before I knew it, I was grinning back.

No. Bad girl. No.

"Follow me. I'll get you something to sleep in," he offered.

The cabin wasn't large. It had a single small bedroom, a separate bath, and a kitchen and living room area with a wood stove.

My sister and I had spent many nights in this cabin with friends, having sleepovers and movie nights.

"You took down the twinkle lights," I stated as I stood in the doorway of the bedroom.

Declan went to the dresser and opened a drawer. "Hmm?"

"The twinkle lights. From the porch."

"Oh. Yeah, well I plugged them in and a few of the bulbs went out and the whole strand went dark." He pulled out a faded gray T-shirt and a pair of flannel boxers. "This okay?"

"I usually know a man's middle name before I wear his boxers," I joked.

"Ah, sorry. You couldn't waterboard my middle name out of me."

"It must be really embarrassing."

"It puts embarrassing to shame," he replied.

I took the clothes from him, our fingers brushing against one another. A tingle of awareness flashed through my belly. "Thanks for this."

"Sure. Bathroom's there." He pointed and then looked sheepish. "Of course you already know where the bathroom is, don't you?"

"Yep. You didn't ask why I showed up in the middle of the night."

"Figured you have your reasons." He shrugged. "Not my business."

Nodding again, I took his clothes to the small bathroom. There was a clawfoot tub and shower, and you could barely turn around. I hit my elbows as I shucked my jeans off. My cell phone clattered to the floor.

It was only 2 a.m., but my body thought it was nearly dawn due to the time change from New York. I was exhausted.

Before I left the bathroom, I sent a quick text to the group chat I shared with my twin sister and two best friends, who were also our roommates back in the city.

ME

Made it home safe. Almost got eaten by a bear. Will explain later.

I opened the bathroom door and saw Declan's sleeping arrangements on the couch.

"You hungry? Thirsty?" he asked.

"Thirsty," I said.

"I've got water and beer. And half and half."

"Water's good," I said, smiling faintly. He made a move to

get me a glass, but I held up my hand. "I've got it. You've already done enough."

"Done enough? By lending you my clothes?" His gaze dipped down my body and shivers prickled up my back.

Prickles I shouldn't have felt. But Declan had three things in his favor: chest hair, a sense of humor, and the fact that he was a cowboy. He was checking off the list of my ultimate weaknesses.

"By saving me from a bear . . . and for giving me your bed. To name a few."

He pretended to doff a nonexistent hat.

Bet he looks good in a cowboy hat and chaps.

Assless chaps.

Shit.

"I am curious about one thing, though," he said.

"What's that?"

"How did you get here? It's an hour and a half drive from the Spokane airport."

"Cab."

He raised his brows. "You got a cab to drive you all the way out here in the middle of the night?"

"I have the power of persuasion," I joked.

More like power of the pathetic.

I'd spilled the truth to a complete stranger. Luckily there still were understanding and empathetic people in this world because not only did the cabbie say he would drive me, but he'd also turned the meter off and given me a flat rate like a car service would've done.

"Huh," he stated. "Okay then."

I went into the kitchen and got myself a glass of water. I drank half of it and then put the glass into the sink.

"You good?" Declan asked.

"I'm good."

"Get into bed," he said. "I'll hit the lights."

"Thanks."

I climbed into the bed of a near total stranger, wondering why I felt more comfortable around him than the man I'd been dating for the last two years.

Not wanting to examine that feeling too closely, I shut my eyes and willed myself to relax.

The cabin went dark, and I exhaled a long, deep breath.

After a few minutes of silence, Declan called out, "Whenever I can't sleep, I count sheep."

"You do not," I said with a laugh.

"I do," he insisted. "I count blacknose sheep."

I closed my eyes and tried as he'd suggested. But every now and again, a picture of a shirtless Declan hauling a bale of hay or riding a horse entered my brain.

Soon, it was just a never-ending stream of Declan doing manly cowboy things and glistening in the sun.

I rolled over and pressed my face into his pillow. The sheets were clean, but Declan had been sleeping in them long enough that his scent was on them. Sandalwood and something else. Something that was uniquely him. Something I couldn't place.

"I'm doomed," I whispered.

There was a hot cowboy who was completely my type sleeping one room over.

It was going to be a long night.

CHAPTER TWO

The Ranch

The coffee pot gurgled, and my eyes flickered open. I held in a moan.

Jet lag combined with a lack of sleep and garnished with a heaping dose of anger had me feeling like a bread truck had hit me. Not just hit me—but run over me, backed up, and done it again for good measure.

But it was a new day. The world had kept on turning. And instead of waking up in the room I shared with my sister in New York, I'd woken up in a wrangler's bed.

And because I was insane, I pushed my head deeper into his pillow and inhaled, needing another fix of his scent.

And then I thought of *him* . . .

Gianni always smelled like expensive Italian cologne. The memory flashed and then vanished.

Realizing what I was doing, I quickly pulled away from the pillow and sat up.

I slid my legs out from underneath the covers. The

wooden floor was chilly on my bare feet. It was late spring, but the bite of winter still hung in the air.

After I used the bathroom, I came out into the living room. Declan was sitting on the couch, bare-chested, having a cup of coffee.

"You're not cold?" I blurted out.

"Nope." He looked at me, a few days of dark scruff covering his jaw. "I brought your suitcase inside. And your keys."

"Thanks."

"Coffee's on. You're welcome to pour yourself a cup."

"I should probably get over to the main house."

"Get dressed, pour yourself a cup, and I'll walk you over there. Consider me bear repellent."

He flashed a grin.

My gaze narrowed.

"What?"

"You're flirting," I said.

"Oh, so you noticed?" His grin widened. "I was flirting with you last night too. And you were kinda flirting back."

I gasped. "I was *not*."

"Hate to break it to you, bear snack, but you kinda were."

"It was late, and my life was in in danger." I crossed my arms over my chest. "But I've had a few hours of sleep now and I'm in my right mind again."

He cleared his throat.

"What?" I demanded.

He gestured with his chin at my chest.

I looked down. Due to the chill in the room, my nipples were standing at attention. Saluting General McFlirty.

"Ah, hell," I muttered. I marched over to my suitcase and grabbed my keys which rested on the handle. "I'm going to change."

"Not on my account, I hope. I like the current view," he said with a cheeky smile.

"Didn't my dad tell you the rules when you started working here?"

"Red sky in the morning, sailor take warning?"

"Powell daughters are off-limits."

"Off-limits for what?"

"Dating."

"Who said anything about dating a Powell daughter?" he inquired.

"Oh, come on." I rolled my eyes. "You've been flirting with me since the moment you met me."

"The moment I met you, you fell on top of *me*. If anything, you've been flirting with me, bear snack."

"Don't call me bear snack," I commanded.

"Why not?" he drawled. "I mean, we do go way back to last night when I saved your life. You actually woke me up out of a sound sleep. I thought I was getting burgled."

Do not smile. Do not smile. Do not smile.

"Look," I said with a sigh. "You work here. I'm going to be visiting for a few weeks before I go back to New York. Let's just be friends."

"You want to be friends?" he asked with a raise of his brows. "Men and women can't be friends."

"Sure they can."

"Hmm. No. I've seen that romantic comedy," he said.

"If we're going to argue, I need caffeine."

"I already offered you coffee. And we're not arguing. This is called banter. We're bantering."

"You were so chivalrous last night," I pointed out. "Where did that go?"

"A gorgeous woman lands on top of me, then sleeps in my clothes in my bed and then wakes up looking like *that*? A man can only control himself so much."

"You think I'm gorgeous?"

"Is that the only part you heard?"

"Nothing else seemed to matter," I murmured, hating that I was staring at his mouth. "This is bad."

"What's bad?"

I gestured between the two of us. "This. I'm talking to you like I've known you for years."

"What's wrong with that?"

"It's just . . . weird."

"Doesn't have to be." He cocked his head to the side. "So, you're visiting your family for a few weeks. And then you're going back to New York?"

"That's the plan."

The idea of going back to New York sounded dreary and tiresome. But my sister and best friends were there.

"Then we can be friends for a few weeks. You'll see, I'm a very good friend," he said.

"You just said men and women can't be friends."

"I like trying new things. Except snails. I'm not doing that."

A reluctant smile spread across my mouth. "I think your idea of friendship is different than my idea of friendship."

"All joking aside, I have no interest in getting on your father's bad side, okay? I respect him, and I like your grandmother quite a bit. And for the record, when I took this job I had no idea you were coming home to visit."

I cleared my throat. "If we're going to be friends, we should set some ground rules. For instance, friends don't walk around topless in front of each other."

"We could start a new trend."

I pointed to his bedroom. "Shirt."

"Bossy women turn me on by the way," he quipped.

"Do *not* make me middle name you," I said, trying not to laugh.

"You don't know my middle name," he reminded me.

"I'll make one up." I sighed. "That coffee really does smell good."

"There's homemade vanilla on the counter and half and half in the refrigerator," he taunted. "Come on, you know you want a cup."

"Caffeine peddler."

"So, friend," he said as he ducked into the bedroom. "Let's get to know each other a bit."

"Hmm. What do you want to know?"

"Age. For starters."

"Twenty-three," I said as I went to the cabinet. "You?"

"Thirty-two."

I didn't make a barb about the age gap between us. It would've been too easy.

"How long have you been a wrangler?" I inquired.

"First job doing it, actually," he stated. "I was a calf roper on the rodeo circuit until about six months ago."

"Rodeo, huh?" I asked as I went to pour myself a cup of coffee. "You quit? Why?"

"One too many injuries. Thought I should quit while I was ahead. What about you? What's a small-town Idaho girl doing in New York?"

"Livin' the dream, man. Just livin' the dream."

He laughed.

"How long does it take for you to put on a T-shirt?" I asked. "It feels weird having this conversation when I can't see you."

Declan stepped out of the bedroom. He'd changed out of his gray sweats into jeans, and he'd put on a black and purple flannel. He was missing the boots and cowboy hat, but thanks to counting Declan-in-chaps in bed last night I was able to visualize the full picture.

"Crap," I muttered.

He frowned. "What?"

"Never mind. My turn to change. Then I really do need to get to the house."

My phone lit up with a slew of incoming texts. Before I had a chance to reply, it vibrated with an incoming call.

"Someone's popular," Declan jested.

"My sister," I explained.

"She doesn't know you're here, does she?"

"She knows." I bit my lip.

Declan took the hint. "I'll be outside."

I took my coffee and ducked into the bedroom, shutting the door.

"What do you mean a bear tried to eat you?" Salem demanded the moment I answered my phone.

"Good morning," I replied. "I slept like shit. I'm in no mood."

"No mood? What about me? I woke up to your text this morning and nearly had a heart attack."

"I was being dramatic," I stated.

"Are you at the house?" Salem asked. "What did Dad say when he saw you?"

"He hasn't seen me yet," I said, setting my cell phone down on Declan's unmade bed. I pressed the speaker button.

"I swear to God, you're the worst storyteller in all the world. Start with the bear."

"Where are Poet and Wyn? I only want to tell this story once," I said.

"Wyn left for Sagaponack this morning with the Carrington family. And Poet's already at the office," she said. "There's no way we can all have a four-way call."

"Kinky," I joked.

"*Hadley*," Salem warned.

"Fine. Fine," I said with a sigh as I slid into my jeans. "I got here at like, two in the morning. I was going to stay in the cabin. Didn't want to wake up Muddy and Dad, you know? A grizzly charged me as I was trying to unlock the door, and that's when Declan pulled me inside."

"Declan? Who the hell is Declan?"

"The new wrangler," I explained. "I crashed in the cabin with him."

"Oh, *really?*"

"Not like that," I said with an eye roll she couldn't see. "He gave me the bed and he took the couch."

She paused for a moment. "Did you know Dad hired a new wrangler?"

"No. He hadn't told me. Neither did Muddy."

"Huh. Well, it wouldn't be like they'd tell me," Salem murmured.

"That's because you never call home."

"I call home," she protested.

"Once every few months?" Now was not the time to get into it with my sister. "Anyway, Declan's waiting to walk me to the main house. I need to go."

"Hold on. What's he look like?"

"Why does that matter?"

"Humor me."

I exhaled a puff of air. "Six three, thereabouts."

"Go on."

"Dark hair," I mumbled. "Scruff . . ."

"No," she gasped.

"Yeah." I sighed.

"Your type."

"I *know*, Salem. He also has tattoos on his pec and arm."

"How do you know he has a tattoo on his pec?"

"I saw it . . . when he pulled me inside the cabin . . . and I fell on top of him. He was—ah—shirtless."

"Well, this just got even more interesting."

"No. No it didn't," I lied. "We're friends. We're going to be friends."

"You're going to being friends with the new hot wrangler who looks like he jumped straight out of *Seven Brides for Seven Brothers?*"

"He doesn't have red hair," I pointed out. "And I didn't say he was hot."

"He's hot," she said with a laugh.

I closed my eyes and remembered the feel of his warm skin beneath my palm . . . and the trail of dark hair disappearing into the depths of his gray sweatpants.

"Might be good for you, you know," she said. "Get over Gianni by getting under a cowboy. I support it."

"Well, I don't," I remarked. "That's the last thing I need to be doing. Hooking up with Declan."

"Send me a picture."

"Absolutely not."

"Come on, you owe me."

"I *owe* you? How do you figure?" I asked with a laugh.

"Just send me a picture," she pleaded.

"And how do you suppose I should go about it? *Excuse me, Declan, can I get a photo of you to show my sister how hot you are?*"

"Ha! I knew you thought he was hot. Is he charming? Funny?"

I held in a sigh. "Yes."

"Oh, yeah, you're screwed. If you can, get a photo of him from the backside. I want to see him in a pair of jeans."

"Bye, Salem."

I hung up on my sister. I made the bed and folded the clothes Declan had lent me and put them at the foot of the mattress.

My coat was laying across the back of the couch and I put

it on. I shoved my cell phone into my pocket and then made sure I had my cup coffee.

I opened the cabin door. Declan was wearing a brown leather jacket with a fleece collar and a worn brown felt cowboy hat. He turned when he heard me, lifting his coffee cup to his lips, his eyes never leaving mine.

"Sorry," I blurted out. "My twin sister's a gabber."

"Twins, huh?" He grinned.

"She's crazier than I am."

"How's that possible?"

"Hey," I said with a laugh. "Be nice."

"Ready?"

I took a deep breath. "Yeah. Let's go." I reached for my suitcase so I could carry it down the steps, but Declan beat me to it.

"I've got it," he said.

"Thanks."

We walked in companionable silence toward the main house. I kept scanning the clearing, but everything was quiet. No sign of the bear.

The early morning sun bathed the mountains and crisp spring air caressed my cheeks. I breathed a sigh of relief at being home.

We passed empty cattle pens, but the smell of churned earth and manure seeped into my nose.

I stepped up onto the porch of the main house and turned the knob of the front door. The aroma of bacon and the crackling of grease in a pan hit me all at once and before I knew what was happening, tears had gathered in the corners of my eyes. I hastily brushed them away, not wanting Declan to see them.

He came in behind me and placed my suitcase in the foyer.

"Dad? Muddy?" I called out.

"Hadley?" Muddy yelled back. "Is that you?"

"It's me," I confirmed. "Declan's with me."

"Hey," Declan said, announcing his presence.

"Can't leave the biscuits," she hollered. "So come on in here."

Declan followed me into the kitchen. It was beautifully stained dark oak with red and white gingham curtains. Salem had tried to convince Muddy to let her redecorate, but she'd been adamant about leaving everything as it was.

My grandmother was a tall, wiry woman just shy of seventy. Her long gray hair was pulled back into a tight braid that hit the middle of her back and she wore one of my grandfather's old flannel shirts.

She set the wooden spoon down and quickly enveloped me into a tight hug. "I'm so happy to see you. But aren't you supposed to be in Italy?"

I glanced at Declan to see his reaction to that announcement, but his face was clear of emotion.

"Change of plans," I averred, pulling away from my grandmother. "Didn't you get my message?"

"Message? What message?" Muddy asked as she picked up the wooden spoon and went back to stirring the gravy.

I rolled my eyes. "I called your cell last night. You didn't answer, so I assumed you'd already gone to bed."

"I don't know where my cell phone is," she said. "It's also on silent."

I sighed. "Great. We'll never find it."

"Never say never," she said. "It's probably in my crocheting chair."

"I also called Dad last night, and his cell went to voicemail. Where is he, anyway?"

Muddy paused for a moment and then said, "Out."

"Out?" I raised my brows. "Dad is out? It's not even seven in the morning."

"You staying for breakfast, Declan?" Muddy asked instead of replying.

"If you'll have me, ma'am," he replied.

Muddy fixed him a heaping plate and did the same for me. We took our food to the dining room table and as I was peppering my gravy, the front door opened.

"Connor," Muddy called. "Your daughter came home."

"Which daughter?" came my father's low, raspy voice.

"Your favorite one," I called out.

"Salem?" Dad teased.

I laughed and scooted my chair back from the table and rose just as my dad came into the dining room. He quickly enveloped me into a bear hug, squeezing me tight.

He pulled back and dropped his arms. "Morning, Declan."

"Morning," Declan said.

"Yeah, good morning, Dad. Where were you?" I asked, hands on my hips.

"Out," he said evasively. He inclined his head. "Why are you home? You're supposed to be in Italy."

"So you didn't get my message either." I sighed.

He pulled out his cell phone and turned it on. A moment later it beeped. "Ah, yep. There's the voicemail." He looked at me. "What time did you get in?"

"Late. I took a flight out of New York around nine."

"And how did you get to the Ridge?" Dad demanded.

"Cab."

"You did *what?* You know I don't trust cab drivers."

"Relax," I said lightly. "It was either take a cab or stay the night in the airport and then have you come get me in the morning."

"I'd have preferred to come and get you," he huffed.

"Your phone was off, and Muddy lost hers," I pointed out. "How would I have gotten a ride?"

18

"I didn't lose my phone," Muddy protested. "It's just momentarily misplaced."

Dad rolled his eyes the same blue shade as mine and grinned at me. "I'm getting a plate of food and then we're having a talk."

He went into the kitchen to speak to Muddy, leaving me alone with Declan.

"So, you were supposed to be in Italy, huh?" Declan asked.

"Yep."

"Going on a solo journey?"

"My dad hates that I took a cab from the airport. How do you think he'd feel about me solo traveling?"

"So, you weren't going to Italy alone . . . Girls' trip?"

His line of questioning would eventually lead to the truth.

"Don't you have things to wrangle?" I asked pointedly.

Declan smiled. "In a bit. I still have bacon on my plate."

I grabbed the remaining slice and put it into my mouth.

His eyes widened. "You ate my bacon."

"Sure did. Now you can get on with your day."

"You ate my bacon," he said again. "Are you trying to start a fight?"

"Who's starting a fight?" Muddy asked as she came into the dining room with a plate of food.

Dad followed her.

"No one," I said.

Declan looked at Dad. "We got a bear close by. Grizzly."

"Yeah?" Dad asked. "You saw it this morning?"

"Last night. When I prevented it from eating your daughter."

I glared at him.

"Hadley?" Muddy asked, her gaze bouncing between me and Declan. "Something you want to tell us?"

"I got home late last night and I didn't want to wake you guys up. I was going crash in the cabin. I didn't realize that the cabin was occupied," I said pointedly. "I was having trouble getting the door open. The bear came out of nowhere and it would've gotten me if Declan hadn't pulled me inside."

"So you slept in the cabin?" Muddy asked with a raise of her brows.

"Yes," I said.

"I gave her the bed," Declan added quickly. "And I took the couch."

Dad looked at Declan, his expression tightening. Declan didn't appear at all put out and I silently cheered him. Not many men could withstand what my dad threw down. He was a tough man. An old-school rancher with the grit and strength to back up his statements. But where his daughters were concerned, he was a big softie. People talk about women, but Hell hath no fury like an overprotective father trying to keep a charming cowboy away from one of his daughters.

"Well, I better get to work," Declan said, rising from his chair. "Thanks for breakfast."

"Leave the dish in the sink," Muddy said. "I'll take care of it."

Declan took his plate into the kitchen and then a few moments later, the front door opened and closed.

"All right," Dad said. "It's just the three of us now. You wanna tell me why you're home and not in Italy with your fiancé?"

CHAPTER THREE

THE RANCH

"Gianni and I broke up," I said flatly. "So, going to Italy with him would've been a *very* bad idea."

Muddy stopped eating and Dad's cup of coffee had been halfway to his lips when I'd dropped the truth bomb.

"When did you break up?" Muddy asked finally.

"A week ago," I said, my chest pinching with pain.

"A week?" Muddy repeated. "A week ago, and you didn't tell us?"

"I wasn't ready to share the news," I mumbled. "After a few days of wallowing, Salem thought it would be good for me to come home for a while. Wyn and Poet agreed."

Dad still hadn't said anything. I looked at him and waited.

He set his coffee mug down and shoved back from the table. Without a word, he strode from the house, the front door slamming shut.

"What was that about?" I asked Muddy.

"Pretty sure your father is about to have some words with the new wrangler."

"About what?"

"About you." Muddy grinned.

"What about me?"

"Not to go near you. Especially now that you're newly single and ripe for the picking."

"Ripe? I'm not ripe. I'm heartbroken."

"Are you?" Muddy murmured.

I glared at her. "Don't do that."

"Don't do what?"

"Get all witchy on me."

Muddy laughed as she picked up her coffee cup. "Don't think I didn't notice how Declan was looking at you. Or how you were looking at him."

"You couldn't have noticed. You were cooking."

"Wasn't looking with my eyes, honey. I heard the two of you. Sparks, m'dear. You two have sparks."

I kept silent.

"I like Declan," Muddy continued.

"Hmm."

"I can see his appeal. Handsome devil."

"I hadn't noticed," I lied.

"Dark hair, too. Tall. Chin dimple. Your type right?"

"*Muddy.*"

Muddy sniggered, but then she sobered. "It's none of my business how you get over your breakup. But I will give you a piece of unsolicited advice—if you want Declan to keep his job, you'll steer clear of him."

"I have no intention of going near him."

Muddy looked at me, steady. Her hazel eyes burned gold with intensity. "Why are you really home?"

"To get over my breakup."

She picked up her fork. "You never were a good liar, Hadley. And living in New York hasn't changed that."

I didn't know how to respond to her, but I didn't have to. The front door opened, and Dad came inside and retook his seat.

"What did I miss?" Dad asked.

"Nothing," Muddy said. "What did you say to Declan?"

"I told him if he didn't want to be gelded, then he needs to stay far away from Hadley."

"*Dad*," I groaned. "You're so embarrassing."

He pointed his fork at me. The end of it was covered in gravy-drenched biscuit. "I don't care that you're a grown woman or that you can make your own decisions. Declan is a wrangler on this ranch first and foremost, and he will *not* be wrangling you."

"Can we please talk about something else?"

"Why did you and Gianni break up?" Dad finally asked.

"Because we realized we wanted different things," I said. It wasn't the whole truth, but it was close enough that hopefully my family wouldn't ask any more questions.

"Sorry, honey," Dad murmured.

"Thanks. I'm moving forward. Can we not talk about it anymore?"

"We've barely talked about it at all," Muddy said.

I looked at her.

"Fine, your prerogative," she said.

"Why didn't Salem come home with you?" Dad demanded.

"Because Salem has to work," I replied. "She can't just take a month off to come home."

"No, maybe not," Dad allowed. "But she could've spared a few days, don't you think?"

"She's up for a big promotion," I said. "She's keeping her nose to the grindstone."

"Good for her," Muddy said. "It's taken her a while to find something she loves and wants to pursue. We should all be supportive of that. Shouldn't we, Connor?"

My father grunted.

"She'll be home for Christmas," I said.

"That's nearly ten months away," Dad groused. "You're staying the full month you were supposed to be in Italy, right? You're not thinking of running back to New York in a week, are you?"

"I'm staying the month," I assured him. "The restaurant is closed for renovations. And I talked to my boss at the stables and he took me off rotation for a while. So, I'm free as a bird."

My phone buzzed with a text from Poet in our group chat. It was quickly followed by Wyn.

I turned my phone over so I couldn't see the screen constantly lighting up.

"I'll take your suitcase upstairs," Dad said. "And put it in your room."

"Thanks." I rose from the table and grabbed my plate. I leaned down and brushed a kiss to my grandmother's cheek. "Thanks for breakfast. Leave the dishes. I'll do them for you later."

"You look exhausted," Muddy said. "You should take a nap."

"Nah. If I nap, I won't be able to sleep tonight." I went into the kitchen and set my plate in the sink.

Dad went to the front room and lifted my suitcase. I followed him up the stairs, stopping off at the linen closet and grabbing a set of clean sheets.

"Here we go," Dad said as he pushed open my childhood bedroom door and placed the suitcase upright by the big window that faced the front of the property. I had an unencumbered view of the pens and corrals. I didn't see Declan, though, and I immediately hated that I was looking for him.

"I'm taking a few of the boys and riding out," Dad said. "I want to get a handle on the bear situation. See what that's about."

Nodding, I set the sheets down on the bed and glanced at my phone.

"You mind if I take the truck to town?" I asked.

"Have at it." He hugged me again. "I'm glad you came home, honey. It hasn't been the same since you and Salem left."

I buried my face in my father's flannel shirt. I breathed in, expecting him to smell like his favorite Oak Barrel cologne and saddle soap.

But the faintest trace of jasmine perfume lingered on his collar.

I pulled away from him.

"I'll bring you something from Sweet Teeth," I said, turning away. "Want anything in particular?"

"Whatever Gracie's newest experiment is," he said. "Tell her I said hello."

"Will do."

Dad left and closed the door behind him.

He'd stayed the night with a lady friend, and he hadn't wanted to tell me.

That was fine. I had secrets of my own.

I turned my attention back to my phone. Because I hadn't answered in a timely manner, Poet had called twice. Wyn texted sporadically.

ME

> Too much to explain via text. FaceTime tonight?

My phone blew up immediately with replies.

25

POET

Yes!

WYN

I'm free after 7 EST. Gotta put the kid to bed first. Can't expect the parents to do it.

SALEM

That works for me.

POET

Me too.

I opened the bedroom window to get some fresh air. I heard the whinny of a horse coming from the stables and I longed to get in a ride.

ME

I'm running on fumes so the conversation won't be long.

SALEM

I'm still waiting on a picture.

WYN

Picture? Picture of what?

SALEM

The new wrangler that saved Hadley from the bear.

POET

Whaaaat?! Details! This can't wait until tonight.

ME

It'll have to.

WYN

Edger. You're an edger of information.

I set my phone on the nightstand and then made the bed

before sitting on the edge of the mattress, staring off into space. My gaze caught on the framed photograph on the nightstand.

A family photo. Salem and I were twelve and making goofy faces at the camera while my mother and father stared at one another in blissful adoration.

I ran a finger across my mother's face. "Miss you, Mom."

My mind immediately went back to the scent clinging to my father's collar.

I wouldn't bring it up to him. Nor would I mention it to Salem. It would only make her lose her cool.

With a groan of exhaustion, I hoisted myself up. I pocketed my cell phone before padding downstairs.

I quickly loaded the dishwasher and set it to run. Then I grabbed the truck keys, my coat, and was out the door.

CHAPTER FOUR

Town

"Hadley Powell!"

I turned at the screech and smiled as a dimpling woman with wrinkles at the corners of her eyes came out from behind the counter.

"Hi, Lucy," I said as the older woman embraced me.

"Your daddy was in here the other day, and he said you were headed off to Italy," she said as she pulled back. "That's so glamorous."

I held in a sigh. "Change of plans. I came home for a bit."

"Hmm."

"I just stopped in to buy some socks," I said, wanting to change the subject away from Italy as soon as possible. "And then I'm headed over to Sweet Teeth."

"Oh, we just got a bunch of socks in. My favorite are the ones with campfires and s'mores on them. Cute as can be." She hiked up her jeans to show off her ankles.

"They are cute," I agreed.

"Let me show you all the new socks and then you let me know if you need anything else."

"I will. Good to see you, Lucy."

General Merc was the town's one-stop mercantile shop for farm and hunting equipment. They sold raw milk and local eggs, too, but for actual groceries you could either go to Dusty's or to Silver Springs, the next town over. For any serious farm equipment or replacement parts you either had to order it or make the forty-five-minute drive to Coeur d'Alene.

I was in the middle of perusing the socks when I heard the heavy clomp of cowboy boots across the wooden floor.

"These are so you," Declan said, reaching in front of me to grab a pair of socks with a pink cow print.

"What are you doing here?" I asked with a frown.

"Connor asked me to pick up some trail cams. For the bear."

"Oh," I said.

"You buying socks?"

"Yep. I forgot to pack them," I said.

In my haste to leave New York, I'd thrown a bunch of clothes into my suitcase without much thought.

"Uh-oh," I murmured.

"What?"

"Nothing."

He raised his brows. "Not nothing."

"Can you go over there?" I asked, pointing to the other end of the store.

"Why?"

"Because I just realized that I also forgot to pack under-wear," I mumbled. "And I need to buy that too."

He let out a low chuckle, but thankfully he didn't say anything flirty. Instead, he sauntered up to the counter and began talking to Lucy.

29

I snatched a few pairs of socks, along with two packages of plain white undies and headed to the register.

"Welcome to Huckleberry Hill, Declan," Lucy said. "Here, have a candy." She held out a glass dish that had saltwater taffy in it.

"How did you know I have a thing for sugar?" Declan asked, looking at me and winking.

I rolled my eyes.

Lucy laughed and then glanced at me. "I can put your things on your father's tab."

"Nah, I'll pay," I said. I reached for my purse and then realized I didn't have it on me. "Never mind. I forgot my wallet."

"Tab it is then," Lucy said. She took my purchases and placed them in a brown paper bag and attempted to hand it back to me, but Declan took it before I could, adding it to his bag.

Lucy's sigh was dreamy as she looked at Declan. "Have a good day."

"We will." Declan winked again and filched another piece of taffy.

We stepped out of General Merc onto the sidewalk. As I headed in the direction of the bakery, Declan kept pace with me. The sun beat down on my face and I breathed in the crisp, cool air.

"Where to next?" Declan asked.

"Sweet Teeth," I said. "The bakery. You been yet?"

He shook his head.

"Gracie's a friend from high school. Her husband's family owns the bakery," I said. "I was going to stop in and say hi."

"I'm yours to command," Declan joked. "So, Italy . . . why were you going to Italy?"

"Italian food," I quipped.

"I've noticed you divert people's attention with humor when you don't want to answer a question."

"Astute of you to notice."

"So, Italy?" he pressed.

"Why so curious?"

"Why so secretive?" he pushed back. "Just trying to get to know you, buddy."

"Inquisitions aren't the way to do it, *friend*."

Declan opened the door to Sweet Teeth, and I walked in first. The bakery didn't look at all like a bakery. It had a rustic, cozy cottage vibe, with heavy wooden tables that were much more suited to a beer hall, several plants hanging from hooks, and a skylight in the A-line roof.

I took out my phone and did a quick video, landing on Declan.

"Say hi."

"Who am I saying hi to?"

"My sister and my friends," I said.

"Hi ladies," Declan drawled.

I ended the video and shot it off to the group text. "Thanks. My roommate Poet loves places like this. I wanted to show it to her."

"Ah."

We stepped up to the counter to order. I didn't recognize the young barista.

"Hi," I greeted with a smile. "Is Gracie here?"

"Who's taking my name in vain?" Gracie yelled from the kitchen.

"The friend that kept your hair out of the toilet on prom night," I called.

A moment later, my old friend popped out from the back, her cheeks pink from the bakery oven and her blonde curls a riotous mass.

She came around the counter and quickly embraced me. "I didn't think I'd see you until Christmas."

I didn't say anything as she released me.

"You have time for a coffee and a chat? Or are you just stopping by?"

"I have a few minutes," I said.

"Excellent." She turned her attention to Declan. "And who are *you*?"

Declan grinned. "Declan Brewer. The new wrangler for Connor Powell."

"Wrangler, huh?" Gracie smiled.

"Just started," Declan confided. "Still getting the lay of the land."

"Well, your first order is on the house as a welcome gift." Gracie looked at me. "Yours too."

"But I'm from here," I said with a smile.

"I insist," Gracie said. "Coffee, Declan?"

"Can't. I rode my motorcycle to town. So I'll take a donut to go, please. Thanks, Gracie."

"Motorcycle?" I asked.

He looked at me, blue eyes twinkling. "If you can ride a Harley, you can ride a horse."

Ride? I wanna ride . . .

I gulped.

He extracted my bag and handed it to me. "Here's your underwear."

"*Declan*," I hissed, causing him to laugh.

"I've got your donut," the barista said to Declan. Her cheeks were pink and they turned a deeper shade of red when he shot her an easy grin and dropped some cash into the tip jar.

"See you later," he said to me.

The three of us watched him saunter out of the bakery.

"Wow," Gracie remarked.

"Yeah," the barista sighed. "Major wow."

"He's not *that* wow," I lied.

"Uh-huh," Gracie said. "Sure. What do you want to drink?"

"A London Fog, please."

"What the hell is a London Fog?" Gracie demanded.

"You know what? How about a chai tea?"

"Coming right up. Abby, will you take care of that?"

"Sure thing."

"And bring an assorted plate of pastries, will ya?"

"Absolutely."

Gracie waved me toward the farthest table tucked back into a corner. "Okay," she said after we sat down. "First of all, did your fiancé come home for a visit with you?"

I rubbed my third eye. "I don't have a fiancé anymore. Gianni and I broke up. That's kind of why I'm home for a bit. To get my bearings, you know?"

"Oh." She frowned. "I'm so sorry. Are you okay?"

Nodding, I also shrugged.

"Are you thinking of rebounding with Declan?"

Abby set the pastries and chai down on the table. "You should totally rebound with Declan."

"I'm not rebounding with Declan," I said adamantly.

"Then what was with all the flirting?" Abby asked.

"He flirts with everyone," I remarked.

"Yeah, maybe," Gracie allowed. "But you flirted back."

"I didn't!"

"You so did," Gracie said. "Plus, he flirted *differently* with you."

"Yeah, he did," Abby agreed.

"Flirted differently? What does that even mean?" I demanded.

"If you can ride a Harley, you can ride a horse?" Gracie repeated. "Come on. That's *so* hot."

33

"Yeah." Abby fanned herself. "If you don't want him, you mind if I ask him out?"

I gritted my teeth and then forced a smile. "He's a little old for you, don't you think?"

Abby lifted her brows. "I'm twenty-one. How old is he?"

"Thirty-two," I said.

"Huh. I'll take him for a test drive. Gotta see about his stamina, you know?"

Her words made my vision flash red. The lizard part of my brain sparked with jealousy. I curled my hands into fists and shoved them into my lap before I did something stupid like wring her neck.

The front door opened and a trio of customers walked in, pulling Abby back to the counter.

"Easy, champ," Gracie said with a wry smile. "Your cheeks are flushed, and you look like you're about tackle my best barista to the ground."

I swallowed. "She's really your best barista?"

"Yes."

"Damn it," I muttered.

Gracie frowned. "You seem more upset about Abby asking Declan out than you do about the loss of your fiancé. Am I reading that wrong?"

"We broke up a week ago," I said slowly, ignoring her comment about Declan completely. "I've already started the grieving process. Don't want to look behind me and dwell."

"That sounds healthy. Why does that sound so healthy?"

"Salem wanted me to donate all his clothes to the thrift store." I grinned. "So when he comes home from Italy, he'll have nothing. She's feral. So, I have to be the healthy one."

"I wouldn't want to get on Salem's bad side." She cocked her head. "Did she come home with you?"

"She couldn't. I took time off work because I was

supposed to go to Italy with Gianni, but yeah . . . I came home instead."

"Ah." She pushed the plate of pastries toward me. "Your dad and grandmother must be happy to have you home."

"They are." I picked up a lady-finger-looking pastry and took a bite. "Oh, this is good. I promised my dad I'd bring home a grab bag of your pastries. So remind me before I leave to get a box."

"Will do," she said. "So, what's your plan while you're home?"

"Ride, spend time with my grandmother and father. Other than that, not much."

Lick my wounds while trying not to lick Declan.

My spine snapped straight, and I forced that unwelcome thought out of my head.

"Well, you can't head back to New York before the mushroom festival," Gracie said.

"We'll see."

I didn't want to commit to anything long-term. I'd had enough long-term to last me a while.

"So, tell me . . . how great is married life?" I asked.

"You think I'm going to talk about how happily married I am when you just ended an engagement?"

"I want you to," I pressed. "I need to remember that there are people who get their happily-ever-afters."

"If you insist, but I'm not bragging or anything," she said with a grin.

"You can brag a little," I said with a laugh.

She pulled out her cell phone. "We're great, actually. I caught Bella napping on Cole the other day and I got a picture."

Gracie swiped through her phone and then turned the screen to me. Her one-year-old daughter was asleep on her husband's chest.

A pang shot through my heart.

"Adorable," I croaked.

Gracie looked up at me, her gaze shrewd. "You okay?"

"Yeah." Emotion tightened my throat. "Just a reminder that I won't have that with Gianni."

"Shit, I'm sorry. I told you I didn't want to talk about this."

"No, don't do that," I stated. "I'm happy you're happy. You've had enough shit happen to you."

She nodded thoughtfully. "Plenty of shit in this world. And we all go through it, don't we?"

"Yeah, we do." I sighed and looked at my phone, noting the time. "I better get home. Box me up your favorite pastries, will ya?"

CHAPTER FIVE

The Ranch

I set the box of pastries on the kitchen table and then stripped off my coat. I stood there for a moment, unmoving.

The front door opened and Muddy walked in.

"You're back," she said unnecessarily.

I nodded. "I brought pastries."

"You look like you're asleep where you're standing," she commented. "Seriously, Hadley. Take a nap. An hour at least."

"Yeah," I murmured.

I still didn't move.

"Stairs." She gently pushed me in the direction of the staircase.

I held up the bag from General Merc. "I need to do some laundry."

"I'll take care of it." She took the bag from me and peered inside. "These are cute." She pulled out the campfire and s'mores socks.

"I thought so too."

She then pulled out the package of underwear. "Are you trying to be celibate?"

"Muddy!" I hissed.

Muddy let out a cackle. "Just kidding. But seriously. I wouldn't even wear these. They're granny panties for sure."

"I so didn't need to know that." I rolled my eyes. "It was all Lucy had on hand. And I forgot to pack underwear." I groaned.

"What?"

"I ran into Declan at the store and he saw me buy these." I buried my face in my hands. "I'm going to shower and then lay down for a bit. I'll help you with dinner prep, okay?"

"Sounds good, sugar." She smirked.

"Stop looking at me that way."

"What way is that?"

"Like you know something I don't."

"When you've been around the sun as many times as I have, you'll smirk like I am too."

"Well, it would be a privilege to have as much wisdom as you."

"Who said anything about wisdom?"

I hugged her. "You're so sassy. I love it."

"You've got a bit of my sass."

"Not as much as Salem," I said, pulling back.

Muddy sighed. "Salem . . . What are we going to do about her?"

"We're going to let her be who she needs to be." I squeezed Muddy's arm and then headed up the stairs.

My bedroom was chilly and I quickly shut the window, but not before I got a good look at the pen outside. Declan was on horseback, his broad shoulders fully displayed.

"Nope. Not doing that." I hastily shut the curtains, but temptation was on the other side of it.

I'd just broken up with my fiancé, a man I'd been

prepared to share my life with. Broken promises and broken dreams aside, there was no reason for me to be lusting after the cowboy who rode a motorcycle, had a smile that made me quiver, and enough swagger that he could give some away to others and still have plenty left over.

There was a full bathroom that was sandwiched between Salem's bedroom and mine. It had a double sink, a huge tub, and enough drawer space for all of our hair products and makeup.

I smiled when I thought about getting ready for school. We'd share the bathroom, talk about the boys we thought were cute, and I'd put the lip gloss in my backpack and she'd stuff the blue eye shadow we weren't allowed to wear in hers.

A pang of longing went through my chest.

My phone rang.

I smiled when I saw the name flash across the screen.

"How did you know?" I asked the moment I picked up the phone.

"Twin thing," Salem said. "I felt the call. So, I called. But also, *hot damn*. Your wrangler is next-level attractive."

"He's not *my* wrangler," I grumbled.

"He could be your wrangler. I want to put my finger in his chin dimple."

"Don't you fucking dare."

"Oh, someone's feeling territorial already. Rawr!"

"I hate you a little bit," I mumbled.

"Only because I'm calling you on your shit. Have Wyn and Poet seen the video you sent?"

"Doubt it. I haven't gotten any calls from them."

"Yet. Give it time. But seriously, talk to me. I have a few minutes before my next meeting. So speak fast."

"I was just in our bathroom, thinking about high school, and how much I miss you."

A beat passed. "I miss you too."

"Should I have stayed in New York?" I asked. "I feel like I ran home with my tail between my legs. But when I'm with you, I'm home, too. Wherever you are."

"How much sleep have you gotten?"

"Only a few hours. I was about to shower and take a nap."

"You need it. You can't think straight when you're tired. That's true for everyone. But let me say this. I would've loved for you to stay here for a month, but to what end? To sit alone and wallow in the apartment?"

"I wouldn't have been alone. You would've been there. And Poet. And Wyn when she came back from the Hamptons."

"Yeah, but you still would've been revolving around us and our lives. For once you need to be the center of your own world. And let's be real, there's no place you'd rather be than the Ridge. You wouldn't even have been in New York if it wasn't for me. So really, it's my fault you met Gianni in the first place and got your heart broken."

"I'm not going to blame you for my terrible taste in men."

"Okay, fine, but what really happened between you two?"

"What do you mean?"

"I mean, one minute you were engaged and ready to go to Italy with him. The next, you two were broken up and he went to Italy without you."

"At least he didn't wait to break up with me until we were in Italy," I lamented.

"Yes, at least the bastard didn't get a chance to ruin Italy for you. Offer still stands. I can go to his apartment and set his suits on fire."

I laughed. "I thought you said you'd donate them."

"Mashed or smashed. Same difference."

"The saying is *potato potahtoh.*"

"We're from Idaho. Mashed or smashed. Never mind,

we're way off topic. Are Muddy and Dad happy as pigs in shit to have you home?"

"Yeah, they're happy I'm here. But they miss you."

She fell silent.

"They want to see you before Christmas."

"Yeah." She snorted. "So Dad can tie a rope to my ankle and keep me on the ranch until I die. No thanks."

"I am to homebody as you are to nomad," I quipped.

"I would fly out there," she said. "My own issues aside—if you really needed me. Do you? Need me?"

I wanted her home with me because she was my best friend. But that would be selfish, knowing how hard it was for Salem to be at the Ridge.

"I think I'm doing okay," I admitted.

She let out a sigh of relief. "Good. I mean, the offer stands. But you know the minute I come home, all the focus will be on me because I'm the drama. You deserve their undivided attention and to be doted on."

"It's true. I do deserve that," I quipped.

"I don't mean to do it, you know."

"Do what?"

"Steal the thunder."

"You never steal the thunder."

"Liar."

"Okay. How about I never *care* that you steal the thunder. And I really mean that."

"That, I'll believe." She chuckled.

"I went into Sweet Teeth. Gracie says hi."

"Ah, now I'm jonesing for the best honey-glazed donut in all the land. Tell her I said hi back."

"I will."

"The apartment isn't the same without you here," she murmured.

"I'll be back."

She snorted.

"What?" I demanded.

"I know you better than anyone. I know you better than I know myself."

"That's because your mind is like a dark attic full of cobwebs and moldy boxes that you refuse to open."

"What a visual. Thanks. I guess the truth is I'd be very surprised if you ever came back."

"I'll be back," I insisted.

"Why?"

"Why? What do you mean *why?*" I asked.

"I mean, you hate New York."

"I don't."

"You do. You *so* do. Hadley, you're a small-town girl and New York is a massive, lonely city full of millions of people you'll never interact with."

"Then why do you like it?"

"Exactly for that reason. I can be anyone here and no one notices or cares. But you, you're always going to be *you*. Small-town ranch girls who love their families and want to raise their kids riding horses don't belong here. Gianni was . . . an experiment. An experiment that went awry."

"The whole damn lab blew up in my face," I muttered. Exhaustion pulled at my emotions, lodging them free. "I wasn't entirely honest with you . . ."

"About what?"

"About why Gianni and I broke up."

"Because he's a douche canoe?"

"No. It's because when I told him I was unable to give him children, he lied and said it didn't matter. That we'd be okay . . . but then two days later he broke up with me. Over the phone."

When she didn't reply, I pressed, "Salem?"

"You can't have children?"

"No."

"But—how did you—when did you find out? And why didn't you tell me?"

"I found out about two weeks prior to my breakup. And I was . . . processing."

Mourning.

"I wasn't ready to tell anyone," I said softly. "Not even you."

"I'm not just anyone. I'm your twin. Fuck, I knew something deeper was going on. I just *knew* it."

"I had to tell Gianni because . . . well, because . . ."

She sighed. "Yeah. Okay. Fuck, Hadley."

"Don't pity me," I commanded. "I can't take pity."

"It's not pity," she assured me. "But how about some empathy?"

"That, I'll take."

"Well, I think this is fucking great."

"*Excuse me?*" I snapped.

"Not the news. The news sucks. But there's a silver lining in all of this. You found out what Gianni was made of *before* you tied the knot."

I sighed. "There is that, yeah."

"Can you imagine being married to him and then finding out something like that? You need a man built of stronger stuff. Gianni doesn't deserve you. I never thought so. This just confirms it."

"Thanks, Salem," I said softly.

"Have you told Dad? Or Muddy?"

"No. I haven't been able to talk about it—until now. They know there's more to my breakup than I'm letting on. They're not stupid."

"No, they're not. You're also a terrible liar. You know how I knew something deeper was going on? You didn't drink," she said. "When you drink you get loose-lipped. I should've

43

gotten you schnockered and then you would've spilled the beans."

"I'm afraid to drink," I admitted. "Because what if I drink and then start crying?"

"Crying is okay. Crying is cathartic."

"Says the girl who hasn't cried in years."

"I prefer breaking dishes to crying. Anger is better. Anger is the fuel for change."

"If I was going to drink, I'd want to drink with you, Wyn and Poet. You guys . . . you make me feel safe, you know?"

"I know," she murmured.

"Don't tell them," I said. "I'm not ready for them to—I'm still coming to grips with it."

"Anything I can do?"

"Just be you."

"Whew, I thought you were going to ask me something hard," she teased. Her tone changed. "I'm sorry, Hadley. About the news."

"Yeah." Tears prickled my eyes. "Me too."

There was a murmur of conversation on the other end followed by Salem saying, "I'm sorry, Hadley. I gotta get to that meeting. I'll talk to you tonight."

"Thanks, twin."

"Any time."

I hung up with my sister, missing her more than ever. I was glad she knew the truth. But I was coated in shame. Shame that my fiancé had left me because I wasn't perfect.

I'm broken.

I hoisted myself off the bed and went to shower. And before I curled up in my childhood bed, I peeked through the curtains of the window, wondering if the dark-haired cowboy biker was the leaving type.

CHAPTER SIX

THE RANCH

My phone vibrated, waking me. I reached for it on the nightstand, wondering who could possibly be calling me.

I looked at the time and realized it was 7 p.m. on the East Coast and my catnap had turned into a three-hour-long coma.

I pressed the answer button. Salem and Poet's faces filled the screen.

"We woke her up," Poet said as she pushed up the black glasses on her nose.

"Hey there, sleepy head," Salem joked. "You ready for our four-way?"

"Can I stay in this exact position?" I asked, my face smushed into the pillow.

"Fine by me," Salem said. "Hang on, Wyn's calling in."

My other roommate's face appeared in the corner. She had a glass of wine in her hand and her blonde hair was in a messy top bun. "Okay, I'm here."

Poet tucked a strand of hair behind her ear. "Okay. Start at the beginning. Now that I have a visual of Declan, I can fully picture the story when you tell it."

"Yeah, like, wow. They grow them hot and tall in Idaho," Wyn said.

"You voluntarily left Idaho?" Poet asked Salem. "You traded chaps for suits? You're insane."

"So this bear," Salem said, glossing past Poet's comment. "How big are we talking?"

I told them the story. Salem kept smirking at me because she already knew the nitty gritty details.

"He was *shirtless?*" Poet gasped.

"He gave you his bed?" Wyn asked. "Did you sniff his pillow?"

"No," I denied.

"You lie." Poet giggled.

"So, when are you having sex with him?" Wyn asked bluntly.

"I'm not," I stated emphatically. "Aside from Dad's number-one rule on the ranch—you don't mess around with a Powell daughter—I'm not ready to date anyone right now."

"Who said anything about dating?" Poet asked. "Get your jollies."

"You are so PG," Wyn said with a laugh.

"You're an idiot," Salem told me.

"I'm not an idiot," I defended.

"You're an idiot if you don't ride that cowboy," Salem added. "He's so your type."

"*That's* your type?" Poet asked. "And you were going to marry Gianni?"

"Hadley was trying to prove something," Salem stated.

"I wasn't trying to prove anything," I defended. "That's your territory."

"Ouch," Salem said lightly. "But yeah, that's true."

"No but seriously," Wyn said. "He's hot. Does he have anything else going for him?"

"He's quippy," I admitted. "A quippy cowboy."

"Ah, so he's smart and masculine," Poet said longingly. "I'm surrounded by oat milk men in skinny jeans."

"When I saw that video of Declan, I swear I could feel the testosterone through the phone," Wyn said. She took a drink of wine. "Hang on a second." She paused for a moment. "Crap. The kid needs me."

She set her phone and wine down and momentarily left our conversation.

"How was your meeting?" I asked Salem.

"Good," she said. "Don't change the subject."

"Have to," I said. "At least while Wyn's gone. Can you do me a favor?"

"What?"

"Go to Gianni's apartment and get the few things I left there, and then leave the key with the security desk. My engagement ring is in the nightstand. Will you take that to his place, too?"

Salem's eyes saddened. "Yeah, twin. I'll take care of it."

"I'll go with her," Poet added. "Wouldn't want her to do something Mount St. Salem like."

Salem wrinkled her nose, pretending to be offended. "What would I do?"

"Your sister just had her heart broken. What *wouldn't* you do in the name of revenge?" Poet demanded.

Salem paused. "Yeah, you should come with me."

The corner square shook and a moment later Wyn appeared again. "Okay, what did I miss?"

"Nothing," I assured her. "How are you liking this new family?"

"It's okay," Wyn said. "The dad is never around. He works like ninety hours a week. The mom is a part-time parent, but whenever she feels guilty, she just gives me money. The kid though. He's a fucking trip. Little boys. Whew. Exhausting."

I caught Salem looking at me, her expression intense.

There was a knock on my bedroom door. "Hadley?"

"Come in," I called to Dad.

He opened the door and stepped into the doorway. "You're awake. I wasn't sure. I checked on you earlier and you were snoring like a buzz saw."

There was laughter on the other end of my phone.

"Who you talking to?" Dad asked. "Salem?"

I nodded. "And Wyn and Poet." I flipped the camera around. "Say hi."

Dad waved.

"Hi, Mr. Powell!" Poet said.

"Looking snazzy, Mr. Powell," Wyn added.

Dad grinned. "You guys coming to the ranch for Christmas?"

"Wouldn't miss it," Poet said.

"Hopefully I can get the time off," Wyn said. "But yes, count me in."

My father and Salem still hadn't actually said anything directly to one another.

"Well, I'll let you get back to your conversation," Dad said, his face blanking. He looked at me. "I'll be downstairs."

Dad retreated and closed the door behind him.

"I stand corrected," Wyn said. "I understand why you won't have sex with Declan. Your dad looks like he could kill a man with his bare hands."

"Elk Ridge is a thousand acres," Salem said. "No one would find Declan's body."

"You're joking," Poet said. "Tell me you're joking."

"About the size of the ranch? Never. You know size always matters," Salem said.

"Okay, I'm seeing myself out of this conversation," I

announced. "Dad looked like he wanted to talk to me about something. I better go find out what it's about."

"Talk to you later," Wyn said. "I'm signing off too and watching Netflix in bed."

"I've got a hot date with the slush pile," Poet said. "Though they really should call it the flush pile. Where creative books go to die."

"What about you?" I asked Salem. "Any fun plans tonight?"

"I actually have to change and go have a drink with my boss. Networking thing," she said.

"So glamorous," Wyn said. "I'm about to put on my under-eye patches."

"Over and out," I said before clicking off.

My phone darkened and I set it on the nightstand. I swung my legs over the side of my bed and sat there for a moment, letting the last of the sleep clear from my brain.

I finally got up and went to my closet to pull out an old hoodie that was two sizes too big. It was worn, faded, and so comfortable. Salem hadn't allowed me to bring it to New York, but every time I was home, I lounged around in it.

Dad was sitting at the dining room table, glasses on the end of his nose as he looked over a stack of papers.

"Tell me why life gets summed up in bills and useless paperwork?" Dad asked without looking up.

"You could have everything sent electronically," I pointed out. "Save on the hassle of having to shred everything."

"And paper cuts," he said, finally giving me his attention. "And do you really think I'm going to switch everything to a computer when I still have a landline?"

"You're a regular time capsule." I leaned down and kissed his cheek.

"You slept hard," he commented. "I thought about waking

you up so you wouldn't have trouble sleeping tonight, but Muddy told me to let you be."

"Thanks," I said. "Need anything while I'm up?"

"Orange juice, please," he said.

I wandered into the kitchen toward the refrigerator. "You wanted to talk to me about something, didn't you?"

"Yeah, I did. I had Declan and the boys ride out and place the trail cams so we can find where the bear is roaming. I don't want you walking to the stables alone at night."

"What makes you think I'll go to the stables at night?" I opened the cabinet and pulled out two glasses.

"I know you," he said. "Whenever you've got something on your mind, you go to the stables."

"So what's the solution?" I poured the orange juice and then put the carton back in the fridge. "I'm not going to wake you up in the middle of the night just so you can walk with me."

"I said I don't want you walking to the stables alone at night, but I also know that's not gonna stop you from doing it."

I brought the glasses of juice into the dining room and set his down away from the stack of papers.

"Promise me you'll take the bear spray with you," he said. "And if you don't take the bear spray, you carry."

"I promise," I said. "Let's hope I don't have to use either."

"From your lips," he murmured. He took off his glasses and then gestured to the chair next to me.

"Oh no, we're having a real talk now, aren't we?" I quipped, but I pulled out the chair and took a seat nonetheless.

"Tell me what happened between you and Gianni," he said.

I pursed my lips. "We ended our engagement."

"Yeah, so you said." He cocked his head to the side. "But why do I feel like I don't have the full story?"

"Because you're smart and I could never lie to you," I said. "Not that I *have* lied to you. Salem says I can't lie."

"Look, this is important. I need you to be a straight shooter right now."

"Oh, goody, here we go—"

"Reel in the snark, would ya?" He smiled, easing the tension.

I mimed a fishing rod and pretended to reel.

"You don't seem too upset," Dad said. "I mean, for a broken engagement, shouldn't you be crying? Yelling? Something?"

"I went through that already."

"You did?"

I nodded. "He ended it a week ago. I got all the tears out of me already."

"He ended it," Dad repeated.

"Yep."

"And you cried."

"I did."

He peered at me. "Salem's right. You're a shit liar."

"*Dad.*"

"Okay, I'll back off. But when my daughter flies home in the middle of the night and then barely says a word about her broken engagement, it makes me . . . concerned."

"Don't be concerned," I said.

"Just tell me why it ended."

"We just weren't . . . compatible. And we both knew it. And we were trying to make something work that was destined to fail."

"Why was it destined to fail?"

"Because he's a restauranteur with deep roots in the city and we're not . . ."

"Compatible," he repeated. "All right. I'll accept that. For now."

"Is the interrogation over?" My lips twitched. "Can I leave?"

"This wasn't an interrogation," he protested. "I just . . . oh, hell. Hadley, you don't seem at all heartbroken. And that worries me more than anything."

"I was heartbroken. But I'm on the mend."

He peered at me, as if he could silently get me to admit the truth. But it wasn't a truth I was ready to discuss. There was so much wrapped up in it.

My infertility.

The fact that Gianni didn't want me because of it.

His love being conditional.

I'd been willing to make a life with him in New York even though I didn't love it there. But I'd loved him enough to sacrifice what I wanted for his dreams and his happiness.

I'd loved him enough to forgo the life I envisioned for myself, willing to build a new one with him. He just hadn't been willing to do the same for me.

"Maybe it's a blessing in disguise," Dad said. "A redirection, you know?"

"Yeah, maybe."

In the darkest part of my soul, if I admitted it to myself, I was more cut up about my infertility than the loss of Gianni. And that said it all.

"So, you were talking to your sister," Dad prodded.

"Yeah."

"Why won't she talk to me, Hadley?"

I loved my father. But Salem was my twin. We'd shared a womb at the same time. And I wouldn't betray her, just like she wouldn't ever betray me.

"She's trying to figure out her life, Dad. Just give her the space to do it. She'll come around."

"I've given her five years," he murmured. "She barely calls. She doesn't come home unless she knows you're going to be here and even then, she makes a last-minute excuse not to come."

I swallowed. "It's harder for her. She was Mom's favorite."

He looked at me. "Your mother didn't have favorites."

I smiled. "Daddy. Come on. It doesn't hurt my feelings."

"Kathleen understood Salem in a way that I never could. And it wasn't just because she was her mother. It was something else."

"Mom was Salem's safe place," I said quietly. "She could be her absolute rebellious, rotten self. And Mom would just . . . love her anyway."

"So did I. Even when she was difficult, I never stopped loving Salem."

"No," I agreed. "You didn't. But the things you loved in Mom were things you didn't understand in your daughter." I placed my hand on his and gave it a squeeze. "And when Mom died . . ."

"She wanted to leave. Salem always wanted to leave."

"Nomad spirit," I said with a rueful smile.

He squeezed my hand. "I hope the nomad comes home. I hope she knows how much I love her."

"She does. Which makes it that much harder for her."

"I hate the reason you came home. But I'm glad you're here."

Emotion thickened my throat. "I'm glad I'm home too."

CHAPTER SEVEN

The Ranch

"They make this appliance called an emulsion blender," I said to my grandmother. "It'll whip the potatoes faster than you can mash them."

She snorted. "This potato masher belonged to my mother. It was good enough for her, it's good enough for me."

"It's gonna give you a splinter," I teased. "The handle is split."

"Are you going to stand there and sass me or are you going to pour me another one of those bourbon things," she commanded.

"It's a bourbon maple martini," I stated.

"From your restaurant, right?"

"Yeah."

"Well, it's good."

The sun had set and dinner was almost ready. Dad was in the sitting room next to the gas fireplace that was currently off. If it had been up to me, it would've been turned on, but I ran cold.

I set the table and helped Muddy bring out the food.

Dad came into the dining room as Muddy served me a heaping plate of steak, potatoes and green beans.

"This is too much," I protested.

"You're too thin," she said. "Living off protein bars, am I right?"

"No. You're not." But between two jobs, I'd become an expert grazer. A snack here, a snack there. And there'd been far too many nights with my roommates and sister that had been wine and cheese boards for dinner.

"You'd think dating a restauranteur, you would've been eating better," Muddy muttered.

I set my fork down. "Okay, let's have it."

"Have what?" Muddy asked.

Dad's gaze volleyed between us, but he wisely focused on his food and stayed out of it.

"You never liked Gianni," I stated.

"No, I never did," she admitted. "Pass the rolls."

With a sigh, I grabbed the basket of bread and handed it to her.

"It seems my intuition about him was correct, though, wasn't it? The engagement ended," Muddy said.

"You know the problem with this family?" I demanded. "No one minds their own business."

"Business. Mind my—you're my granddaughter. Do you think I was happy when I heard you were going to marry some slick Italian restauranteur who was going to keep you thousands of miles from home?"

"Well, that's no longer the case, now, is it?" I said, my tone bitter.

"You dated how long?" Muddy asked.

"Two years."

"Two years," she repeated. "And he never once found the time to come meet us. That says a lot about a person. You spent how many holidays with his family?"

"Several."

So many I'd lost count.

Gianni's large Italian family were constantly having baptisms, confirmations, birthdays, and anniversaries. It had been exhausting and I'd always been expected to attend.

Our relationship had been completely unbalanced.

"What did Salem think about him?" Muddy pressed.

I clamped my mouth shut.

"Wyn and Poet? Did they feel the same way?"

It had been staring me in the face, and I'd been too blind to see it. I hadn't *wanted* to see it.

My afternoon conversation with my father came roaring to the surface. Maybe our breakup really was a blessing in disguise.

I wasn't ready to concede. To concede meant I had to let my entire reality crumble to the ground before I built it back into something stronger, more resilient.

I shoved back from the table.

"Where are you going?" Muddy asked. "You haven't touched your food."

"I'm not hungry." I marched toward the front door.

"Let her go, Mom," Dad said. To me, he called out, "Bear spray."

I swiped the can of bear spray and my coat and headed out the door. My boots were on the porch. I slid into them and put on my jacket on the way to the stables.

Spending time with horses was the only thing that seemed to straighten out my brain. I could be alone with big, majestic, emotional animals that just seemed to *get* me.

Mom had loved to ride. Salem wasn't much of an equestrian, so it was something Mom and I had shared. Her brown spotted Appaloosa mare was in her stall. She lifted her head, blew out a breath of air, and came toward me.

I patted her nose. "Hey, Goldie."

The sound of clopping hooves had me turning my head. Declan was leading a handsome gray stallion into the stables.

"Hadley," he said in surprise.

"Hey," I greeted. I smiled at the spirited stallion who attempted to say hello by moving its head over Declan's shoulder toward me. "Who's this handsome guy?"

"I'm Declan," he teased. "We've already met."

I rolled my eyes.

Declan patted the stallion's nose. "This is Merlin."

"Hi Merlin," I murmured. I looked at Declan. "May I?"

"Sure thing."

I reached out and stroked his nose. He bumped my shoulder, causing me to laugh.

"Beggar," Declan stated. "He's looking for a treat."

"I was just about to feed Goldie a carrot," I said.

"Merlin loves carrots," he said.

I reached into the metal bucket hanging on Goldie's stall door and offered my palm to Merlin. The carrot was gone in two chomps.

"Were you putting up trail cams?" I asked.

"Nah. Merlin and I haven't had a quiet moment since the two of us got here. Thought I owed him an evening ride."

"He's beautiful," I commented.

"Yeah. Good 'ol Merlin. He was on the rodeo circuit with me." Declan led Merlin into a stall next to Goldie and then began taking off his saddle. "What are you doing out here? I thought it was dinner time."

"It is. But Muddy and I . . . we kind of got into it."

"Into it? About what?"

"About me and my fiancé."

Declan kept his head down, but I saw his shoulders tense. "You're engaged?"

"No. Not anymore."

His shoulders relaxed. "That why you came home?"

"Yeah," I admitted.

"Italy."

"What about it?"

"You were supposed to go there with him, yeah?"

"Yeah." I turned back to Goldie. "I could've stayed in New York, but I'd already taken off work, so I would've just been sitting around, stewing."

"Nothing like getting some clarity under an Idaho sky."

I smiled. "Yeah, nothing like it."

"What did you do in New York? For work, I mean."

"You know the horse-drawn carriages around Central Park?"

"Yeah."

"I worked in the stables. And then a few nights a week, I served in an Italian restaurant. It's how I met Gianni. He owns the restaurant. Well, his family does. He came in one night and I spilled sparkling water on him." I paused. "I don't know why I'm telling you this."

"Sometimes you can talk to a stranger the way you can't talk to people who know you," Declan said.

"You're easy to talk to," I said. "Maybe it's because you have no preconceived ideas about who I am. Who I'm supposed to be."

"You don't have to be anything other than what you are."

I smiled. "My sister would like you."

"Yeah? Why's that?"

"Because she's spent her whole life trying to justify who she is."

He shrugged. "Your dad, Muddy, they love you. Just

remember that's where they're coming from when they talk to you."

I patted Goldie's nose.

His words had me pondering, but the stables were no longer empty, and I had the desire to be alone.

"Have a good night, Declan."

"You too, Hadley."

I strode from the stables and forced myself not to look back. There was more to Declan than met the eye.

For all his joking and teasing, I knew there was depth to him.

When I returned to the house, I kicked off my boots and left them on the porch and then I set the bear spray on the foyer table.

"I left a plate for you in the microwave," Muddy called.

I went into the sitting room. She was resting in a patchwork chair that she refused to have reupholstered. The fireplace was on, the fake logs glowing under the flames. She had a brandy on the end table next to her and her crocheting project in her lap.

"I'm sorry," I said, taking a seat on the couch.

"Ah, sugar, don't apologize. I was baiting you." She shot me a smile. "I was hoping it would get you to open up."

"I'm not ready to open up."

"Yeah, I got that message loud and clear. Say the word, and I'm on the first plane to New York." She held up her crochet hook. "This can do some serious damage, you know."

"I know." I grinned. "But he doesn't deserve the energy. Trust me on that."

She bent her head and went back to her task. "He was never good enough for you. I think you know I feel that way. But I won't say anything more about it until you tell me. Okay?"

"I love you, Muddy. I really do." I sighed. "Where's Dad?"

She paused for a moment and then she said, "Out."

"Out." I rose from my seat. "Guess we all have our secrets, huh?"

CHAPTER EIGHT

THE RANCH

The next morning, I woke up with the sun. I hadn't set an alarm—I didn't need to. Something about being home had my inner clock functioning like I'd never left.

I got up and quietly padded downstairs, not wanting to wake my grandmother and father. I'd told Muddy before going to bed that I'd feed the chickens and collect the eggs.

As the coffee gurgled into the carafe, I watched from the kitchen window as the morning rays gilded the mountainside.

I took out my phone from my pocket and snapped a photo. I sent it to the group chat.

Poet's reply was almost instant.

> POET
>
> Your morning view is better than my morning view. I saw a homeless guy throw up on the train.

WYN

How did you ever leave that place?

SALEM

She had to follow me to make sure I didn't lose any limbs.

Smiling, I put my phone away and poured myself a cup of coffee. I splashed heavy cream into the cup, and then I went outside onto the back porch to sit in the silence of the early morning.

I nuzzled down into my coat, my cold fingers wrapping around the hot mug.

The back door creaked open, followed by the clod of heavy boots. Dad took the chair next to me. He wore a down vest, but his flannel shirt sleeves were rolled up to reveal muscular forearms.

"You're up early," he said.

"So are you."

"I'm always up early," he pointed out.

"I'm falling back into the old rhythm," I said with a smile. "After I feed the chickens and collect the eggs, I'm going to muck out the stalls and wash the saddle blankets."

"It's like you never left." He lifted his black coffee to his lips.

I paused. "Sometimes I wish I hadn't."

"It's good you left," he said. "It's good to experience different things in life. So you know what you're coming back to."

"Yeah, I guess," I murmured.

"Are you missing New York?"

"It's only my second day of being home," I said with a laugh.

"So?"

I sighed. "I miss this place when I leave it. When I'm in

New York, I have this . . . this aching feeling for the Ridge. I've always felt that way."

"I'm glad you're home. I am," he said and then fell silent.

"But? There's a *but* just waiting to come out."

"*However*," Dad grinned, but it slipped. "I don't want you to . . . hide here. You get what I mean?"

"Yeah." I sighed. "I get what you mean." I took a sip of coffee. "I don't think I miss New York. Poet texted that she saw a homeless man throw up on the train. Who would miss that?"

"There are other things to love about a big city."

"Really," I drawled. "Like what?"

His brow furrowed. "Fine, I'm the wrong person to talk to about the pros and cons of city life."

"I miss my friends," I admitted. "I miss Salem. I miss our tiny eclectic apartment and the four of us running around a city trying to make our dreams come true. I miss the random nights when all four of us happen to be home and we sit on the floor and drink wine and eat cheese. That, I miss. That, I can see myself missing if I . . ."

"If you what?"

"If I don't go back," I admitted. "Do I have to go back?"

"You don't have to do anything you don't want to do."

"But like you said, I can't stay here and hide. And what am I going to do the rest of my life? Live and work on the ranch?"

"You would've done that if you hadn't followed Salem to New York," he pointed out. "You've been in New York for five years, honey. That's long enough to know if a place is good for you or not."

I tapped the rim of my mug. "I'm not like them. Salem, Poet, Wyn . . . they love New York. They thrive there. To me, it's just . . . exhausting."

I looked away from my father and stared out over the land.

"I can't breathe there," I said quietly. "And I think I lied to myself that I could."

"So, again, maybe this is a silver lining from your breakup?"

"Yeah maybe. How can it be, though? Home for barely two days and I'm feeling more stable than I have in months."

"You said it: *home*. This is your home. This will always be your home. This place is in your blood."

"Salem's my home, too," I pointed out.

"You're allowed to choose yourself," he said. "You're allowed to be happy."

I looked at him. "What about you, Dad? Are you happy?"

"Am I happy," he repeated. "Million-dollar question, huh? I get to wake up every day doing what I love. One of my daughters came home. Now, if we could get your sister here, I'd want for nothing."

It was on the tip of my tongue to ask about his romantic life, but if I didn't want him prying into mine, I couldn't be a hypocrite and pry into his. So, I kept my thoughts to myself.

"I'd love it if Salem came home to stay. And if I'm honest about it, I'd love it if she brought Poet and Wyn and the four of us lived here forever." I smiled. "You'd love that wouldn't you?"

"I would, yeah." Dad grinned back. "You four would cause a ruckus. Shake up this little town for sure."

"You make it sound like we're living *Footloose*," I said with a laugh.

"I saw that musical," Dad drawled. "When your high school put it on, remember?"

"Oh, I remember." I laughed.

Two boys had gotten into a fight over Salem. Fists went

flying and one of them had gone through the set piece. The curtain had come down early.

"What's even more hilarious is that the school let her be in the musical the next year despite the chaos she created," I said.

"It's endearing chaos, apparently."

I stood up. "I bet the chickens are hungry."

"Probably," he said, also rising. "I'm going to check on the new mare. She's due to give birth any day now."

"I was going to take Goldie out for a ride. Is that okay?" I asked.

He frowned. "Of course that's okay. Why wouldn't it be okay?"

"Because she's Mom's horse."

Dad's eyes softened. "And she would love nothing more than for you to ride her. I sure as hell don't ride her enough."

Or at all.

He couldn't bring himself to.

"Goldie needs some spoiling," Dad said. "It's good you're home to do it. Just do me a favor. Don't ride the trails alone. Not until we have a handle on the bear situation."

"Any sighting of it?" I asked.

He shook his head. "No. Nothing on the trail cams either."

The mention of trail cams made me think of Declan and the cup of coffee he'd offered me yesterday morning. I never did return his mug.

"To the chicken coop," I stated.

I kissed my father's cheek and then I headed inside. I set my half-drunk cup of coffee into the sink, grabbed Declan's mug from the dish drain, and went out front.

The ranch was stirring to life. I waved to the few men I saw on horseback who were riding the opposite direction of the house, no doubt to check on fences and the grazing livestock.

I marched up to the guest cabin and knocked on the door. There was no answer, but I knew Declan was home because his muddy cowboy boots were lined up next to the welcome mat.

I knocked again, louder this time. When it was clear he wasn't going to answer the door, I decided to leave the mug on his doormat. I was just setting it down when the door opened—my gaze immediately meeting a pair of bare shins.

My eyes traveled upward to take in a wet, nearly naked Declan who was currently wearing nothing but a towel.

A towel and a smirk.

"Uh, hey."

"Hi ya, bear snack." His smirk widened.

"Aren't you cold?" I blurted out.

"Hmm. Getting there. Come on in."

"Oh, that's not—"

"You were pounding on my door, so clearly it was something important. Come in and I'll get dressed."

I wish you wouldn't.

I scooped up the mug and followed Declan into the cabin, closing the door behind me. He turned and went toward the bedroom, giving me a view of his sculpted back and damp skin.

"I brought your mug," I called out to him.

"Thanks. You can set it on the counter."

I wandered farther into the cabin, noting the lack of clutter or personal belongings—no photographs, no knickknacks.

"So, I'm gonna go," I said.

"Hang on, I'm almost done changing."

"The chickens really need their breakfast."

He popped out of the bedroom, buttoning up his flannel shirt. Declan was barefoot and for some reason I found that incredibly endearing.

"You're going to feed the chickens?" Declan asked.

I nodded.

"I'll walk with you."

"Why?" I asked with a frown.

"Why what?" Declan asked.

"Why do you want to walk with me?"

"Because we're friends," he said. "But I gotta say, the way you were looking at me, wasn't a *just friends* look."

"I didn't expect you to answer the door in a towel." My cheeks heated.

"It's barely seven in the morning," he said. "How did you expect me to answer the door?" When I didn't reply, he went on, "How are you doing?"

"I'm fine."

"Yeah?"

"Yeah."

"You sleep okay?" he asked.

"I slept fine."

Nodding, he ducked back into the bedroom. "Socks."

"Socks, right."

"Speaking of socks, which pair are you wearing?"

"The ones with the donuts," I said, fighting a smile.

"Cute."

He came back out and sat on the couch to put on his socks. "I didn't expect you to be up this early."

"Habit," I stated. "But also, my sleep is erratic from the time difference."

"You woke up this early in New York? Well, of course you did. The horse stables."

I blinked. "Yeah. That's right."

He cocked his head to the side. "You like it, though. Getting up super early. Maybe before the sun is even up. When it's just you and a cup of coffee. And the silence."

I held up my hands. "You have me figured out."

Declan smiled. "I imagine it's hard to find a quiet moment in a city of eight million people."

"Eight point three," I remarked.

"That's insane."

"You said it."

He got up from the couch and went to the hook on the wall that had his jacket on it. He threw it on, grabbed his felt cowboy hat, and gestured for the door.

I stood on the porch as he pulled on his boots. "So I guess that means you don't like big cities?"

"I don't even like big towns that could fall into the category of small cities," he explained.

We headed in the direction of the chicken coop, our jackets brushing every now and again.

"Where did you grow up?" I asked.

"Bonner's Ferry."

"Ah. So you're basically Canadian," I joked.

He laughed. "Thirty minutes from British Columbia. It was closer to go there than to look for trouble in Cocur d'Alene."

"You like trouble," I concluded. "Shocker."

"I ride a motorcycle and worked the rodeo, and now I wrangle cattle for a living. Did you really think I wasn't trouble?" He flashed me a flirty grin.

"I'm not looking for trouble."

"You look like you could use some trouble," he said. "Besides, I'm the good kind of trouble."

"Innuendos begone." I waved my hand at him.

"Innuendos? Get your mind out of the gutter, Hadley." He shot me a wink that had my cheeks burning.

We arrived at the chicken coop and Declan picked up the basket hanging on the fence and handed it to me. I took it and he opened the latch of the gate. After he stepped in behind me, he closed it.

"You're such a flirt," I accused, maneuvering around the chickens to the back of the coop.

"Guilty. So, if you're not into trouble, what are you into?"

"Sitting at home, having a bottle of wine, eating charcuterie."

"What the hell is charcuterie?"

I began to collect the eggs while Declan filled the trough feeders with grain. "Charcuterie are cured meats."

"You spelled barbecue wrong."

"Let me guess, you're also into mircobrews?"

"Mock all you want, but microbrews are actually good."

I bit my lip as I looked at a green egg before setting it gently in the basket. "Have you been to the Copper Mule yet?"

"No. What's the Copper Mule?"

"The town's only bar and local microbrewery," I said.

"I'll have to check it out." He gestured with his chin at the basket in my hands. "How's the haul?"

"Pretty good. We've got happy hens. Thanks for feeding them."

He opened the gate and held it for me. "No problem."

We both stood at the coop, neither of us making a move to go about our day.

"So I'll see you later, I guess," he said.

"Sure." I nodded.

"Okay." Declan turned in the direction of the stables.

"Declan?" I called out.

He stopped walking and turned. "Yeah?"

"I was going to go for a ride this afternoon," I said. "Dad doesn't want me on the trail alone until the bear thing is resolved. Would you, maybe, want to—"

"I'd like that," he said, a smile blooming across his face. "Four o'clock?"

I nodded.

69

He winked. "It's a date."

CHAPTER NINE

The Ranch

"Hello?" came a muffled voice.

"Poet?" I asked into the cell. "Are you okay?"

She sniffed. "Yeah, I'm okay." And then she promptly burst into tears.

"Hey," I soothed. "What's wrong? Where are you?"

It took a few moments for Poet to get herself under control, but she finally managed to pull herself together.

"I'm in the women's restroom at work, hiding from my boss so she won't see me cry."

"Who made you cry?" I demanded, angry on behalf of my sensitive friend. "Was it Alba?"

"Yes."

"What did she say to you?"

She exhaled a rickety breath. "We were in a meeting with Candace and . . . and . . ."

"And?" I pressed gently.

"You know that manuscript I was reading?"

"The one you couldn't put down? I remember."

"Yeah, well, I stupidly left it out on my desk with my notes and I was going to tell Candace I recommend she read the manuscript for herself because it was a real diamond in the rough. Alba took the manuscript off my desk and presented it to Candace as if she'd found it. Candace read it on her lunch break and told Alba *good work* and that she was going to present it at the editorial meeting later this week."

"Oh, Poet," I said softly. "I'm so sorry."

"It's fine."

"It's *not* fine. You're crying in the bathroom stall at work. Tell Candace the truth."

"I can't," she said. "You know publishing is cutthroat. It'll look like I'm a whiney tattletale. And at the end of the day, all I care about are good stories getting their day in the sun."

"You also want the job title of senior editor," I reminded her.

"Yeah," she admitted. "But people like Alba usually give themselves enough rope to hang themselves. I just have to give it time."

Poet had been working as a junior editor for a major publishing house for the last two years. She loved her job—but she hadn't planned on people wanting to step on her on their way to the top.

"You called me," she reminded me.

"I did."

When I fell silent, she urged, "Go on."

"I'm sitting in my bedroom closet so I can have this conversation in complete secrecy."

"I'm intrigued," she teased.

"You know the cowboy wrangler?"

"The one you're determined not to sleep with? Yes. How's that going, by the way?"

"I went to his cabin to give him back his coffee mug and he answered the door in a towel."

There was a pause.

"You slept with him, didn't you?"

"What? No!"

"But you're thinking about it."

"Am I allowed?" I blurted out.

"Allowed? Allowed to what? Be an adult and sleep with a guy? Yes. You're single. He's single. I don't see a problem."

"It hasn't even been two weeks since Gianni and I split up," I pointed out. "Doesn't that make me . . ."

"Make you what?"

"You know."

"A slut?"

"I was going to say *terrible*, but thanks," I drawled.

"I'm not calling you a slut. And you're *not* a slut," she stated. "Why didn't you call and ask Salem for advice? Or Wyn?"

"Because Salem might be my twin, but Salem and Wyn are feral twins in spirit. Both of them would've told me to go for it. You and I though . . ."

She sighed. "Yeah, I get you. We're kinda prudish."

"I wouldn't say prudish."

"I would. I'm okay with that though. You . . . I think you're not okay with that. Otherwise, you wouldn't be calling me asking me for advice."

"I asked him to go riding with me this afternoon."

"Riding, huh?"

"Horseback riding," I clarified. "Jeez. You're just as bad as Salem."

"Why are you going horseback riding together?"

"Because I don't feel comfortable riding alone while there's a bear so close to home."

"You could've asked your dad to go riding with you. Or

your grandmother. She's still spry at her age. And if I recall, she's a better shot than your dad, too."

"No lies there." I laughed.

"So why did you ask Declan?"

"Because I wanted to." I paused again. "Poet, there's something I need to—"

"Hang on," she interrupted. "The bathroom door opened. Someone else is in here."

It was muffled on the other end and then Poet came back on the line. "I've got to go. Let me know how your ride goes."

She hung up before I had a chance to reply.

My screen went dark.

I reluctantly opened my closet door and crawled out.

"Okay," I said out loud. "You're going to go on this ride, but you're not going to do anything to look pretty."

I had to force myself not to glance in the mirror because there was no doubt that I would've primped. Earlier in the morning, I'd braided my hair and it was still intact, so that had to be good enough.

I'd spent the day outside and in the stables, breathing in fresh mountain air. I loved the familiarity and routine of ranch chores.

Maybe I had been deluding myself into thinking I could settle long term in the city. I'd made it work because I followed my sister on her adventures, and then I'd forced myself into a box because of Gianni. But now that I no longer had the tether of a fiancé, the only real draw to return was my sister and my friends.

And those relationships were important to me.

But what about what *I* wanted?

On my way to the stables, my phone buzzed in my jacket pocket.

I pulled it out and saw Gracie's name across the screen.

GRACIE

Are you busy two nights from now?

Snorting, I texted back.

ME

No.

GRACIE

The in-laws are willing to watch Bella. Cole is working, so how about you and I go to the Copper Mule for a drink and some dancing?

ME

I'm in.

I stuck my phone back into my pocket and entered the stables. Declan was already saddling Merlin.

"Hey," I greeted.

"Hey." He looked at me, a slow smile creeping across his lips.

"What?" I demanded.

Without a word, he headed toward me. He reached out and gently stroked a finger down my cheek. "Dirt."

My hand flew to my face. "Dirt?"

"Yep." His grin was wide.

I groaned.

"What?"

"Never mind," I muttered.

I saddled Goldie and then she trotted behind Merlin out into the late afternoon sunshine.

"Season is going to turn soon," I said.

"What was that?" Declan called back.

"Oh, I just said the season is going to turn soon. Winter's got its last grip, but I give it two weeks and the air will be warmer."

"How can you tell?"

I smiled. "I've lived here all my life. I just know."

He inclined his head. "So, which way do you want to go?"

"North," I said. "The land has all been cleared that direction and if the bear is anywhere around, we'll be able to see him before it's a problem."

"I'll follow you."

I took the lead. We rode across a meadow and a small stream, silence falling between us as we enjoyed the outdoors. Eventually, Declan brought his mount next to mine and we slowed the horses.

"If you go that way," I pointed, "you'll find the hot spring."

"The hot spring? You're kidding."

I shook my head. "Nope. The original cabin that my great-great grandfather built was only a few hundred feet from the spring. It's why he settled here."

"I don't think I know the story of the ranch," he said. "I didn't realize it's been in your family that long."

"Dad didn't tell you?" I asked in surprise.

He shook his head.

"My great-great grandfather, Eamon Powell, was an Irish prospector," I recounted. "He struck silver in this valley in the early 1880s. He homesteaded the first 160 acres, and as the years went on he used the silver to buy as much land as he could around the original ranch until the mine went dry. He spent the rest of his life here, and the ranch has been in my family since then." I shot him a grin. "There's a myth about the hot spring on our land, too."

"Oh yeah? What's the myth?" Declan asked, his blue eyes bright in the sunshine.

"That it has healing powers." I shrugged. "Eamon cut his leg once. It was bad enough he thought he'd have to have it amputated—but he went to the hot spring and soaked it, and somehow it healed and he was able to keep the leg."

"How'd that story make it down the generations?" Declan asked. "Was it written down?"

"Like in the family bible?" I shook my head. "No. It was passed down orally."

Declan nodded thoughtfully. "Do you believe it?"

"No." I scoffed. "Of course I don't believe it."

"Why not? It could be true. Why don't you believe it?"

"Because it didn't heal my mother," I said quietly.

Declan's expression fell. "Hadley—"

"Come on, I'll race you back to the stables."

CHAPTER TEN

The Ranch

"Ow, ow, ow, ow." I hobbled down the stairs, grimacing with each step.

"Is that you, sugar?" Muddy called.

"Yeah," I replied, slowly making my way into the kitchen.

Muddy was at the stove, wearing her faded strawberry print apron. She looked at me over her shoulder and grinned.

"Stop it," I said with a laugh.

"Want me to get you some aspirin?"

"I'd prefer bourbon," I replied.

"That, I can do." Muddy fixed me a stiff drink and brought it to me and ran a soothing hand across my back. "A little out of practice working the ranch, huh?"

"It's like riding a horse," I quipped. "Literally. It's a good sore. I miss it."

She returned to the stove, her back to me. "Saw you out riding with Declan."

"Yeah. I didn't want to be out alone with the bear, you know?"

Muddy made a non-committal noise.

"What's that mean?" I demanded.

"It means nothing."

"Liar." I laughed. "You have an opinion about everything."

"The last time I gave you my opinion, you walked out of the dining room."

"Well, I promise I won't leave the room if you speak your mind. I can hardly move anyway, so I'm kind of my own hostage."

Muddy didn't say anything for a moment and then she said, "Why didn't you ask your father to go riding with you?"

"Didn't think about it."

"Hadley."

"Muddy."

"You like him."

"Yeah, I like him."

"No, I mean you *like* him."

"I'm not ready to like anyone," I stated. "I'm still getting over my engagement ending."

"Are you?"

"Yes."

I frowned even though she wasn't looking at me. "Declan and I are friends. Friends ride horses. Friends talk."

"What do you talk about?"

"Stuff."

"Stuff?"

"Yeah, stuff. I told him about New York and what I was doing there."

"And?"

"What do you mean, *and?* That's all."

"He really listens," Muddy murmured. "Declan, I mean. He listens when you talk."

79

"Yes," I admitted. "He does. Is dinner going to be ready soon?"

"A few more minutes."

"Is Dad joining us?"

"Yes."

"You promise not to talk about Declan when he's here?"

"I thought nothing was going on between you and Declan?"

"Nothing *is* going on. But you know Dad. He'll make a mountain out of a mole hill."

I fell into silence as Muddy continued to cook. I nursed my drink and thought of the afternoon ride with Declan. I internally winced when I remembered how abrupt and short I'd been about the hot spring.

We'd raced back to the stables and then worked in silence, tending to our horses. He hadn't tried to speak to me again.

Guilt swamped me.

Dad came home and poured himself a drink. He sat at the table, laughing and chatting with me. Being home was like being wrapped in a warm blanket.

I felt safe, protected.

My phone chimed in the middle of dinner. It was Salem. Her message made all good thoughts suddenly flee.

"What's wrong?" Dad asked as he reached for the bread basket.

"Nothing," I lied.

"Who texted?" Muddy demanded. "Gianni?"

I shook my head. "No. Not Gianni. I haven't heard from him since he . . . it was Salem. She was just telling me she'd gone to Gianni's apartment and packed up the things I had there. And left the key with the security guard."

My finger absently stroked my left ring finger.

She'd returned the engagement ring, too. Leaving it in a box on his nightstand.

Dad and Muddy didn't say anything.

What was there to say?

I picked up my plate and walked to the sink. "Thanks for dinner. I'm going to go upstairs for a bit."

After I made it to my bedroom, I closed the door and flopped down onto the bed, half my face smushed into a pillow. I texted Salem back.

A moment later, she called.

"Hello," I mumbled.

"You sound exhausted."

"I am exhausted. I got soft in my city life."

"Ah, you went for a ride today."

"Yep."

"By yourself?"

I paused. "Nope."

"You went with the hot wrangler in Wranglers, didn't you?" she teased.

"How long have you been sitting on that one?"

"It just came to me. What can I say, I'm a genius."

I chuckled. "Hey, thanks for getting my stuff from Gianni's. Did the security guard give you any trouble?"

"No. None."

I sighed. "One less thing I have to deal with. Thanks, Salem. I appreciate it."

"No problem."

"Did Poet go with you?"

"No . . ."

I paused. "What did you do?"

"Do? I did nothing."

"I don't believe you. You were supposed to take Poet so she could make sure you were on your best behavior."

"Relax. I didn't do anything crazy. Except write asshole in silver sharpie on every mirror in the apartment. And on the glass stove top."

"You didn't slice his mattress?"

"No."

"You didn't accidentally on purpose leave a faucet running with the sink plugged?"

"No."

"Huh, you must be mellowing in your old age," I teased.

"Hey. I'm only four minutes older than you. If I'm old, so are you."

I paused. "I feel old. Tired."

"That's the breakup talking."

"Maybe."

"You'll spring back. Also, take some vitamin D. It'll help your mood."

"Not a bad idea," I said. "The winter has been long and gray."

"I wasn't talking about *that* kind of vitamin D."

"What were you—*Salem!*"

"I got you to laugh, didn't I?" she asked, bursting into giggles. "You like riding. I volunteer Declan as tribute."

"How much wine have you had?"

"Just poured my first glass. Come on, there's nothing to do there except ride a cowboy. It'll bring you more joy than riding a horse, I'll tell ya."

"You're shameless."

"I'd like that on my tombstone, please."

"There are other things to do here," I protested.

"Like what?"

"It might be time I let Muddy teach me how to crochet."

"Stop. Please stop. You just aged thirty years in once sentence."

"I'm going to the Copper Mule with Gracie."

"Great, when? Tonight?"

"No. In a few days. Her in-laws are watching the baby and Cole is working."

She was silent for a moment and then she said quietly, "Are you ready to talk about it?"

I swallowed. "No."

"I'm the one who buries stuff she doesn't want to talk about—not you."

I once again thought of my earlier conversation with Declan.

"Salem, I gotta go," I said.

"Go? Go where?"

"None of your beeswax."

"I want details!"

"There won't be any details," I said with a laugh. "Bye."

I hung up and tossed my phone aside.

Muddy and Dad were in the sitting room with the TV on. I felt like I was sneaking out, and I had a moment of teenager flashback. I grabbed my coat from the hook and put it on and then slid into a pair of comfortable outdoor slippers before quietly closing the front door behind me.

I was halfway to Declan's cabin when I realized I'd forgotten the bear spray. I picked up my speed and breathed a sigh of relief when I saw the front porch of the cabin lit up and Declan sitting in a chair, nursing a beer.

"Hey," I greeted. "Sorry to interrupt your night."

He looked at me and smiled. "You're not interrupting. You want a beer?"

"Oh." I paused for a moment. "Sure."

"Sit," he said, rising. "I'll grab a beer and the other chair."

I headed up the porch steps and didn't protest. I settled into the seat and hunched lower in my coat.

Declan came back outside and handed me a beer in a koozie and then went to grab the other chair at the end of the porch.

"Cheers." He clinked his bottle neck beer against mine and then sat down.

"Thanks for this," I said and took a sip. "Oh, that's good. What is it?"

"A huckleberry microbrew."

I laughed. "Stop."

"Seriously." He grinned. "Gotta love the grocery store in town. They only have local beer. Can it even be called a grocery store? It's got like eight aisles. Can you even buy sandwich meat there?"

"It has a deli counter," I said. "A few years ago, a giant corporate chain wanted to build a grocery store here. The town regulations for chains are intense and the company lawyers started to get nasty. The people in town went to the mayor and eventually they tucked tail and ran. After that, Huckleberry Hill passed a law—no corporate chains are allowed to build here. Locally owned businesses only. No fronts, no foreign corporations. If you own a business in this town, you have to live here and prove it."

"I kind of like that. Keeps the small town small."

I nodded. "Yeah."

He ran a hand through his dark hair but otherwise didn't reply.

"I'm sorry," I blurted out. "For earlier."

He frowned. "Sorry for what?"

I licked my suddenly dry lips. "When we were talking about the hot spring. And my mom."

"No apology necessary." He looked at me. "I didn't know. About your mother. Connor never mentioned . . ."

"He doesn't talk about her often," I said quietly. "So it's not a shock that you didn't know. I still feel guilty for how I spoke to you."

"You shouldn't."

"But I do." I shot him a wry grin. "I'm a people pleaser. And I never want to make anyone feel . . ."

"Uncomfortable?"

I nodded.

"Maybe you should."

"Should what?"

"Make people feel uncomfortable. Not care so much about what other people think." He shrugged. "You can become a recovering people pleaser, you know."

"I wouldn't even know where to begin."

"For starters, you can try not apologizing for your feelings."

"I'm not apologizing for my feelings," I explained. "I'm apologizing because of how I talked to you."

"Oh, okay." He smiled. "I accept your apology."

"Just like that?"

"Just like that, bear snack."

His jokey nickname sent warmth curling through me.

I took a sip of beer. "It's peaceful out here, isn't it?"

"It is," he agreed. "Nice to be able to hear yourself think."

"Hmm, yeah. I guess."

"You don't want to be able to hear yourself think?"

"When does too much thinking become overthinking?"

"When you ask that question." He lifted his bottle and took a drink. "So, what are you thinking about?"

"My sister called. I asked to her go to my ex's apartment and get my stuff. She returned the ring for me."

"Good sister."

"It's just weird, you know? One minute, you're going along and there's a plan for your life. And then you hit a brick wall. It all changes. Why does it do that? Why does life change without your permission?"

"It's designed that way."

"What's happened in your life that hasn't gone your way?" I asked. "Anything?"

"Several things, actually."

"Like what?"

"Ah, misery loves company, is that it?" he teased.

"Something like that."

He paused for a moment and then he said, "When I was sixteen, I found out the man who I thought was my father wasn't."

"You're kidding."

"Nope." He fiddled with the beer label. "My stepdad was a good man. And he never treated me like I wasn't his. But when he died . . ."

"Oh, Declan," I murmured.

"Yeah." He sighed. "Mom came clean. Told me my real father was actually a well-known bull rider on the circuit. She never told him about me. She was a buckle bunny. That was a shocker, too. Finding out my mom was a rodeo groupie."

"And your stepfather . . ."

"He was a biker, actually." He grinned. "I thought I was going to patch into his club when I turned eighteen, but I liked riding horses more than a motorcycle, so . . . I chose the rodeo circuit."

"Have you met your biological father? Do you have a relationship with him now that you're an adult?"

"We've met. He's not a family guy. He said as much when we met and he wasn't at all angry at my mom for letting him off the hook. And for all intents and purposes, my stepdad—the man who raised me—I consider him my father."

"That's a lot of baggage to saddle a sixteen-year-old with," I murmured. "How'd you handle it?"

"I didn't." His laugh was sardonic. "I became a menace. Drinking and fighting . . . and other things."

"Women?" I guessed.

He inclined his head. "Yeah. There was some carousing going on. I'll leave it at that."

"It's left," I said. "So, how did you snap out of it?"

"My manager. He wanted to sign me, but he didn't want a troublemaker. He saw potential in me. He told me that if I didn't want to wind up exactly like my father—my biological father—with a kid I'd never met and no family—that I needed to get my shit together. His words got through my thick head. So I got my shit together."

"His loss, you know," I said quietly. "Your dad. For not wanting to be a part of your life, even now."

He shrugged. "I'm okay."

"How can you just let all that go?"

"I don't know. I guess I realized that parents are human first. And we're all just a bunch of teenagers in grown up bodies. And some of us know how to communicate our emotions better than others."

"That's actually very . . . emotionally mature."

"It's not like I got there overnight. Like I said, I fought and drank my way through it first. And when that was no longer working, I guess I had to figure stuff out."

"And your mom?"

"Remarried to a nice, boring guy. Lives in Florida. I talk to her once a week. We're good."

"Sweet."

"Yeah." Declan finished off his beer. "Another?"

I shook my head. "I'm still nursing this one."

He set his bottle down next to the chair but made no move to get up.

"Do you miss it? The rodeo circuit?" I asked.

"Parts of it. The adrenaline, the attention . . . the money. As far as the crap food and constant travel? No, I don't miss that part."

I smiled. "Yeah, I can see how that would be exhausting."

"I'm old now." He winked. "I need a comfortable bed and a solid eight hours of sleep a night."

"On that note." I stood.

"I didn't mean you had to go," he protested. "Stay. It's still early."

"Thanks, but I'm tired. I'm out of practice working on a ranch."

He stood up. "I'll walk you home."

"That's not—"

"Where's your bear spray?" Declan demanded.

I sighed. "Okay, you can walk me home."

We ambled side by side in silence. I shoved my cold hands into my coat pockets and pretended I couldn't see Declan glancing at me every now and again.

When we got to the front porch, we stopped. I turned to him. "Thanks, Declan. For the beer and . . ."

"Sure thing, bro."

"Have a good night, buddy."

The warm glow of our conversation enveloped me as I was getting ready for bed. I realized he hadn't pressured me into talking about my mom, choosing instead to be open and honest about his own childhood.

And that's why I wanted to tell him about mine.

CHAPTER ELEVEN

TOWN

The Copper Mule smelled like grease and paprika. It was dim, with lodgepole pine ceilings, a scarred wooden bar, pool tables and an old juke box that didn't play country music past the year 2000.

"Hadley?"

Grinning, I sauntered up to the bar. "Hey, Wade."

"What are you doing here?" he asked.

He came out from behind the bar to give me a hug. His dark hair fell over his forehead, giving him a boyish appearance, but he was anything but. He'd played football in high school, and he'd been tall and muscular even back then. Now, he had a few more years of seasoning to him and he looked good.

"I'm meeting Gracie for a drink," I explained.

He shook his head. "I mean what are you doing home?"

"Came for a visit," I lied. "How are you doing? How's business?"

"Mom finally convinced Dad to enter semi-retirement, and they promoted me."

"To what? You've been bar manager since we graduated high school," I teased.

"Just a title." He winked. "Drinks are on me tonight."

"You don't have to do that," I protested.

"Yes, I do," he said. "Did Salem come home with you, too?"

I shook my head. "Just me."

"Is your fiancé joining you later?" His eyes went to my left hand, letting the question linger.

"No," I stated. "I don't have a fiancé anymore."

"Glad I'm covering your drinks tonight then. Maybe some shots later, yeah?"

"Sure," I said with a smile. "Thanks."

"I got a new cider on tap. You want to try it?"

"Sounds perfect. Thanks, Wade."

I took the stool at the end of the bar. Wade poured my cider and put the pint in front of me.

"So how long are you in town for?" he asked.

"To be determined," I said.

"We should grab dinner one night. Catch up."

My phone vibrated in my jacket pocket. "Oh, sorry. Hold that thought."

I pulled out my cell and read the text. With a sigh I texted back and set my phone down on the bar.

"Problem?" Wade asked.

"Gracie had to cancel. Bella came down with the flu."

"That sucks," he said.

"Yeah." I looked at my pint. It was no fun to drink alone. "I think I'll head out."

"What? You just got here."

"I know, but I don't want to just sit here and be a barfly."

"Stay for one drink. I already poured it. It'll just go to waste. And you haven't even tasted it yet."

I picked up the pint and took a sip. "Oh, wow. That's really good. What is it?"

"Thimbleberry cider. Dad's creation."

"What was that about your dad retiring?" I said with a laugh.

"You're right. He's spending even more time brewing now that he's got me to run the bar. I'm thinking of having an amateur cocktail competition. Get some new bodies into the bar, you know? Not everyone wants beer and cider all the time."

"That could be fun."

My gaze wandered toward the front door which had opened. A tall, familiar body in a cowboy hat stepped inside.

Declan looked around the room just as I slid off the stool.

"What are you doing here?" I asked as I went to him.

"You told me about this place. I came to check it out." He shrugged. "What are *you* doing here?"

"I was supposed to meet Gracie for a drink, but her daughter got the flu. So I'm flying solo."

"You want some company?"

My stomach swirled with pleasure.

"Sure."

We headed back to the bar. Wade's gaze was steady as he watched Declan approach.

"Wade, this is Declan Brewer. He's the new wrangler at Elk Ridge."

"Nice to meet you," Wade clipped. "Get you something to drink?"

Declan looked at me. "What are you drinking?"

"Thimbleberry cider. Wade's dad brewed it himself." I handed him my pint and gave it to him to taste.

He took a sip and nodded. "That's fucking delicious. I'll take one of those."

Wade's expression cracked and he smiled. "I'll tell my dad

you said so." He went to pour Declan a pint and then handed it to him. "You want to start a tab?"

"Sure." Declan reached into his jeans pocket and extracted his wallet.

Wade took Declan's credit card.

"Table?" Declan asked me as he put his wallet back into his pocket.

"Sure." I grabbed my pint and cell off the bar. "See ya, Wade."

Declan followed me to the corner of the bar and we took the vacant booth. I slid in and immediately took off my coat.

"What's that smell?" Declan asked.

I frowned. "What smell?"

"The bar smell. It's like grease . . . and something else, but I can't figure it out."

"Paprika," I explained.

"How do you know that?"

"The bar serves barbecue. Paprika is in the butt rub."

"Look at you—knowing all the things."

"Wade was my high school boyfriend," I explained. "I have the inside scoop."

"Ah that explains it."

"Explains what?"

"Explains the death-glare he gave me."

"He didn't death-glare you," I protested.

"*Right*," he said with a wry smile. He lifted his pint class. "Cheers."

"Cheers," I said, clinking my glass against his before taking a sip.

"So, you've been avoiding me."

"What? No."

"Yes," he said. "Be honest with me."

"I really haven't been avoiding you," I promised. "It's just worked out that way. I swear."

"Okay." He lifted his pint and took a sip. "You don't have to be a stranger, you know. You're welcome to enjoy a beer and talk anytime you want."

My gaze narrowed. "Talk."

"Yeah, talk. Like what we did the other night when I told you my dad wasn't my dad."

"I remember."

"If anyone should be embarrassed it should be me."

"Why should you be embarrassed?"

"Because I told you some personal shit and people get weird when you tell them personal shit."

"I appreciated that you told me about your parents. And I . . ."

"Yes?"

"Realized that I didn't tell you anything."

"I didn't ask. I figured if you wanted to talk about it, you'd talk about it." He shrugged. "I've got nothing to hide, Hadley."

"Have you ever been married?" I blurted out.

He smiled slightly. "No."

"Serious relationships?"

"None of those either."

"How is that possible?" I demanded.

"What do you mean?"

"I mean, you seem emotionally mature and very self-aware. How are you not taken?"

"I became self-aware only about a month ago," he joked.

"Declan."

"I don't know, Hadley. The rodeo circuit didn't really allow for long-lasting relationships and I wasn't really looking for one either. What about you?"

"What about me?"

"You were engaged, so clearly that was serious. And what about Wade?"

I looked at my high school boyfriend who was currently

93

helping a customer before glancing back at Declan. I shook my head. "No. It wasn't serious. It was high school."

"Some high school relationships last."

"Yeah, but not ours. It was amicable. We were together until graduation, but that summer I left with Salem to move to New York."

"He still carries a torch for you."

"I wish he wouldn't."

"So you don't have any unresolved feelings for him?"

I raised my brows. "I was going to marry another man. I do not have any unresolved feelings for my high school boyfriend."

"Good to know."

My gaze narrowed.

A customer walked up to the jukebox and pressed a few buttons. When the song didn't change, he kicked the side of it. With a warble, an old-school country song blasted from the speakers.

"Come on," Declan said, scooting out of the booth.

"Where are we going?"

"We're going to dance."

"You dance?" I asked in surprise.

"Guess you'll find out." He held his hand out to me.

I looked at it for a moment and then took it. He helped me up and led me toward the dance floor.

He pulled me close, one hand splaying across my back, his other hand holding mine. I tripped over my own two feet, but Declan didn't laugh at me. And soon the nerves disappeared. He twirled and whirled me, keeping a strong, firm grip.

His flannel shirt was soft beneath my fingertips and when he pulled me close, I could smell the saddle soap and hay clinging to his skin.

The song changed to a slower one, but Declan didn't

release me. Instead, his large hand pressed against the small of my back and urged me closer.

Our hips brushed against one another, and quivers of longing sparked in my belly. A startled gasp escaped my lips.

My head whipped back so I could stare at him. He was looking down at me, his blue eyes banked with heat. His head dipped . . .

I shoved away from him, almost colliding with another couple on the floor.

"Air," I blurted out.

I ran for the front door and yanked it open. After stepping outside, I bent over, placed my hands on my thighs, and gulped like my life depended on it.

The door opened and I turned my head. Declan strode outside, holding my coat.

"Thought you might be cold," he said.

"Thanks," I mumbled.

He held my jacket up to me, silently offering aid. I shoved my arms into the sleeves. My coat slid on, but Declan didn't let go. Instead, he stepped behind me, reached down and zipped it up for me.

"Hadley, look at me."

When I didn't comply, he gently placed his hands on my shoulders and turned me to him.

"Declan, don't," I begged.

"Don't what?" he asked, his voice husky, his hands grasping the collar of my jacket.

"Don't look at me that way."

"What way?"

"Like you want to kiss me."

"I do want to kiss you."

"You can't."

"Why not? You want me to kiss you. I can see it."

"No, I don't," I lied.

He smiled.

"*Declan*," I groaned.

He took a deep breath.

"What?" I demanded.

"Hearing you say my name like that . . . it's giving me fantasies."

"Well, stop."

"Can't." The lights from the street and the building made him easy to see.

His gaze was intense, and he hadn't let go of my coat.

"You work for my father," I said, trying to reason with him.

He frowned.

"You work for my father," I said again.

"I'm aware." He cocked his head to the side. "Is that really the only reason you don't want me to kiss you?"

"It's a pretty big reason," I said. "I don't want you to get fired."

"Thanks for thinking of my livelihood," he drawled. "I like you, Hadley. And I know you like me, too."

"We said we'd be friends," I reminded him. "That's all this can be, Declan. Please don't make it harder."

He stared at me for a moment and then released me. "Let me walk you to your car."

"I drove the truck. I'm parked right there," I said, pointing to the street spot outside the Copper Mule.

He walked me to the truck and opened the driver's side door for me.

I wasn't sure what to say to him. Small talk seemed stupid when my heart was racing and all I wanted to do was close the distance between us.

"Get home safe," he said.

"You too."

With a nod, he shut the door and then crossed the street to his motorcycle.

I started the truck as I watched Declan lift his long leg and straddle his bike.

"I'm so screwed," I muttered, putting the truck into gear. "So damn screwed."

CHAPTER TWELVE

THE RANCH

Muddy looked up from her crochet project and raised her brows. "You're home."

"Yes."

She glanced at the clock on the mantle. "You're home before nine."

"Yep."

"What happened?" She picked up the remote and muted the TV.

I sighed. "Gracie's daughter got sick, so she bailed. I stayed for a drink and then I left."

"You see Wade?"

"Yeah. He was working the bar."

"How's he looking?" Muddy asked with a raise of her brows. "Still cute?"

"Still cute," I said with an amused smile.

"Still pining for you?"

"No," I scoffed.

"You sure about that?"

"No."

She laughed. "He isn't dating anyone."

"How do you know?" I demanded.

"Because our town is eight hundred forty-three people," she drawled. "So, I know. Was he happy to see you?"

"Yes. Surprised too." I paused, my brow furrowed. "I don't want him to pine for me. I want him to date someone else and move on."

"How noble of you."

"Muddy!"

She grinned. "What? It's nice to be wanted."

He isn't the man I want.

"Can I ask you something?"

"Sure," she said.

"Why didn't you ever remarry after Grandpa died?" I asked. "I'm sure many men were sniffing around you."

She picked up her crochet hook and bent her head to her task when she answered the question. "A few. But I wasn't interested in taking care of anyone else again. The ranch was enough work."

"You took care of me. And Salem."

"You're my granddaughters. It's different than caring for a dying spouse." She shrugged. "There is the other issue, also."

"What issue is that?"

She looked at me. "I wasn't going to marry for companionship, and I only fell in love once."

"Once?" I asked.

"Once. You're young, though. You'll love again."

"You were young," I protested. "When Grandpa died."

"I was older than you. By a decade."

"But didn't you miss . . . ya know . . ."

Her lips twitched but she didn't raise her head. "Miss what, Hadley?"

EMMA SLATE

"Are you really going to make me say it?" I grumbled.

She cackled. "Yeah. I'm gonna make you say it. Especially if you expect me to answer."

"Didn't you miss sex?" I stage-whispered, feeling my cheeks heat.

"You don't have to be married to enjoy sex."

I gasped.

Muddy looked up and winked. "Like I said, there were several marriage proposals."

"Several? You said *a few*."

"Several, a few." She shrugged. "I've lost track."

"You're a trip," I said with a laugh.

The front door opened, and I heard the plodding of boots across the wooden floor before my father appeared in the doorway.

"Hey," he greeted, his gaze bouncing between me and Muddy.

"Hey," I said.

"What are you guys talking about?"

"Nothing," Muddy and I said at the same time, causing us both to laugh.

I stood up and went to my dad and hugged him.

"Thought you'd be out with Gracie until the wee hours of the morning," Dad said.

"Thought so too," I admitted. "Her baby got sick."

"Everything okay?"

"Yeah, just the flu."

He made a noise in the back of his throat. "I checked on Mirabelle. She's gonna foal soon. In a few days, I think. I'll call Dr. Swanson tomorrow and make sure she's aware we might need her in the middle of the night."

"I'll give Mirabelle some extra love tomorrow," I said. "I think I'm gonna turn in early. Gotta get up and feed those chickens, you know?"

"Have you seen Declan?" Dad asked Muddy. "I want to tell him about Mirabelle."

"Nope. He said he was going to the Copper Mule for a drink." Muddy looked at me. "Did you see him while you were there, Hadley?"

My gaze narrowed at her, and a devilish twinkle entered her hazel eyes.

"No, I must've missed him," I said. "Good night."

I escaped to my bedroom and closed the door.

My grandmother was a sly one. She saw all. She knew all. And I was sure she realized that there was something going on between me and Declan.

I grabbed my cell phone from my sweater pocket and debated on whether or not to text Salem. It was near midnight on the East Coast, but I was in desperate need of advice.

> ME
>
> You awake?

Salem's reply was almost instant.

> SALEM
>
> Unfortunately.

> ME
>
> I need help.

> SALEM
>
> that encompasses a lot.

> ME
>
> Call me you loon.

A moment later, my cell phone rang and I went into my closet and closed the door to muffle the sound.

"Hey," I greeted, smiling at Salem. Her red hair was messy and pulled back into a lopsided ponytail.

"Hey," my sister said. "What's going on? I thought you were out with Gracie."

"How did you know that?" I demanded.

"Muddy told me when I talked to her earlier."

"You talked to Muddy?"

"Yeah, I called her. I had a question about the chocolate cupcake recipe. I was blanking on one of the ingredients."

"Brewed coffee, right?"

"Yes, how did you know?"

"Twin tingle," I said. "Gracie's daughter got sick. So it was just me and Wade at the bar."

"He's still in love with you, you know."

"Not you too. Muddy said the same thing. But I don't want to talk about Wade."

"What do you want to talk about then?"

I paused and then said, "Declan showed up."

"Did he?"

"Yeah." I sighed.

"Oh my God, something happened between you two, didn't it?"

"No. I mean, well, yes, but no."

"Hadley . . ."

"We two-stepped."

"I'll alert the church elders," Salem drawled.

"No, you don't understand. We *two-stepped.*"

"Unless you did it naked, I'm failing to see the issue. And that's not really an issue, that's a good idea actually. Naked two-stepping. It's the new cardio craze."

"Salem," I hissed. "We almost kissed. In public."

"Really?"

"Yes."

"But you didn't."

"But we *almost* did."

"Why didn't you?" she demanded.

"Because I came to my senses."

"You're entirely too sensible. That's your problem."

"We can't all be feral hyenas," I mocked.

"That hurts . . . kind of."

"It does not," I said with a laugh.

"I'm getting Wyn on the phone and we're taking a vote. Let me go get Poet."

"A vote? What do you mean a vote? A vote on what?"

"Hang on."

"Salem—"

"*Hang on!*"

A few moments later, Poet grumbled, "I was almost asleep." She took a seat on the couch next to Salem. "What's this meeting about?"

"Wyn?" Salem asked.

"Here," Wyn said, her face appearing on the screen.

I leaned forward. "You have something on your shirt."

"It's puke. The kid puked on me."

"Ew." Salem wrinkled her nose. "You should really shower."

"I was going to," Wyn said, "but you called, and I answered."

"We have been summoned," Poet stated. "So, what's this about?"

"Hadley almost kissed Declan," Salem announced.

Poet and Wyn were silent, but their mouths dropped open in unison.

"Almost?" Wyn asked, regaining her voice. "Why almost?"

"Because she's a big fat chicken," Salem said. "So, we're taking a vote."

"A vote?" Poet asked. "About what?"

"About if she should kiss him for real," Salem said.

"I vote yes," Wyn said.

"Me too," Poet added.

I glared at her.

"Sorry. I need to live vicariously through you," Poet said.

"Same, I'm in a major dry spell," Wyn said. "These days, my eye candy is nothing but balding middle-aged men trying to recapture their youth. And hairlines."

"Let's talk about why this is a bad idea," I said.

"Let's not," Salem replied. "We love you, Hadley. But you'll always find a way not to do the scary things."

"Kissing Declan isn't scary," I denied.

"No?" Wyn asked. "Then why won't you do it?"

"Well, because he works for my dad. And there's the rule. I don't want him to lose his job."

"Were you going to kiss him or was he going to kiss you?" Poet asked.

"What do you mean?"

"I mean, if he was the one who was going to make the move, then he's obviously throwing caution to the wind and deciding it's worth the risk," Poet said. "Ergo . . ."

"Yes, *ergo*," Salem agreed. "If he kisses you then it's not on you if he loses his job."

"That's so cavalier," I stated.

"Is this because you'd feel guilty?" Poet asked quietly. "Like, would you feel like you're betraying Gianni?"

I thought about her question for a moment and then reluctantly shook my head. "No. It doesn't really have anything to do with Gianni."

"That's interesting," Salem said.

"I know this sounds weird. Like really weird. But since I haven't heard from him and I've been back here . . . it feels like it happened in another life already."

"I don't think that's weird," Poet said. "If anything, it proves we were right in telling you to go home to heal."

"There are two types of healing. Emotional and physical.

It's time to jump back in the saddle, woman," Wyn said. "Get your groove back or whatever."

"I'll think about it," I lied. "Thanks for the advice, peanut gallery. I'm gonna go now."

"One more thing," Salem said.

"What?" I asked.

"Do it scared," she said, her eyes meeting mine.

I groaned. "That's not fair."

"I think it would be good for you," she said. "Live a little."

"Why? You live enough for both of us," I replied.

"Mommy and Daddy are fighting," Wyn said. "I'm out."

"Me too," Poet added.

The two of them left and it was just me and my sister.

"I'm worried about you," she said.

"Why? Why is me being cautious something to be worried about?"

"Because you're always cautious," she said.

"And the one time I wasn't, I got my heart broken," I pointed out.

"Did you? Did you *really* get your heart broken?"

"Now you're doubting how much I loved Gianni?"

"Loved? It's already in the past?"

I fell silent.

"Is it?"

"I don't know," I admitted. "Because if I say yes, then did I really love him at all? And if I say no, am I pathetic?"

It was Salem's turn to fall silent.

"I just wish . . ." I stopped.

"Go on," she pressed.

"I just wish I wasn't so confused."

"What are you confused about?"

"Everything. Nothing." I sighed. "I like Declan. But I'm so angry at Gianni that I don't trust that I'm seeing straight. I don't want to make another foolish decision and then have to deal with the fallout. You know?"

"Yeah. I know." She paused. "Does anyone else know? The real reason you and Gianni split up?"

"No. You're the only one. I almost told Poet, but she was in the middle of a crisis when I called."

"Her co-worker taking credit for her work. Yeah, she told me."

"Coming home was the right choice," I said. "But I miss you. And I miss Wyn and Poet."

"But you don't miss your life here."

"No, I don't think I do," I admitted. "New York doesn't fit me the way it fits you."

"It's okay, you know. If you decide to stay. I'll be okay."

"If I decide to stay," I said quietly. "New York doesn't fit me, but maybe the Ridge doesn't fit me anymore either."

She snorted.

"What?" I demanded.

"It's not a failure on your part for loving home, for wanting to be home. For needing the big blue sky and the mountains."

"But what's *here* for me?" I asked.

"What's in New York?"

"Touché." I scratched my forehead.

"Have you mourned?"

"Mourned? Mourned Gianni and the loss of that relationship, you mean?"

"Kinda. I meant about . . ."

"My infertility," I remarked bitterly. "No, I don't think I have. I can barely stomach thinking about it. All I've ever wanted was to have a family. I'm not ready to let go of what I thought my life was going to look like. I'm not ready to say goodbye to that dream."

I thought about Declan. Was he the type of man to leave,

to walk away when things didn't go according to plan? Gianni had done exactly that. Even worse, he'd promised me it didn't change how he saw me and our life together, but it had been a lie. Because in the end, he'd left.

"I'm tired," I said quietly.

"Okay." Salem's voice sounded so far away. Too far away. "Get some sleep. I'll talk to you later, yeah?"

"Yeah," I agreed.

Neither of us hung up and because Salem was Salem, she knew I needed another moment.

"You might be okay without me in New York," I said. "But I don't know if I'll be okay without you here."

"I can't go back there, Hadley."

"I know. I'd never ask you to."

"Love you."

"Love you too."

"Things will look better in the morning," she promised.

"Lie."

She grunted. "Well, they'll look how they'll look. It's your decision on what lens to look at life through. Good night, twin."

CHAPTER THIRTEEN

THE RANCH

Late the next morning, I opened the front door and smiled in surprised confusion. "Hey, Wade."

"Hi," he greeted. "Sorry I didn't call."

"That's okay." I stepped back to let him inside and closed the door behind him.

"Did I catch you at a bad time?"

"Bad time?"

He pointed to my face. "You've got dirt on your cheek."

My hand went to my face and I rubbed it absently. "I was in the garden."

"Ah, yeah. The get up makes sense now." He winked.

I was wearing a pair of patchwork overalls, and my hair was parted into two French braids.

I headed into the kitchen. "Something to drink?"

"No. I'm good."

I opened the fridge and pulled out a pitcher of iced tea. "So, what brought you to my neck of the woods?"

"Two things," he said. "One, I wanted to check on you."

"Check on me? Why?" I went to the cupboard and got a glass.

"You left the bar last night without a word," he explained. "And I saw Declan run out after you."

"Ah," I said, keeping my back turned.

"That's all you've got to say?"

"What do you want me to say?" I asked, finally facing him, my eyebrows raised.

"I want to know if you're okay. It looked intense."

"I'm fine," I lied.

"Okay." He nodded and then reached into his pocket to extract his wallet. "Declan left his card. I thought maybe you could give it to him."

"Oh. Yeah, I can do that. Thanks, Wade."

He set the card down onto the kitchen table and then put his wallet back into his pocket. "So what's going on with you and Declan?"

I choked on my iced tea. "Going on with Declan? Nothing."

He cocked his head to the side and studied me. "Something's going on there."

"Nothing is going on there," I assured him. "He works for my dad. He's a friend. That's all."

Wade suddenly smiled. "Good."

"Good? Why is that good?"

"I know your engagement just ended," he said, running a hand through his dark hair. "So I don't want to pressure you into anything. But I was wondering if you want to have dinner. With me."

"Dinner," I repeated slowly. "With you."

The front door opened, and someone tromped through the house into the kitchen.

"Wade," Muddy said in surprise.

"Hey, Muddy." Wade smiled.

She looked at me and then back to Wade. "You staying for lunch?"

Wade shook his head. "I gotta get going." He glanced at me. "Call you later?"

I nodded absently.

Wade walked from the kitchen and after a moment, the front door opened and shut.

"What was he doing here?" Muddy asked.

"He came to return Declan's credit card," I said, gesturing with my chin to the table. "And to ask me to dinner."

"Declan left his card at the bar last night?" Muddy asked slowly. "The bar you were at last night? The one where you said you didn't see him?"

"*Muddy*," I warned.

"Well, it looks like you have two fine options in helping you get over Gianni."

I rolled my eyes. "How's Mirabelle?"

"Restless," she said. "Your father's right. She's going to foal any day now." Muddy picked up Declan's credit card. "He's out in the barn now, so you can go return this to him."

I took the credit card. "Playing matchmaker, are you?"

"I don't know what you mean," Muddy said, hazel eyes twinkling.

"Salem and I might be twins, but she's cut from the same cloth as you," I said with a laugh.

Muddy patted my cheek as I passed by her.

I walked to the barn, my heart hammering in my ears. Declan was setting up a cot in the empty stall across from Mirabelle.

"What are you doing?" I asked.

Declan slid a pillow into a pillowcase. "Mirabelle's gonna foal soon, so I'll be sleeping in the barn until she does."

"You? Why you?"

"Because I have experience birthing horses."

"Oh, I didn't realize."

"I'm more than just a pretty face," he joked.

I smiled slightly. "I know."

"Do you?" He looked at me, pinning me with a blue stare.

I held his gaze for a moment and then reached into my pocket. "Wade came by and asked me to give this to you."

He looked at the credit card for a moment before taking it. "I'd forgotten I even opened a tab."

I took a deep breath. "About last night—"

"Forget it," he said. He shoved his credit card into his back pocket.

What if I don't want to forget it?

The words tangled my tongue, and they wouldn't come out. They dared not be spoken.

I turned around and walked out of the barn. My conversation with Salem played in my head. Was I still raw from my broken engagement? Yes. Even under the anger, there was deep-seated hurt that wasn't going to go away just because I found Declan attractive.

But I knew that if I kissed Declan, my relationship with Gianni was truly over. Along with the dreams of the life I'd planned on building with him. My present was murky. My future undecided. And I wasn't ready to leap without looking. That was Salem's territory. I'd never been that way.

Every time I was around Declan, I felt foolish. I rebuffed and rejected.

I needed a ride to clear my head, but I wasn't going to go back into the barn to saddle Goldie.

So I decided to grab the truck keys and go for a drive. Two hours later, I was no closer to working out my feelings.

My eyes flipped open, staring into the darkness of my bedroom. Anxiety clogged my throat, but I wasn't sure where it was coming from.

I sat up and waited for my pulse to stop racing. I looked at the clock. It was just past midnight.

Before I knew what I was doing, I was flinging off the covers and getting dressed in an old pair of jeans and a flannel shirt. I tied my hair back and pulled on a pair of thick wool socks. I quietly turned the knob of my bedroom door and crept down the wooden stairs, making sure to skip the second stair from the bottom, which was known to creak.

I lifted my coat from the hook, picked up the bear spray, and then unlocked the front door. I crept outside and breathed in the crisp night as I shrugged into my coat and then slid into my boots.

My strides were long and brisk. I felt the tension in the barn as a horse huffed out a breath of air.

I padded toward Mirabelle's stall. She was pacing, her black tail swishing back and forth.

"What are you doing here?" Declan asked from the stall behind me.

I turned to look at him. He was sitting up on the cot he'd set up earlier, his feet touching the ground. He was in a pair of jeans and a black thermal. His dark hair was mussed, but his eyes were clear.

"I don't know," I admitted. "I just . . . woke up and . . ." I rubbed my chest. "I can't explain it. It's weird." I gestured to Mirabelle. "How long has she been like this?"

"About an hour," he said.

"Ah. Has her water broken?"

"Not yet."

"It's not her first baby. When she gets going, it's going to be a fast delivery." I peeked over the stall to watch Mirabelle for a moment. She was pacing and pawing the fresh hay. Her tail kept swishing back and forth.

We were at the back of the barn, away from the draft, but Declan had set up a heater to keep the foal warm.

"Someone else is more than a pretty face," Declan said. "You know what you're talking about."

Pleasure at his words skated through my belly.

"So I'm guessing you've assisted with deliveries before?" Declan asked.

I nodded. "I helped my mom from time to time. She was a vet."

"Interesting," Declan murmured. "You didn't have any interest in following in your mother's footsteps?"

"No," I admitted. "A big part of being a vet is being with people on one of the worst days of their lives. It wears on you after a while. I saw that with my mom."

"Here, take a seat," Declan said, gesturing to his cot. "I didn't think I'd have company, otherwise I would've brought a chair."

"Thanks." I sat on the cot with my back against the stall.

Declan leaned against the far wall that faced me. "Nothing to do now but wait."

"Yeah."

"You need anything?" he asked. "Something to drink?"

"I'm good."

We fell into a companionable silence, listening for the sounds of Mirabelle's impending birth.

"Was I right?" he asked suddenly.

"About what?"

"About Wade."

I paused for a moment and then nodded. "Yeah, you were right about Wade. He asked me to dinner."

"You gonna go?"

"No."

"Why not?"

My heart drummed in my ears. I forced myself to meet Declan's gaze when I replied, "You know why not."

His hands clenched at his sides.

Mirabelle grunted and then there was the sound of whooshing water.

Declan pushed away from the wall and grinned. "Showtime."

CHAPTER FOURTEEN

THE RANCH

Forty minutes later, the birthing was finished. The foal was nursing while his mother recuperated.

I was covered in gunk and so was Declan. Both of us were elated and a bit slaphappy.

"It never gets old," I said with a satisfied grin. "Especially when everything goes according to plan."

"Mirabelle is a champion," Declan said as I helped him clean up.

"I earned a shower—and a drink," I said as I looked at my clothes. "But I'm also starving."

"I've got a bottle of fifteen-year-old bourbon I haven't opened yet," he said. "And I make a mean quesadilla. You can shower while I make food."

"Oh, that's not a good idea—"

"You want to wake up the entire household tromping in at two in the morning? I've got a shower and spare clothes."

My stomach rumbled.

"Let's go," I said with a smile.

We checked on Mirabelle and the foal one more time and then left the barn.

Declan's porch was devoid of light, and I nearly tripped up the stairs. He reached his hand out and caught me before I fell.

"Thanks," I muttered.

His grip was firm, but then suddenly it was gone and I wished it wasn't.

Declan opened the front door and flipped on the porch light. We took off our boots and left them on the mat outside and then we headed into the small guest cabin.

"Sorry it's cold in here," he said, immediately going to the thermostat. "I keep it at sixty-four. I run hot."

I rubbed my hands together and wisely kept my thoughts to myself, remembering all too well the warmth of his skin.

"Let me get you a towel and some clean clothes to change into."

"Thanks," I said. I stood by while he gathered what I needed and set them in the microscopic bathroom.

"Save some hot water for me, yeah?" he asked with a wink.

"Will do," I said, feeling my cheeks turn pink.

I closed the bathroom door and turned on the shower. As it steamed, I quickly shucked my clothes and scooted them into the corner with my toes.

My hair was tied back, and I kept it out of the water. I washed quickly, using Declan's sandalwood-scented soap. I didn't linger—my stomach continued to rumble in demand.

I shut off the water and quickly wrapped myself in a faded, soft towel and then I pulled on the clothes Declan gave me. It was reminiscent of the first night we'd met.

I gathered up my soiled clothes and wondered what I was going to do with them when I stepped out of the bathroom.

The scent of butter and cheese hit my nose, and I began to salivate.

"Do you have a plastic bag or something I can put these in?" I asked Declan.

"Yeah, under the sink." He stood at the stove and flipped a quesadilla.

I grabbed a grocery bag and stuffed my clothes into it and then set it down by the front door. "That smells incredible."

"Sit," he commanded.

I perched on the couch. He turned off the burner and slid the quesadilla onto a plate. After grabbing a fork, knife and a napkin, he brought the food to me.

"Thank you," I said.

"Sure thing. Let me get the bourbon."

He went back into the kitchen and grabbed the bottle on top of the fridge. He cracked it open and poured a splash into two glasses.

"Cheers," he said, clinking his glass against mine.

I took a sip of the bourbon and nodded. "Yep, that's incredible."

"Aged in charred American oak barrels and finished another year in a former sherry barrel," he said. "I've been saving it for a special occasion."

Warmth at his words—and the bourbon—poured through me.

"You good if I shower real fast?"

I nodded.

"You need any hot sauce or salsa to go with that quesadilla?"

I shook my head.

"Okay then." He took another sip of his drink, left the glass on the coffee table, and then went to shower.

By the time he returned to the living room, the quesadilla was gone and I was nursing my drink.

Declan took the spot at the other end of the couch and picked up his bourbon. His dark hair was wet and even though he'd put on a pair of sweats and a long-sleeved shirt, he'd left his feet bare.

"You really do run hot," I blurted out, pointing to his toes.

He wiggled them. "Yep. I do."

I shuddered. "My hands are always cold. So are my feet. I sleep in socks even in summer."

"That would drive me crazy," he said. "You know what I love?"

"What?"

"When it's winter and the wood stove is lit, and I'm under a heavy blanket, but there's still a slight chill to the air."

I closed my eyes. "Yeah. Nothing like falling asleep next to the fire."

I opened my eyes and stared at him. He leaned over and unscrewed the bourbon and picked it up. Declan gestured to my glass. I held it out to him, and he topped it off.

Despite my full belly, my head was already starting to buzz. My skin was humming, warmth spreading through me.

"What's your favorite thing about New York?" he asked after he topped off his drink.

"My sister and my friends."

"You miss them?"

"Yeah," I admitted.

He took a hefty swallow. "Have you talked to your ex since the split?"

All the warmth I'd been feeling suddenly disappeared. Bitterness coated my tongue. "No. I haven't talked to him. Why would I?"

"I don't know." He shrugged. "I thought he would've come to his senses and begged you to take him back by now."

"That'll never happen."

"What? Him begging you to take him back, or you going back to him?"

"Both," I replied.

We fell silent, but I could tell he wasn't done prying.

"Ask," I said gruffly.

"Ask what?"

"Ask whatever's on your mind. Because something clearly is."

"It's not so much a question as it is an observation."

"Go on," I urged.

"You just don't seem all that bothered by it," he said. "The ending of your engagement, I mean."

"Not bothered?" I repeated. "How do you figure?"

"I don't know. I guess you just seem so . . . put together. Not losing your shit at all."

"And I should be losing my shit?" I asked in wry amusement.

"Aren't you mad?" he blurted out. "Don't you want to yell and throw things?"

"And that would prove what, exactly? That I'm feeling my breakup on a deeper level?" I tossed back the rest of my drink, trying to wash away the bitterness.

"Why aren't you angry?"

"Who says I'm not?"

"Are you?"

"Hell yeah, I'm angry." My eyes narrowed and heat filled my cheeks. "But I'm not angry at Gianni. I'm angry at myself."

"What? Why?"

"Because I was stupid to believe him," I said. "I was stupid to believe he loved me. I was stupid to believe that love conquered all. I was stupid to believe we had anything lasting. I was stupid to think I'd found a love like my parents."

I hastily shot up from my seat and stared down at Declan,

who didn't appear at all put out by my sudden bout of emotion.

"I was stupid to even dream of a life with him. It was right there in front of me the whole time," I went on as I began to pace. "He always had some excuse about not being able to come home for a visit with me. And when I threw out the suggestion of a small wedding here, he balked. Our relationship was always about him and about how I could contort myself into *his* life and *his* family. It's no wonder it ended."

"What was the final straw?" he asked quietly. "What made you finally walk away?"

"I didn't walk away. He did. My self-esteem is in the toilet."

"It shouldn't be," he said. "Fuck him."

I smiled slightly. "Yeah. If only I could convince myself not to feel bad. But it's raw, you know? Someone rejects you and then you start to wonder if you're . . ."

"If you're what?"

"Desirable." I sighed. "Ignore me. It's the bourbon. It's loosened my tongue."

"Good. No use in being emotionally constipated."

His words made me laugh. And then he laughed. The warmth that was missing bloomed between us again.

Declan's gaze suddenly softened as he looked at me. "You really think you're not desirable?"

I shrugged.

"You are desirable."

My eyes widened. "What?"

"You are desirable," he said again, slowly this time. His gaze raked over me from head to toe. "It's been damn near impossible to keep my hands to myself around you, Hadley."

Tingles erupted all over my skin.

And the way he was looking at me made me feel as

though he'd slowly stripped me out of all my clothes and was memorizing how I looked naked.

Maybe it was the bourbon. Maybe it was my deflated ego that needed stroking.

Or maybe it was that I'd been denying what had been brewing between us since the first night we'd met.

Instead of replying to him I set my glass down onto the coffee table and then I did something completely out of character.

I scooted across the couch and then straddled his lap.

His blue eyes burned bright as his hands came up to cradle my hips.

Banked desire roared to life. Flames of need rushed through my blood, sweeping away all resistance.

I suddenly needed to know how he felt inside me.

"This is a bad idea," I murmured, my fingers sinking into the hair at the base of his neck.

"I don't care," Declan said as his strong, warm hand slid underneath my T-shirt.

"My whole life I've always done the right thing . . . tonight I'd like to try something else and see how it feels."

Declan grinned. "You'll like being bad."

"Yeah?"

He nodded slowly. "I'll make sure you like it."

Declan's words were a promise, and I shivered in anticipation.

His hand continued to glide up my back lightly, without urgency. I scooted even closer and then slowly eased down to press against him.

We were hindered by our clothing, but I felt his erection at my cleft.

Declan's other hand cradled the back of my head, and he urged my mouth toward his.

"You want me."

It wasn't a question.

I licked my lips and nodded.

"I need to hear you say it," he said, his voice raspy and deep. "I need to know you want me as much as I want you."

I placed my hand on his chest. The powerful beat of his heart pulsed beneath my fingertips, and I itched to feel his warm skin against mine.

"Yes, Declan. I want you."

That was all the confirmation he needed.

His lips covered mine. Warm, insistent, passionate.

I opened my mouth in invitation. His tongue thrust between my lips to duel with mine. I rubbed against him, rocking my hips, instinctively needing more from him.

His breath smelled of bourbon and mint, and I savored the taste of him.

"Off," he grunted, tugging on my shirt.

I lifted my arms, and he slid the T-shirt up over my head and tossed it aside.

"Fuck me," he whispered in reverence as his hands reached up to cradle my breasts.

He held the weight of them in his palms and then his thumbs slid across my nipples. Declan bent his head and took one of them into his warm, welcoming mouth.

I closed my eyes and moaned in pleasure as he released my nipple from his lips.

"You like that."

I didn't reply, I just pushed my breast back into his mouth.

He nipped and tugged, sending a shot of desire straight to my core. With his fingers, he twirled my other nipple. A blush of a fever spread through me.

I wanted more. I needed more.

My nipple popped from his mouth again and he leaned back, gazing at me with languid eyes.

"My turn," I whispered, reaching for the hem of his T-shirt.

He lifted up and away from the couch, grabbed the back of his shirt and hauled it off. He tossed it where he'd tossed mine.

"It's just as beautiful as I remember," I said as my hand grazed down his pectoral, across the tattoo.

"My muscular chest?"

I smiled at his sass. "That too. But I meant the tattoo."

"I'll tell you about it later," he said gruffly. "So you were looking at me the night we met?"

"Kind of hard not to," I admitted. I wiggled on his lap, causing him to groan. I pressed my lips to his sternum and then peppered my way across toward his nipple.

"I couldn't stop staring at you either." His fingers sank into my hair and his breath caught when my teeth gently bit his nipple.

"No more talking."

"Yes, ma'am." He leaned his head back against the couch and closed his eyes.

My fingers glided up his chest that was covered in dark hair. I giggled.

Declan's eyes flipped open. "Are you laughing?"

"Yes."

"Are you laughing at me while I'm half naked?"

"Maybe."

"Woman, you want to talk about an ego killer?"

I buried my face into the side of his neck and started to laugh again. "I'm sorry, I just—you've got a pelt."

He wrapped his arms around me. "A pelt?"

I placed my hand on his chest and all but ran my fingers through his chest hair. "A pelt."

"A pelt," he repeated, turning his head and grazing his lips across my ear, causing me to shiver.

He held onto me as he stood and then he walked us toward the bedroom. Declan didn't turn on the light, but there was enough illumination from the living room that I was able to see the curves of his shoulders and his tapered waist.

Declan gently lay me in the middle of the bed.

"I like it," I said.

"Like what?"

"Your pelt."

He wheezed out a laugh. "Woman, how am I supposed to make love to you if you're making me laugh?"

"I don't know," I said wickedly. "Guess you'd better get creative."

"Guess I'd better," he agreed as he reached for my sweats.

I lifted up my hips and let him drag them off me so that I was splayed out naked.

Without a word, he bent his head toward the apex of my thighs. "Fuck."

Anxiety rippled through me. "What?" I asked, trying to clamp my legs shut.

He placed his large hands on my inner thighs to keep me open. "You smell incredible."

"What?"

"Yeah, I can smell your arousal and it's fucking diabolical. I can't wait to taste you."

His gaze was trained on me for a moment and then he bent his head and gave me a slow, long lick. Declan was gentle, taking his time to savor me, to react to what I liked.

He listened when I gasped. He touched me where I needed. He paid attention to every nuance of my body—my body that had no choice but to follow the path of pleasure Declan laid out for me.

"Declan," I moaned.

"I know, baby."

He slid his hands beneath my ass and urged me to rest my legs on his shoulders. My back bowed off the bed when he gently sucked me into his mouth.

I was wet and writhing, trembling with need but Declan didn't stop. He spurred me on, forcing me to give in to the pleasure waiting for me.

The tingles started at the top of my scalp and shot down my spine, spreading out through my core and then I was erupting around his tongue. Convulsing with my release, crying out my joy.

It wasn't until I was gently floating back into my body that I realized my legs were still up on Declan's shoulders and my thighs were squeezing his ears.

I slid them off his shoulders and stared at him. His mouth glistened with my release and with a swipe of his tongue across his lips, my desire flamed to life again.

"I want you inside me," I whispered.

He stilled. "Fuck."

"What?"

"I don't have a condom."

I swallowed. "You don't have to worry about a condom. I —I can't get pregnant."

His jaw clenched. "You sure?"

I nodded.

He closed his eyes for a moment and then nodded.

I reached for him.

CHAPTER FIFTEEN

THE RANCH

Declan rolled off the bed and stood. He grasped the band of his sweats and shoved them down his legs.

My eyes widened in surprise.

He grasped his erection and gave it a few long, slow pumps.

"You worried about my size?" he asked gruffly. "Don't worry, you can take me."

"I wasn't worried about your size," I stated. "I was just surprised you weren't wearing underwear. Were you just hoping to get lucky?"

"If I was hoping to get lucky, don't you think I would've bought condoms?" His eyes pinned me with a stare. "You sure you're okay with this? If not, say the word and I'll get creative and find other ways to make you come again."

I wasn't sure if it was the bourbon or just Declan, but I didn't want to turn back. I wanted all the pleasure he could offer me.

"Hadley?"

"I want you, Declan," I assured him. "And I want you now."

He squeezed his shaft and then released it before climbing back onto the bed. His crown glistened and my mouth watered. I wanted to taste him and almost vocalized my desire, but he slid the head of his shaft against my entrance, and I forgot to think.

"You're fucking beautiful," he growled.

The tip of him glided in and then he sank all the way inside me to the hilt. We both groaned in pleasure. I could feel every bit of him. He was big and girthy, and when I clenched around him, he shuddered.

He cradled the back of my neck with one hand and grabbed my leg with the other. I lifted it and wrapped it around his hip.

I took him deeper, meeting him thrust for thrust. My nails scored his back as he drove into me. Relentless. Ruthless.

The bed frame smacked against the wall with each robust movement. Our skin heated, our breaths mingled, our kisses were torrid.

"Hadley," he rasped.

I lifted both my legs straight in the air and widened them. He angled inside me, hitting the exact spot I needed, and I cried out my release.

As the waves of pleasure tore through, Declan slammed into me one final time and came. He gasped and shuddered with the force of his orgasm.

I felt the heat of him deep inside me.

Declan gathered me into his arms and pressed a kiss to my forehead, and then my nose, and then my lips.

He then slid out of me; I quivered as he went.

"Don't move," he stated.

He padded naked to the bathroom. After a few moments, I heard running water. Declan returned with a washcloth.

I held out my hand for it, but he batted me away and gently tapped my thigh. "Open."

"You don't have to do that," I said, embarrassment coating my voice.

"Yes, I do. Open," he commanded again.

I did as he bid, my cheeks flaming in heat.

"Why are you embarrassed?" he asked as he chucked the soiled washcloth into the laundry bin in the corner of the room.

"I just have never had anyone . . ." I sat up and looked around for my T-shirt, only to realize it was still in the living room. I folded my arms across my chest. "Can I get a shirt?"

He raised his brows and then sat down on the bed next to me. "What's going on, Hadley?"

"What do you mean?"

"I mean, why are you being shy? There's no reason for you to be shy. I was just inside you."

"Declan!"

He grinned. "Come on, let's get under the covers and get at least a few hours of sleep."

"I can't sleep over. I've got to get back to the main house before my dad wakes up."

"So wait, you come over here, drink my bourbon, seduce me, and then you won't even spoon me?"

"Who seduced who?"

"Let's just call it an equal opportunity seduce-fest." He grinned again. "And if you give me the chance, I'll do it again."

"As much fun as that sounds, I don't think it's a good idea."

"Why not?"

"Well, for the obvious reason."

"My job and The Rule?"

I nodded.

"A little late for that. We crossed the line."

"Yeah." I sighed. "It's my fault we crossed the line."

He raised his brows. "How do you figure?"

"I shouldn't have come back here with you. I could've—should've—gone back to the main house. I definitely shouldn't have let you make me food or drank your bourbon. And I definitely shouldn't have . . . well, ya know."

"Come on my tongue?"

"*Stop,*" I hissed.

"Oh God, this is going to be so much fun."

I frowned. "What's going to be fun?"

"Making you blush. I plan on finding out at least three new ways to make you blush by the end of the week."

"Declan," I began. "We can't."

"Why not? We've already done it. Do you regret it already?"

"I really wish I wasn't naked having this conversation," I muttered. "And I definitely wish you weren't naked."

"Why? Because you're distracted by my virile man-pelt?" He ran his hand across his chest. "Touch it. You know you want to."

"Oh my God," I moaned. "You're never going to let me live that down."

Declan leaned over, all but tackling me to the bed. He caged me in, propping himself up on his elbows so he didn't crush me.

"I'm willing to risk sneaking around if you are," he said.

"Why?" I asked with a frown. "Why would you do that?"

"Uh, hello. I've got you naked in my bed. Why *wouldn't* I do everything in my power to keep you naked in my bed?"

I bit my lip to stop my smile. "But what about your job?"

"There will always be other jobs. Besides, I did okay on the rodeo circuit. I've got a bit of nest egg."

I ran my hand along his jaw and up through his hair. "I'm not worth the trouble. I've got a lot of stuff going on upstairs." I tapped the side of my head.

"You think you're not worth the trouble?" His expression clouded. "Why the hell would you think that?"

"Declan, it's nearly four in the morning. Do we have to do this right now?"

"No," he admitted. "We don't. But at some point we're going to talk about it and we're going to talk about what the hell happened with you and your fiancé because he—"

I lifted up and quickly covered his lips with mine.

"Are you trying to distract me?" he murmured against my mouth.

"Yes."

He deepened the kiss, and I sank into it. Declan was warm and comforting and he smelled like us—the unique scent that could only come from two people's intimacy.

"Declan," I murmured. "I've really got to go."

He sighed but reluctantly released me. He reached for his sweats and quickly pulled them on. "Hang on, I'll get your clothes."

Declan went out to the living room and then returned to the bedroom with his T-shirt and sweats.

I quickly threw them on and then followed Declan out into the living room.

"Socks," he said. "Hang on."

He went and grabbed me a pair of wool socks and then opened the door to get my boots. I sat down on the couch and put them on. Declan held up my coat and I shoved my arms into the sleeves.

Instead of releasing me, he clasped my shoulders and turned me around. He kissed my lips before pulling back.

"Don't be shy with me, Hadley."

"Okay." I hunched my neck so my chin disappeared, causing him to laugh. He hugged me to him.

"We'll work on it. Let's go."

"Go where?"

"I'm walking you back to the main house."

"I've got bear spray. Besides, if you walk back with me at this hour it'll raise questions if anyone hears us."

He raked a hand through his hair. "I don't like that."

"Tough."

I kissed him one last time and then wiggled out of his embrace. I quietly trekked to the main house and took off my boots when I got to the front porch. The house was dark and I listened for sounds of movement.

There were none.

I shut the door quietly and then padded upstairs, grimacing when I forgot to avoid the squeaky stair.

When I got to the second floor, my grandmother's bedroom door opened and I came face to face with her.

We stared at one another but neither of us said a word. She looked me up and down and then she walked past me to the hall bathroom, like I wasn't even there.

I went into my bedroom and shut the door. I stripped out of Declan's clothes and shoved them into the back of my closet and then changed into my own pajamas. I climbed into bed and pulled the covers up to my neck.

My phone was resting on the nightstand, and it lit up with a text but didn't vibrate because I'd put it on silent. I grabbed it and opened the screen.

DECLAN

Good night, bear snack.

I set my phone back on the nightstand.

"Crap."

CHAPTER SIXTEEN

THE RANCH

My face was smushed into the pillow when I cracked an eye open.

"Morning, sunshine," Muddy greeted from the chair in the corner of my bedroom. She was crocheting, but she looked up from her hook.

"What time is it?" I asked, still refusing to move.

"A little after eight. Thought I'd let you sleep in, what with your late night out. Or early morning."

"What are you doing here?"

"Waiting for you to wake up so we can talk."

"Talk." I closed my mouth and squeezed my eyes shut. "What do you want to talk about?"

"Declan texted Connor early this morning about the foal's birth," she said. "He said you helped him."

"Yeah," I said carefully. "I woke up last night and had a feeling Mirabelle was going to go into labor. I went to the barn and sure enough, she was antsy."

"And the birth went fine. No complications?"

"None." I frowned and finally sat up. "Where's Dad?"

"With Dr. Swanson. She came out to check out Mirabelle and the foal."

"Oh, good." I cocked my head to the side. "Is that all?"

"Do you think I'd be sitting in your bedroom waiting for you to wake up if that's all it was?"

"I'm really tired. So can you please—"

"I won't lie for you," she said.

"Excuse me?"

"To your father. I won't lie to him about what you and Declan are doing."

"Declan and I aren't doing anything."

"*Hadley*."

"*Muddy*," I replied.

"I'm not an idiot."

"Okay? What do you want me to say?" I demanded. "So you won't lie for me. I never asked you to. And what about Dad?"

"What about him?"

"You're lying for him, aren't you?" I asked. "Since when does Dad stay out late at night, or come home during the early morning hours smelling like perfume?"

"Your father's business is his business."

"And my business is my business."

She shook her head. "No, your business is your father's business—especially if one of his ranch hands is putting his hands all over you."

"I thought you were for it."

"I am." She shrugged. "You're a grown woman who can make her own choices. But that doesn't mean there aren't consequences to those choices."

"I'm a little old to be getting this kind of lecture, don't you think?"

"You're never too old." She leaned back in her chair. "What you two are doing isn't as simple as knocking boots. He works for your father. And you just broke off an engagement."

"I'm aware of all those things," I said. "Thanks for the reminder."

"You don't do casual," she said softly. "And I don't want you to get hurt . . . again."

My anger softened. "I know."

"And you know how cowboys are."

I raised my brows. "Your son is a cowboy."

"And he married your mother four months after meeting her," she said with a smile. "Powells are built differently."

"Yes, we are," I agreed.

Muddy gathered her crochet project and rose. "I've said my piece. You're an adult and you're going to make your own decisions."

"That sounds like you don't trust me to make good ones," I remarked flatly.

"Take it however it sounds." She shrugged. "Word of advice?"

"If I say I don't want it, will you tell me anyway?"

"Sassy Sasserson," she said with a chuckle. "If you're going to be sneaking around with Declan, don't do it in town. There's no sneaking around in a small town. Someone's bound to see you and tell your father."

I sighed but reluctantly nodded.

Muddy left the bedroom and shut the door behind her.

I continued to sit on the end of my bed, weighing the words she'd spoken. What was I doing? I'd snuck into the house like a teenager not wanting to get caught after curfew.

Exhausted and rethinking everything from last night, I pulled myself up and trod to the bathroom. I stood in the shower, letting the water remove the scent of him from my skin.

I closed my eyes, remembering the pleasure I'd shared with Declan. It was hard to have any sort of regret over it.

But would I do it again? That was asking for trouble.

If you had to sneak around to do something, didn't that make it wrong?

I groaned in frustration.

Why couldn't I be like Salem? Salem, who asked for forgiveness and not permission. Salem, who didn't do regrets. Salem, who'd somehow broken free of the box society tried to dictate for her.

But here I was, twenty-three years old, worried that my father would be disappointed in me if he found out I broke one of his rules.

I turned off the shower and wrapped a towel around me.

My phone was lighting up when I walked back into the bedroom. It was still on silent.

When I saw it was Wade calling, I silenced it and let it roll to voicemail. I felt bad. I hadn't been firm enough with my boundaries.

I gritted my teeth in frustration.

While I got dressed, I practiced saying no.

As I sat on the edge of the bed and I was pulling on a pair of clean socks, there was a knock on the door.

"No!" I called out.

"Hadley? You okay?" Dad asked.

I took a deep breath and called back, "Sorry, yes, come in."

He opened the door, his brow furrowed. "You okay?"

"Fine," I said. "I was thinking about something. What's up?"

"I just checked on Mirabelle and the foal. They're both doing great."

"Glad to hear it."

"The birth went okay, then?" Dad studied me.

"The birth went fine. Declan did an amazing job. He has a good bedside manner."

"He does." Dad scratched his jaw. "He told me you went back to his cabin to get cleaned up?"

I nodded. "I didn't want to wake you by coming in late and showering. I know you're a light sleeper."

His expression cleared. "Thoughtful."

"That's me. The thoughtful one." I rubbed the side of my head.

"You okay?"

"Hmm? Oh. Yeah. Just tired. I only got a few hours of sleep."

"You do look a little wrecked."

"Thanks," I said with a laugh. "Did you just come in here to tell me I look like a car ran over me?"

"No that's not why I came up here. I'm heading out of town tomorrow for the livestock auction in Three Forks."

"Oh." I frowned. "I didn't realize that was happening . . . but that makes sense. It's that time of year isn't it? So you want me to ride shotgun with you?"

"What?"

"Ride shotgun," I repeated. "I always go with you to the stock shows, Daddy. Now that I'm home . . ."

"Actually, I'm taking Henry and Josiah. I'll be gone for a week. I need you here to keep an eye on Muddy. Don't tell her I told you this, but she's slowing down a bit. If you can help around here—maybe pick up the slack—that would help a lot."

"Sure, no problem," I said.

"Thanks, Hadley. I know I can count on you."

"You can, for sure."

Muddy hadn't slowed down in the least. But my father

was trying to come up with a plausible reason for why he didn't want me going to the stock show.

I wondered if he was taking his new secret lady friend, and he wanted some uninterrupted alone time with her.

If my father was gone for a week, that meant Declan and I . . .

My stomach rumbled.

Dad raised his brows. "You might want to do something about that."

I laughed. "Yeah. That leftover shepherd's pie is calling my name. I meant to ask about the bear. Any sign of it?"

Dad shook his head. "Nah, I think he moved along. Still, make sure you're carrying if you go for a ride, yeah?"

"I will. Are you going to bring me home a present from the stock show?"

"What kind of present do you want?" he asked.

"Something cute and cuddly. How about a baby goat?"

"You gonna take the baby goat back to New York with you? I don't think your roommates would appreciate the smell."

My heart fell at the thought of going back to New York, but I didn't want Dad to know how I truly felt. Not yet. It would invite questions I wasn't ready to answer.

CHAPTER SEVENTEEN

THE RANCH

My phone buzzed in my jacket. I slowed Goldie to a walk and unzipped my pocket and extracted my cell.

I pressed a button and put the phone to my ear. "Hey."

"Entertain me," Wyn said. "I'm at the Bridgehampton station leaving Sagaponack and the train has been delayed so I'm standing on the platform with nothing to do."

"I'm flattered you called me," I said with a laugh.

"Well, Salem and Poet are both at work."

"Ah, so I'm your last resort."

"Not really. I wanted to catch up. It's hard to get a grasp on the situation with a four-way video call."

"Grasp on what situation?"

"Your situation with Declan."

I closed my eyes as I remembered my experience just a few hours ago.

"Hello? Did you cut out?" Wyn asked.

"No, sorry. I'm here." I flipped my eyes open and took in

the beauty of the place I'd grown up in. "Wait, why are you on the train platform? I thought you were in the Hamptons for another week."

"Change of plans. The dad surprised the wife and kid with a trip to Paris. They're taking the other nanny. The one that speaks French."

"If only they'd decided to go to Norway, you could've gone," I said.

She sighed. "Yes, if only. So anyway, I'm headed back to the city and I have a week to myself. Whatever will I do?"

"You could fly out and see me. I miss you. I miss all of you, really."

"What about Declan?"

"What about him?"

"I thought you were going to go for it," she said. "That was the plan."

"That was the plan the three of you wanted for me," I said. "I'm still not entirely sure it's a good idea."

For some reason, I couldn't bring myself to admit to her what had happened between me and Declan. And it wasn't because I was ashamed or embarrassed. I wasn't entirely sure why, but I wanted to keep it just between me and Declan.

I heard the sound of clopping steps behind me. I turned in the saddle, phone still to my ear and saw Declan approaching on Merlin. Declan was wearing a cowboy hat, but his eyes were shielded by sunglasses.

"I gotta go," I said hastily.

"Why? What's wrong?"

"Nothing's wrong. I just need to go."

"Damn, we were just getting to the good stuff," she said.

"No we weren't. There isn't any good stuff."

"Get on that. Get on Declan."

"Bye, Wyn." I hung up and shoved my phone into my pocket and zipped it up.

Declan slowed his mount as he neared me.

The breadth of his shoulders had me sighing internally. And then I remembered my legs thrown over those wide shoulders . . . and my cheeks immediately flamed with heat.

"Hey," he greeted. "What are you doing out here?"

"Going for a ride," I said. "What are you doing out here?"

"I'm mending fence today." He faced my direction, but I couldn't see his eyes. "How are you?"

"Fine."

"No, I mean *how are you?*"

His question had a deeper meaning. Like, *how are you after I've come inside you,* deeper meaning.

"I'm fine, Declan."

"You don't look fine."

"How do I look?"

"Like you're trying to find a polite way to leave. I'm right, aren't I?"

I swallowed. "Can we not do this?"

"Do what?"

"Whatever this is."

He sighed and rubbed the back of his neck. "I told you I didn't want you to be shy."

"Declan," I began. "It's broad daylight on the ranch. There are things you can say in broad daylight and things you can't."

"You didn't text me back."

"What do you mean?"

"I mean, I texted you good night and you didn't reply."

"I was already asleep."

He grinned. "You little liar."

"Fine, I wasn't asleep."

"You were overthinking, that's what you were doing." He gestured with his chin to the hill. "Ride with me to the fence."

He didn't give me a chance to reply. Instead, he nudged Merlin and turned toward the hill.

With a sigh, I reluctantly followed. Goldie was interested in Merlin, so she trotted a few steps to keep pace with him, putting me right next to Declan.

"Who were you talking to on the phone?" he asked.

"Wyn."

"Which one is Wyn?"

"The nanny," I explained. "She was on the train platform, and I was supposed to entertain her."

"I see." He fell silent for a moment. "Your dad is leaving tomorrow for the livestock auction."

"Yeah, he told me." I bit my lip. "Can I ask you something?"

"You can ask me anything." He turned his head to look at me.

"Do you know if my dad is dating someone?" I blurted out. When he didn't reply right away, I pushed on, "I used to go to the livestock auctions with Dad all the time. It was kind of our thing. Salem would stay home with Mom and Muddy . . . and even after Mom died, Salem would stay home and I'd go with Dad. He made the lamest excuse for why he didn't want me to come this time. He said Muddy was slowing down and he wanted me to look after her."

Declan let out a chuckle. "Muddy? Slowing down?"

"That's what I'm saying. It was a flimsy argument. But I didn't push him to take me."

"Why not?"

When I remained silent, he pressed, "Hadley, why didn't you insist on going?"

I groaned.

He smirked.

"You trapped me," I muttered. "You trapped me into admitting the truth."

EMMA SLATE

"Which is what, exactly? That you can't get enough of me. That you want to feel my huge di—"

"Is it your mission in life to embarrass me?" I demanded with flaming cheeks.

"No, it's my mission in life to get you to be honest. And for the sake of honesty, I'll go first. If your dad is gone for a week, we have an entire week of you sleeping in my bed."

"Sleeping, huh?"

"Among other things. Lots of other things."

I couldn't stop the shiver that raced down my spine. I swallowed and then unzipped my jacket.

"Can I take you to dinner tomorrow night?" Declan asked.

"Take me to dinner where? We live in a microscopic town and if we show up at one of the two restaurants that exist, it'll be all over the news."

"You think they'd print it in the Huckleberry Hill Crier?" Declan asked.

"I think I don't want to draw attention to you and me."

He grinned.

"What?" I asked with an eyeball.

"You said *you and me*. There's a *you and me*."

My lips quivered. "You're impossible."

"Impossible to ignore," he quipped. "Well, if you won't let me take you to dinner in town, that leaves one of two options."

"Go on."

"We drive separately to Silver Springs, meet at a restaurant, not drink too much because we have to drive back. Or . . ."

"Or?"

"Or you come to the guest house and let me cook for you. And then you let me take you to my bed again. And you spend the whole night with me this time."

"You cook?" I asked in surprise.

"I'm fond of this thing called eating, so I learned how to take care of myself. Ergo, I cook."

"You're going to cook me dinner after a long, hard day on the ranch?" I asked.

He frowned. "Well, yeah."

Do it for the plot, Hadley.

"Dinner sounds wonderful," I said. "But I'm bringing the drinks."

"You know what this means, don't you?"

"What?" I asked with a smile.

"We're dating."

My smile slipped. "Declan, I can't—"

"Tomorrow night," he interrupted. "Tomorrow night we'll iron it all out."

"Iron what out? What's there to iron?"

"Tomorrow night," he said emphatically. "Wait until tomorrow night. Red."

"Red," I repeated in confusion. "Red what?"

"Wine."

I blinked. "I thought you were a microbrew kind of guy."

"We're having steak," he said. "And you like red, don't you?"

"I do."

"If you like it, I'll try it and see how it is. If I don't like it . . ." He shrugged.

"You'll try it and see," I parroted.

"Trying new things is fun." He flashed a wicked grin. "You'll see."

CHAPTER EIGHTEEN

TOWN

I was setting the brown bag on the floor of the passenger side of the truck when someone called my name. I looked over my shoulder and saw Wade jogging down the sidewalk toward me.

"Oh, hey," I said awkwardly, realizing I'd never returned his phone call.

"I didn't think you'd be here," Wade said, shoving his hands in his jeans pockets.

I frowned. "In town? I had to run some errands."

"The livestock auction in Three Forks is going on, isn't it? I thought you'd go with your dad . . ."

"Oh, right," I said. "He asked me to stay home and look after Muddy."

Nodding, he looked at me. "Listen, no sweat about dinner, okay?"

"What are you doing right now?" I asked suddenly.

"I was going to the bar to count inventory."

"You think you can put that on hold for a moment and get a cup of coffee with me?"

"You don't have to do that," Wade said.

"I know, but I want to. There are some things I want to—we're old friends, okay? I don't want you to think—just have coffee with me? Please?"

"You don't have to beg," Wade said with a grin. "I'll have coffee with you."

I closed the truck and locked it.

"You locked your truck," Wade said.

"Yeah, so?" I frowned and looked at him.

"Nothing it's just—well, it reminds me that you haven't lived here in a long time."

We fell silent as we walked shoulder to shoulder to Sweet Teeth. He opened the door to the bakery, and I walked inside first, greeted by Abby's friendly smile and the scent of warm, buttery croissants.

Wade tried to pay, but I said, "My treat. You bought my drink the other night."

"My family owns the bar," he pointed out. "It hardly counts."

I handed over my card and looked at Wade sternly.

"Fine," he relented.

We took our orders to the corner table and sat down. My latte was too hot to sip, but I tore apart the croissant and popped a buttery bite into my mouth.

Wade watched me intently, his hand wrapped around his coffee cup.

"What's New York like?" Wade asked suddenly.

"Loud."

"Is that all?"

"Congested."

"You sound like you hate it."

I paused for a moment and then I shrugged. "I don't know

if *hate* is accurate. But it's just so *hard*. Everything is a fight. And at the end of the day, you shouldn't fight where you live."

"So why did you stay so long? I mean, obviously you stayed because you got engaged, but before that. What made you stick it out?"

"Salem. And Wyn and Poet. My roommates and best friends," I clarified.

"Ah." He lifted his mug and took a sip. "So now that you're no longer engaged . . . do you plan on going back?"

"I don't know," I admitted. "The idea of living far away from my sister . . . I don't know if I can handle it. And my friends . . . they might as well be my sisters."

But what else was *there* for me?

I'd been asking myself the same question since the first night I came back home and slept in my childhood bed.

"I'm sorry I didn't stay in touch," I said quietly.

"Hey, don't be sorry. We broke up five years ago. You were living your life, moving forward. It's not your fault I haven't gotten over you."

I reached across the table and took his hand. "You were a good boyfriend. A good friend. I shouldn't have cut you out."

"You didn't cut me out," he said, squeezing my hand. "Life took you in a different direction. What were you supposed to do? Call me every night? Promise me a future? It wasn't realistic."

He sighed and let go of my hand.

"Even if I don't go back to New York, you and I—"

"Oh, I get it." He smiled slightly. "Heard you loud and clear."

"You're better off anyway," I said with a winsome smile. "I'm a mess."

"Why do you do that?"

"Do what?"

"Put yourself down like that?" He frowned. "Your ex must be a real piece of shit, because any man would be lucky to be with you. Mess and all."

"You're a good friend, Wade. One of the best."

He sighed. "Yeah, that's always been my problem. Friend-zoned for life."

"Have you tried dating apps?"

"I'd rather stick my head in a vise," he drawled.

"Have you tried a mail-order bride?" I teased.

"It might come to that. There are no datable women in this town. They've all paired off or moved away. I've all but taken a vow of celibacy. Actually, the celibacy has been thrust upon me."

"That's no good. Tell you what. We'll go to a bar one night and I'll be your wingman. Nothing makes a woman want a man more than when she thinks he's already paired up."

"Name the time and the place. I'm in."

"Knock on the door," I muttered to myself. I raised my hand and then stopped. "Hadley, come on. This is ridiculous. He's seen you naked. You can have dinner with him."

Anxiety shot up my throat and I lowered my hand. I hastily took the steps down off the guest cabin porch and headed back in the direction of the main house.

"No, come on. You can do this. There's no reason to be nervous."

The sun was setting and the temperature was dropping. And I'd made the mistake of wearing a cute sundress with a denim jacket and cowboy boots.

I'd shaved my legs—past the thigh.

And now I was psyching myself out.

I started to pace toward the cabin.

I was muttering to myself like a crazy person while carrying a bag with wine and a dessert from Sweet Teeth.

The door to the cabin opened. Declan was barefoot, his hair was damp, and his shoulders looked miles wide in his black and blue flannel button down.

"You want to come in or should I give you a few more minutes to gather your courage?" he asked with a smile as he leaned against the doorframe.

I groaned.

"You've been out here five minutes," he said. "You could've been well into your first glass of wine already."

"Yeah . . ."

"Come inside, Hadley. I promise I won't bite. Unless you ask me to."

I pointed at him. "That, right there, that's why I'm nervous."

He grinned and pushed away from the doorframe and then went inside, leaving me to contemplate if I wanted to follow him.

With a sigh, I tromped up the stairs and into the cabin. I closed the door behind me. My mouth instantly watered.

"Something smells incredible," I said as I set the bag down so I could take off my boots.

"I kind of changed the menu on you," he said from the kitchen. "This morning, I put a brisket in the slow cooker."

"Oh, I love brisket." I picked up the bag and padded into the kitchen to set it down on the counter. I pulled out a bottle of wine.

"We're not just having brisket. We're having my famous kitchen-sink nachos. I was in the middle of grating the cheese when you couldn't decide if you wanted to come in."

"Let's forget that, okay?" I asked. "Wine opener?"

Instead of replying, he walked over to me and caged me in against the counter. "Hi."

I looked at him and swallowed my nerves. "Hello."

His hand sank into my hair to cradle the back of my head. "You had to wear a dress . . ."

I frowned. "I don't get it."

"All I'm going to be able to do during dinner is fantasize about your skirt hiked up around your hips, your hands gripping the counter while I fuck you from behind."

My eyes widened and I sucked air into my lungs.

Declan leaned down and gently kissed my lips before releasing me and stepping back. He opened a drawer and pulled out the wine opener and held it up.

"Open the wine," he suggested, kissing me quickly again before moving away.

I did as he said and popped the cork. "Glasses?"

"Let me get them." He opened the dishwasher and pulled out two sparkling clean wine glasses and handed them to me.

"These are pretty," I commented.

"Yeah? I thought you'd like them."

I frowned. "Thought I'd like them?"

"Yeah." He looked at me. "I didn't have wine glasses in the cupboard, so I went to town and bought a set."

"You went to town?" I asked.

"Hmm, yeah."

"When? I was in town earlier today."

"I know. You went to Sweet Teeth with Wade."

I set the bottle of wine aside.

"You guys were looking a little cozy," he said, his blue eyes steady on me. "Anything you want to tell me?"

"Like what?"

"Like, are you dating him too?"

I lifted a glass of wine and held it out to him.

He took it and then I took mine. I sipped it and nodded. "That'll do."

"Hadley," he said quietly.

"Try the wine," I suggested.

"*Hadley*."

I grinned. "Are you jealous?"

"No. Jealousy is stupid and destructive."

"You sound jealous," I remarked. "You really should try the wine."

He took a sip. "Happy?"

"Delighted. And not just that you tried the wine."

He opened the oven and slid the nachos into it before closing the door again. He set the timer and then grabbed my hand to lead me to the couch. "You're completely evil."

"What? No, I'm not."

We sat down next to each other, and Declan pointed to my painted toenails. "I call bullshit. You're totally evil."

I wiggled my toes. "What? These? How is this evil?"

"Your toes are kind of adorable."

"Oh no."

"What?"

"You're a *foot* guy? Please tell me you're not a foot guy."

"You can be a pelt woman, but I can't be a foot guy?" he asked with a raise of his brows.

"I knew you'd never let me live it down," I muttered.

"I'm not a foot guy. I just think you have cute toes. We can move past this conversation if you want."

"I want."

"Back to the evil thing. You wore a sundress."

"Yeah . . ."

"*Evil*," he stated seductively. "And now you won't answer a simple question. Are you also dating Wade?"

I sighed. "No, I'm not dating Wade."

"Was that so hard to admit?"

"No." I paused. "Is that all?"

"Is that all what?"

"Do you believe me?"

"Of course I believe you. Why wouldn't I believe you?"

"I don't know." I shrugged. "You're not going to ask me what we talked about?"

"I'm guessing if you want to tell me what you talked about, you'll tell me. But I'm good just knowing you don't have several of us in rotation."

"Several of you—*what?*"

"Hmm. Maybe I am a little jealous." His gaze strayed to my mouth. "The idea that you'd kiss someone else . . . Yeah, I don't like thinking about that."

"I'm not kissing anyone else," I said softly.

"Good."

We stared at one another, and I felt the back of my neck flush.

The timer on the oven dinged.

"Dinner's ready." He got up and went to deal with the nachos. He pulled them out of the oven and set them on a trivet.

"Declan?"

"Yeah?"

"You know what I love?"

"What's that?"

"Cold nachos."

He'd been reaching for the spatula when I voiced my announcement. Declan set it down and looked at me.

"You like cold nachos?"

"Love them," I replied with a smile. I set my glass of wine onto the coffee table and stood up. I then slowly removed my denim jacket and tossed it onto the couch. Then I went for the straps of my yellow and blue sundress.

"Leave it," he commanded, voice gruff. He stalked toward me and scooped me up into his arms. "Best fucking date ever."

CHAPTER NINETEEN

The Ranch

My heart pounded.

Declan carried me into the bedroom and flipped on the light. "I'm leaving it on this time. I want to see every bit of you."

I shivered and nodded.

He placed me in the center of his neatly made bed.

I scrambled up to sit on my haunches and faced him. And then my hands went for his belt buckle.

"What are you doing?" he asked.

"I want to . . . what you did to me the other night." I looked up at him through the sweep of my lashes. "I want to taste you. Please?"

His jaw clenched as he stared down at me, and then he nodded.

My fingers shook as I slid off his belt. And then I went for the button of his fly. It popped open. I slowly tugged down his zipper.

He let out a frustrated groan. "Evil."

"Hmm. Maybe I do have a cruel streak," I said with a husky laugh.

Declan's pants dropped down to his ankles and he was tenting his navy-blue boxer briefs. I gently stroked him over the fabric.

He shuddered with pleasure.

I slowly grasped the band of his boxers and lowered them so that he was completely revealed to me.

A sigh of pleasure escaped my lips.

I gently grasped the root of him and slid my hand up his engorged shaft. I swiped my finger across the head, feeling the bead of pre-come and then I placed it on my tongue.

"Fuck, Hadley." Declan's voice was strangled and his eyes were lit with desire.

Grinning, I bent my head. Slow—achingly slow—I took him into my mouth. He was large, but I was determined.

I felt him at the back of my throat, but it wasn't enough. I wanted to make him lose control the way he'd made me lose control the first night we'd been together.

As I teased and sucked, changing the rhythm so he was always on edge, I gently cradled him. And then I glided my fingertips up and down his thighs, tantalizing him with a teasing touch.

I took him as far into my throat as I could and then backed off. I tongued the crown of his shaft before engulfing his length once again.

Finally, Declan couldn't stand the torment any longer. His hands sank into my hair and grabbed my head and ruthlessly began using me.

"I'm gonna come."

And with a groan, he emptied himself into my welcoming mouth.

He was warm and salty and I swallowed him down.

Declan's hold on my head loosened and he backed up a step. He slid out of my mouth, and I licked my lips.

"You swallowed every bit of me," he said gruffly.

I nodded.

"Show me. Open your mouth."

I did as he commanded.

His hand softly cradled my jaw and he skimmed a finger across my cheek. "So fucking perfect."

Declan let go and then his hand wandered down my neck and teased the strap of my dress. "I'm hungry."

"Let's eat." I made a move to get off the bed.

A low laugh escaped his lips. "I wasn't talking about food, Hadley."

"Oh." My cheeks flushed with heat.

He continued to tease my strap until it fell off my shoulder. He slid the other down as well. And then he went for the buttons at the front of my dress, slowly undoing them until the garment fell off me, baring my breasts to him.

Declan leaned forward and captured a nipple in his mouth, sucking it into a hard pebble. A thread of pleasure shot from my breast to my core. He released my nipple and then gently urged me to lie down on my back.

He slid off my panties.

His grin was wolfish. "Now it's my turn to be completely evil." And then he bent his head and made good on his word.

My stomach rumbled.

Declan laughed and held me tighter. "I'm a terrible date. I promised to feed you."

I stroked a finger across his pelty chest. "You fed me. You fed me *good*."

"Did you just—tease me? With an innuendo?"

"Maybe."

He kissed the top of my head, his hand stroking down my back. "You've got to get up."

I snuggled closer. "But I'm comfortable."

"It'll be worth it, I promise."

With a sigh, I rolled off him and sat up, my back facing him.

"What's this?" Declan asked, brushing my hair off my shoulder and touching the ink on my shoulder blade.

"My tattoo," I said. "I'm going to wear your shirt. Where is it?"

"I'll get it for you. And I know it's a tattoo. I just didn't know you had one." He swung his legs over the side of the bed and reached for his shirt to hand me.

"Well, I was on my back. So how could you see my hummingbird tattoo?"

"Just . . . you didn't seem like the type to have any ink."

"Everyone has ink," I said. "Even my friend Poet has a tattoo. And she's not the tattoo type."

I slid into his flannel shirt and buttoned it. I stood. It fell to the middle of my thighs and I rolled up the sleeves.

"You look good in my shirt," he said gruffly. He grabbed his discarded boxer briefs and pulled them on. "You care if I get into sweats, or is it too early for me in our relationship to get comfortable?"

My hands stilled and I looked at him. "Relationship?"

"Bad word choice," Declan said.

"Hmm." I went back to rolling up the sleeves and then I found my underwear. I didn't like Declan's casual use of the word *relationship*. I wasn't sure what we were doing, but I wasn't ready for anything resembling a relationship—not after what I'd just gone through.

"Why a hummingbird?" he asked, pulling me back to the present.

"Nachos, and I'll tell you."

We padded barefoot into the kitchen. He turned on the oven. "I'm going to throw the nachos back in for a few minutes. Let's sit. It'll take a bit for the oven to heat up."

I took my glass of wine and sat at the end of the couch. Declan's shirt rode up my legs, but I didn't mind, especially because Declan couldn't take his eyes off me.

He patted his thigh. I lifted my legs and placed them on his lap, and he held onto my ankle.

"You turned up the temperature," I remarked.

He smiled. "Yeah. I'll turn it down before we go to bed so we can sleep."

My heart went gooey. "Thanks."

He tweaked my big toe. "The hummingbird."

"My mom . . . she loved hummingbirds." I shrugged. "One drunken girls' night, Salem pitched the idea that the four of us should get tattoos to solidify our friendship. So the next day, after a greasy diner breakfast, the four of us went to a tattoo parlor in the East Village and got inked."

"The hummingbird has meaning for you—but I doubt your friends got the same thing, right?"

"Right. They got something that mattered to them. And my sister got something different too."

"Tell me about your sister."

"Why?"

"Curiosity. Are you identical twins or fraternal?"

"Fraternal. She's about five inches taller than me. She's got hazel eyes like Muddy and bright red hair. We both had the same shade of red hair when we were younger, but mine went chestnut. I got the blue eyes from Dad."

The oven beeped and Declan let go of my ankle. I lifted my legs so he could get up and slide in the nachos. When he returned, I put my legs back on him and settled down.

"Do you have siblings?" I asked.

"No. Just me." A phone began to ring.

"Not mine," I said. "Mine's on vibrate."

"That would be mine." He made no move to get up. "It can go to voicemail."

"What if it's important?"

"Nothing is more important than this moment. With a gorgeous woman wearing my shirt, sitting on my couch."

I smiled.

The oven timer beeped, and Declan once again got up. I followed this time. I refilled our wine glasses while Declan served us and then we took our plates back to the couch.

"Well, dig in. I hope it's good," he said.

"It's perfect," I said before I even took a bite.

We fell silent while we devoured the nachos. When I'd had my fill, I pushed my empty plate away and settled back against the couch.

"Your turn," I said as I took a sip of wine.

"My turn what?"

"You get to explain your tattoos and their meanings."

"The horseshoe," he pointed to the spot on his chest, "is for luck. I got it when I was eighteen. Riding motorcycles and roping calves . . . there was a good shot I was gonna find an early grave, ya know? I'm not superstitious by any means, but I thought, what the hell."

"Kind of like a talisman."

"Exactly."

"And the arm brand?"

"Drunken stupidity." He laughed. "My best friend has one too."

"Ah, so it's not just me and my friends who make drunken mistakes."

"Nope." He looked at me. "This is nice."

"Yeah. It is."

"Kinda feel like I'm shafting you though."

I raised my brows. "You haven't shafted me yet. Well, not tonight anyway."

He grinned, but then his smile slipped. "No, I mean, this is great, don't get me wrong. But you deserve more."

"More than what? Good nachos, good conversation, good sex?"

"Good? Better than good," he said.

"You're right. The nachos were diabolical."

He pinched my toe, causing me to laugh. "I meant you deserve a real date."

"This is a real date."

"No, this is the kind of thing you do when you're settled with someone. Cozy night at home. You know, that kind of thing. And we're not settled."

"No, we're not." I sighed. "Look, it is what it is. We can't really be out and about in town. This is fine. Better than fine."

He ran his hand up and down my calf. "I still feel like you deserve more."

"That's sweet," I said. "But if I'm being honest, I don't want to do anything like it's normally done. I played by the rules. I got burned."

"What rules?"

"The relationship rules. But I don't want to talk about my past. Not when our present is so good. Let's not spoil it, okay?"

"Okay."

"Speaking of sweet." It was my turn to get up. I went to the bag I'd brought over and pulled out a pastry box. "I got us a little tart medley."

Declan's phone rested on the counter next to the bag. It was lit up with a voicemail. I grabbed it and brought it and the box to the couch. I handed him his cell.

"Thanks," he said, glancing at the screen. "It's my buddy.

I'll call him back later. See? Nothing that needs my immediate attention."

"Your buddy?"

"From the rodeo circuit."

I opened the box and lifted one of the banana cream tarts toward Declan. A glob of pudding fell onto his lap.

He raised his brows. "Well, this could get interesting."

I scooped the pudding off his lap and stuck it into my mouth. "I'm game if you are."

CHAPTER TWENTY

THE RANCH

It was still dark out and I was half asleep when Declan slid inside me from behind. I winced at the angle—I was sore—but I didn't make a sound of protest. Instead, I lifted my legs and took him deeper.

He kissed my naked shoulder as he rocked into me, his hand snaking across my hip to rest between my legs. Declan played with me, his fingers slipping through my wetness.

I was warm and feverish, caught up in the magic of us. It wasn't long until I shattered around him. He gently thrust into me, gripping my hip as he came. Declan stilled.

I sighed in delight.

He slid out of me.

"We made quite a mess," Declan murmured. "You want to shower?"

I stretched and then hastily covered my mouth when I yawned. The idea of showering with Declan felt . . . intimate.

Too intimate.

"No." I sat up. "I should get back to the main house."

"Oh, so *that's* how it's gonna be." Declan climbed out of bed.

"What do you mean?"

"You got what you wanted and now you want to rush out in the morning. You're making me feel cheap." He looked over his shoulder and grinned cheekily, letting me know he had no hard feelings.

I brushed my hand down his back. "Can we do it again tonight?"

He leaned over and kissed my forehead. "Absolutely."

My insides hummed at the prospect.

"Let me at least make you a cup of coffee for the road," Declan said.

"Not necessary. The road is short."

"Trying to sneak back into your house before your grandmother wakes up?"

"Not even. Besides, she knows what's going on between us."

"Does she?"

"Yeah, not officially, but she's a smart cookie. She won't tell my father—but she said she won't outright lie to him either. Strange though, considering she knows my father's personal business but is keeping his confidence."

Declan fell silent. He scratched his bare chest and my eyes drifted toward the swath of inked skin.

"So tonight, yeah?"

I nodded. "But I'm cooking dinner this time."

He shook his head.

"Why not?"

"Because this isn't a tit-for-tat situation. I'm happy to cook."

"Okay." My brow wrinkled. "But I'm still bringing dessert."

He reached his hand out and gently cradled my breast and slid a thumb over my nipple, causing me to shiver.

"You are the dessert."

His words were delicious and sent a thrill through me.

"I better get up and shower before I get distracted," he murmured.

"Hmm. Probably."

He sighed and reluctantly dropped his hand. "Tonight."

"Tonight."

"You mind if I . . ."

"Shower," I urged. "I'll see myself out."

Declan got up and padded naked to the bathroom.

I glanced at the clock. It was just past five in the morning. My body was sore and tired. But I smiled the entire walk back to the main house.

The scent of frying bacon immediately hit me along with the strong brew of coffee.

My mouth watered as I entered the kitchen.

Muddy stood at the stove, wearing her faded blue and white striped apron, her gray hair tied back in a long braid.

"Morning," Muddy said.

"Good morning," I said, going to the coffee pot and filling a cup.

I was a grown woman and I refused to be embarrassed, waltzing into the house after spending the night with Declan.

"You've got razor burn on your neck."

I groaned. "*Muddy*."

"What?"

"Can't you at least pretend you don't know what I was doing?"

"Kinda hard to do that, sugar." She looked at me and grinned. "You look exhausted."

My cheeks heated. "Some grandmothers don't comment on their granddaughter's private lives."

"Some granddaughters at least pretend to sneak in after being out all night," she pointed out.

I sighed. "We never could get anything past you."

"Salem was pretty good. You, my dear, don't have that gene."

"What gene is that?"

"The rebel gene."

"I can be a rebel," I protested, my spine snapping straight.

"You're twenty-three-years old. You make your own choices, and yet you're still standing here trying to defend them. Salem plows ahead and when she gets into trouble, she asks for forgiveness. Never permission."

"As you said, I'm twenty-three and I don't have to ask permission."

"True. How do you want your eggs this morning?"

"Poached, please."

She nodded. "I just want you happy. You know that right?"

"I do."

"And you look happy."

I rolled my eyes. I looked well-fucked, but I wasn't going to say that to my grandmother. There were some things you just didn't say.

"Remember the night of the bonfire, you caught us trying to climb the tree outside my window to get into the house?"

"I remember." She grinned at me. "Peppermint schnapps on your breath."

I laughed. "You said if we were going to get caught drinking, then we at least needed to drink something we wouldn't be embarrassed about in our later years when retelling the story. And the next night you made us drink straight bourbon. Does Dad know that story?"

"Doubt it. He was out of town when that happened. And I certainly never told him."

"Neither did I. And I know Salem wouldn't have squealed." My smile dimmed.

"Have you told her yet?"

"About what?"

She gestured with her chin in the direction of the cabin.

"It was her idea," I said with a rueful shake of my head. "Wyn, Poet and Salem all voted and told me I had to go for it."

"Voted? You're making life decisions based on a committee?"

"Just this life decision," I said with a grin.

"Hmm."

"Hmm. What's that mean?"

"It means hmm."

"You never keep your opinions to yourself. Why are you now?"

"I'm not keeping my opinions to myself. I'm mulling over what you told me. I guess I didn't realize . . ."

"What?"

"They're your tribe," she said. "Your village. And it must be really hard being separated from them."

"Yeah," I said slowly, nodding. "It is."

I felt like I was on a raft in the ocean and a storm was throwing me about. Wave after wave crashed over me, and every time I managed to poke my head above water, another would engulf me once again.

My friends, my sister—they were the lighthouse on land.

Would all that change if I didn't go back to New York?

Muddy scooped the poached eggs from the water and gently set them on the plate, along with several pieces of bacon.

"Eat," she commanded.

I took the plate to the kitchen table and sat down. "It's funny, you know? Salem and I moving into a strange apartment. Nothing but each other, a suitcase each, and a lot of gumption. I'd never have guessed Poet and Wyn would become our best friends."

"You should invite them out for a visit," Muddy said.

"I invited Wyn," I admitted. "The family she nannies for went to Paris and took the French-speaking nanny. She has a week off."

"Is she coming?"

"I don't know. I kind of threw out the invitation willy-nilly."

Though it would be wonderful to see one of my friends, I hated to admit that I was enjoying my private time with Declan. And if Wyn was here, I'd feel pulled in two different directions. It wouldn't be fair to have her come out and then bail on her to spend time with a man I barely knew.

I ate my breakfast and then helped Muddy clean up.

"I already fed the chickens," she said. "And collected the eggs. I'm headed into town. You need anything?"

"Town? This early in the morning?" I raised my brows. "You don't have a town fella, do you?"

"Oh you." She laughed. "No. I'm meeting Lucy for coffee before the store opens."

"Tell her I said hello," I said.

"I will."

I sprayed off the counter to get rid of the grease splatter and began wiping it off.

She leaned over and patted my cheek. "Don't think too hard about the future, Hadley. It has its way of working itself out."

"Yeah."

"Well, I'm off. Call me if you need something."

"Okay."

Muddy walked to the foyer, grabbed her keys and jacket and was gone. The house was quiet except for the hum of the dishwasher. I went upstairs and headed immediately to my bedroom. My cell phone was charging on my nightstand. I had a missed text from Dad with some photos of livestock he was contemplating purchasing, and several messages in the group text.

It was just past nine on the East Coast which meant that Poet and Salem were at work already.

I called Wyn.

"Are you coming to visit or not?" I demanded.

"Good morning, how are you? I put vanilla in my coffee this morning and did Pilates."

I sighed. "Good morning."

"No, I'm not coming for a visit. Though I wish I was."

My heart sank. "Why can't you come? You have a week off."

"Yeah, see, about that week off . . . the housekeeper called and said the Carringtons' mini dachshund was having separation anxiety, so she asked me if I would take care of her. Mildred becomes destructive and has a habit of leaving fecal gifts in random places when she's left alone."

"Mildred is the housekeeper or the dog?"

"The dog. She's a good girl, she just needs an emotional support human."

"And where is the good girl right now?" I asked with a smile.

"Not snuggling me . . . in bed . . . under the covers . . ."

"Ah," I said with a laugh. "I see."

"Mildred and I are hanging for the week at our place. Poet and Salem are excited to have a part-time dog."

"Dogs are good," I said.

"Sorry I can't visit."

"It's fine."

"Are you getting bored?"

"Bored? No. There's plenty to do on the ranch to keep me occupied."

"Plenty to do, huh? Like mucking out stalls? Feeding chickens?"

"And sleeping with Declan."

There was silence on the other end of the phone.

"Wyn? Hello? You still there?"

"I'm here. I'm in complete and utter shock, but I'm here."

"Why are you in shock?" I demanded. "You guys told me to go for it!"

"Yeah, but I didn't think you would actually do it," she said.

"Well, why not?"

"Because you're Hadley. And you're very thoughtful about your decisions."

"I was thoughtful about this."

"Hm. No, you weren't. Which is fantastic news, actually. You're only impulsive after too much to drink and that rarely happens. Wait, so when did this start?"

"Couple of nights ago," I admitted. "I helped him give birth. Wait, no. I helped him help Mirabelle—the mare—give birth. I went back to his cabin to shower. He made me a quesadilla and we drank bourbon and then we . . . ya know. And last night he cooked me dinner and I stayed over."

"Oh my God!" she squealed.

I smiled even though she couldn't see me. I was giddy talking to a best friend about a guy. The last time I'd been this excited, it was because of Gianni . . .

My good feelings slipped away at the memory of him.

"So, are you going to gush or let me speculate?"

I laughed. "I haven't told Poet or Salem yet, so I'm thinking we need to have a charcuterie and video hang-out. Do me a favor and keep it between us for now, ya?"

"Will do. But let's have that chat soon," she said. "It won't be the same as you being here, but we'll make it work. If you can pull yourself away from the awesome get-over-your-ex sex."

"I'll find the time," I assured her.

"So, it is awesome, right? At least tell me that much."

I sighed. "Yeah, it's pretty awesome."

She squealed again. "Oh, sorry, Mildred. I woke the beast and now she probably has to go outside. Later, gator."

Wyn hung up and I set my phone aside. I stripped off my dress and underwear and threw them in the dirty clothes bin before padding into the bathroom.

As the shower steamed, I looked at myself in the mirror. My lips were swollen and even though my skin was wan from lack of sleep, there was a definite sparkle in my eye. And just maybe a jaunt in my step. A lifting of my spirits. A reason to smile.

CHAPTER TWENTY-ONE

The Ranch

"Oh my God." My eyes immediately watered, and I pinched my nose as I approached the cabin porch.

Declan was in the middle of taking off his boots when he saw me. "Don't come any closer."

"Too late. I can smell you from here. Is that cow dung all over you?"

"Yeah." He sighed. "Merlin got uppity and knocked into me. I fell into a pile of wet cow shit."

I covered my mouth but couldn't stop the laughter that escaped. It only worsened when Declan began hopping around on one foot in an attempt to remove his boot.

"I was about to spray myself off outside and then shower before you came over. Bad news, though, Merlin's antics cost me my grocery shopping time. I don't have anything to cook."

"Oh." I bit my lip.

"I'd kiss you hello, but . . . yeah."

I stifled another laugh and moved toward the side of the cabin where the hose was. "Come on, I'm hosing you down."

"You're going to derive pleasure from this, aren't you?"

"Probably. Strip down, cowboy."

He began to unbutton his shirt. "I'm about to show off my pelt. Don't get overly excited."

I smirked. "Thanks for the warning."

Declan stripped down to his army green boxer briefs, showing off a lot more than just his pelt.

I fiddled with the knob on the spigot. Cold water gushed from the hose. I picked it up and held it like a gun. "Are you feeling lucky, punk?" I asked in my best Clint Eastwood impression.

"Not even a little bit. Aim away from my crotch. I don't want shrinkage."

I hit him with water and he let out a garbled, "Ahhhhhhh!"

When he was rinsed off, nary a smear of cow dung on his skin, he ran toward the cabin.

"Fuck, I'm freezing!"

"Make sure to wash twice!" I called as I trailed after him.

Declan beelined for the bathroom. "Make yourself comfortable."

The door to the bathroom closed and I was alone. I went to the kitchen and opened the refrigerator. It was bare bones despite the fact that he'd made nachos for me last night. There was a third of a block of cheese and a few eggs. We could make do with a cheese omelet, but that wasn't what I was in the mood for.

I looked in the freezer. Two mini frozen pizzas.

My cell phone buzzed. I pulled it out of the side pocket of my overalls and looked at the screen. Nerves skated through my belly. I glanced at the bathroom and heard the faintest sound of the shower.

I marched to the front door and closed it behind me as I answered the call.

"Hello?"

"Hey . . . Hadley," Nico greeted awkwardly. "How are you?"

"Fine," I said, my heart pumping rapidly in my chest. "How are the renovations going?"

"They're going," he said.

He fell silent for a moment.

I closed my eyes, wondering why Gianni's cousin was calling me.

"Is there a reason you called?" I asked.

He cleared his throat. "Yeah, I was just—I'm making out the server schedule for when we open again and I was wondering about your availability."

"Ah," I said. "Because I'm not in Italy."

There was some shuffling of papers in the background and then I heard the sound of a shutting door.

"Gianni hasn't said much," Nico stated. "I mean, he told the family you guys ended things and that he was going to Italy alone, but that was all."

Well, at least he hadn't aired our dirty laundry. I could thank him for that at least.

"I like you, Hadley. You're a good server and I'm sorry shit didn't work out with Gianni. I just wanted you to know that. And you can have whatever shifts you want. I'll make it happen."

The idea of returning to Gianni's family restaurant and seeing my co-workers gossip behind my back—to see Gianni's cousins and sisters, hell to even see Gianni himself, was not something I was going to subject myself to.

"I quit," I said.

Nico sighed. "Yeah, I had a feeling it would come to that. I don't blame you. If you want, I can make a few phone calls. I know people. I can get you another serving job if you're interested."

"Why, because you feel bad?" I asked with a wry snort.

"Yeah, I feel bad. But like I said, you're good at what you do. You shouldn't not have a job because my cousin is a dick. You were really good to him. You were a part of the family."

My throat thickened. I'd mourned Gianni and the life we were supposed to share together. I hadn't thought about everything else I was losing. His big, amazing, nosy Italian family.

"Don't call around," I said. "I'm not sure when I'm coming back to New York."

"Back to New York?" he repeated in confusion. "What do you mean *back to New York?* Where are you?"

"I came home for a visit."

The front door of the cabin opened, and my spine tensed.

"Thanks for calling." I hung up and shoved my cell phone back into my pocket. I didn't turn around, choosing instead to grip the wooden porch rail until my knuckles turned white.

Declan sidled up next to me. The scent of lanolin and tea tree oil wafted toward me.

"No trace of cow dung," I said, forcing a smile and looking at him. His hair was damp and his five o'clock shadow looked more like three-day stubble.

His brow furrowed as he adjusted the collar of his flannel shirt. "You okay?"

I shrugged.

"You want to talk about it?"

I bit my lip. "It'll ruin our date."

"Not possible."

I wanted to tell him, but it wasn't fair to dump all my feelings onto him. Especially when it was about another man—a man I'd been planning on sharing my life with.

He went back inside for a moment, but quickly returned, carrying a pair of clean boots and socks. Declan took a seat on the porch steps and pulled them on.

"Come on," he said, rising, holding out his hand.

"Where are we going?" I asked.

"We're going for a ride."

"A ride?" I asked in confusion. "Why?"

"Because you need it. It'll clear your head. And then you can decide if you want to confide in me."

I blinked. "It's not that I don't want to confide in you. It's just I don't want to talk to you about my ex. It's not fair."

I let him tug me toward the direction of the stables.

"You're all tied up in knots. So we'll go for a ride. And then we'll get back to my place. You'll shower, wear my clothes, and I'll make you a frozen pizza. Come on, bear snack. Let's go."

We rode long enough for my brain to clear and my mood to lift. As if Declan could sense the change, he turned Merlin back in the direction of home. Goldie happily trotted after him.

I was beginning to feel like Goldie was mildly obsessed with Merlin. She threw a fit when they were separated. And like the horses' attraction to each other, Declan was becoming a calming, protective beacon that I was gravitating to as well.

After we stabled the horses, fed, watered and rubbed them down, we went back to Declan's cabin. The moon had risen and it lit the path to his porch. He took my hand and guided me up the steps.

We hadn't spoken on our ride, but Declan didn't push to fill the silence.

"How did you know that was exactly what I needed?" I asked as I took off my boots.

"Just did." He shrugged. "Oh shit, I forgot to throw my clothes into the washer. Go ahead and get in the shower. I'll get you some clean clothes." He fingered the strap of my overalls. "I like these."

"Yeah?"

"Yeah." He leaned down and captured my lips with his. "I have a pretty vivid fantasy involving these overalls."

I grinned. "Don't tell me. Just surprise me with it."

He swatted my butt playfully. "I'll oblige."

I went into the cabin and unbuckled the straps on my way to the bathroom. As the water heated, I stripped down.

While I was in the middle of washing my face—and lamenting the fact that I was washing off all my makeup—the bathroom door opened.

I thought it was Declan just leaving me a pair of his sweats and a T-shirt, but when he yanked back the shower curtain, I yelped in surprise.

"Easy," he said, his hands going to my hips as he pressed his chest to my back.

I whipped my head around, lashing my wet hair against his skin. "What are you doing in here?"

He raised his eyebrows. "I thought it was obvious."

"You didn't say you wanted to shower with me. That wasn't the plan."

"It wasn't?" His hand slid from my hip to my belly and then traveled upward to cup a breast.

"No." I batted his hand away. "You said go shower. Nothing about you following me in here."

"It's just a shower. Why are you getting bent out of shape?"

"Bent out of . . ."

His finger flicked across my nipple as his other hand pressed my hip, silently urging me to lean against him.

"Showering is intimate."

"Intimate." His hand wandered toward the apex of my thighs, sliding between my folds and finding my clit. "What's wrong with intimate?"

I clawed at his wrist, more to hold on than to stop him.

"Intimate is . . . *intimate.*" I closed my eyes as his fingers spread me, teased me, pleasured me.

"Failing to see the problem," he rasped as he plunged a finger into me.

I shuddered and clenched around him.

He gently bit my ear. "You think showering together is a bad idea? You're wet. I want you to come on my fingers, Hadley. I want you to fucking drench them."

I moaned as he added another finger and began to thrust them inside me. I clung to him, my body begging for release.

Declan was relentless and sure enough, I came on his fingers. When I stopped shaking, he slowly removed them.

"Any more complaints?" Declan asked.

"Bite me."

He bit my shoulder.

"Hey!"

"You told me to bite you. Just following orders, ma'am."

"Hmm. Following orders." I slowly turned in his arms to face him and then I gently urged us to switch places to give him the water. "What other orders can you follow?"

He grinned. "I don't know. Let's find out."

CHAPTER TWENTY-TWO

THE RANCH

"You feeling better?" Declan asked as he pushed the last piece of pizza toward me.

"Full, sedated and satiated," I remarked. "No, you eat the last piece."

"You sure?"

"I'm sure."

"Don't have to twist my arm." He took the piece and got up. "Another beer?"

"Sure."

He went into the kitchen and while his head was stuck in the refrigerator, I said, "I quit my restaurant job. Back in New York, I mean."

Declan chewed his bite of pizza and after he swallowed he looked at me. "Yeah?"

I nodded. "That's who called me."

"Your ex-fiancé called you? I thought he was in Italy."

"He is. He wasn't the one who called. His cousin

manages the restaurant I work at. Nico called to ask me what shifts I wanted when we all came back to work after the renovations. The idea of seeing them again after Gianni told his family that we broke up . . ." I shook my head. "So, I quit."

He pulled out two beer bottles and shut the fridge. "I don't blame you. Who the hell would want to see their ex's family, let alone work for them."

"They're good people," I murmured. "And I didn't think . . . that when my relationship ended, I'd lose them too. That's what really got to me, you know?"

He cracked open both bottles and returned to the couch, holding one out to me.

I took it. "Thanks."

"So you haven't talked to your ex? Since it ended?"

I paused and then shook my head. "No. I haven't talked to him. Why would I?"

"I don't know. Maybe there's some unresolved stuff there."

"No. It's resolved," I said with finality. "It's over. It's done. Dead and buried. Ain't coming back."

"What's that saying? Thou doth protest too much?"

I raised my brows. "It's not me protesting. I don't want him to call. I don't want to talk to him."

"So, if he came back—"

"He won't."

He cocked his head to the side. "What's fascinating is that you didn't even pause to think about it."

"Nothing to think about." I shrugged. "You have to look forward, not behind. And we didn't work. It's all hypothetical anyway because he'll never come back and I wouldn't want him to."

He took a drink of his beer but didn't reply.

"You look like you want to say something," I remarked.

"I want to say a lot of things. But I don't think you'll like what I have to say."

"Probably," I agreed.

"So I'm keeping my thoughts to myself."

"No, don't do that."

"What?"

"Dangle the carrot. Now I have to know."

"I don't think you're being honest," he said.

My heart drummed with nerves. "About what?"

"About what you want," he said.

"You think I'm lying about my ex? That I actually want him back?"

He paused and then shook his head. "No I think you're telling the truth about that, but I think you're not being truthful about being over it."

"I said *it's over*, not that *I'm* over it. And just when I think I might be over it, something wallops me in the face."

"Like the call from his cousin and you quitting the restaurant, so you don't have to face the family that's not your family anymore."

I swallowed and felt tears sting my eyes. "Ouch. What is it you want from me, Declan?" I asked softly.

"For you to be honest with yourself."

"About what?" I was ready to tear my hair out. "That I enjoy being with you, but that I can't handle anything serious right now? That I'm more devastated about my breakup than I want to be?"

"You're still in love with him." His jaw clenched. "Aren't you?"

"No, I'm not, but how do you expect me to get over a two-year relationship in a month?" I demanded.

"I don't expect that. But Jesus, I thought I was okay with whatever you had to give me, but I'm not. I want more. I want more of you. I want more of us."

"I told you this was a bad idea."

"Because you actually like me?"

"Yes," I snapped. "I actually like you, and I don't want to hurt you by being emotionally unavailable. So I know I should stop having sex with you, but I don't want to stop having sex with you because it's really good sex and it blows out all the clouds in my brain where nothing makes sense and when you're inside me suddenly the world is quiet and I feel like I'm not drowning."

My words came to a halt and the horror was immediate. I hastily clapped my hands over my mouth, as if that could somehow put all the words back inside me where they belonged.

Instead, they hung in the air between us.

"I have to go," I blurted out.

"Why?"

"Because I just emotionally splattered all over you and I need a chance to—"

His lips covered mine and his hand tore through my hair. I closed my eyes and pressed a palm to his chest. I sank into him for a moment before ripping myself away, before putting distance between us. I scrambled back and stood.

I placed my fingers to my swollen lips. "I can't, Declan. I'm going back to New York."

"Are you?"

"Yes," I said, even though I was hardly sure.

"You're going back to New York after admitting you don't like it and there's nothing for you there." When I remained silent, he stood up and nodded. "You don't want to go back to New York. But you're willing to run back there because there's something for you here now. And that scares the ever-loving shit out of you."

I didn't reply, my head crammed too full of thoughts that were taking root and not letting go.

Without another word, I turned and left the cabin. I grabbed my boots and didn't even bother putting them on. A grave mistake when I stepped on a rock that dug into the arch of my left foot.

The main house was dark and quiet, and I breathed a sigh of relief. I didn't want to run into Muddy and explain to her why I was coming home at ten o'clock when she knew I had plans to spend the night with Declan.

I trod quietly up the stairs and into my bedroom and ensured my door closed without a sound.

And then I went to the closet, flipped on the light, and shut myself inside.

I stared at my cell phone for all of two seconds and then I called my sister.

"This better be an emergency," she groused. "I was just about to fall asleep."

I winced. I hadn't even thought of the time difference. "I slept with Declan a few nights ago and now I'm afraid that I like him. Like, *like him* like him."

She paused and then said, "I'm waking up Wyn and Poet. And then I'm calling you back."

The line went dead, and my screen flashed before going dark. A few minutes later, it buzzed.

"Hello?"

"You're on speaker, and we've congregated," Salem said.

"Mildred is here, too," Wyn added.

"So tell them what you told me," Salem commanded.

I sighed. "I slept with Declan a few nights ago and I think I actually like him."

Silence reigned.

"Of course you like him," Wyn finally said. "I knew that would happen after you told me you slept with him."

"Wait, you knew?" Salem asked. "When did she tell you?"

"The other day," Wyn said. "She asked me not to say anything because she wanted to tell you herself."

"Why does no one call me?" Poet demanded. "I feel left out."

"The last time I called you, you were crying in a bathroom stall at work," I reminded her.

"You were crying at work?" Wyn asked. "When?"

"I'll tell you later. After we get off the phone with Hadley," Poet said. "It's not that good of a story."

"It's a good story," I protested.

"Are we riding at dawn?" Wyn asked.

Poet laughed. "No. Now let's get back to Hadley's problem."

"Yeah, is there a reason you're sitting here talking to us instead of naked wrestling with the wrangler?" Wyn asked.

"Whoa, before you reply to that, I want the details. When did you hook up with Declan?" Salem demanded.

I quickly explained the night Mirabelle gave birth and what had happened between us, following it up with our plan for this evening that had gone to shit.

"So like, a few nights ago," Poet said. "And now you're already in a fight?"

"We're not in a fight," I denied.

"You were there and now you're here, talking to us instead of being with him," Wyn said. "Sounds like a fight to me."

"So you like him," Salem said. "What's the problem?"

"The problem is she doesn't trust herself," Poet said. "She thinks she can't like someone so soon after her engagement ended. And she's worried she's going to get her heart broken again."

"This is so charcuterie and wine talk," Wyn said.

"We don't have any charcuterie, but we have the rest of the wine," Poet mentioned.

"I'll get the bottle," Salem offered. "Don't say anything until I get back."

"This is so exciting," Poet said.

"Not a word," Salem called out.

"I didn't say anything important," Poet replied.

"I'm back," Salem said a few moments later.

"No glasses?" Wyn inquired.

"I figured we'd just pass the bottle around," Salem said.

"Oh, that's better," Wyn agreed. "Gimme."

My heart ached. The three of them were together, no doubt cuddled up on Wyn's bed with a dog to pet and a bottle of wine to share.

And I'm here, in a place I love with a man I have no business having feelings for.

"Okay, let's continue," Salem said. "Mama's gotta get to sleep, but this is monumental. I want to know what you guys talked about that had you leaving his cabin instead of staying the night."

"She already said," Poet replied. "He called her out about having feelings for him."

"Before that," Salem said. "What led up to that? Because I know something did."

"That damn twin thing," Wyn remarked.

"Yep," Poet agreed.

"Nico called this afternoon," I blurted out. "Asking about what shifts I wanted when the restaurant reopened. It was awkward, and he said Gianni told the family we'd split up and I just kinda lost it. Not on him. But like, I didn't realize that whole part of my life is really over. Done. Not just my engagement to Gianni, but my involvement with his family. And the idea of going back to work for them and seeing his cousins, and letting them all speculate about why we broke up . . . I told Nico that I quit. That I wouldn't be coming back."

"Thank God," Salem muttered. "We wondered when you were going to realize that you couldn't go back there."

"Yeah, well, like I said I haven't been thinking clearly." I rubbed my forehead. "Nico offered to call around and get me a job at another restaurant. And I said no."

"You said no?" Wyn asked. "Why?"

"Because she doesn't think she's coming back to New York," Salem said softly. "Right, Hadley?"

"Not coming back?" Poet asked, her voice sounding confused, broken. "You have to come back. We can't be the four of us without you."

"Oh, that's why you're worried about having feelings for Declan," Wyn realized.

"Am I allowed to talk?" I intervened. "Or do you guys want to keep having a conversation like I'm not here?"

"But that's just it. You're there, not *here*," Poet stated. "And it sucks. It sucks so bad."

"I fully agree," Salem said. "It sucks a big one."

"I can't live in New York for you guys," I said. "As much as I love you all. I don't even like New York; that's not a shock. But I also can't stay here because of a man I hardly know."

"The Ridge is your home," Wyn said. "Forget Declan for a second. If he wasn't there, would that change the way you feel about coming back to New York?"

"No."

"So why does Declan's presence change it for you?" Wyn went on. "Unless . . . oh no."

"What?" Poet asked.

"She more than likes him," Wyn said. "Don't you?"

When I didn't reply, Salem asked, "Hadley, are you falling in love with Declan?"

CHAPTER TWENTY-THREE

THE BAR

"The blonde," I said, lifting a pint of cider to my lips.

"Yeah?" Wade asked, arching a brow. He rubbed his jaw and discreetly angled his head in the direction I'd rolled my eyes.

"This is why you needed me to help you get laid," I quipped. "You're completely unaware. She's been eye-fucking you since the moment we sat down at the bar."

He glanced at the woman and flashed a grin.

"Go," I urged.

"I'm not going to ditch you."

"The whole point of going out with you was to get you some action. You can't get action if you stay by my side all night. We drove separately for a reason. You're a free agent."

"You're a good friend." He finished off his drink and set the empty pint down. "You sure?"

"I'm sure."

"Okay." He grinned. "Wish me luck."

"You don't need luck. But maybe put a little more swagger into your walk. Girls like swagger."

"You should teach a class. Okay, here I go." He saluted me and then headed in the direction of the blonde.

I watched him approach her, smiling when she nodded and stood up from the booth where she sat with a group of friends and went to the pool table with him.

Wade had called in the morning, asking if I wanted to venture out for a little jaunt in the next town over from Huckleberry Hill. I'd agreed. Mostly to get my mind off Declan and the fact that we hadn't spoken since the previous night when I walked out of his cabin.

I hadn't been able to turn my brain off—especially after the late-night conversation I'd had with my friends and sister. When Salem had asked me if I was falling for Declan, I'd hung up and turned my phone off.

Mature? No.

Self-protective? Yes.

I was staring into my pint of cider when Wade came back to the bar, the blonde a few steps behind him.

"Hey," he said. "I'm buying a round. You want another drink?"

I shook my head. "I'm good."

Wade reached back and grabbed the blonde's hand and pulled her up. "This is Chelsea. Chelsea, this is my friend from high school, Hadley."

"Nice to meet you," Chelsea said with a genuine smile. "Do you want to play pool with us?"

"Oh, that's okay," I said, returning her smile. "You guys have fun. I'm probably going to leave after this drink."

"Stay," he said, though his tone lacked any force behind it.

I held in a smile. "We'll see."

Wade turned his attention to the bartender and Chelsea

blocked the view of the doorway. I dug into the pocket of my hoodie and extracted my cell. No missed calls or texts.

Sighing, I shoved my phone back into my pocket and slouched down. I wanted to make sure Wade and Chelsea were Velcroed before I left, but I was ready to get into a pair of sweats, chow down on chocolate, and watch a movie.

"If you change your mind, come find us," Wade said, handing a glass to Chelsea.

The door to the bar opened, momentarily pulling my attention. My eyes widened when I recognized the broad shoulders in a flannel shirt and leather motorcycle jacket.

"Hadley?" Wade asked.

My mouth dropped open in surprise as Declan swaggered toward the bar and came to stand between me and Chelsea.

"What are you doing here?" I demanded.

Declan didn't reply. He placed his arm across my shoulder and pulled me to him before looking at Wade and then Chelsea.

"Hey, Declan," Wade greeted, a knowing smile blooming across his lips. "This is Chelsea."

"Uh, hi." Chelsea frowned in confusion, shooting a look at Wade for explanation.

"Come on," he said to her. "If you beat me, I'll take you out to dinner."

She laughed. "What happens if you beat me?"

"I'll still take you out to dinner."

The two of them wandered toward the pool table, leaving me alone with Declan. I threw his arm off and glared at him.

"What are you doing here?" I demanded again.

"What am I doing here," he repeated, raking a hand through his mussed hair. "Million-dollar question." He pointed to my cider. "Yours?"

I nodded.

He took it and drank the rest of it in a few swallows before setting the glass down with a forceful clank.

"Let's go," he growled.

"I'm not going anywhere with you. I came with Wade. I'm having a friends' night out."

"Wade is trying to sink his ball into a corner pocket," Declan said, moving his body so his leather jacket brushed against my hoodie. "And you're coming home with me so we can fuck the anger out between us. Got it?"

His words shivered down my spine and my belly fluttered.

I put a hand to his chest and pushed him back. He took a step away to give me space and I was able to get off the stool. "How did you know I was here?"

"Muddy told me."

I closed my eyes and groaned.

"Hadley, you're trying my patience."

"I'm trying *your* patience? Rude."

"You've got two choices. Either you walk out of here and get on the back of my bike, or I carry you out of here and you get on the back of my bike."

"I thought you didn't do jealousy."

"I don't. This isn't jealousy. This is—fuck I don't know what it is."

"Possessive brute," I stated, crossing my arms over my chest. "You're being a possessive, stalkery brute, and I don't like it."

"We can talk about that back at my cabin. Option two it is." He bent down and scooped me up and flung me over his shoulder, caveman style.

I squawked and pounded on his back. My cheeks flamed with heat when I realized everyone in the bar was staring at us.

"Have fun, Hadley!" Wade yelled.

I stuck my tongue out at him and then I buried my face against Declan's back in embarrassment.

When we got out to the sidewalk, I said, "You can put me down now."

He ignored what I said and continued to walk toward his bike.

"Declan, I drove," I stated. "I can't just leave my truck here."

"We'll come back for it tomorrow. I need you on the back of my bike, Hadley." He finally set me down and then gripped the collar of my hoodie. "I need to feel your arms wrap around me."

I looked up at him. "What's going on, Declan? Where's this coming from?"

"You'll think I'm insane."

"There's a good chance I already think you're insane."

His mouth flickered like he tried not to smile. "I wanted to talk to you—about everything that happened last night. And I wanted to do it in person, so I went to the main house and your grandmother told me you went out with Wade. That's all I heard. *Went out with Wade*. She told me where you were. Before I knew it, I was getting on my motorcycle and I . . ."

"You thought I was lying," I said quietly. "When I told you I wasn't dating Wade, you didn't believe me. And why would my grandmother tell you where I was and not clarify that I'd gone out with Wade to be his wingman?"

"I don't know." His brow furrowed. "I just know I got . . ."

"Jealous?" I supplied.

He sighed. "Jealous."

"Has your frontal lobe returned from vacation?" I teased.

"Starting to." He kept his hold on my hoodie. "I know you can drive home. And you probably should."

"I'll ride your motorcycle with you on one condition," I said.

"Name it."

"You tell me the truth."

He frowned. "Truth about what?"

"About why you really came here tonight. You know I was telling the truth about Wade, so why are you here?"

"You're right." His hands released the hoodie, but only so they could cradle my cheeks. "I just wanted a reason to see you. Especially after how we left things last night."

We stared into each other's eyes, but even in the dark night with the illumination of the streetlamps, I saw the intensity in his gaze.

I squeezed his wrists, and he let go.

"Home?" he asked.

I nodded. "Home."

CHAPTER TWENTY-FOUR

The Ranch

The motorcycle ride was exhilarating, and unlike any experience I'd ever had. Declan had put a helmet on me, made sure it was tight enough, and then told me to climb on behind him. I'd wrapped my arms around him, enjoying the feeling of his strength beneath my fingertips.

He guided the motorcycle with ease, and I felt safe despite the danger. In a way, it was no different than riding a horse. You trusted that a thousand-pound animal capable of throwing you wouldn't, and on the motorcycle you trusted going seventy-five miles per hour wouldn't be the end of you.

We zoomed up the driveway to the ranch and he parked the motorcycle on the side of the cabin. He cut the engine and put down the kickstand.

I sat there for a moment, letting the silence of the night soften the buzzing in my ears. I unclipped the helmet and climbed off the bike.

"Well?" Declan asked, unclipping his helmet and removing it before getting off.

"Incredible." I handed him the spare helmet. "My teeth are still vibrating though."

He grinned.

I shivered.

"Fuck, you're cold."

"I'm always cold."

"Yeah, but you were wearing nothing but a hoodie and there's still a bite in the air. I should've gotten you a leather jacket. We'll get you some riding clothes."

I took a deep breath. "You have to stop."

"Stop what?"

"Stop saying things that allude to a future together," I explained. "That's exactly why I freaked out last night."

"I know," he said easily. "I'm not an idiot. Of course you're freaked out. You don't need glasses to see that you're freaked out."

He put the helmets on the seat and then took my hand. I let him lead me to the cabin. We took off our shoes and left them on the porch and then we went inside.

Declan flipped on the light and turned to me. I closed the door and locked it.

His gaze narrowed.

"What?" I demanded.

"That." He pointed to my chest.

"That what?" I looked down. "I'm confused."

"You're wearing a man's hoodie."

"Yes. It's Wade's. I got cold."

He took a deep breath and then he walked to his bedroom.

I didn't follow him, choosing instead to stay in the living room. He returned a few moments later holding one of his gray hoodies.

"You can wear this," he said.

"Not jealous, my ass," I muttered.

"We're dating. Ergo, you wear *my* clothes, no one else's."

"Are we dating?" I demanded. "Because it feels like we've jumped about fifteen steps ahead of where we're supposed to be."

"And where are we supposed to be?"

"Getting to know each other."

"We know each other. Intimately."

"That's not what I mean," I snapped.

"Hoodie," he reminded me. He laid the hoodie he'd brought out for me on the back of the couch and reached for me. "Arms up."

I lifted my arms and let him strip me of Wade's hoodie. He gave me his and I quickly put it on. My nose brushed against the collar, and I closed my eyes.

"I saw that," Declan said with a sultry laugh.

My eyes flew open. "Saw what?"

"You were sniffing my hoodie. Don't bother denying it."

"I wasn't gonna deny it," I lied.

He took my hand.

"Where are we going?" I asked.

"The couch."

"Oh."

"Oh?" he asked. "What's that mean?"

"I mean, I guess if we went to your bed we wouldn't talk. On second thought, let's go to your bed."

"Hadley."

"Declan."

"You like me."

"I do," I admitted.

"And you weren't expecting to like anyone so soon after your breakup."

"Correct," I agreed.

"But you do. And I like you back, and I'm not bullshitting you."

I frowned. "I never thought you were bullshitting me."

"Maybe not, but that doesn't mean you trust me or my intentions." When I didn't reply, he went on, "If I wanted to get my rocks off, I didn't have to do it with the daughter of my employer where my job is at stake."

"Yeah, I guess I never thought of it that way." I bit my lip. "We don't have to overcomplicate things. We could just end it before my dad gets home—"

"No," he said flatly.

"But it would be so much easier if—"

"Tell you what," he said. "We've got a few more days until your dad gets home. Let's enjoy our time together until then. Okay?"

"Okay."

"Now, come to bed with me."

"True or false," Declan whispered as he curled around me, our naked bodies pressed together. "You hated when I showed up at the bar."

"False," I murmured. Our hands were linked, and I held them to my chest.

"You hated that I hauled you over my shoulder."

"False." I leaned down and brushed a kiss to the back of his hand. "Hmm, you're like a warm snickerdoodle right out of the oven."

He chuckled, the rumble from his chest vibrating against my back. "Is that your new nickname for me?"

"Snickerdoodle? Yeah, I think it might be." I sniggered. "I'm going to get so much shit from Wade, though."

"Because I carted you out of the bar like a Neanderthal?"

"Oh yeah."

"You think he went home with the blonde?"

"Yes. That was the plan all along. You don't deviate from the plan."

"Sometimes you gotta pivot. Pivoting needs to happen sometimes."

"Hm. Why do I feel like you're talking about me?" I asked.

He fell silent for a moment, but I knew it was because he was gathering his words. "Did your ex tell his family why you guys broke up?"

I thought about how Nico treated me. He was sympathetic and kind. But there had been no pity in his tone.

"I think Gianni kept it vague. Not wanting to air his dirty laundry."

"Kept it vague? In an Italian family? That's hard to do."

"Hmm. Yeah."

"Speaking of keeping it vague, you're still vague with me about why you guys broke up."

"Sometimes relationships just run their natural course," I dodged. "Okay, your turn in the hot seat."

"What hot seat is that?"

"You know about both of my past relationships. I want to know about yours."

"Wait, you've only had two relationships?"

"Yes."

"Wow."

"Wow what? Is that weird?"

"Wow, that's—*how?*"

"Well, Wade and I dated through high school, and we broke up when I moved with Salem to New York. And then I was single for a few years. I went on a couple of dates, but I wasn't really interested in anything serious, and then I met Gianni. And we were together for two years." I unlinked our hands and rolled over in his embrace. I poked his bare chest. "Now you."

"I've had my share of girlfriends, but nothing serious."

"Nothing serious?"

"Life on the circuit is time consuming and the schedule doesn't allow you to form lasting bonds."

"Ah, so you hooked up with a bunch of women."

"Yeah . . ."

"Okay, riddle me this," I said. "You said you left the circuit because of potential injuries. Is that the only reason?"

"What do you mean?"

"I mean, you're a man of a certain age," I drawled. "Were you thinking about something more out of life? Your mortality, perhaps? Your legacy?"

"Ah, you speak of progeny." Declan laughed. "I don't know if I thought about it in that way, but yeah. I was getting tired of the circuit. I wanted something different. Some stability."

The words I wanted to ask were clogged in my throat. If I asked them—if he wanted a wife and kids—I had to be ready for whatever he said. And I wasn't sure I wanted to know.

What did it matter, anyway? My father was going to come home and this thing with Declan was going to end.

Declan stifled a yawn.

"You're tired," I said.

"Exhausted," he admitted. "I didn't really sleep much last night after you left."

"Same," I proclaimed.

"Roll over. Let's go to sleep."

For once, I didn't argue. For once, I shoved the questions to the back of my mind. For once, I pretended I was enough, and it didn't matter why my fiancé had left me.

Declan's breathing soon evened out, his hold on me tight.

I fell asleep, and dreamt of dark-haired, blue-eyed babies being ripped from my arms only to disappear into the shadows.

CHAPTER TWENTY-FIVE

I set the basket of newly collected eggs onto the counter. My phone buzzed in the pocket of my overalls, and I pulled it out. I unlocked the screen and saw Wade's selfie and a thumbs up.

"Nerd," I muttered with a soft chuckle.

"Who's a nerd?" Muddy asked as she came into the kitchen. She gestured with her chin to the basket. "Looks like a good haul."

"Very good haul. We've got happy hens. And it's Wade who I'm calling a nerd," I replied. I shoved my phone into my pocket. "You and I need to have a wee chat."

"Do we?" Muddy grinned cheekily.

"Why did you let Declan think I was on a date with Wade?" I demanded.

"I did no such thing," she protested. "I told him where you were and who you were with. He drew his own conclusions."

197

I cocked my head to the side. "And when Declan drove out of here like a bat out of hell? Do you know he came into the bar, picked me up, threw me over his shoulder and brought me back here? Oh, shoot, that reminds me—I need to go get the truck. I left it parked overnight. Can you drive me to the Wagon Wheel?"

"He *what?* He carried you over his shoulder?" Muddy's grin was slow and devilish. "I'm loving this more and more."

"I thought you didn't want us together!"

"When did I say that?" Muddy demanded. "I never said that."

"I think you have selective amnesia."

"I think if you want a ride to the Wagon Wheel you'll be nice to me."

"Yeah, you're right. Can we go now?"

"Sure. But I demand a stop at Sweet Teeth."

She grabbed her keys and the two of us loaded into the truck. It was newer, black, shiny, with an automatic transmission. Muddy hated it. But Dad insisted she drive it because of all the new safety features. If I stayed, no doubt he'd insist on getting me a new truck too.

"So, tell me how it went last night," Muddy said.

I'd been staring out the passenger window and swiveled my head to look at her. "I already told you what happened."

"No, you told me he picked you up and hauled you out of there. I want to know what made Declan have a personality transplant. He's normally so good-natured. Unflappable."

"Well, he was flapped last night."

"Clearly." She fell silent, obviously waiting for me to talk.

I sighed. "Two nights ago, we kind of got into a fight. Not a fight, but a disagreement, and I left his cabin and slept in my own bed."

"Hmm? What was the fight about?"

"I think it was about feelings," I said.

"And that you're feeling them?"

My gaze narrowed. "You think I'm catching feelings?"

"Aren't you?"

"Yeah, I am." I groaned. "I don't want to, though."

"There's what we want and then there's reality."

"You're a regular fortune cookie."

"Just for that, you get to buy me a cruller."

Muddy drove us downtown and found a spot outside Sweet Teeth. She parked and we hopped out of the truck. I held the bakery door open for a couple who was exiting just as we were about to go inside, and then Muddy and I entered.

Gracie was behind the counter, and she waved when she saw me but then began tending to the people in front of us.

When we stepped up to order, Gracie said, "Good morning, ladies. How are you doing today?"

"We're doing great," Muddy said. "How's Bella feeling?"

"She recovered quickly. Unfortunately, Cole got the crud and he's at home," Gracie said. She looked at me. "Sorry I bailed the other night."

"Completely understandable," I said.

"We need to go out and catch up. Really catch up. I think you have things to tell me," she said with a wide grin.

I frowned. "Do I?"

"You do." She nodded. "Didn't Declan hoist you over his shoulder and cart you out of the Wagon Wheel last night?"

I blinked. "How did—did Wade go around telling everyone my business?"

"Wade? Why would Wade be the one to tell me that?" Gracie asked.

"Because he and I were hanging out when it happened."

I glanced at Muddy, whose expression had gone

completely blank. But I could see the gears turning in her head.

"If Wade wasn't the one who told you, who did?" I asked.

"My egg delivery guy," she said.

"Your egg delivery guy is from Silver Springs?"

She nodded. "He was at the Wagon Wheel last night. Said it was the most excitement he'd seen in a while."

"How did he know it was me and Declan?" I demanded.

"He heard someone call you Hadley, so I asked him what the guy looked like who carried you out of the bar and sure enough, he described your new hotness."

"Lovely." I wrinkled my nose.

"Yeah, Larry likes to gossip," she said, biting her lip and looking worried.

"What?" I demanded. "What aren't you telling me?"

"Larry delivers to several of the businesses in Huckleberry Hill. I wouldn't be surprised if that story is making the rounds."

I groaned and rubbed my temple.

"Can I get a latte?" Muddy asked. "With a few pumps of cinnamon? We're actually on our way to the Wagon Wheel now to pick up the truck. She came home last night on Declan's motorcycle."

"Ohhh," Gracie said.

"You're fired," I said to Muddy. "Why are you telling people my business?"

"Gracie isn't *people*, she's Gracie. And besides, this is girl talk. I miss girl talk."

"You said you weren't going to get involved in my love life."

She grinned. "I lied. I like Declan."

"I like him too," Gracie said. "I don't know him well, but everyone says he's really nice and he helped Lucy pull some heavy boxes from the stockroom when he was in General

Merc the other day." She looked at the other barista, who was listening intently. "You got Muddy's order, Abby?"

Abby nodded. "No wonder Declan turned me down when I asked him out. Sorry, Hadley. I didn't know."

"Nobody knew," Muddy said with a cackle. "Guess they do now."

"People are talking about Declan?" I asked, panic creeping into my chest.

"It's the most action we've gotten in months," Gracie said. "A hot new wrangler at Elk Ridge? Yeah, we're going to talk about him."

"That's not the only action being got," Muddy quipped, elbowing me in my side.

My cheeks heated.

"You do look . . ." Gracie cocked her head to the side. "I don't know."

"Like the stick from her butt went somewhere else," Muddy quipped.

"What's gotten into you?" I asked. "You're extra sassy this morning."

"Someone has to be."

Abby handed Muddy her drink.

"Thanks, sugar," Muddy said. "How about that cruller?"

"What can I get you to drink, Hadley?" Abby asked.

"Double shot latte, please." I shook my head. "And a new grandmother."

"This is the most fun I've had in ages," Muddy stated.

"You need a hobby," I muttered. "Join a book club or something."

"That's a good idea," Muddy said. "But I don't want to read any memoirs or non-fiction. Give me the spicy stuff."

"Lord help me," I said, glancing up at the ceiling.

"So really, when can we hang out?" Gracie asked.

"I'll text you," I said. "I'm not sure about my schedule."

"Oh, I see how it is." Gracie nodded.

"See how what is?" I demanded.

"This thing with Declan is new and all you want to do is wrap yourselves in a bubble. I remember new."

Muddy sighed. "So do I."

"How's my drink coming, Abby?" I called out.

"Nearly finished," the barista yelled back.

Gracie put the cruller into a brown pastry bag and looked at me, eyebrows raised.

"The chocolate eclair. Better make it two." I sighed. "How much do I owe you?"

"On the house," Gracie said with a wink. "You paid in gossip."

I dropped a few bills into the tip jar for Abby. I took my drink and the bakery bag, and we left Sweet Teeth.

Muddy climbed into the truck and set her drink in the drink holder. "Give me that cruller. My mouth is watering."

I dug it out of the bag and handed it to her, along with a paper napkin. We sat in the parking spot and devoured our sugar fix.

"Have you talked to Dad?" I asked after I polished off one eclair.

"Briefly," she said. "But he's busy. Hasn't he called you?"

I shook my head. "Texts. Photos of goats. But that's it." I paused. "He took her with him, didn't he?"

"Her who?"

"*Muddy* . . ."

"Yes, he took the woman he's dating with him," she admitted and looked at me. "Are you mad?"

"That he's dating someone? No."

"Are you mad he hasn't told you about her?"

"I don't know," I admitted. "I know whoever she is, she won't replace Mom. But I kind of wish . . . I kind of wish he wasn't hiding it."

"But you have no plans to tell him about Declan, do you?" she asked.

I frowned. "Why would I?"

"Because it's serious."

"It's not serious," I scoffed.

"Hadley," she said softly, reaching over and taking my hand. "Be honest with yourself."

"Oh no. Not you too."

"Not me too what?"

I licked my lips. "Declan told me to be honest with myself just the other night. But it *can't* be serious."

"Why not? Everyone already knows you ended your engagement with Gianni—"

"No, Muddy. No. I didn't tell you the real reason why it didn't work out with Gianni," I said quietly. I forced myself to look at my grandmother. She was a pistol, a firecracker. Sass and brass, for sure. But she loved me. And it was time to tell her the truth. Because I needed perspective. As much as I loved Salem and my friends, they hadn't lived seventy years on this planet. With age came wisdom. Trauma did the same thing, but . . . it was different.

"I found out I have fertility issues," I blurted out. "I went to another doctor to get a second opinion and it was confirmed. I—I can't have children . . . and when I told Gianni . . ."

"He broke up with you?"

"Not right away," I admitted. "He said it didn't matter, that we'd adopt or it could just be the two of us. And I . . . I believed him, Muddy. He gave me no reason not to. And then right before the trip he said he wanted to go alone. That he wasn't sure he could have a life with me. So he went to Italy without me."

I swallowed, tears forming in my eyes as my grandmother let me talk.

"I haven't made my peace with it," I stated. "Not even a little bit. I haven't thought much about it, really. Because I'm not ready to mourn a life I didn't even have—but could've. Does that make sense?"

"Yes," she said softly. "It makes sense."

"So, it can't be serious with Declan. Because even if the feelings are real, they'll go away when he realizes I can't— that I can't give him children."

"You don't know that," she said. "Not unless you tell him. I know you think he'll be just like Gianni, that he'll react the same way, but Declan is different."

"Different," I said. "How can you possibly know that?"

"Honey, sometimes you just get a feeling about people. I don't know how I know, but I do. Does Salem know?"

I nodded.

"And your friends?"

I shook my head. "No. I wasn't ready to . . . Gianni's cousin—Nico—he called the other day to ask what shifts I wanted when the renovation of the restaurant is over. His family knows Gianni and I split up, but they don't know the reason why."

"You sure they don't know?"

"Yeah, he would've said something. Gianni's mother would've called. His sisters. But so far it's been radio silence. I'm mourning the loss of them too."

"What did you tell Nico? About the shifts?"

"I quit over the phone." I smiled, but it was bitter. "I do have *some* pride and I wasn't willing to work there and see everyone and stew in my own dirty laundry. Nico offered to call other restaurants and get me a job, but I said not to bother because I didn't know when I was coming back to New York. I told him I was home for a visit."

"Do you want to go back to New York?"

"Not particularly."

"But you're not sure staying here is the right choice either," she finished.

"You get it," I said.

"I get it." She took a sip of her coffee. "Do you want my advice or do you just want to vent?"

I raised my brows. "You're asking for permission? Instead of offering it freely? That's new."

She tweaked my nose and smiled. "We all have opinions. Very few people actually want to hear the truth."

"I'm not sure I'm ready for the truth." I sighed. "Lay it on me."

"This is your home. In good times and bad. Sure, you might've come home to heal and maybe to hide a little. But this thing you're doing with Declan . . . that shouldn't be the reason you run back to New York. It shouldn't be the reason you stay, either. Stay because you love it. Stay because this is the right place for you. Stay because this place is in your blood."

I thought about what she said and nodded slowly. "Can you not—please don't tell Dad what I told you. I'll tell him—in my own time. When I'm ready to face it. Right now, I just . . ."

"I understand. This stays between you and me."

I sighed in relief.

"But it seems the town now knows you're running around with Declan. It's only a matter of time before Connor finds out the truth. And he should hear you're with Declan from you before he hears it from someone in town."

"Ugh. You're right about that. He's going to fire Declan, isn't he?"

"Probably." She shrugged. "But that was a risk you were both willing to take. You're adults and you can make your own decisions. That doesn't mean there aren't consequences to those decisions."

"Adulting. Zero out of ten, do not recommend."

She gently patted my cheek. "You're going to be fine, Hadley. You'll figure it out."

I wasn't sure if she was talking about my relationship with Declan or my infertility.

CHAPTER TWENTY-SIX

THE RANCH

"So we kinda have a bit of a problem," I said to Declan the moment I walked into the cabin.

He closed the slow cooker lid and came to me. "Hi."

"Hi." I looked up and wrapped my arms around his neck and brushed my lips against his.

"So, what's the problem, bear snack?" Declan asked as he pulled back but didn't let me go.

"Apparently, Larry, Gracie's egg delivery guy from Silver Springs, saw us at the bar last night. And he told her about you carting me out of the bar over your shoulder . . ."

I went on to explain the details and then he raised his brows. "Huh."

"Yeah."

"So, the problem would be . . ."

"The townsfolk." I smiled wryly. "People are talking about us."

"Ah, and you're upset the cat is out the bag."

"No, not really. It's just that my dad doesn't know yet and I don't want him coming home and having someone else tell him before I get a chance to."

"I see," he murmured, dropping his arms from around my waist.

"So, I think we need to tell him. Or I need to tell him," I said.

"Actually, I should tell him. Man to man."

I shook my head. "He's probably gonna fire you. But if I tell him maybe I can dissuade him. But only if I talk to him before he hears about it from anyone else."

"No, Hadley. I should tell him. He'll respect that I wasn't a coward about it. And if he fires me, so be it."

"What will you do if he does fire you?" I asked, biting my lip in concern.

"No idea. Maybe Wade will hire me as a part-time bartender."

"Oh, yes, because you really missed your calling slinging drinks." I laughed and shook my head. "Maybe Lucy will hire you on as a stock boy at General Merc. I heard you helped her out the other day."

"You're hearing all sorts of things," he said. He took my hand and led me to the couch. "Sit. Put up your feet. I'll get you a drink."

"I'd really love a cup of tea," I said.

"Tea it is. I think I have some Earl Grey."

"Perfect."

He moved around the kitchen, filling the copper tea kettle and setting it on the stove.

"So can I run something by you?" he asked.

"Run it."

"I've never seen the hot spring. What do you say we take the horses out tomorrow night, camp out under the stars, and come back in the morning?"

"Night trail ride? Oh yeah, I'm down," I said. "But it's still kind of chilly."

"I'll make sure you're warm."

The way he said it had my blood simmering.

"Can I ask you another question?" he inquired.

"Yes."

"If you're worried about someone else telling your dad about us, does that mean there *is* an us?"

"I guess so, yeah." My brow furrowed. "Well, that's weird."

"What's weird?"

"Usually when I have anxiety, I get a feeling right here." I pressed a hand to the spot right below my rib cage. "I don't have that feeling of an angry rodent burrowing inside my belly."

"That's good. We don't want angry rodent burrowing." He opened a cabinet. "I lied about having Earl Grey. All I have is English Breakfast."

"That's fine. This is so strange."

"Or you could try *not* rationalizing every single thing. You could just let it be. You like being with me. I like being with you. We'll deal with whatever fallout comes because of your dad. But I'm not worried."

"How can you not be worried? He has a shotgun."

He looked at me over his shoulder. "Of course he has a shotgun. He's a rancher."

"Are you purposefully being obtuse?"

"Yes." He grinned. "Hadley?"

"What?"

"There's an *us*. That makes me really happy."

"It does?" I asked softly.

"It does."

I sighed. "This is all happening really fast."

"I know."

"I wasn't supposed to like you."

"I'm a very likable guy."

"Too likable," I groused. "I'm pretty sure the town is going to name you Huckleberry Hill's Townsperson of the Year."

"Does it come with a plaque?" he joked.

"Yes."

"Wait, seriously? I was kidding."

"I wasn't," I said. "You know who the head of the committee is who decides this sort of thing? Lucy."

"Oh, then I'm so in." He fixed me the tea, adding a ton of honey, and brought it to me.

We sat next to each other, his arm around my shoulder.

"Your dad finding out about us isn't the worst thing in the world," he said. "It means I can finally date you in public. For a while, it seemed like you were embarrassed to be seen with me."

I laughed. "Yeah right. I never did tell you that I've got a weakness for dark-haired cowboys that are the human equivalent of a snickerdoodle. A snickerdoodle that looks diabolical in a pair of jeans."

"You wanna take some selfies and blast them all over social media? You're welcome to use my hotness to get back at your ex."

"Ah, you *are* the jealous type," I teased.

"Just when it comes to you, sweetheart. Just when it comes to you."

This is the moment.

"Declan, we need to—"

His cell phone vibrated on the coffee table.

He leaned over to see who it was. "It's Bowman. You mind if I grab this real quick?"

I shook my head, internally breathing a sigh of relief.

"Thanks."

He grabbed his phone and pressed the screen and put the cell to his ear. "Hey, fuckface." Declan looked at me, a smile taking over his expression as he set a hand on my thigh. "Just sitting here having a beer with my girl. What's up?"

My girl.

Would I still be his girl after I told him the truth?

A sick feeling swarmed through my stomach. I set my tea down on the coffee table and gently moved away from his touch so I could get up.

He looked at me in confusion, phone still to his ear.

Bathroom, I mouthed.

Nodding, he turned his attention back to his conversation.

I went to the bathroom and closed the door. Leaning against it, I closed my eyes and tried to calm my churning stomach. I breathed through the nausea and when it passed, I splashed cold water on my cheeks.

When I got back to the living room, Declan was off the phone, his expression furrowed.

"Bad news?" I asked, taking a seat next to him.

"No. Not bad news. Bowman got a brand deal."

"And you're not happy for him?" I pressed my fingers to his wrinkled brow and sank my fingers into his hair. He turned his head and kissed my wrist.

"No, I'm extremely happy for him." He fell silent.

"So what's the issue?" I placed my hands in my lap.

"The brand—a coffee company—is looking for other riders to sponsor. Bowman floated my name and there was . . . interest."

"Interest."

"Yeah. A lot of interest, actually. I'm only a few months off the circuit and my name still rings out. I left at the top, Hadley. He said they'd be calling me to discuss an offer."

"Oh. Oh wow," I murmured.

He took a deep breath. "I'm going to say no."

"Because you're retired?" I asked.

"Yeah, because I'm retired. That's not the life I want anymore." He looked at me, his gaze steady. "Doesn't matter how much money they throw at me."

"When are they supposed to call you?" I asked quietly.

"Next few days, probably."

"Don't tell them no," I said. "Not right away. Give yourself time to think about it."

"I don't need time to think about it." He cupped my cheek in his hand. "I already know what I want."

His voice turned husky, and my insides melted.

"How much longer do we have on that slow cooker?" I asked.

"About twenty minutes."

I stood slowly, his hand dropping from my cheek. "Better make the most of the time."

He shot up from the couch, a huge smile on his face. "I can be efficient."

I placed my thumb on his lips. "Oh yeah?"

"With twenty minutes I bet I can make you come three times."

I dropped my finger and stepped back. "You love a good challenge, don't you?"

He laughed. "This isn't a challenge, sweetheart. This is just a warmup."

CHAPTER TWENTY-SEVEN

THE RANCH

"Declan and I are going on a ride tonight and we're going to camp near the hot spring," I said to Muddy the next morning.

"You'll bring protection?" Muddy asked.

"Muddy!" I laughed.

She rolled her eyes. "I meant a pistol. And bear spray."

"Yes, we'll bring those. It seems the bear cried off though. So that's good."

"It is good." She nodded. Her eyes met mine. "Are you doing okay? Yesterday was a lot."

I took a deep breath and nodded. "I'm okay. I've decided I'm going to tell Declan the truth tonight."

"Good."

"We'll see." I shrugged. "I can't keep it to myself any longer."

I thought about his conversation with Bowman and the brand sponsorship that was on the horizon. He said he didn't want that life anymore, but what would happen when he learned I couldn't give him a family? Hell, I didn't even know if Declan *wanted* a family. I'd been too chicken shit to ask him.

"Did I ever tell you about your grandfather and me getting together?" Muddy asked, setting her crocheting into the basket underneath the end table near the fireplace.

I paused as I searched my memory. "I don't think so."

She nodded. "Thought so. We got married after sixteen days of knowing each other."

I gasped. "No!"

"Yes." She smiled, her eyes misty as she clearly thought about her late husband.

"How did you two meet?"

"I was a waitress in a nothing town. His truck broke down outside the diner where I worked. He came in to use the phone to call a tow truck, but . . ."

"But?" I pressed.

She grinned, her eyes flashing with wickedness. "He forgot completely about calling for the truck because the moment we looked at each other, that's all either of us saw. He stayed with me until the diner closed and then . . ."

"Muddy!"

"Yeah, sugar. Your grandpa came home with me. And the next morning, he called the tow truck and then started packing my bags. He brought me here and we were married fifteen days later."

"Wow. That's intense."

"Yes, it was. You're probably asking yourself why I'm telling you this now. Well, I'm telling you this story because it's not the norm. But it was right for us. And we were *so* happy."

I smiled. "Thank you, Muddy."

"What time are you guys leaving for the hot spring?"

"Probably dusk," I said. "He's never been to the hot spring."

"Well, it's about time you showed it to him. It's special, that spring. I swear it's got a little bit of magic in it."

"Does it?" I asked wistfully. "It didn't help Mom."

"It helped her the way it was supposed to."

"What do you mean? The cancer still took her."

"You don't know, do you?"

"Know what?"

"That your father took her out there every night for two weeks before she passed. He picked her up out of bed and carried her to the truck and drove her out there. They sat underneath the stars and talked. They talked so much that your father's voice went hoarse."

"I remember that—the hoarse voice, I mean."

"They talked about you and Salem. About their life together. It was like . . . each night they renewed their vows." She took my hand in hers. "Death isn't the end, you know. It's just another beginning. With their feet in the pool of the hot spring, they said goodbye."

I brushed the tears from my face. "I didn't know. Dad never . . ."

"Never talks about her. I know. It doesn't mean he doesn't think about her all the time. Think about those final two weeks." She looked at me. "We did okay, didn't we? We did okay without her?"

"We did okay," I agreed. "You know it's weird . . . Mom's ovaries killed her, and mine don't work."

Muddy took my hand and gave it a squeeze.

Tonight, at the hot spring that had no name, I'd confront the ending of a life I was supposed to have. I'd mourn it once and for all. I'd tell Declan the truth and face the aftermath no matter what it was.

Tonight, I'd make peace.

Declan took my bag and strapped it to his saddle. "What do you have in here?"

"Jammies, a change of clothes, three pairs of socks . . ."

He laughed and leaned close, brushing his lips across my ear. "You won't need your jammies."

"*Sir*," I gasped. "I'll gladly skinny-dip in the hot spring, but sleeping without my jammies? No way. Not happening."

"I'll keep you warm," he promised.

My cheeks heated.

Making love underneath the starry sky? Yeah, I couldn't wait for that.

Unfortunately, my happy mood was tinged with anxiety.

"Did the coffee company reach out to you?" I asked.

"Not yet." He looked at me. "Promise me one thing."

"What's that?"

"We won't talk about it tonight, okay?"

"Okay."

We mounted our horses and then I took the lead. "You don't know where we're going."

"I know where we're going," he said. "I had Muddy show me earlier today."

"What?" I gasped. "But I wanted to be the one to show it to you for the first time!"

"You'll understand why I needed her when we get there." He winked. "Come on, bear snack. I want to see you in your birthday suit."

He took off at a quick pace and I followed. It was dusk and the sun would be completely set soon. The sky was clear of clouds.

"We might see the aurora tonight," I said, looking up.

"I've never seen it."

"Never?" I asked, coming up next to him.

He slowed his pace.

"Never," he said.

"You grew up in Bonner's Ferry and never saw it? How is that possible?"

"Never worked out that way I guess."

"Well, tonight will be your lucky night."

"In more ways than one." He winked.

Fifteen minutes later, I saw the old red farm truck parked near the hot spring.

"What's that doing here?" I asked in surprise.

"I'll show you," he said. He brought Merlin to a halt and dismounted. "I had to bring hay and water for the horses. Plus . . ."

I descended Goldie and walked over to the bed of the truck and saw a mattress, along with a huge sleeping bag and two pillows.

"This is glamping," I stated.

"Yeah."

I laughed. "I love it."

"Let's tend to the horses and then I'll tend to you," Declan said huskily.

My insides quivered.

We got the horses comfortable and settled. Declan took off his hat and opened the passenger side door and stuck it on the dashboard.

"Not to make you swoon," he said. "But I also packed us a charcuterie dinner."

"Stop."

He lifted the picnic basket that rested on the seat. "Yep. Got us a nice bottle of local cider to split."

"Perfect."

"Not yet, but it will be." He placed the picnic basket back on the seat and then closed the door.

The sun was halfway gone, and the moon was starting to make its appearance. Soon, the stars would be out.

I went for my jacket and tossed it onto the hood of the truck. "Last one in . . ."

We began to strip, and Declan almost fell over in his haste to get his boots off. I was already thigh deep in the water by the time he came in. He pressed his chest against my back and wrapped his arms around me.

"There's a makeshift bench," I told him. "On the other side."

We waded farther into the pool that was only about ten feet wide. Declan sat down on the bench and then pulled me onto his lap to face him.

I draped my arms around his neck and stared at him.

"So I asked the other ranch hands about the hot spring and they had no idea about it," Declan said. "Why is that?"

"Because this place is special."

"You ever brought anyone else here?" he asked, his hand dragging up and down my back.

I shook my head.

"Really?"

"Really." I lowered my lips to his.

His tongue entered my mouth as his hand slid to the small of my back, pushing against it so that I came even closer to him.

He sipped at my lips, drinking all that I offered him.

I gave him everything I was feeling. My worry, my pleasure, my joy.

His free hand cradled the back of my head, and he held onto me as he switched our positions, so that I was the one sitting on the bench. We continued kissing, our hands caressing one another.

My body temperature skyrocketed from the heat of the water, the heat of him.

He lifted me up and set me on the edge of the pool, widening my legs and stepping between them.

"I want to make you come," he rasped. "I want to make you come underneath the stars."

"Yes," I breathed. "I want that too."

"Lay back, Hadley."

I did as he commanded, my back hitting the earth. Declan lifted my legs and placed them on his shoulders, raising my body so that my core was near his mouth.

I gazed at him, heavy lidded, my nipples taut from desire and my skin steaming in the cool air.

Declan licked me; slow, long, perfect.

His hands gripped my ass, holding me to him. My body wanted him, and I felt myself grow even wetter from his tongue.

"Sweet. So fucking sweet," he growled before he went back to his purpose.

My eyes flew to the sky. Stars winked above. The sky streaked with the faintest traces of pink and green. So subtle you could almost miss it if you didn't know what you were seeing.

With Declan's tongue between my legs, my back bowed underneath the aurora borealis in the sky.

There was no one to hear me cry out my pleasure, just the wind in the trees and the two of us alone in this magical place.

When I came, I yelled from the depths of my soul. And while I was still shuddering, Declan lowered my legs from his face.

He grasped his erection and lined himself up at my entrance and then he slid home.

We curled around one another, thrust for thrust. He was so deep inside me I felt as though we'd become one person.

When I came for the second time, I couldn't stop the tears

from streaming down my face. I couldn't stop the rush of emotion swirling around my heart.

He looked into my eyes, his gaze saying he understood, but he remained quiet. Instead, he used the talents he'd been given, wringing another round of pleasure from me.

Declan angled his hips, driving into me, and gave me his release.

I felt it inside me, and in the warmth of it I found solace in my body.

He gathered me in his arms and pulled me back into the hot spring. We were still joined, and it was as if neither one of us had the desire to be separated ever again.

I buried my face in the crook of his neck and cried. I cried for all the things I'd lost. I cried for a second chance at happiness, and I cried even more for the fear of losing it.

Losing it for real this time.

Because I thought I'd loved Gianni . . .

How wrong I'd been.

"Don't let me go," I hiccoughed.

"Never." He pressed his lips to my shoulder. "I'll never let you go."

A fresh set of tears burst from my eyes, streaming down my cheeks. I forced myself to pull back, just enough so that I could look at him.

I traced his brow, his cheek, his jaw, the shell of his ear. "You might let me go when I tell you the truth."

"The truth," he murmured. "The truth about what?"

I took a deep breath. "That I can't have children, Declan. I'm infertile."

CHAPTER TWENTY-EIGHT

I stared into his eyes after I admitted the truth to him.

He said nothing, he just continued to hold me. His gaze was unyielding.

"Say something," I blurted out when the silence became unbearable.

His hands reached up to cradle my cheeks. "I love you."

My eyes widened. "What?"

"I love you."

"You can't love me."

"Why can't I?"

"For the reason I just said."

His expression morphed from tenderness to intensity. "I do love you. And I don't care that you're infertile."

"Declan, stop," I begged. "You don't mean it."

"I don't?"

I shook my head, my hands going to his wrists, gently squeezing and tacitly asking him to let me go.

"You can't love me," I said again.

"Explain that to me, because I'm sure that I do."

"But how?" I blinked. "We've only known each other . . ."

"Two weeks."

"Two weeks," I agreed. "You can't possibly . . ."

"I could possibly. And I do."

I tried to move—but he was still inside me. And he wrapped his arms around me and forced me to stay caged within his embrace.

"You love me too," he declared. "And that scares you. But that's okay. You can be scared all you want. I'm not running. I'm not taking the brand deal. I'm not leaving *you*, and I never will."

Emotion screamed through my chest, clawing up my throat. "You say that now. But you'll change your mind. I know you'll change your mind."

He stared at me and his expression cleared. "That's what happened with your fiancé, didn't it? You told him about your infertility."

I bit my lip and nodded. "He said it was going to be okay. That we'd still be together and have a life. And then . . . he left me and went to Italy alone. He said he was okay with it, but he wasn't. Having children of his own was more important to him than having a life with me."

"He's a son of a bitch and stupid to let you go. Well, his loss is my gain and I'm not making the mistake of ever letting you go. You're mine and I'm yours, and nothing else matters."

I wanted to believe him. I wanted him to be everything that Gianni wasn't, but my heart had been broken once before by a man who was supposed to love me unconditionally.

"I'm not Gianni," he said quietly, leaning forward and brushing his lips against mine. "And if you want a family, we'll find a way to have one. I promise. Adoption, surrogacy, whatever you want, Hadley."

"How, Declan?" I whispered. "How is this going to work?"

"It just will," he vowed. "Because when it's right, it's right. And we're right. More than right."

"I want to believe you. But how can I?"

"Time. You take all the time in the world to come around to the idea that I'm not leaving you."

"I'm broken—"

"No."

"All I've wanted—since as long as I can remember—is a family. It may not be enough for some people, but it's enough for me. I always dreamed of a loud house with a large family."

"Not all families are blood. Some are made. We can make any kind of family you want."

Fresh tears gathered in my eyes, and they streamed down my cheeks. He kissed them away with his lips.

"You want to know when I fell in love with you?" he asked, kissing my forehead.

"When?" I sniffled.

"The moment you fell on top of me the very first time I ever laid eyes on you. You were adorable and embarrassed and blushing. And I just felt like . . . like I'd been knocked off my feet."

"You *were* knocked off your feet," I pointed out with a smile. "You're telling me it was love at first sight?"

"Yup."

"Oh."

"Oh, what?"

"That's why you never cared about telling my father, right? I mean, you never even thought of putting your job before me."

"There is nothing before you. There's you, and then there's everything else."

I sighed. "You're not love-bombing me, are you?"

"No. I've never said those words to another woman."

"Thirty-two-years old and in love for the first time?" I cocked my head. "No wonder you carried me over your shoulder like a caveman."

"Had to get what was mine."

He shifted under me, rearranging me a little. The warm water swirled between us, and I let out a low chuckle.

"What?" he asked.

"Muddy tried to tell me."

"About what?"

"She told me she married my grandfather sixteen days after meeting him."

"Did she now?" He smiled.

"Yeah."

"That woman knew what was going on long before you did, huh?"

"Not *that* long before." I rolled my eyes. "Considering we've only been dating a couple of weeks. This is insane. You get that, right?"

"Why is it insane?"

"Well, because who says *I love you* this fast?"

"People who are lucky enough to find the one they want to share the rest of their life with. And when you find that, you want your life to start immediately."

"Immediately." I sighed dreamily. "I guess it's not so crazy. I mean, I was with Gianni two years before we got engaged. Look how that turned out."

"Exactly."

My fingers threaded through the hair at his nape.

"So, New York . . ." he trailed off.

"What about it?" I asked.

"You can't really go back there. Not now."

A heavy boulder that had been weighing my heart down

suddenly shifted. I took a deep breath and nodded. "I'm not going back to New York. I think I've always known that."

"If you really loved it, I'd go with you," he said quietly. "If your heart was really there, I'd follow you."

"And be completely miserable," I said with a deep belly laugh. "You'd hate it worse than me, I'm sure."

"Most definitely," he said, leaning forward and kissing me again. "But how can I hate any place where you are?"

"Stop, you're making me swoon."

He pressed his forehead against mine. "Swoon away, bear snack."

"I'm ready to get out of the spring," I said. "But we forgot the towels."

"Ah, yeah, in my haste to see you naked, I forgot to grab them. I'll get them for us. You stay warm."

I lifted myself off him, achingly slow, causing us both to groan in pleasure.

"That has to happen again," I gasped.

"After I feed you," he said. He stepped up onto the bench and out of the pool. "Be right back. Shit, it's cold!"

I giggled and dunked myself up to my chin to stay warm.

Declan glanced at me, the light of the moon and stars showing the heat of his gaze. And then he dashed toward the truck, disappearing from my sight.

"I'm getting dressed first!" he called out. "Give me a minute!"

I floated on my back in the hot spring, my eyes on the sky. A wave of peace settled over me. I'd always been the good twin, the one who did the right thing. I wasn't loud or bold. I wasn't ostentatious. I was downright modest.

I'd lost myself. I'd accepted Gianni's excuse for ending things, thinking there was something inherently wrong with me.

But Declan . . .

Declan showed me that I could be loved for exactly who I was.

Declan proved to me that I was deserving of a family, of having my dreams come true. And that I didn't have to sacrifice a part of myself to feel worthy of that love.

I was crying again by the time he returned with a big fluffy towel.

"No, you're crying again," Declan said. "What happened? I shouldn't have left you alone and given you time to think. Come out of there and let me hold you."

His words only made me cry harder. "Happy tears," I blubbered.

"They don't sound like happy tears. You're a very loud bawler, did you know that?"

I laughed through my watery gaze. "Are you trying to distract me?"

"Yes, is it working?"

"Kinda." I waded through the pool to the edge and got out. I'd barely begun to shiver before Declan had the towel wrapped all the way around me. He rubbed his hands up and down my arms to warm me up and then he slowly led me back to the truck. He'd lit an oil lamp that rested on the roof. Between that and the moon, I could see fairly well. I changed into my pajamas and then climbed up into the truck bed, sliding into the sleeping bag to keep my lower half warm. I'd never given Declan back his hoodie and I'd packed it with me for the night. I threw that on, too.

He came around to the back of the truck and set the picnic basket down onto the sleeping bag and then climbed up, taking a seat next to me.

I opened the picnic basket and pulled out the goodies and arranged them on the cutting board between us. The cheese, fruit, and baguette had been pre-sliced, the jams set in their own containers with several serving spoons.

"Can I ask you something?" he asked as he took a piece of apple and brie and put them together.

"Sure."

"The first night we were together, and you said you couldn't get pregnant . . . you weren't talking about birth control, were you?"

"No," I admitted. "I wasn't."

Nodding slowly, he took a bite of his cheese and apple combination.

"Are you mad?" I asked quietly. "That I didn't tell you right away?"

"Not even a little bit," he said. "Look, I can't imagine what it must feel like, finding something like that out. No, Hadley. I'm not mad you kept it to yourself. I'm glad you told me tonight, though."

I ate a piece of bread and let it settle in my belly. "I promised myself I'd tell you the truth tonight. But I didn't expect . . ."

"What?"

I shrugged. "I didn't expect your reaction."

"It's not bullshit. I'm not a liar."

I reached out and cupped his jaw. "I know that. You've been honest about who you are from the beginning. Even though I didn't trust it at first."

"I should be offended, but I'm not. You didn't want to get burned again. I get it. We often don't see things when we're right up on it."

"My sister and friends are going to have a field day." I laughed. "That'll be a fun conversation."

"Which part?" he asked. "When you tell them you've fallen in love with me, or that you're not going back to New York?"

He looked at me, his gaze steady. As confident as Declan was, he still wanted to hear the words.

"Both," I said quietly. "I think they'll be more surprised

about me falling in love with you so quickly. It goes against every bit of my cautious nature."

He smiled and held up an apple slice to me. I bit off half, and he demolished what was left.

"That's why you told me not to give the brand deal an answer right away," he said suddenly.

I frowned and nodded. "I wasn't sure how you would take my news. I didn't want you to feel . . . trapped. I didn't want you to miss out on something without having the whole picture."

"You are the whole picture." He pulled out the container of olives. "I know this is a lot."

"The food? No, it's the perfect amount. Let's crack the cider open, while we're at it."

He handed me the olives and reached for the bottle of hard cider. "No, I didn't mean the food."

"Oh." I paused. "Yes, it's a lot for sure. My head is spinning. But I kind of wonder . . ."

"Yeah?"

"If I've been living in black and white . . . until you."

Smiling, he popped the cork on the bottle of hard cider. "Cheers, bear snack. Here's to living in full color."

CHAPTER TWENTY-NINE

THE HOT SPRING

We finished the food and split the cider. Then we blew out the oil lamp and snuggled down into the sleeping bag, our faces peering up at the sky.

Neither of us said anything, but our hands met underneath the bag and we linked our fingers.

I was a bit tipsy, giddy even; as light as the carbonation in the cider.

"Would you consider the brand deal?" I asked quietly. "Even if we weren't together?"

He was quiet for a moment and then he replied, "When I was younger, it was all I wanted. Big brand deals, flashy clothes . . . a ton of money."

"Buckle bunnies throwing themselves at you?" I teased. "Oh, wait, I'm pretty sure that part already happened."

"I'm a gentleman, and a gentleman never kisses and tells," he stated.

"Uh-huh, I'm *so* right."

He pulled our linked fingers closer, forcing me toward him. He extracted his hand, but only so he could put his arm underneath me and cradle me close.

"As I was saying," he drawled. "That was the dream for a long time."

"And it stopped being a dream because of the injuries?"

"That was part of it," he admitted. "But I think I was just tired, you know? Working toward those things. To what end? When I was in my twenties, my priorities were different and that was okay. But I don't know. When I got to be about twenty-eight, I started thinking about how I could get out of that life. The endless cycle of injuries, and the potential that one would be the last . . . It all felt . . . meaningless, I guess. It used to be fun, and then one day it wasn't fun anymore. I wanted something else. I just didn't know what *something else* was." He paused. "I envy you, Hadley."

"Me? You envy me? Why?"

"Because you've always known what you wanted. And you didn't waste time like I did."

I snorted. "Yeah, I knew what I wanted . . . a home and a family. And then life was like, *oh just kidding*. You don't get any of that."

"You can still have all that. It just might look different than what you expected."

I was silent for a moment and then asked, "Was your time on the circuit a waste? I mean, it led you to Elk Ridge, but was it worth it?"

"I met you here, so yeah, it was worth it."

"Would you go back and do it differently?"

"Nah. I don't believe in regrets. Plus, like you said, it all led me to you."

I turned toward him and bathed his chin in kisses. "Thirty-two is still young, Declan."

"Tell that to my body." He chuckled. "It feels beat to shit. I've used it hard."

"And what a hard body it is," I teased, but then I sobered. "I understand, though. Hindsight is everything, isn't it?"

"It really is."

"I like the idea of not living with regrets. I thought I regretted my move to New York, my relationship with Gianni. I just felt like a colossal failure on all fronts. But if I'd never been dumped by Gianni, I never would've wanted to come home. I never would've met you."

"And that would've been a real tragedy. Don't you think?"

"The biggest." I sighed. "I never wanted a big life. I never had big dreams. And for a while, I let the outside noise from other people make me feel like I was wrong for wanting a simple life. But finding someone who loves you—who *really* loves you—and making a life with them . . . isn't that the biggest dream there is?"

"I think so," he agreed. "And so many people never get that."

"Muddy lost my grandfather so many years ago. Dad lost Mom . . . I don't want . . ."

He hugged me tighter when I didn't go on.

"We don't know how long we've got on this earth," he said. "So that's why we have to live our lives to the fullest."

I swallowed. "People don't understand, do they? About losing a parent. You kind of lose your way for a while."

"Yeah. That can be true. It can really put shit into perspective, you know? About what's really important."

I placed my hand on his chest and snuggled my nose against him. He was warm, vibrant. He smelled like the outdoors, like life.

"Make love to me, Declan," I purred. "Make love to me under the stars and tell me you love me."

His hand slid down my body to rest at the apex of my thighs. "I'll do one better. I'll show you, instead."

One of the horses nickered, startling me awake. My eyes flipped open into the early dawn, and I attempted to sit up, but Declan's arms tightened around me.

"Just Merlin wanting his breakfast," Declan said softly. "Impatient fucker."

The warmth of his thighs seeped onto my skin. I was bare from the waist down, never having bothered to put on my pajama pants before falling asleep tucked into Declan's embrace.

He ground against my backside, hard and ready. His hand slid down my body, between my legs.

I'd never been so wet in my life. Without a word, I bent my knees and lifted them toward my chest.

The crown of his shaft teased me before slipping into me. He glided his finger between my folds, finding the spot that needed his attention. Sparks shot along my nerve endings.

"I can't stop thinking about you in those overalls," he whispered in my ear as he thrust. "I want you to wear them for me without underwear. And when I find you, alone in the barn, I'm going to unclasp the straps and let them drop to your ankles. And then I'm going to bend you over and fuck you from behind. I'm going to fuck you so hard and so deep, you come like a volcano. And you're going to cream all over me. Would you like that, Hadley? Would you like it so raw and deep you feel me for days after?"

"Yes. *God yes*," I moaned. His filthy words painted a graphic image of the two of us.

"Come for me, baby. Come for me now." He pressed his fingers against my clit.

I did.

I came all over his girth, my nails gouging crescent moons into the skin of his neck as I reached behind me and gripped him with all my might.

"Fuck," he growled as he came.

He stilled inside me, the beating of his heart slamming against my back. I closed my eyes and lazily drifted into a half comatose sleep.

Declan slid out and I felt the wetness we created on the back of my thighs.

"More mornings like this," he said, kissing my cheek.

"Hmm. I say yes to that," I agreed, looking at him over my shoulder and smiling. "Not to mention the overalls fantasy."

"We'll make that a reality." He reached for his boxer briefs. "We should probably pack up."

I sighed but didn't move. "Yeah."

He kissed my hair. "You stay exactly where you are. I'll pack up and saddle the horses."

"What do we do with the truck?"

"You'll drive it home. I'll ride Merlin and tether Goldie to him."

"Sounds good."

We saddled the horses and made sure all our trash was in the truck. He tossed me the keys and I climbed into the driver's side.

"You good?" he asked, meeting my eyes.

I smiled, relief curling through me. "Perfect."

He chuckled and kissed me quickly. "Let's get back and shower. Then we should grab breakfast in town."

"Sounds great," I said.

"We're going to enjoy my day off," he said heatedly.

"You insatiable maniac. I have an idea of how you want to enjoy your day off."

He chucked my chin and then swaggered toward Merlin.

I watched him mount, appreciating how he looked in a saddle.

I started the engine and then drove in the direction of home, Declan and the horses disappearing in the rearview mirror.

It was a faster drive than you could ride on a horse, and I got home several minutes ahead of Declan. I parked the truck out front of main house, leaving the mattress for the time being.

I cut the engine and removed the keys. I got out of the truck and was about to head to the barn to meet Declan to help with the horses when the front door of the house opened. Turning, I smiled, expecting to see Muddy.

My eyes widened in surprise when my father stepped out onto the porch.

"Morning, Hadley," he greeted, appearing calm and stoic.

"Uh, hi, Dad." I frowned. "You weren't supposed to get back until tomorrow."

"Change of plans," he said, his blue eyes narrowing. "Where are you coming from this early in the morning?"

"Nowhere," I lied.

"You're a terrible liar." He took a step down off the porch and came toward me. His gaze took in my disheveled hair and my appearance.

"Nice hoodie. It looks familiar."

I took a deep breath. "Dad, let's go inside. We need to have a talk."

"Damned right we need to have a talk," he said, his expression morphing into anger. "Right after I fire Declan."

"Dad, don't—"

"Where is he?"

"He's . . ." I pointed in the direction where I'd come from.

Like a ghost, Declan suddenly rounded the bend and appeared. He didn't stop off at the barn, instead he let Merlin trot toward us, Goldie tethered to his saddle. Declan's eyes went to me and then to Dad. He dismounted and patted Merlin's neck.

"Connor," he greeted, inclining his head.

Dad didn't take his eyes off him. "You son of a bitch."

"*Dad*," I snapped.

"No, Hadley, stay out of this," Dad said, turning on his heel and heading up the porch steps.

"Where's he going?" Declan asked me. "Why is he going inside?"

My brow furrowed. "I think he might be getting his shotgun."

"For dramatics, right?" Declan asked.

"Where the hell is my shotgun!" Dad yelled from inside the house.

I winced. "Eh, sure?"

"I hid it," Muddy yelled back. "You will not make a gelding out of that boy!"

"That's not a boy," Dad bellowed. "That's a man. That's a man who seduced my daughter!"

Declan took a step toward me and wrapped an arm around my shoulders. "I think someone from town might've told him."

"I think you're right." I turned to him. "You should take Merlin and go for a ride. I'll talk to my dad. I'll calm him down."

"No." He cupped my jaw. "We do this together." He suddenly looked up. "You might want to move."

"Why?"

He gently pushed me out of the way. I turned and saw my father striding across the lawn. When he got to Declan, he clenched his fist and slugged him right in the jaw.

Declan took it like a man.

But when Dad wound up to give him another punch, I yelled, "Dad! I love him!"

Dad's hand stopped mid-flight and he looked at me, astonishment on his face. "You *what?*"

"I love him," I said, taking a hesitant step toward Declan. "We love each other, Dad."

Dad cursed under his breath. He looked at me and then glanced at Declan. "You're fired."

Declan nodded. "I'll get my things." He stared at me and placed his hand on my shoulder. I gripped his wrist and then gave it a squeeze before letting go. My father and I both watched him grab Merlin's lead and urge the horses to follow him.

"Connor." Muddy had come out some time during the altercation to stand on the porch. "Come inside."

Dad looked at me, his jaw clenching, but then he reluctantly did as his mother bid.

I followed at a slower pace, glancing over my shoulder to see Declan, still tall, still proud. He didn't look at all put out by my father's decision. Then again, it wasn't much of a surprise.

I stepped into the house and closed the front door. "Dad, we need to have a talk."

CHAPTER THIRTY

THE RANCH

"Coffee, Hadley?" Muddy asked as she stood in the kitchen.

"That would be great, thanks," I said.

"Start talking," Dad commanded.

"I will not," I said, crossing my arms and glaring at him. "You will not bully me into talking about this until I have a cup of coffee in my hands and you calm down."

"I won't calm down," he seethed. "I stopped in town at General Merc and you know what Lucy told me? She told me you and Declan were dating. I've been gone five minutes and—"

"For the record, we had planned to tell you the moment you got home," I said. "But things kind of spun out of control."

I took the coffee Muddy offered me. "I assume you're staying for this conversation?" I asked her.

"Damn right I am," she said with a sassy grin. She glared

at her son. "Listen to your daughter and by God, if you make her cry, *I'll* get the shotgun."

Dad looked duly chastised. I bit my lip to hold in my laughter.

"Sit," she commanded. "And really listen to her. Okay?"

"Okay." He sighed, sounding tired. "Wait, you don't seem surprised by any of this. Why not?"

"I already knew about them." She shrugged. "And anyone with two eyeballs and a brain cell or two could see they were sniffing around each other from the moment they met. God, they're no better than two cats in heat."

"Not helping," I told her.

"Ferrets in heat, then."

"*Really* not helping," I stated.

The three of us sat down at the kitchen table. Dad opened his mouth to speak, but then thought better of it.

"Declan did not seduce me," I told him.

"You're fresh off a broken engagement," he said. "You're not in your right mind."

"That's just it," I said. "I *am* in my right mind. I've never been more right about anything in my whole life."

"You were in bad shape when you got home," he stated. "You're telling me you're in love with someone two weeks after meeting and—and—"

"I married your father after sixteen days of knowing him," Muddy reminded him. "And you married Kathleen four months after knowing her."

"That's different," he said in frustration.

"How?" I demanded. "At this point, falling in love quickly with the right person is clearly in the Powell DNA. I came by this genetically. You have no one to blame but yourself."

"It's different because you're my daughter," he rasped. His hands were on the table, and they were clenched.

I reached over and took one of his fists, forcing it open so

I could hold his hand. "I didn't tell you the full story of why Gianni and I broke up."

"No, you didn't," he allowed. "You kept that one close to the vest."

I glanced at Muddy, who smiled at me with encouragement. I took a deep breath. "I found out I—I can't have children, Dad. I went to two different doctors who both confirmed it. And Gianni couldn't handle that, so he ended things with me."

"Hadley . . ." His hand tightened on mine.

"Yeah." I nodded. "It was bad. The breakup. I didn't get out of bed for days. I came home to heal. I didn't expect to meet Declan. I didn't expect to fall so hard and fast for him, but he's just so . . . you know who he is. You hired him, for crying out loud."

"Cow-wrangling lothario," Dad muttered. He raised his brows. "And does he know? What you just told me?"

I nodded. "I told him last night. And he told me he loved me *after* I told him."

"And you believe him?" he asked gruffly.

"Yeah. I believe him." I smiled. "You think he'd risk your anger and losing your respect for a few rolls in the hay if he didn't really love me?"

He closed his eyes. "*You* don't roll in the hay. You're still six years old with pig tails."

"Dad," I said softly.

Dad opened his eyes and sighed. "I'm going to have to be okay with this, aren't I?"

"If you want to be okay with me, then yeah," I said. "Please, Dad. Go to him. Un-fire him."

"High road, Connor. Hadley fell in love and now she's not going back to New York," Muddy said. "Actually, you should be thanking Declan."

Dad looked at me. "Is that true?"

"How did you know?" I asked Muddy.

"I'm Muddy." She shrugged.

"Hadley?" Dad pressed.

"I'm not going back to New York," I said slowly. "I'm right where I want to be."

"One more question, and then I'll let it rest," Dad said.

"Shoot."

"Would you stay even if you weren't with Declan? What I mean is, are you staying for you as much as you are for him?"

"You're worried this is just another Gianni situation," I said in understanding. "That I stuck it out in New York because of him."

He nodded.

"Yeah, Dad. I'm staying as much for me as I am for him. But I'm staying for you and Muddy, too. I'm staying for the mountains. I'm staying for the huckleberries. I'm staying for the mushroom festival. I'm staying because this is where I belong, and I don't want to be anywhere else."

Dad rose from his chair. "Excuse me, will you?"

"Ask him to come for breakfast," Muddy said as she got up from the table.

Dad sighed but reluctantly nodded and then he walked out of the kitchen. The front door opened and then closed, leaving me alone with Muddy.

"You get on upstairs and shower. You've got sex-hair." She winked.

"*Muddy!*" My hand went to my head, and I laughed. "Are you going to tell Dad where you hid the shotgun?

"Hmm. Let's give it a few days."

CHAPTER THIRTY-ONE

THE RANCH

Breakfast started off super awkward. Muddy and I tried to fill the silence with inane chatter. Declan sat next to me, and he placed his hand on my thigh, which instantly calmed me.

I looked at Dad, who was watching me and Declan like bugs under a microscope. I straightened my spine and raised my brows. He sighed and went back to eating his bacon.

"So why did you come back early?" I asked.

"I saw all I needed to see. I purchased what I wanted to purchase," he said. "Henry and Josiah are loading up the livestock and coming home."

"You drove home by yourself?" I asked. "All alone?"

Dad narrowed his gaze. "What does that mean?"

"It means, I'm wondering if your special lady friend came with you," I said with a wide smile.

"Lady friend?"

"Give it up, Dad." I rolled my eyes. "I know you're seeing someone."

Dad's gaze went to Declan. "You told her."

"Told her," I repeated, my gaze bouncing from Dad to Declan. "You knew?"

"Guess he didn't tell her," Muddy said, picking up her cup of coffee. "For the record, I didn't tell her anything either. But she's a smart cookie, and if you ever wonder where she gets the bad lying gene from, well that's all you."

"I'm still stuck on the fact that Declan knew Dad was dating someone." I looked again at the man sitting next to me. "Oh, I remember now."

"Remember what?" Declan asked, his expression tight.

"I asked you about it days ago and we never picked up the thread of conversation again. You distracted me."

My dad made a noise.

"I didn't want to betray his confidence," Declan said finally.

"How'd you find out?" Muddy asked Declan.

"He saw me kissing her in the barn." Dad rubbed the back of his neck.

"Well, well, well, now whose turn is it to explain?" I demanded. I glanced at Declan. "I'll deal with you later."

"Looking forward to it," he said lightly.

"I get that I have to accept this relationship," Dad stated tightly. "But can you try not to flirt with each other in my presence?"

"We'll try and tone it down," I said.

"Thank you."

"No, we won't," Declan drawled. He pulled my chair closer to him.

"Atta boy," Muddy said, raising her cup of coffee to him.

Dad's gaze narrowed at Declan but softened when he looked at me. "You don't seem mad," Dad said to me.

"I'm not mad. She's the reason you didn't want me going to the livestock auction with you, wasn't she?"

"Yes," he admitted. "I wasn't ready to—anyway, we're done now."

"Done?" Muddy asked. "Really?"

"Why?" I asked.

"Because she wants to get married and I don't," he stated. "So, there you have it."

"Dad," I said softly. "Mom would want you to be happy again."

"I'm not having this conversation." He pushed his chair back from the table and stood. Without another word, he strode from the house, the front door slamming shut.

I looked from Muddy to Declan. "Who is she? Let me guess. The veterinarian. Dr. Swanson."

Declan nodded. "Yep."

"What do you make of all this?" I asked Muddy.

"If I had to guess, I would say Dr. Swanson *does* make him happy. And that's why he ended it."

"Oh," I said softly.

"Let him be, sugar. It's for your father to figure out." Muddy rose. "You kids mind cleaning up?"

"Not at all," Declan said.

"You're a good boy," Muddy said, coming to him and patting his cheek. "Treat her well, or I'll use the shotgun myself."

"Yes, ma'am," Declan said formerly.

Muddy left, grabbing her jacket on the way out.

I stood up and began gathering the dishes.

"You're mad at me," Declan said. "For not telling you."

"No."

"Annoyed?"

A smile flickered across my lips. "Annoyed is a better word for it, and I am annoyed—just not for the reason you think."

243

"Tell me then." He went to the sink and grabbed the scrub brush.

"You know how to clean cast iron, right?"

"Yeah, I do."

"Okay, because that pan has been seasoned for sixty years. My grandmother will kill you if you ruin it."

"I know how to clean cast iron," he assured me. "Back to what we were talking about."

"I'm annoyed because you knew and instead of telling me you didn't want to divulge what you knew, you misdirected me. Don't misdirect me. Next time I can't know something, then tell me that."

"And you'll just accept that as a viable answer?"

"Well, of course not." I rolled my eyes. "But once I calm down, I'll respect your decision to be an iron vault."

"All right."

"But you do know now that I'm your girlfriend we're not supposed to have secrets, right? You're supposed to tell me everything you know. Especially when it pertains to gossip."

"So, if Salem tells you something in confidence, does that mean I get to know too?"

"Hell no. Salem isn't just my sister. She's my twin."

"So let me get this straight; I have to tell *you* someone else's confidence, even if they swear me to secrecy, but you won't do the same."

"That's right." I nodded.

"That's not fair."

"I don't make the rules, Declan. But what's yours is mine and what's mine is mine."

His lips turned up in a smile. "Is that right?"

"That's right." I nodded.

"Hadley?"

"Hmm?"

"You called yourself my girlfriend," he said.

"Oh." I nibbled on my lip as I began loading the dirty breakfast plates into the dishwasher. "I just assumed—maybe I shouldn't have assumed."

"Assuming is good," he said.

"Yeah?"

He grinned at me and then leaned over and brushed his lips across mine. "Yeah."

I sighed. We finished cleaning up the kitchen in companionable silence. It made me think about doing this with him forever, but my heart saddened when I thought about no sounds of children's laughter echoing through the house. No Christmas mornings of squeals when they realized Santa had come the night before.

"Hey," I said, feeling emotion jam my throat. "I know we were supposed to have a day together, but I really want to call Salem and my friends and tell them . . . well, everything."

"Everything?" he asked, wrapping his arms around me.

"Not *everything*. But enough that they understand." I placed my head against his chest and closed my eyes. He smelled like bacon, and I nuzzled my nose against his shirt.

"Stop that," he whispered against my hair.

"Or what, my big, delicious snickerdoodle?"

"Or I'm carrying you out of here and taking you back to the cabin. And then I'll have to make love to you on the hardwood floor with nothing but blankets because the mattress is still in the back of the truck."

"That doesn't sound so terrible," I whispered, peering up at him.

"Hmm. No, it doesn't." He kissed me and then let me go. "Call Salem and your friends."

"I want you to take me for another ride on the back of your motorcycle soon," I said. "But I don't have the clothes."

"We'll get you some clothes," he promised. "And some hot boots."

"We better be careful," I whispered. "We don't want anyone walking in while we're flirting with each other."

"We're at the beginning of a relationship. If we can't flirt now, how are we supposed to cement it for years to come?"

"Valid question, Declan." I stood on my toes and kissed him again. "Get out of here. And walk away from me. Slowly. I want to enjoy the view."

"Your wish is my command, ma'am." He pretended to doff his hat and then he turned and with an exaggerated swagger, walked away from me.

The front door closed, and I was alone.

With a deep breath, I went up the stairs to my bedroom. My cell phone was on my nightstand. I swiped it and immediately went into my closet. Even though my relationship was out in the open now, I didn't want my dad to accidentally hear anything I said through the walls. Especially anything sexual.

I groaned in embarrassment when I remembered that he'd seen me with sex-hair.

"Don't think about it," I muttered aloud.

I turned on the closet light and closed the door. And then I dialed Salem.

"We're on our second bottle of Prosecco," she said in lieu of greeting.

"Oh, that's fun," I said. "Boozy brunch at the apartment?"

"Yep," Salem said. "None of us wanted to get dressed. Wyn cooked."

"Reluctantly," Wyn called out.

"Hang on, let me put you on speaker. Okay, can you hear me?"

She was a bit echoey, but I could hear her. "Yep."

"Hey, lady," Poet said.

"How are you doing?" Wyn asked.

"I'm good." I cleared my throat. "Really good, actually."

"Mood stabilizer?" Wyn joked.

"Yeah, in the name of Declan," Salem quipped.

"Guys, let her talk," Poet said with a laugh.

When I stopped chuckling, I said, "So do you want the good news or the bad news first?"

"Bad," Salem said.

"Yeah, bad," Wyn agreed.

"No, good," Poet stated.

"You're outnumbered," Salem said. "Sorry, Poet. Go on, Hadley, what's up?"

I swallowed and felt my heart leap into my throat. "I'm not coming back to New York."

There was silence on the other end of the phone followed by Wyn saying, "We know. We already started packing up your stuff."

"*What?*" I asked in shock. "You can't be serious!"

"We're serious," Poet said. "The moment you told us you quit the restaurant, we went out and got boxes. You don't have that much stuff, so we'll send it to you in a few days."

"Oh." I frowned. "That seems anti-climactic."

Salem still hadn't said anything.

"Salem?" I pressed.

"I'm here," she croaked.

"Are you . . . okay with my decision?"

She fell silent for a moment and then said, "Selfishly, no. I'm not okay with it. Unselfishly, I understand completely."

"You're not mad at me?"

"Why would I be mad at you? We all knew this place wasn't for you. It was only a matter of time . . ."

There was silence again and then Poet asked, "So what's the good news?"

"Yeah, and is it dirty?" Wyn teased.

I laughed. "Positively filthy."

"I'm sat," Wyn said. "With bubbly. Tell us *everything*."

CHAPTER THIRTY-TWO

THE RANCH

"Hey, come here, I want to show you something," Declan said, taking my hand and leading me to his bedroom.

"Seriously, can you feed me first? I need protein for energy before we—"

Declan laughed. "I'm not showing you my dick. I want to show you this . . ." He gestured to his dresser.

"What about it?" I asked in confusion.

"Open the top drawer."

I opened the top drawer to find it empty. "There are no clothes in here."

"No, there are not."

I looked at him and then the drawer. "Oh . . ."

"Yeah. That's for you. Your underwear, some socks. You know, so you don't have to do the walk of shame back to the main house in soiled undies."

My cheeks heated. *"Soiled undies?"*

He leaned forward and brushed his lips across my ear. "From my cum dripping out of you."

I gripped his arm and swayed. "Declan!"

"I love it, Hadley," he said, wrapping another arm around me. "I love looking at you and knowing that."

"I need to sit down," I murmured.

"Or lay down?" he asked wickedly.

"I can't lay down," I said. "We're having dinner at the main house in a few minutes. Propriety. I can't show up with sex-hair again."

He sighed. "Fine. But when dinner's over, we're coming back over here."

"Declan . . ."

"Yes?"

"I think I should sleep in my own bed tonight," I said.

"Why?"

"Because."

"*Because* is not a reason," he said. "You're an adult."

"I know."

"We already told your dad, and I'm pretty sure Muddy is cheering us on. So what's the problem?"

"That sassy pants has done nothing *but* cheer us both on," I agreed. "But I don't want—I know this is stupid. But I think my dad is hurting more over his breakup than he wants to admit."

"So what? You're not allowed to be happy if he's unhappy?"

"No, that's not it. It's just . . . I don't want him to think . . ."

"That you're choosing me over him," he finished.

My eyes widened. "How do you do that?"

"Do what?"

"Know exactly what's in my head and spit it out for me?"

"I don't know. I just get you. I get where your mind is at. I also know you're a recovering people pleaser." He grinned.

249

I grinned back. "Just for tonight, I promise."

He sighed. "I understand. But the next time you sleep over, bring some socks and underwear. Preferably the black, lacy kind."

"Okay. I'll have to go buy some." I looked down at his crotch to the bulge he was sporting. "If I thought you wouldn't touch my hair and mess it up, I'd get on my knees for you and take care of that problem."

"Hmm. You know I can't stop myself from touching you."

I bit my lip and then boldly met his gaze. "Maybe I should tie you up and have my way with you."

"Please, God, *yes*." He kissed my lips and tried to deepen the moment.

I gently pushed away from him when all I wanted to do was pull him closer. "We need to get out of here."

"Yeah, we do," he agreed. He took a deep breath. "You go on ahead. I'll take care of this problem and then join you at dinner."

"Can I watch?" I blurted out.

"You want to watch me jack myself off to the thought of you in black lacy panties?"

"Please?"

His eyes darkened. "Fuck yeah you can watch, but I'm gonna want to come all over you. And once again that defeats the purpose of not showing up at your family's house looking like we got into trouble."

I swallowed, my mouth watering at the thought of tasting him. Of us tasting each other.

"Go," he urged. "I need a cold shower. I'll be there in fifteen."

"Fifteen minutes? Seriously?" I asked.

He grinned. "Time me."

I pulled out my phone. "Okay. I will." I set the clock and with one last kiss goodbye, I forced myself to walk out of the cabin. I headed back to the main house, keeping an eye on the time.

Dad and Muddy were in the kitchen, having cocktails. I shook my head at my father's offer of bourbon and grabbed water instead.

"Where's Declan?" Muddy asked.

"Showering," I said. "He'll be along in a bit."

I was in the middle of setting the table when my phone alarm went off. I silenced it just as the front door opened.

"Hey," Declan greeted, his eyes finding mine. "Was that your alarm?"

"It was." I bit my lip to stifle a giggle.

He arched a brow and then turned his attention to Muddy. "What can I do to help?"

"Nothing. Pour yourself a drink. Connor's in the den."

"That was pointed," I said with a laugh.

"It sure was," Muddy agreed. She handed me a basket covered with a napkin. "Biscuits."

Declan went into the den and straight to the liquor cart. I watched out of the corner of my eye as he sat on the other end of couch and didn't say anything to my father.

"This is going to be fun," I muttered.

"Give them some time. They were buddies before you got between them."

I gasped. "I didn't get between them."

Muddy raised her brows.

"Fine, but I didn't mean to."

"Green beans, and mashed potatoes," she said, pointing to the dishes. "And take a trivet. I'm bringing the tenderloin right from the oven."

"On it," I said.

"We're ready," Muddy called out.

Dad wasted no time getting up from his seat and bringing his drink to the table. Declan was slower. I took the chair next to Declan and we all sat down. Muddy brought in the beef tenderloin and poured gravy over the top of it.

"Smells amazing," Declan said.

"It does," I agreed. "Doesn't it, Dad?"

Dad grunted.

After Muddy took her seat, I picked up the basket of biscuits and handed it to my father. "How was your day?"

"Fine," he said.

"I think a storm's on its way," Muddy said. "One of our famous late spring storms."

"Muddy has a sense about these things," I said to Declan.

"I like storms," Declan said awkwardly.

God, are we really talking about the weather?

"What's your favorite season?" I asked.

"Winter," he said. "Christmas, especially."

"Winter is long here," I said. "But there's an ice sculpture festival. I'm so glad I don't have to miss it this year."

"We should enter," Declan said. "It would be fun."

"Yes," I said in excitement.

"You'll have to take him sledding on Maple Mountain," Muddy added. "And ice skating on Lavender Lake."

"Oh, I can't wait." I looked from Declan to my dad.

Dad held his fork in his hand and his brow was wrinkled in thought. A slight smile appeared on his lips. "You can't forget hot chocolate and chocolate fondue at Sweet Teeth."

I nodded. "You have to reserve tickets. They do seatings."

"Winter in Huckleberry Hill sounds kind of amazing," Declan said.

My hand rested on the table and Declan covered it with his own and gave it a squeeze.

The tension around the dinner table eased and conversation began to flow.

"I bought you a present," Dad said to me. "It should be here tomorrow."

"What did you get me?" I asked in excitement.

"I'm not telling you." He looked at Declan. "She loves surprises."

"Does she?" Declan asked. "Good to know."

"No, don't do that," I moaned. "Don't tell him that."

"Don't ever tell her what you're planning," Dad went on. "Because if she knows too early, she gets really happy, but then she gets really sad."

"It's a dopamine thing," I said. "When the surprise is no longer a surprise, I kind of crash."

"I'll remember that."

"You're really not going to tell me?" I asked Dad.

Muddy laughed. "You just said not to spoil it for you."

"I am my own worst enemy." I sighed. "I talked to Salem and the girls today."

"Yeah?" Dad perked up.

I nodded. "I told them I wasn't going back to New York. None of them were surprised. In fact, they already started packing my boxes."

Dad nodded, his expression turning solemn.

Declan noticed and looked at me.

Later, I mouthed.

He inclined his head and went back to eating. "I need this recipe," Declan said. "It's fantastic."

"It really is," I agreed.

"I'll write it down for you," Muddy said.

Declan frowned. "You don't have it written down?"

Muddy shook her head and tapped her temple. "It's stashed up here."

"Along with many other great dishes," I said. "Everything I know about cooking I learned from her."

"Why haven't you cooked for me?" Declan asked.

"Because you always offer to cook for me," I reminded him. "And you're no slouch."

"You've cooked for her?" Dad asked.

"Yes," Declan replied.

"When?"

"Dad," I muttered.

"I'm just curious."

"He made me his kitchen-sink nachos on the night of our first date. With homemade brisket."

"Brisket?" Dad asked.

Declan nodded. "Yep."

Dad paused. "I love brisket."

"Yeah?" Declan asked.

"And beer," Dad added. "I like bourbon better, but I like beer. Local beer. With pool tables."

I frowned in confusion and looked at Muddy. She shook her head and shrugged.

"I like pool," Declan said.

Dad stood up from the table, his plate only half finished.

Declan did the same.

"I'm driving," Dad announced. To me he and Muddy he said, "Don't wait up."

The two of them left the room without another word.

"What's that about?" I asked in confusion.

"If I had to guess, I'd say that's your father's olive branch," Muddy said. "He's taking Declan to the Copper Mule."

"Oh," I said with a sigh. "That's good."

She frowned.

"What?" I demanded.

"There's no pistol in the glove box, right?"

"Muddy!"

"Well," she shrugged, "there's two ways this can go. We'll just have to wait and see which one your father chooses."

CHAPTER THIRTY-THREE

THE RANCH

It was three in the morning, and I'd read the same page of my book four times. I finally cast it aside and turned on the TV.

I was in the den, curled up on the couch, waiting for my father and boyfriend to come home.

Muddy had gone to bed hours ago and I'd eaten half the Boston cream pie in one sitting.

I heard the engine of the old farm truck. I waited a few minutes to see if Dad would come inside, but he didn't.

Frowning in confusion, I got up to investigate. I looked out the window and saw the truck parked outside Declan's cabin.

My fingers fell from the curtain and I went back to the couch. Twenty minutes later, the front door opened and closed softly.

There was the clod of footsteps across the wooden floor and then my father appeared in the doorway of the den.

"I thought you'd be asleep," he said.

"No, you didn't." I lifted the remote and turned off the TV.

He smiled lightly. "You're right. I hoped you'd be asleep. Not the same thing, I guess."

Dad came into the room and sat down on the couch next to me.

"What did you do to Declan?" I asked.

"Got him stinking drunk and then asked him a bunch of questions," he said, running a hand across his stubbly jaw.

"Dad," I groaned. "You didn't."

"I did. He thought we were drink for drink. But I had Wade pour apple juice in mine instead of bourbon. I took Declan to the cabin. Got him in his bed. Made sure to put water, aspirin and a trash can nearby. There's a real good chance he's going to vomit. Though he swore up and down he wasn't a puker."

I rubbed my eyes.

"You should probably spend the night over there, just to make sure he's okay."

"Dad," I whispered, lunging for him and wrapping my arms around his neck.

I pulled back and wiped the tears from my eyes.

"No one is going to be good enough for you, Hadley," he said, his voice sounding suspiciously thick. "But I have to let you make your own decisions. I have to let you choose. And of all the men you could have chosen, I'm glad it's Declan."

"Had to get him drunk and talking to admit that, huh?" I asked with a laugh.

He swallowed but didn't smile. "You know what he said to me?"

I shook my head.

"I asked him about you being—being infertile. Fuck, I feel like I didn't even give you the right reaction to that. We just glossed right over it. I know it's tearing you up inside. I know how much you wanted a family of your own."

"Declan said there are plenty of ways to make a family," I said quietly.

Dad nodded. "That's what he told me too. He told me that he only wants you to be happy. And he'll do whatever it takes to make that happen. And I believe him. Not because he was drunk, but because I remembered meeting him for the first time before he ever even knew you existed. I had a good feeling about him. And my intuition has never let me down. It's what made me propose to your mom so fast. And look what we made together. A beautiful life, and you girls."

"I'm going to cry," I warned.

"That's okay," he said with an endearing smile.

I burst into tears and reached for my father. He held me while I cried, patting my back like he did when I was little.

When my emotions had run their course, I pulled back and wiped my cheeks.

"Go on, now," Dad said with a sigh. "Make sure he doesn't choke on his own tongue."

"Dad," I said with a laugh.

"He's not a drinker. He can't hold his liquor for shit. It only took him three shots to get sloppy. That's a good sign. He's got a good head on his shoulders and he's been solid as a rock since he's been here."

"So, we have your blessing?" I asked quietly.

"Would it matter if you didn't?"

"No." I smiled to take the sting out of it. I kissed his cheek. "Sleep well, Dad."

"I will."

I bit my lip as I stood up. He looked at me and waited.

"You've got a lot of life left in you, old man," I said gently. "It would be a shame not to share it with someone. Just think about that, okay?"

He didn't reply as I walked toward the front door. I slid into my outdoor slippers and grabbed my jacket. I knew the path to the cabin by heart and traversed it easily.

I walked up the porch steps and took off my slippers before going inside. I locked the door and turned off the main light—the lamp in the bedroom was on.

Standing in the doorway, I watched Declan, asleep on his back. His boots were still on. I crouched down and gently removed them and set them aside.

He was too heavy for me to lift so I left him in his jeans and shirt. I crawled into bed next to him and placed my hand on his head.

"Hadley," he slurred.

I smiled, glad that even in a drunken delirium, he thought of me.

Me, and no one else.

"I'm here, cowboy," I whispered.

"Love you," he muttered before falling back to sleep.

"I love you too."

"Fuck. My. Life." Declan appeared in the living room, looking pale, disheveled, and downright terrible. "What time is it?"

"Eleven a.m.," I said, taking a sip of my lukewarm coffee.

He was in a pair of boxer briefs and a white T-shirt. He must've stripped down before coming out because he hadn't moved all night once he'd passed out.

"Your dad is a cruel, cruel man." He swiped a hand down his face, wincing when he touched his jaw. "He punched me in the face and then got me drunk."

"You let him do both those things," I reminded him.

"I was hoping it would get me in good with him."

"Mission accomplished."

He cocked his head to the side. "Why are you here? I thought you were sleeping in your own bed last night. Or did you sleep in your own bed last night and come over this morning and wait for me to get up?"

"Coffee?" I asked, rising from the chair. "Toast?"

"Orange juice," he begged. "And dear lord, don't mention food."

"Okay." I went to the kitchen and opened the fridge. "Dad got you to bed and he and I had a brief talk. He told me to sleep over here. He was worried about you choking on your own tongue."

Declan sat down on the couch. I handed him the orange juice and he took a sip. He waited a moment, no doubt to see how his stomach reacted, and then he took another bigger swallow.

"Well, at least he didn't try and kill me. It would've been so easy for him to do that," Declan muttered.

"He gave us his blessing," I announced. "It wouldn't matter if he hadn't, though."

"No?" He raised his brows. "You would've defied your father to be with me? Very Romeo and Juliet."

"They died," I said blandly. "No one's dying in my story."

He smiled and then his expression slipped. "I didn't do anything embarrassing, did I? Did I say anything embarrassing?"

"Not to me," I said. "You were really sweet. Told me you loved me and passed out. It was kind of adorable."

"Adorable." He squinted. "You can't turn down the sun, can you?"

I giggled. "No. But I can find your sunglasses."

"Please, God. The aspirin hasn't kicked in yet."

"You really should eat something. You shouldn't take that stuff on an empty stomach."

"What's it going to do? Make me nauseous? Too late for that."

I got up and brushed a kiss to his forehead and then went to the bedroom to the nightstand. I picked up his aviators and brought them to him.

"So I was wondering," I said, retaking my seat.

"Wondering what?"

"Wondering if you wanted to go out to dinner with Gracie and her husband, Cole. Like a double date thing."

"Sure." He turned his head. "Not tonight, right? Please, not tonight."

"Not tonight," I assured him. "But maybe when Cole has a night off?"

"That sounds good." He settled down on the couch and rubbed his jaw. "I think I told Wade we should be friends. Though I can't be completely sure. It's all kind of fuzzy."

"You're a nice drunk, aren't you?"

"Yeah, I'm super friendly. Not friendly with the ladies though, I promise."

"I'm not worried. Dad vouched for your character."

"Is your dad hurting this morning?"

"No. Wade was pouring him apple juice in whiskey glasses the whole night."

"I knew it!" he yelled and then immediately winced. "Ow."

"You really sure I can't make you toast before I go?"

"Where are you going?"

"I figured you'd want to go back to bed. After all, hangovers at your age must be debilitating."

"Cruel woman. Making fun of my age."

I grinned. "Dad said it only took you three shots to get completely trashed. You know that's endearing, don't you? A cowboy who isn't a huge drinker is hard to find."

"I aim to please. And when I'm feeling better, I'll do just

that." He sighed. "Toast would be good. Dry, though. The idea of butter makes me want to throw up."

CHAPTER THIRTY-FOUR

Midmorning the next day, I parked downtown a block away from Sweet Teeth. When I got to the bakery, I saw a line out the door, snaking down the sidewalk.

"What's going on?" I asked the woman who was in front of me. "Why's there a huge line?"

"You don't know?" she asked in surprise.

"I don't."

"Sweet Teeth went viral on social media. I drove here from Sandpoint. I hope they don't run out of cinnamon rolls."

I raised my brows. "I had no idea." I stepped out of the line and then headed toward the door.

"No cutting!" someone shouted.

"I wouldn't dream of it," I said back. "I just need to use the restroom."

It was a lie. With a line winding out onto the sidewalk, I was sure Gracie was overwhelmed. When I went inside, I saw her at the register. Her hair was in a lopsided ponytail and her cheeks were flushed.

"Gracie," I greeted. I attempted to sidle up to the bakery display, but there were four customers squashed together in my way. "Hey, Abby."

"Hadley!" Abby sent me a panicked look.

"Put me to work." I rolled up the sleeves of Declan's flannel shirt.

Gracie tossed me an apron. "You know how to work an espresso machine, right?"

"Absolutely," I said with a grin. "I worked at an Italian restaurant, remember?"

"Great. I'm moving Abby to the register so I can get to the back and make some more donuts."

"Hey, we'd like to order," a middle-aged man grumbled.

"Absolutely, sir," I said, working my way behind the counter. "Tell me what I can get you."

Gracie handed me a marker and said quietly to me, "Abby posted on social media and we went viral."

"So I've heard," I said. "You need reinforcements."

"I need more hands," Gracie agreed.

I pulled my cell phone out of my pocket. "I'll make some calls."

"Bless you."

"I'm still waiting," the man said.

"Right," I said. "What would you like?"

He rattled off a drink order with five different customizations. I glanced at Gracie and cocked an eyebrow.

"City folk," she mouthed.

I nodded and smiled. And then I got to work making his drink. Abby started taking orders and ringing people up and getting them their baked goods. She wrote drink orders on the to-go cups and set them in a line at the espresso machine. I was a decent barista and while I was steaming milk, I called

Wade and told him to get over here and help. I called Muddy next.

I picked up a cup and glanced at the drink order and frowned. "What's a Huckleberry Mist?"

"Our version of a London Fog," Abby explained. "Instead of Earl Grey we're using local berry tea."

"A London Fog, huh?" I asked with a wry smile.

"We were curious and looked it up." Abby shrugged and turned her attention to the next customer.

Wade showed up ten minutes later with Chelsea in tow.

"Holy cow," Wade announced.

"Tell me what to do," Chelsea said.

"Talk to Gracie." I pointed to the back kitchen.

Muddy arrived ten minutes after that and began to help Gracie. Chelsea cleaned the tables and made sure the coffee bar was well supplied. Wade checked that the bathroom was clean and there were enough paper towels. Then he was on trash detail.

More trays of baked goods came out of the kitchen, much to the delight of the eager customers who were no longer annoyed because the line had begun moving at a good pace.

Time blurred and by the time it was 3 p.m., all of us were exhausted. The line was only five people deep. We finished serving them and then had a much-needed lull.

Gracie walked over to the front door and closed it, locking it and flipping the sign over to read *Closed*.

"I was not ready for that," Gracie said as she pulled out a chair from a café table and took a seat. "Nothing like that has ever happened."

"I need food," Abby said. "But I'm too tired to move."

"There are a few meat pies left over from the rush," Gracie announced.

"Tell me where they are and I'll get them," Chelsea said.

"Counter in the back." Gracie stood. "I need to use the restroom."

"Should I heat them up?" Chelsea asked.

"Don't bother," Muddy said. "I'm starving. I'll eat mine room temperature."

"Same," I said.

Chelsea headed to the back, and I looked at Wade. "So that turned into something?"

Wade grinned and shrugged.

I kicked his foot. "That's for getting my boyfriend drunk last night."

"I'm guessing he doesn't need a place to crash," Wade said.

"A place to crash?" I repeated. "What do you mean?"

"He texted yesterday, midmorning, I guess. And asked if he could sleep on my couch."

"He didn't tell me that," I said. "He just said he asked you to be his friend. But that was last night at the bar."

"I told him I would be his friend," Wade said. "So he doesn't need my couch anymore?"

"He doesn't need your couch."

"What did I miss?" Gracie asked, when she returned.

"My dad got my boyfriend drunk last night—with Wade's help."

Gracie raised her brows. "Boyfriend?"

"Declan," I clarified.

"Well, well, well," Gracie said with a grin. "It looks like that test drive turned into a buy. I'm going to need all the details to that story. Not just the headlines."

I laughed. "I'll tell you everything later."

"Someone's standing at the door," Gracie said as she looked to the front of the bakery.

"We're closed," Muddy announced. "Tell them to go away."

"I will, but politely." With a groan, Gracie got up and went to answer it. She unlocked the door and opened it.

"Hi, Dr. Swanson," she greeted.

My ears perked up and I looked at Muddy.

"We're closed to the general public after a crazy fluke of a rush," Gracie said. "We all needed to catch a break."

"I drove by earlier and saw the line," Dr. Swanson said. "I thought I'd come back. But you're closed now, so I'll come back tomorrow."

"Nah, come on in. We have a few pastries left and the espresso machine survived the gauntlet."

"You sure?"

"You're a local." Gracie stepped back and let Dr. Swanson through the door. She was a beautiful woman with high cheekbones, dark brown hair, and bright blue eyes.

She also looked no older than thirty.

Gracie took her hand and led her farther into the bakery.

"Hi, everyone," Dr. Swanson greeted. Her gaze turned to me. "Sorry, I don't believe we've met."

I stood up from my chair and held out my hand to her. "I'm Hadley Powell."

"Hadley," she murmured. "Nice to meet you."

"Nice to meet you too, Dr. Swanson."

"Please. Call me Jane."

We stared at each other for a moment.

Muddy jumped in, "You know Abby, right?"

"Of course I do." Jane smiled at the young woman. "Every morning she makes me a latte with a leaf pattern drawn in the foam."

I looked at Abby. "You have to teach me that."

"Sure thing." Abby beamed. "Would you like a latte now?"

"Sounds great," Jane said. "And whatever pastry is left over."

"There are a few." Abby got up. "How about I make up a box for you?"

Chelsea finally returned with the individual meat pies on several plates. "Sorry, I decided to heat them up in the toaster oven. They'll be better that way."

She set the plates down along with a stack of napkins.

Wade introduced Chelsea to Jane and the rest of us dug into the food.

"How much do I owe you?" Jane asked.

"On the house," Gracie said through a mouthful of meat pie. "Damn, who made this batch?"

"I think it was Muddy," Abby said, handing off the coffee to Jane, along with the bakery box.

"These are better than the ones I make," Gracie said.

"Secret ingredient," Muddy said with a wink. She tapped her temple. "All up here, too."

"You really do need to write those recipes down," I said.

"Make a cookbook," Chelsea suggested. "Because these pies are insane."

"A cookbook," Muddy murmured. "Hmm. That's an interesting idea."

Jane took a sip of her latte. "Guess I better get going. Nice meeting you, Hadley. Chelsea."

"Bye." I waved at her.

Jane left and Abby locked the door after her.

The moment she was gone, I looked at Muddy. "How old is she?"

"I don't know," Muddy remarked. "I didn't ask."

"Why does it matter how old she is?" Gracie asked.

I didn't want to air my family's business, so I lied and said, "She's a vet. Vets are in school a long time. I'm just wondering if she skipped a grade or something."

Abby reached for her meat pie. "She's thirty and divorced."

Gracie looked at her. "How do you know that?"

Abby rolled her eyes. "I make her coffee every morning. We talk."

"And she told you she was thirty and divorced?"

"Her ex-husband called her to wish her a happy birthday last month," Abby said. "She was in the bakery when it happened."

"What else do you know?" I asked.

"I know a lot of things," Abby said loftily. "But I'm not at liberty to share."

We finished off our meat pies and then we helped Gracie clean up the destruction of the bakery.

"What are you going to do if there's a line tomorrow?" I asked.

"Call for reinforcements?" Gracie asked hopefully.

"I don't mind coming in early," Muddy said. "Help you prep. If you want."

"I want," Gracie begged.

Muddy looked at me. "You'll feed the chickens and collect the eggs?"

"Sure thing," I said.

"I'm not a fan of early morning hours," Wade said. "But I can get another bartender to cover me for a few nights and help you out, too. Better count on me midmorning, though."

"And me," Chelsea said.

"You guys are incredible," Gracie said, breaking down in tears. "Sorry, I'm just exhausted. Ignore me."

We said our goodbyes and then Muddy and I left the bakery.

"Where did you park?" I asked.

"Few blocks down. There weren't any spots on the street," Muddy said. She pointed in the direction she'd parked.

"I'm down that way too." We walked together. "So, Jane's nice."

"Very nice." She looked at me and grinned. "And almost twenty years younger than your father."

"She could be my older sister," I muttered.

"But she's not," Muddy said. "Does it change how you feel about your father dating?"

I thought for a moment and then shook my head. "I was just surprised. I thought he'd be with someone closer to his age. I didn't think he'd go for a younger woman. A *much* younger woman."

"She's pretty."

"She is," I agreed. "Good with animals."

"And sexually at her peak."

"Muddy!"

"What?" She shrugged. "It's true."

"I know, but ew. I don't want to think about *that*." I paused. "You think he'll get back together with her?"

"Not unless he decides marriage is on the table."

"Does she want kids?" I asked.

"I don't know. Probably."

"Probably?"

"Well, why would she care about marriage if kids aren't on the table?"

"People get married and don't have kids."

"Yeah, but more people get married to have a family. It's just the way of it." She looked at me and quickly looped her arm through mine. "I'm sorry, sugar. I wasn't thinking. Ignore me. I've entered the phase of my life where I have no filter and I say whatever's on my mind."

My lips twitched. "You've been that way for as long as I can remember. So you can't use the age excuse."

"Still, I'm sorry about what I said. It was thoughtless."

"No." I shook my head. "I have to get used to hearing things like that. From people I love as well as strangers. I can't expect people to curb what they say."

She fell silent and didn't say anything else. We got to the truck and I opened the driver's side door.

She hugged me and held me for a long moment before letting go. She pulled back to look at me. "I'm proud of you, Hadley."

"For what?"

"For being you."

She squeezed my shoulders and then dropped her hands.

"See you at home," I said. "Drive safe."

I got into the driver's side seat and shut the door. My phone pinged with a text.

DAD

Your present got here.

ME

On my way home.

CHAPTER THIRTY-FIVE

THE RANCH

"You didn't," I said as I got out of the truck.

"I did," Dad said with a rueful grin.

"You *didn't!*" I squealed. I ran to the front porch and held out my hands.

He lifted the kid and placed it in my arms.

"It's a she," he said. "A Nigerian Dwarf goat."

She was black and white with black socks, and I hugged her to me. "You got me a baby goat!"

"You've wanted a goat for years," he said. "And now that you're staying . . ."

Tears gathered in my eyes. "Thank you, Dad."

He smiled. "What are you going to name her?"

"Don't know yet." I stroked a hand down her head, and she bleated.

"I've got her stall and pen all set up," Dad said. "And Dr. Swanson already checked her out at the livestock auction."

I couldn't hold back. "I just met Dr. Swanson at Sweet Teeth not even an hour ago."

He sighed. "Yeah?"

"She's young, Dad."

"Not that young."

"She's thirty."

"Yeah. So?"

"And you're forty-eight," I pointed out.

"I'm missing the point of this conversation."

"That *is* the point of the conversation. She doesn't just want marriage, does she? She wants a family, too."

"She does. And when I realized I wasn't going to be able to give her that, I let her go so she could find someone else."

"Find someone else?" I raised my brows. "In a town of eight hundred people. With maybe three unmarried men in her age range."

"You said I was too old for her," he pointed out. "So, which is it?"

"I know why you like her. She's beautiful and smart. And she's a vet. A lot of similarities to Mom."

His jaw ticked. "She's not a stand-in for your mother."

"I know." I looked down at the baby goat in my arms. "Just like this baby goat isn't a stand-in for the baby I can't have."

He flinched. "Hadley, I—"

"Thank you, Dad. I love her already. And you didn't know about my . . . until after you bought her for me. It's why she's so perfect."

"Let's show her the new digs."

"New digs." I snorted. "You're so old."

"Not that old."

A few hours later, Declan found me sitting in the baby goat's stall.

"What do you have there?" Declan asked with a grin, leaning over the stall door.

"My present from Dad," I said with a laugh. "Come meet her."

Declan opened the stall door and closed it quickly. He then took a seat next to me on the straw bedding.

The baby goat went to investigate him right away.

"I know how this is going to go," I said with a smile. "She's going to love you more than me."

"Nah." He scratched her head, and she leaned into his touch. "She's cute. What are you naming her?"

"Tempest." I offered my hand to her and she nibbled on my fingers. "Hungry again, I see."

I reached into the bucket next to me that had some starter grain and held it out to her in the palm of my hand. She devoured the grain quickly and then immediately began exploring for more. I gave her some and then she went to drink water.

"She's going to need a buddy," Declan said. "They're social animals."

"Yeah." I nodded. "A buddy would be good."

I leaned my head on his shoulder.

"What were you up to today? I texted several times and didn't get a reply," he said. "Were you out of cell range?"

"Nah. I went to Sweet Teeth this morning and there was a line out the door. Abby posted something on social media and it went viral. They weren't prepared. People drove all the way from Sandpoint, can you believe it? Anyway, I jumped behind the counter to help Gracie and then I called Wade and Muddy for reinforcements. We're all going back tomorrow to help."

"Ah," he said, taking my hand and linking his fingers through mine.

"Sorry I didn't get back to you."

"It's all good. I figured something was up."

I lifted my head and looked at him. "Wade brought Chelsea to Sweet Teeth to help too. Looks like that's sticking. Everyone's falling in love."

"Just in time for the Mushroom Festival," he said with a smile. "You want to go to that with me?"

"Absolutely."

"So, what exactly happens at a mushroom festival?" he asked.

"Well, there are booths, and everyone is selling something to do with mushrooms. Everything from leather mushroom totes to small, sharp knives for harvesting and even fresh and dried mushrooms themselves. Usually morels since they're the most prevalent in the area. I'd love to get out and forage for some, but . . ."

"But?"

"That's something Salem and I used to do together." I sighed. "Damn, I miss her."

"I bet you do."

"It's weird, you know? I love being here. I *want* to be here. But this is the first time we're ever going to live apart. It just doesn't feel right. I'm off kilter, you know?"

"Twin thing?"

"Definitely a twin thing."

"How's she taking your decision?"

"She says she's fine with it." I shrugged. "She'd already started packing up my stuff, so she knew before I did that I was coming home for good. But she's not fine with it. I mean she'll be okay . . . as much as she can be."

"Will she come home for a visit soon?"

"If I ask her, maybe. But it's hard for her to be here. There's a lot of unresolved . . . issues. For her."

"You want to tell me about them?" he asked softly.

"I want to tell you, yes. And I probably should tell you. But I don't want it to color how you see her. When you meet her—whenever that is—I don't want it tainted."

"Fair enough."

Tempest wandered to the corner of the stall and started pawing at it.

"Is she secretly a dog?" Declan asked.

"Maybe."

Goldie was in the stall next to us, and she nickered. Tempest perked her head up.

"I think they want to meet each other," Declan said.

I scrambled to a stand and then I picked up Tempest and walked out of the stall with her. I trekked to Goldie's stall and held the goat up for the mare to inspect.

The two of them sniffed each other and then my heart melted right out of my chest when the two of them touched noses.

"I'm pretty sure Goldie just became a surrogate mother to a goat," Declan said with a soft laugh.

I patted Goldie's neck and then brought Tempest back to her stall. I set her down. "I don't want to leave her."

"I know. But my cabin isn't set up to house-train a baby goat. Not yet anyway."

"Not yet?" I raised my brows.

Declan leaned down and gave Tempest a good side scratch. She pressed against his leg. "Yeah, a litter box, some wood shavings, some positive reinforcement—she can be an indoor house goat."

"Declan." I sighed.

He looked at me. "I just want to make you happy, Hadley. That's all I want to do."

A week of pure bliss went by. I gave my nights to Declan and my days were spent at Sweet Teeth. The fervor hadn't died down. In fact, it had grown, amplified by word of mouth and customers posting their own videos of how good the treats were on social media.

Gracie was in the process of hiring some extra help, and I was grateful because as much I loved helping her out, dragging my butt out of bed at the crack of dawn and driving to town was hard on me. I'd always been a morning person, but lately I'd been tired and the caffeine jolt in the middle of the afternoon just wasn't doing anything to pick me up.

Plus, attempting to house-train a goat when neither Declan nor I were there full time was a chore. During the day, Tempest was either in her stall or her pen. She needed a routine and at the moment, she didn't have one. After an accident in the middle of the night, my good-natured boyfriend had grumbled and insisted that she had to go back to the barn. He took her while I cleaned up the mess on the wood floor.

"I have to be up in three hours," I moaned, collapsing back onto the bed.

"I have to be up in two," he said.

"Oh, so it's a contest now of who suffers the most?"

He turned off the lamp. "Let's not argue—let's just go back to bed." He pulled me against his chest, and I fell asleep.

His alarm woke me up and in my frustration, I hit him with a pillow. He wrestled it from me and somehow it ended with him inside me.

The two orgasms he gave me before finding his own release had me sedated and mellow. I drifted off again, but my alarm never sounded and when I woke up naturally at ten a.m., I was completely horrified.

I looked at my phone; I had a few missed calls and texts from Gracie. I scrambled to the bathroom and reached for the toothbrush Declan had given me and called Gracie.

"Hey, are you okay?" she asked. "I couldn't get a hold of you, and I was worried."

"Sorry," I said around the toothbrush. "My alarm never went off. I'm getting ready as we speak. I can be in the truck in ten minutes."

"Don't worry about it," she said. "I have more than enough help now. I was just concerned."

My heart rate began to slow. "Did Muddy go in today?"

"Nope. I let her off the hook, too. You guys were my knights in shining armor coming to my rescue the way you did."

"Call me Dame Hadley," I joked.

"Okay, sorry, but I gotta hop off now."

"Happy baking," I said and hung up.

I set my phone aside and brushed my teeth. I looked in the mirror, grimacing in horror. My hair was a rat's nest. I looked like I hadn't slept at all, and my skin was pale.

"Burning the candle at both ends," I said to my reflection.

I got into the shower and ten minutes later, I was dressed. I went and checked on Tempest, who was happy in her stall with fresh hay and bedding. The ranch hands pitched in and helped take care of her, just like they did for all the other animals.

I went to the main house. My head was in the fridge when there was a knock on the front door. I went to answer it and saw the postman I'd known since I was a child. He was delivering my boxes from New York. I signed for them, thanked him, and then maneuvered them into the foyer. There were six in all, and they were too heavy for me to cart up the stairs. I'd wait for my father or Declan and use them for their muscle.

I was in the middle of eating my breakfast when Muddy came in. "There's a maze of boxes in the foyer," she said in greeting.

"I can't get them up the stairs. I need Dad or Declan."

"Your stuff from New York, I'm guessing?"

"Yep."

"Knowing Salem, there might be a gag gift in there as well," Muddy said. "I'd open the boxes in private."

"Hmm, thanks for the reminder."

I set off a text to the group chat that I got my boxes and thanked them for their timely delivery. Salem replied almost immediately.

SALEM

tell dad I used his credit card for the astronomical shipping costs.

ME

tell him yourself

SALEM

tongue stuck out emoji

WYN

have you opened them yet?

ME

No. They legit just showed up. Should I be worried?

SALEM

Depends.

ME

that terrifies me

POET

We just threw in some stuff as a going away present. Since we didn't really get to have a party and all.

WYN

yeah, Salem and I kinda added some more
stuff after you went to bed.

POET

Sorry Hadley. I tried to keep them contained.

SALEM

We are uncontainable.

ME

Dad got me a baby goat.

POET

WHAT I NEED PICTURES IMMEDIATELY.

WYN

Him? Her?

ME

Her. Name is Tempest.

Grinning, I sent them photos of Tempest. Several of them
with Declan in them.

WYN

I need to get me one of those.

ME

I know isn't she cute?

WYN

No, a cowboy

ME

He also rides a motorcycle . . .

WYN

How does it feel to be living my dream?

POET

Definitely God's favorite.

. . .

I set my phone aside and finished my meal. Dad came inside and carted the boxes up the stairs. I closed the door of my bedroom and sat on the floor, reaching for the first box.

Clothes and a few keepsakes. A framed photograph of my parents on their wedding day. The hot spring during a sunset. A black and white photo of Huckleberry Hill in the 1800s.

I put away my winter clothes in the back of my closet. But when I found a men's button-down shirt, I inhaled sharply.

There was a knock on the bedroom door, followed by it opening. "Hadley?"

There was nowhere to put the blue-button down shirt, and I knew Declan would see it when he entered the closet.

"I came to see if you wanted to get some lunch." His eyes dropped to the shirt. "What's that?"

I cleared my throat. "My boxes came with all my stuff. Including one of Gianni's shirts."

His smile slipped.

"I'm throwing it away," I said hastily. "I wasn't expecting to see it."

"You weren't expecting *me* to see it either, were you?"

"Definitely not." I sighed. "Seriously, Declan, this isn't a big deal. I don't want to keep it."

"You kept Wade's hoodie," he pointed out. He raked a hand through his hair.

"He gave that to me when we were in high school, but I'll throw that out too. I don't want to wear anyone's clothes but yours."

"I'm trying to stay levelheaded here," he said. "It's not working."

"You're angry."

"Not at you."

"What then?"

"You can throw away the clothes of relationships past, but what about pictures? Memories?"

I went to him and placed my hand on his heart. He covered my hand with his and stared down at me.

"I don't know if I'll ever be ready to get rid of photos. Because when I look at them, I don't think about my relationships. With Wade's photos, I remember high school, I remember bonfires, I remember sneaking in past curfew with Salem."

"And Gianni's photos?"

"I don't know yet when I look at them what I'll feel . . . or remember. It's fresh. As for the memories—"

"Those are yours to keep." He kissed me gently. "It's okay to remember. I just . . ."

"What?"

"Don't want you to look at them and wonder *what if*."

"What if? You mean what could have been if I'd stayed with him?"

"Married him. Had a whole life with him."

"I won't ever look at photos and wonder *what if*," I vowed.

"You don't know that."

"I do," I insisted. "Because he didn't want me. And you do. And that's what matters."

He took a deep breath.

"Better?"

"Better," he agreed.

"Less homicidal?" I teased.

"Barely." He smiled. "But it's a start."

"What were you saying about getting lunch?"

His eyes darkened as he closed the closet door and then he gently pushed me against the wall. "I know what I want for lunch."

His fingers reached for the button of my pants.

"You better find something to stuff into my mouth," I replied huskily. "I'm a screamer."

He opened a drawer and pulled out a pair panties. With a wicked grin, he shoved them into my mouth. "Yes. I'm aware."

CHAPTER THIRTY-SIX

THE RANCH

The rain started two days later. It woke me up in the middle of night. I was naked and sprawled atop Declan when I heard the quiet patter of raindrops.

"I love that sound," he whispered. "Rain on a tin roof."

Tempest bleated from the living room.

"I'll check on her," he said, kissing my forehead.

I rolled off him and he got up, putting on a pair of boxers. He went to check on the baby goat in her makeshift pen to keep her confined, but the cabin was not big enough for a baby goat, a six-foot three cowboy and a five-foot-four brunette.

It was fine in the interim, but I was sleeping over every night. My clothes were finding their way into the closet and dresser.

But everything was perfect, and I didn't want to shake up our rhythm.

Declan came back holding Tempest to his chest. "She

used her litter box, had a snack and some water, but I thought she could use some cuddles."

"You really want a dog, don't you," I joked.

"I do," he said. "But she's a good substitute for the time being."

I pulled on Declan's discarded T-shirt and reached for the baby goat. I set her on my lap and she immediately laid down and put her head on my knee.

"Why don't you guys have dogs? Ranches always have dogs."

"We had a dog," I said. "When I was younger. She was Mom's dog. She passed away our last year in high school, and after losing Mom, it kind of broke us. So we didn't get another one." I looked down at Tempest. "Maybe it's time, though."

"If your dad isn't going to get married again, he needs a furry companion."

"Did I tell you I met Dr. Swanson?" I asked. "At the bakery when I was helping Gracie?"

"Ah, no you didn't."

I pinched his side. "You didn't tell me she was nearly twenty years younger than my dad."

"What can I say that won't get me into trouble?"

"Hmm. You are a wise man, Declan Brewer." I cocked my head to the side. "I think it's time you told me your middle name."

"Nope."

"Is it really that embarrassing?"

"Yes. It's really that embarrassing. What's your middle name?"

"Sullivan—my mother's maiden name. Come on, you have to tell me. Is it something like Mortimer?"

"No."

"I won't make fun of you."

"Oh, you will. I'd expect nothing less from you actually."

"We're not supposed to have secrets, remember?"

He sighed. "Copernicus."

I blinked. "Copernicus. Like the astronomer?"

"Yep."

I attempted to swallow my own lips to keep the laughter inside.

"Go ahead."

I burst into laughter, startling Tempest who looked up in confusion. I patted her head, and she settled down immediately.

"That's the most endearing thing I've ever heard," I said. "Copernicus? How did you get that name?"

"I don't even know," he admitted. "It's not like it's a family name. My mom just liked it."

"I think I'm going to like your mother quite a bit," I said with a shake of my head.

He stilled.

My smile dropped. "What? What did I say?"

"You said you'd like my mom."

I frowned. "Should I not have said that?"

"No, I mean—you'd be okay . . . with meeting her?"

"Of course I'd be okay with meeting her. Declan, what's this—"

Declan leaned forward and covered my lips with his. "You're incredible, you know that?"

"Why? Because I want to meet your mom?"

"Yes."

"People meet each other's parents when they're in a relationship. It's just what they do. Hell, you sit at family meals with mine on a regular basis at this point. My dad got you hammered! I'm sure your mom would be a cakewalk, comparatively."

He smiled slightly. "Maybe I'll invite her out this summer."

"Summer's a gorgeous time here." I nodded.

Declan touched my forehead. "Just seeing if you have a fever."

"Why would I have a fever?" I laughed.

He dropped his hand. "Because not too long ago, you refused to have any sort of conversation about the future, or feelings for me, or calling our relationship a relationship. Now, you're all about meeting my mother."

I rolled my eyes. "Once I gave myself permission not to worry about what other people thought, it suddenly became very freeing."

"You no longer care what other people think?"

I bit my lip. "Well . . ."

He chuckled. "Yeah, I thought so."

"I'm a recovering people pleaser. But I'm a work in progress. And you know what? Life is a hell of a lot easier when you finally admit what you want."

"And actually allow yourself to be happy?" he asked.

"Yeah."

"And you are, right? Happy?"

"Yeah, I'm happy."

"Mostly happy," he said quietly. "But not completely happy."

"I'm still coming to terms with . . . my issue," I admitted slowly.

Declan glanced down at the baby goat on my lap. "I've never slept with a goat on the bed before."

"Nor have I," I said.

"She smells okay."

"Better than okay. She got a bath earlier."

"Scoot over."

I moved toward the wall and set Tempest down onto the

comforter. Declan climbed back under the blankets and then turned off the lamp.

The sound of the rain on the tin roof was soothing, lulling me back to sleep.

But then Tempest got up and started pawing at the covers.

"What's she doing?" Declan asked.

"I think she wants underneath the blanket," I said.

"No. Absolutely not. She can sleep on top of the covers or she can go back in her pen."

But Tempest was stubborn and adorable, and eventually Declan sighed and lifted the covers. Tempest wormed her way beneath them and plopped down between us and didn't move.

"This is bad," Declan said. "We're teaching her this is okay."

"You were the one who brought her in here in the first place," I said with a laugh. "Not to mention, you lifted the covers and let her under."

"Have you seen her face? *You* say no to her. Try it, I dare you."

I laughed again, reaching out to pet Tempest, but I encountered Declan's hand instead.

He gave my fingers a squeeze. "We're going to need a bigger bed if we're going to be sharing ours with a baby goat."

"A bigger bed." I snorted. "In this room? It's already getting crowded."

He fell silent for a moment, but then he said, "It's too soon to have this conversation, isn't it?"

"Yes, definitely." I paused. "What conversation?"

"The *you and I finding a bigger place so we can live together comfortably* conversation."

"Oh, *that* conversation. Yes, it's too early."

"You do realize that you kind of already live here, right?"

"I don't."

"No? When's the last time you slept in your own bed?"

"Uh . . ."

"You took over half my closet with your clothes."

"You don't sound mad about that."

"I'm not. I like seeing our clothes hanging up together. You've also used up your entire drawer and you're encroaching on another one."

"Well, I have a lot of socks . . ."

"And that bathroom—it's a nightmare showering with you."

"Hey!"

He laughed. "I just meant, every time we try and move around each other, one of us nearly tumbles out of the tub. And now we're raising this goat together . . . Goat things take up a lot of space, Hadley."

"How did I move in here without actually having that conversation with you?" I asked.

"Evolution." He paused. "How long did you live with Gianni?"

"I didn't live with Gianni. We were waiting until after we got married to move in together."

"Huh. That's kind of weird."

"It's not that weird," I said.

"I guess not. But why didn't you live together?"

I thought about his question and then replied, "We talked about it every few months. But he liked his space, and I liked mine. I also loved living with my sister and friends. And I didn't want to be that kind of girl."

"The kind of girl who moves in with her fiancé?"

"The kind of girl who forgets she had a life before a guy," I said. "It's so easy to get lost in a relationship, you know? I thought if I continued living with Salem and my friends that

I'd maintain some sort of identity. With you . . . it feels different."

"Different."

"I like being in your space. And you never make me feel . . ."

"Feel what?"

"Like you want time away from me. So naturally, that just makes me want to be with you even more."

"I always want to see you."

I smiled. "Very golden retriever energy."

"Did you just insult me?"

"No. I gave you the highest compliment. We're not going to talk about officially moving in together tonight—but if we were, I would say, there's not really a better place than this cabin. It might be small, but there's no commute to work."

"And it's still on your family's land, which means you get to see your family as often as you want."

"There is that."

"So in the meantime, we just have to trip over each other's stuff? And sleep in a bed too small for two people and a goat?"

"I don't see another solution at this point, Declan. Do you?"

"No, I guess I don't."

My hand snaked out to touch his chest. He immediately covered my hand with his.

"It's an adventure, isn't it?" I asked.

"Oh yeah. You can definitely say that."

CHAPTER THIRTY-SEVEN

The Ranch

The rain persisted and it went from a pleasant sprinkle to downright pouring. It was two days of slogging to the barn with wet boots, damp socks and scalding showers in the evenings in an attempt to get warm.

"We haven't had this much rain at this time of year in five years," Dad said, worry crossing his brow. "And we had a long winter with a lot of snow."

Muddy took a sip of her coffee. "You're thinking what I'm thinking . . ."

Dad nodded. "The southeast corner of the ranch is going to flood bad. I've been doing this long enough to recognize what's coming. The rain hasn't let up and the snowpack is warming faster than the land can handle the water that's coming down from the mountains. The grazing land is a giant mud pit right now and the creek is swollen and getting deeper by the minute. We've got to get the cattle to higher ground and move them to the northwest side of the ranch.

And we need to move fast. All hands on deck. It can't wait any longer."

I finished the last bit of my coffee and set my cup down. "Just tell me where to be."

Declan nodded. "Goldie and Merlin are bonded at this point. I'll ride with Hadley so the horses stay calm. Just put us where you want us."

"Declan, I need you to get the boys together. We need a plan. We have way too many cattle for the number of hands, and conditions are already bad," Dad said. "We can only cross at the rocky portion of the creek without losing cattle. If we try to cross too far up stream where it's deep and muddy they'll get stuck in the muck and freeze and drown. I'll call Clint and Max and ask for their help. If they can come we just might be able to move the whole herd at once. And I need to call Jane and her team and let them know we're forcing the cattle across the creek."

I wisely held my tongue when he mentioned calling Jane. Yes, she was a vet and we needed a vet in case the animals were stressed or injured, but I wondered if he wanted to have a personal reason to call her.

"I'll get changed," I said. "I just hope I can find my water-proof clothes."

"I'll help you piece an outfit together," Muddy said. "And I'll get the walkie-talkies and make sure they all work."

"Thanks," Dad said. "And you'll—"

"Hold down the fort here," she said.

I looked at Declan. "Tempest. I don't want her to be alone."

"Bring her here," Muddy said. "She can keep me company."

"If that goat pisses in this house, you're cleaning it up," Dad warned me.

"She's slept the last two nights on the bed without a problem," Declan announced. "She's smart."

Dad looked at Declan and then to me.

"What?" I demanded. "You got me a pet goat. Was I not supposed to potty train her?"

"Fair enough. Declan, let's get the boys together and make this plan."

Dad and Josiah took the lead of the herd. They'd set the pace and ensure the cattle would follow. Henry, along with several other ranch hands, would flank as many cattle from the herd as they could at one time and keep them moving. Declan and I would be the drag riders. We'd watch out for injured animals and calves getting separated. A few swing riders from the neighboring ranches would join us, moving between the flank and drag riders, going where they were needed and steering the herd.

We were all seasoned, which was why I was on horseback in the rain with a bunch of men who did it for a living. Our walkie-talkies were clipped to our rain slickers and the volume turned up to max.

Between the calls of cowboys, the din of heavy rain, and the fearful mooing of the cattle, it was a struggle to hear much of anything. We relied on hand signals and motions for a lot of communication. Every now and again, Dad would come through on the walkie with instructions.

I'd done this once before, several years ago. Salem had stayed behind with Muddy. So much had changed in a short of amount of time and yet some things would always stay the same. I'd always lend a hand on the ranch; I'd always climb on horseback or get myself dirty. I didn't care. I loved this life.

The herd crossed the rocky creek bottom one by one as the team worked to move them to high ground. There were a few stragglers from the herd, but we urged them on.

Things were going well, and it wasn't until Declan and I got to the rocky crossing area of the swollen creek that we had our first problem. The water in the creek was moving fast and had washed out many feet on either side of what was usually a calm, foot-deep crossing. Now, banks were forming on either side as the earth washed away and the water carved out a deep trench in the ground. The creek was raging, seeming much more like an angry river, and I knew we didn't have much time to finish crossing.

A lone bull calf got caught in the swift current as it tried to follow its mother across and nearly lost its footing, but Declan roped him and safely led him across the water to the other side.

When he hit the bank, the calf shook himself uselessly in the pouring rain and then trotted to catch up to his mother.

The sky was nearly black with steady, dark clouds. Thunder boomed, lightning flashed; rain marred my vision.

Goldie needed no urging—Merlin was already on the other side of the river, and she was determined to get to him.

She splashed into the river but took a slight turn to the left, veering away from the path the rest of the animals had used to cross. The water swirled around Goldie's knees and then rose higher as she sank into the muddy bottom. But she was a steady girl and kept a good pace despite the rush of the current and the suction of the ground beneath her. She was three quarters of the way across the river when a hoof caught on something and she lost her balance. She tossed her head and attempted to regain her stance, but she was unable to move forward. Despite my urging, she came to a halt.

She tossed her head again and neighed in distress.

I looked across the river to see Declan about ten feet away

from the bank. He saw me and raised his hand over his head and then I heard through the walkie, "What's wrong?"

I pressed my walkie button. "She's stuck, I think. I need to get down and see what's going on."

"Wait, I'll be right there."

But I couldn't wait. The river was starting to rise. Even though we'd been immobile for just a moment, the water had started to froth and the current was picking up speed.

Flash flood. Fuck.

I swung my leg over the saddle and gingerly felt for the bottom of the river. The water came up to my crotch and it was ice cold. I held on to Goldie's harness as I got my footing, and then I leaned over. I stole a hand down her left leg and delved into the river.

Something poked me through the tip of my glove.

I cursed.

I guessed it was barbed wire from a fence post that had been pulled lose.

"Hadley!" Declan called from the bank. "What the hell are you doing?"

"She's stuck!" I yelled back. "The water's rising fast—I think it's a flash flood! We have to get her out!"

Declan kicked his spurs and rode back into the river toward me as fast as Merlin could take him. He got near me and dismounted.

"Hadley, get back on your horse. I'll get her free."

"No! I've got this," I said as Declan grabbed Goldie's bridle to steady her. I reached into my saddlebag for my fence pliers. I bent over, feeling my way around the barbed wire, and made a cut. When nothing happened, I felt around farther and realized it was attached to a fence post just beneath the water's surface. I ran my hand down Goldie's leg for the wire that was still holding her and made another cut, and when Goldie realized she was free, she took a step toward Merlin. In her haste to get out of the river, she knocked into me.

I dropped the fence pliers and lost my balance. I fell into the water and the force of the current pushed me directly into the fence post beneath the surface. All the air left my lungs.

"Hadley!" Declan yelled.

My head went under water.

The shock of the freezing current momentarily stupefied me, but my brain forced my limbs to work—they pumped and my legs kicked and I broke free from the river and rose to the surface.

I was being carried away. I attempted to swim toward the bank, but my side burned in agony.

"Declan!" I cried out, praying he'd hear me over the rushing water and pouring rain.

My head bobbed up and down as I tried to regain my footing, and through the slanted rain I could see Declan on Merlin's back galloping along the bank. He had his rope out and he was building a loop over his head, preparing to throw. When he was close enough, Declan threw the rope.

It missed the mark, but my fingers touched it briefly before I was pulled under again.

I broke the surface, sputtering and coughing, and that's when Declan's second throw caught me. He dallied the rope to the saddle horn to slow me down and I began to tread water as I was being pulled to the bank by Merlin.

As I got to the edge of the creek, Declan dismounted and ran toward me. I thought about attempting to stand, but my body was cold and I was injured.

He waded into the shallow water toward me. I could tell he wanted to go faster, but if he lost his footing, the raging creek would just sweep him away too.

My heart pounded in relief when his arms came around me.

I cried out in pain.

"Hadley! Are you okay?"

"No—my ribs—" I gasped.

"Hang on to me, okay? Whatever you do, don't let go."

My arms wrapped around his neck and my legs around his waist. He waded us out of the water as he carried me, and I clung to him with all my might.

We finally made it to solid ground, and Declan set me down.

He kissed my wet cheeks, my wet forehead, my wet lips.

"You're okay. You're going to be okay. You're okay." He repeated it like a mantra, an affirmation for him to believe.

"I'll be okay," I chattered. "But I'm so cold . . ."

CHAPTER THIRTY-EIGHT

The Hospital

The left side of my body screamed in pain. I gritted my teeth. Declan saw my grimace and took my hand while we waited for the doctor.

"Squeeze my hand," he said. "Hard as you want."

"I'm fine."

"Liar. Terrible, terrible liar."

"Have you talked to Dad? How are the cattle? Was anyone else injured?"

"We don't have to talk about that now."

"Distract me, please," I begged.

"I didn't ask," he said. "My first and only priority was getting you to the hospital."

He was still in his rain gear. After Declan had fished me out of the floodwater, he'd ridden Merlin hard toward the main house, with me in front of him on the saddle. When Muddy saw us, she immediately snapped into drill-sergeant mode. She commanded Declan to get me warm and dry.

Muddy tried to get hold of Dad to let him know what was going on, but cell service was spotty in even the best of circumstances at the ranch, and because of the weather he was with the rest of the boys and the cattle on the northwest side of the property.

Declan had helped me change, but when he saw the bruising on my body, he'd wrapped me in a wool blanket and carried me to the truck and driven me to the hospital. Terror had been etched on his face every time he looked at me.

The curtain around the exam table slid back and a middle-aged doctor with fine lines around her eyes and brown hair streaked with gray appeared.

"Hi there," she said. "I'm Dr. Novak. I'll be taking care of you today. Tell me what's going on." She glanced at Declan and his attire, but her focus returned to me.

I quickly explained that Declan was my boyfriend and what had occurred. "I'd love some painkillers."

"I'm sure you would," she commiserated. "Please lay back for me, so I can do an exam and see what we're dealing with here."

I laid back and lifted my shirt.

"Ouch," Dr. Novak said as she put on a pair of gloves. She gently touched the left side of my abdomen and worked her hands up to my ribs.

It took everything in me not to howl in pain.

"You've got a lot of bruising. I don't know if there's any internal bleeding or broken ribs, so I'll need to get some images. Before I administer pain meds, I need to know if you're pregnant."

I hadn't been prepared for the question. "No," I rasped. "I'm not pregnant."

"Any chance you might be?"

"Doubtful," I whispered.

She patted my shoulder. "You can sit up. Do you remember the date of your last period?"

"No."

I hadn't bothered tracking my period after finding out I couldn't have children. What was the point?

"All right." She nodded. "I'm going to have you take a pregnancy test anyway to rule it out. It's protocol. I'm going to order a rush on it, okay?"

"Okay." I nodded.

"I'm just going to get someone to draw your blood, but—" She handed me a cup for a urine sample. "Bathroom is right over there."

Declan immediately came to my side and helped me off the exam table and guided me to the bathroom.

"I don't know why I need to pee in a cup," I muttered. "We both know it's negative."

"Protocol, like she said."

"Fuck protocol," I moaned. "I'm in pain."

I went into the bathroom and did my thing. I returned to the exam table and handed off the sample to the phlebotomist, who wrote down the information on the label and then drew my blood.

She took the samples and left us alone.

My mind was bouncing from one thing to the next. Declan's cell phone rang, and he unzipped his jacket and reached for it in the inner pocket.

"Your dad," he said.

"Answer it," I suggested.

"Connor," he said in greeting. "Yeah, we're at the hospital. A doctor has just seen Hadley. She's going to do some x-rays." He paused. "Sure. Here."

He handed me the phone which I put to my ear.

"Hey," I said.

299

"Hey, honey. How are you doing? You hanging in there?" he asked.

"Yeah, I'm okay. How's everything where you are?"

"Rain's finally letting up. Goldie got a decent laceration from that barbed wire, but Jane's taking care of it."

I let out a sigh of relief. "That's good to hear. Any of the cattle hurt?"

"No. We got them all to safety. Even though the rain is letting up, the snowmelt from the rapid temperature shift combined with the rain is going to be crazy the next several days."

"I'll bet."

"Muddy's taking care of Tempest, so don't worry about anything. Put Declan back on for me. Love you, Hadley."

"Love you too." I handed the phone back to Declan.

"Yeah, it's me," Declan said. He paused and then nodded. "Right. Will do. Bye."

"Will do what?" I asked after he hung up.

He put his phone back into his pocket. "I told him I'd keep him posted."

I smiled.

"What?"

"That's Dad speak for *he's on his way.* He'll be here in about half an hour."

Dr. Novak pushed the curtain aside and then closed it to give us privacy. "How we doing?"

I sighed. "I'd really like those pain meds. Please tell me that's why you came back so quickly."

Dr. Novak smiled. "I came back quickly because your pregnancy test came back positive."

"*Positive?*" I repeated.

"Positive?" Declan parroted.

"Positive," Dr. Novak said again. "Congratulations, Hadley. You're pregnant."

"But that's impossible!" I blurted out.

Dr. Novak looked Declan up and down. "Impossible. Really?"

"*Really*," I insisted. "Really, really."

"Have you two been having sex?" she asked.

I blushed. "Yes."

"Have you been having *unprotected* sex?"

"Yes." I squirmed. "But only because I was told I was infertile."

"Pregnant?" Declan asked again.

"You might want to sit down," Dr. Novak said, rolling a stool toward him which he immediately collapsed on. "As far as infertility goes . . . well, sometimes these things happen. Couples believe they can't get pregnant, they don't use protection, and boom. You get a baby."

"A baby," I whispered.

"I'm lightheaded," Declan murmured.

"Me too," I said.

"Put your head between your knees," Dr. Novak advised Declan.

Declan did the motion easily, but I couldn't due to the pain in my side.

There was a chime from a device, and Dr. Novak reached into her lab coat pocket to pull out a tablet. She tapped the screen. "It's your blood test results. Yep, you're definitely pregnant."

Declan lifted his head from between his legs and scooched the stool closer to the exam table and took my hand. I squeezed his fingers with all the force I had.

He winced, but otherwise said nothing.

Dr. Novak smiled and said, "Let's get you to radiology and make sure that bruising isn't something to worry about."

I had no internal bleeding and no broken ribs. Just a lot of bruising. They'd admitted me to the hospital though because Dr. Novak wanted to monitor me for a few hours in case anything unforeseen popped up.

She asked if I wanted any pain meds that were safe for my condition, but after finding out I was pregnant I refused them.

I'm pregnant.

Declan and I hadn't had a chance to talk about it.

I was currently laying in a bed, hooked up to a bunch of monitors, and Declan was sitting in the chair next to me.

Neither one of us had spoken and the air was filled with tension.

A sudden thought bounced into my mind.

"I had my period in New York last month," I blurted out. "And then Gianni went to Italy. There's no way the baby is his."

His expression softened. "Is that what you thought I was thinking about?"

"I don't know what you're thinking about." I bit my lip. "You haven't said anything. What *are* you thinking about?"

"Honestly?"

"Honestly." I braced myself for something terrible.

"I'm thinking about the fact that there's no way in hell we can live in that cabin. Not with a baby goat and an actual baby. Sorry, bear snack. But we're going to have to move whether you like it or not."

I blinked. And blinked again.

"Declan," I began.

"Yes, Hadley?" he asked with a wry grin.

"Why are you smiling at me that way?"

"Because I can feel a lecture coming on."

"No, no lecture. I don't lecture."

"You're right, it's more like a monologue. So, tell you

what, you tell me all the reasons why we can't move to a bigger place and why we can't be happy and in love and have a baby and I'll sit here and listen. But if you think I won't be a good father then I'll remind you about Tempest. I'm a good goat dad. How much harder would a baby be?"

My lips wobbled. "You really want to have a baby with me?"

"I do, Hadley. I really do. But in all honesty we really should've put a condom on the banana. I think I may have missed that day in sex ed."

I stole a hand across my belly. "I didn't think this was possible. If I thought it was, you know we would've used a condom."

"Well, we've failed to use condoms every time so far," he said. "I've never been so happy to be a failure at something."

"You're really not mad?"

"Why would I be mad?"

"Because you and I—we just—and infertility—and—"

"Hey, it's okay. You may have been infertile, but now you're not."

I sighed in relief. "A baby."

He smiled. "A baby."

The door to my room opened and Dr. Novak returned, only this time she brought my father. His boots were muddy, and he was still in his rain gear and his expression immediately softened when he saw me.

Dr. Novak quietly saw herself out and closed the door behind her.

"You're okay," he said, immediately coming to my bedside. "I'd hug you, but I'm wet."

"Hug me," I instructed. "But gently. My side is really sore."

He enveloped me in his arms, and I pressed my head to his rain jacket lapel and closed my eyes.

Dad pulled back and released me. "So, what did the

doctor say? She didn't tell me anything. Only that you were healthy and your injuries will heal, but she wanted to keep you for a few hours for observation. Why would she want to keep you for a few hours if you're okay?"

Declan rose from his chair. "Take my seat."

"I don't want to sit," Dad said.

"You should probably sit," I urged.

Dad looked between me and Declan. "What's going on?"

"You should really sit," I said. "Please?"

"Okay." He shrugged and took Declan's chair. "Now tell me what's going on."

I reached for Declan and he took my hand, bringing it to his lips.

"Hadley?" Dad pressed.

I gave him a nervous smile. "Congrats, Dad. You're going to be a grandpa."

CHAPTER THIRTY-NINE

THE HOSPITAL

"Dad?" I asked. "Did you hear me?"

"I heard you," he said, his brow wrinkling. "But how is that possible? I thought you couldn't . . ."

"Well, apparently I can." I glanced at Declan. "Declan and I are going to have a baby."

Dad looked at Declan but didn't say anything.

"Please don't hit me again," Declan said, grimacing.

Dad stood up from the chair. And then before I knew it, I was being hugged again. And when he pulled back, my strong, stoic father had tears in his eyes.

"This is damn good news," he said gruffly. "Congratulations to the both of you. When's the wedding?"

"Excuse me?" I asked.

"The wedding," he said, looking from me to Declan, focusing hard on Declan. "There will be a wedding, right?"

I looked at Declan too, unsure of what to say. Declan

didn't take his eyes off my father when he replied, "Whenever she wants one."

Dad nodded and his expression relaxed. "Good."

"You're not going to stand behind me with a shotgun, *Seven Brides for Seven Brothers* style, are you?" Declan asked.

"No," Dad said. "I still don't know where the damn thing is hidden."

"Hold on a second," I voiced.

Two pairs of eyes looked at me.

"Don't I get a say?" I demanded. "About a wedding?"

"Of course you get a say," Declan said with a cheery smile. "You get to set the date."

"Aren't you forgetting something?" I asked.

"No, I don't think I'm forgetting anything." Declan frowned. "Oh, wait. The ring."

"Not the ring, you goober. The *question*," I said. "You never asked me if I wanted to marry you."

"Hadley, will you marry me?" Declan asked.

I crossed my arms over my chest and turned my head away from him. "No."

Dad slapped Declan on the back. "I better leave you two alone to iron out some stuff. I need to call Jane and let her know you're okay."

"Jane?" I asked. "There's a Jane?"

"I was with her when Muddy got hold of me," he said. "So she knows you're in the hospital. Don't worry. I won't spoil your good news. You can tell everyone in your own time."

Dad shook Declan's hand and then left the room, leaving me alone with the man who had just given me the worst marriage proposal in history.

"I'm not marrying you," I said to Declan.

"Sure, you are," he said, looking far too cheery.

"I won't say yes to such a lukewarm proposal."

"Oh, that wasn't my proposal." He took the chair and

scooted closer. He tried to take my hand, but I kept tugging it free.

"Then why did you tell my dad we were getting married?" I asked in exasperation. "And why did you just literally ask me to marry you in front of him?"

"Because your father wants to know if I'm a man of my word. My *drunken* word. I told him that I was serious enough about you to marry you when he got me drunk at the Copper Mule. He also knows I can provide for you financially. That proposal was for your father. I knew you'd say no, at least here in this room. You haven't gotten your real proposal yet."

I felt myself softening. "I don't want you proposing just because we're having a baby. We can be together and not get married."

"Nope. Not happening." He shook his head. "I want you to have my last name. And I want our baby to have my last name. We're going to be a family."

Tears misted my eyes. "Was that your proposal?"

He scoffed. "Not even close."

"Oh. Well, the sentiment was nice."

Declan grinned. "I promise you when I propose, you'll know. And you'll be really happy you waited for me to surprise you."

"I stand by what I said. I don't want you to feel like you have to marry me just because we're having a baby."

"I was going to marry you regardless." He shrugged. "But the little sprout kind of pushed the timeline forward."

My insides went gooey like a chocolate chip cookie fresh out of the oven.

Hmm. Chocolate chip cookies.

He linked our fingers together and brought my hand to lips. "We're going to be here for a few hours. Can I get you anything?"

"What are you, a mind reader? I could kill for chocolate chip cookies."

He stood up and gently released my hand. "Mission accepted."

"You mind if I call my sister and friends and share the good news with them?"

He kissed my forehead and then my lips. "Absolutely. Share the joy."

I watched him walk out of the room, my heart fluttering with happiness.

Even though I wanted to call my sister and friends, I wanted just another moment to revel in news.

A baby.

With Declan.

Wow.

For the first time in my life, I was completely content. I was getting everything I'd ever dreamed of. A man who loved me. A baby. And living with family who would be there for me.

My phone buzzed, startling me out of my reverie.

"Hello," I blubbered.

"You're crying," Salem said. "Why are you crying?"

"Because I'm happy."

"That's weird. You usually cry when you're sad."

"Well, I've done enough of that already. Now I get to cry because I'm happy."

"I'm happy you're happy then."

"Don't you want to know *why* I'm happy?"

"Of course. Did you open your boxes yet?"

I was momentarily thrown by my sister's boomerang in conversation.

"I opened a few of them, but things have been kind of crazy here, so I didn't get to your inappropriate present, whatever that might be."

"Why has it been crazy there? It's Huckleberry Hill. Nothing ever happens there."

"Not true," I said. "Sweet Teeth went viral on social media and Gracie had a line out of the door for several days. So Muddy and I and a few others pitched in to help. And then a late spring storm came through and we had a flash flood and now I'm in the hospital."

"*What?*" she nearly yelled.

"I'm okay," I hastened to say. "Just a little bruising."

"Holy hell," she muttered. "You are terrible at giving news, you know that? You're in the hospital right now?"

"Yes."

"Oh hang on. Poet and Wyn just got home. Let me call you back and we can video chat and you can tell us everything."

She hung up on me. A moment later, my phone rang again. I pressed the button, and the screen filled with their three faces.

"Hey," Wyn said. "What's this about you being in the hospital?"

"There was a late spring storm and we had to move the cattle to higher ground on the ranch so they didn't get trapped. It was pouring rain and Goldie got caught on an old fence post covered in barbed wire under the waterline. I cut her free, and when I did she bolted toward Merlin and knocked me into the water. I fell on the fence post and bruised my side really bad and the water washed me away."

The three of them were silent, their eyes wide.

"And you say nothing happens here," I said, directing my statement to Salem.

"So then what happened?" Poet asked.

"Declan was right there. It was so fast," I explained. "He saw me go under, but the current swept me away before he could get to me, so he got on Merlin and came after me. He roped me and dragged me up onto the bank like I was a cow." I was trying to give them the headlines because I knew any moment Declan would return with the cookies, and I wanted to tell them the most important news.

"He took me to the hospital to get me checked out. No broken ribs or anything, just a lot of bruising," I said.

"So you're okay then?" Salem asked. "When do they release you?"

I took a deep breath. "Well, the doctor wanted to keep an eye on me for a few hours due to my . . . extenuating circumstances."

"Extenuating circumstances?" Wyn's blonde brows slashed together in confusion. "What does that mean?"

"It means I'm pregnant."

Silence reigned across the screen.

"Pregnant?" Salem asked. "But how?"

"I think we know how," Poet teased. "It's Declan's, right?"

"It's Declan's," I assured her. "I had my period in New York last month before I came home. And Gianni and I hadn't been . . . not since the news about my infertility."

"Infertility, you say," Wyn said. "Nature clearly called bullshit. That cowboy has some powerful ding-a-ling juice."

"Ew." Poet wrinkled her nose. "Can you not?"

"I'm just saying," Wyn said.

"Hold on a second," Salem stated. "Are you telling me you and Declan have been raw-doggin' it this whole time? Because I know you. You're captain safety."

I felt my cheeks heat and then cleared my throat. "I didn't think I needed protection."

"You put the ho in Idaho." Salem suddenly smiled. "I'm going to be an aunt!"

"Aunties!" Wyn hollered.

Mildred barked in the background and Wyn leaned down to scoop her up.

"Oh my God, she's the cutest," I said with a smile. "Like a mini golden retriever puppy."

"She's pretty great." Wyn snuggled Mildred's ear and then set her down.

"Wow, Hadley," Poet said with a teary smile. "I'm so happy for you."

"We all are," Salem said. "Really."

"When are you due?" Wyn asked.

"Don't know yet," I admitted. "I'll have to go to the doctor, and they'll have to figure it all out. When I know, you'll know."

"A baby!" Poet squealed. "This is so cool."

"There's more," I said shyly.

"More?" Salem asked. "How can there be more?"

"I'm getting married."

Silence.

"When?" Salem demanded.

"Yeah, I need to take off work," Wyn said.

"And look at flights," Poet added with a nod.

"Hang on, guys, I don't know when I'm getting married."

"I'm confused," Wyn said.

"Declan hasn't actually asked me to marry him yet. But he and Dad kinda . . . you know Dad, Salem."

"I do know Dad, yes," Salem agreed. "So there's a wedding happening but we don't know when because Declan hasn't officially asked you, but he's told you he will?"

"Pretty much." I sighed in happiness.

"You'll say yes though, right?" Wyn asked. "Or are you going to hold out and be stubborn?"

"Why would I hold out and be stubborn?" I demanded.

"I don't know, this is all just kind of crazy fast," Poet said. "Romantic as hell, but still kind of crazy."

Salem looked at the screen and grinned. "Crazy perfect. Maybe Hadley is the craziest of us all."

CHAPTER FORTY

THE RANCH

"Easy," Declan said, holding his hand out to me.

I grasped it and scooted across the seat, wincing as I put my feet to the ground.

My side ached and I wanted to get inside and rest. Even though I'd been sitting for several hours in a hospital bed, recuperating at home on the couch was the best form of medicine.

Dad had left the hospital an hour after we'd given him the news about the baby. He wanted to stay, but I insisted he go. There would be damage from the storm, and he might need to lend a hand to one of our neighbors since they'd done the same to help with our cattle. He left with great reluctance, but I assured him I was fine—I had Declan, and despite Dad's reluctance, he knew that Declan was more than capable of taking good care of me.

"I can carry you up the porch steps," Declan offered.

It was late afternoon and even though the rain had

stopped, the sky was still gray, and everything was slick and muddy. The last thing I wanted was for him to lose his footing and have us both go down.

I shook my head. "I just need to go slow."

We finally made it up the porch steps and without a word, Declan crouched down to help me take off my shoes so I didn't have to bend over.

Bathing was going to be interesting.

The front door opened, and Muddy stood at the threshold. "Thought I heard the truck. Wasn't sure though. Hours of rain has my ears buzzing."

"Did you talk to Dad?" I asked.

"Briefly," she said. "He told me about your injury. Come in and sit down. I've got the salve ready."

"Salve?" Declan asked as he closed the front door. He began helping me out of my jacket.

"Old family recipe," I explained. "We put it on everything from scrapes to bruises to goose eggs on the forehead. It cures everything."

"Fair warning, it stinks," Muddy said.

I heard the clop of tiny hooves on the wooden floor before Tempest appeared. She immediately trotted over to me and pressed her head to my leg. I wanted to lean down and pick her up, but there was no way I could.

Declan scooped her up and held her toward me. I rubbed her head and sighed.

"How did she do during the storm?" I asked.

"Slept right through it," Muddy said with a smile. "She's a cute thing. Kept me company and didn't cause any trouble. Well, she did eat a part of my crocheting basket, but I've forgiven her."

"No accidents?"

"No accidents," she said. "You should probably take her out though. It's been a few hours since she's gone."

"I'll take care of it." Declan kissed my cheek and then headed for the front door with the baby goat in tow.

"You need to sit," Muddy said, gently taking my arm and guiding me to the den. I eased down onto the couch and slowly lifted my shirt.

Muddy whistled. "Look at that battle wound." She unscrewed the mason jar, the scent of the salve hitting my nose and making my eyes water.

"You gave us all a good scare, Hadley." She scooped a finger into the salve. "I'll be as gentle as I can."

"I know." I inhaled sharply at the touch of her finger. The salve was room temperature, so thankfully it didn't chill my skin. "So Dad told you about my injury. Did he tell you anything else?"

Muddy shook her head which was bent to the task. "No. I'm sure he wanted you to be the one to tell me you're having a baby."

I gasped. "How did you know?"

She looked up and smiled at me, her eyes clear with wisdom. "I had a feeling."

"A feeling?"

"A dream, actually," she said. "Oh, about five days ago I had that dream."

"What dream?" I asked.

"I saw a little baby with dark hair and blue eyes. Spitting image of Declan."

"How do you like that?" I asked with a laugh. I winced as she rubbed the salve into my skin. "Ow, that hurts."

"There." She screwed the lid back on. "Now I'll wrap it and we'll get you settled on the couch. You need anything, you tell me and I'll get it for you."

"Wait a second," I said. "You know I'm having a baby and you're being pretty calm about it."

"Ah, honey." She cradled my cheek with the hand that

hadn't been drenched in smelly salve. "I know it's what you've always wanted. Now tell me how your father reacted. Don't leave out any details."

I smiled, but held in another laugh, not wanting to jostle my side which had begun to tingle from the homemade ointment.

"He was very happy," I said. "But also demanded that Declan and I get married right away."

"Uh hmm. Not surprising."

"Not surprising at all."

"So? Is there going to be a wedding?"

"Eventually," I said. "Declan hasn't officially asked me to marry him. But he told Dad we were getting married so right now Dad is happy."

"It won't take him long to propose." She wrapped my abdomen loosely with an old sheet that had been cut down and then lowered my shirt. "He's crazy about you."

"I'm crazy about him."

"So he's happy then, about the baby?"

"Very." I sighed. "I called Salem and the girls to tell them the news. So as far as people go, everyone knows who needs to know. It's so weird. Not that long ago, I was at rock bottom. It's insane how fast things can change."

The storm had blown itself out, but not without causing a fair bit of damage to the ranch. Several fence posts needed repair, along with washed out roads and a creek bed that had shifted ten feet in one spot and rerouted itself to a new location. We were lucky, though. All our livestock survived, and we had no water damage to any of the buildings. The same couldn't be said for some of the neighboring ranches.

Declan and I were staying in the main house, me in my

childhood bed and Declan in Salem's room. And it had nothing to do with my father's watchful eye or any antiquated rules about not being married and sharing a bed. This time it was for my comfort as well as the fact that Declan was up before dawn. Everyone agreed I needed my rest.

Not just to heal but because of the baby. Apparently, I was supposed to live life on easy mode after finding out I was pregnant. Not that I was complaining. Especially since Muddy brought me breakfast on a tray while I lazed on the couch and watched TV, Tempest curled up at my feet.

We had family dinners, laughing and joking and my world felt complete. But every now and again, I'd look at the empty chair where Salem was supposed to sit, and I'd have a twinge of sadness. Not to mention the absence of my mother. I imagined that as my pregnancy progressed, I'd miss her more and more.

I made an appointment with an OBGYN in Coeur d'Alene. Huckleberry Hill had a small family practice, but no specialists. I was desperate to know how far along I was. I was worried. My infertility might have suddenly disappeared, but it had left a bad taste in my mouth and I was waiting for the other shoe to drop.

One night a few days after I'd gotten out of the hospital, Declan and I were getting ready for bed, brushing our teeth in the joint bathroom.

He spit into Salem's sink. "God, I love how big this bathroom is."

"Yeah, it's pretty great," I admitted. "I do miss our cute little cabin, though."

"Well, we'll be able to move back in there once you're on the mend." He looked at me. "How are you feeling?"

"Better. That salve is a godsend. It tingles and numbs the area. It does make my eyes water, though."

"It's not that bad."

"It's horrible." I wrinkled my nose.

"I can hardly smell it, actually."

"Really? Huh. I wonder if I've got pregnancy nose already."

"Probably." He set his toothbrush down and then dropped to his knees.

"What are you doing?"

He wrapped his arms around me, low enough on my hips that he didn't touch my injury. Declan placed his ear on my belly.

I sifted my fingers through his hair. "A little early to be feeling any kicks."

"I'm listening for sounds of the ocean," he teased. He turned his head and kissed my stomach. He dropped his arms and rose. "I miss sleeping next to you."

"Me too," I admitted.

He stepped closer and lowered his voice. "I miss having you against me in the middle of the night. I miss sliding my fingers into your panties and stroking you until you're wet. I miss thrusting into you from behind, both of us half asleep but desperate for each other."

I shivered and placed a hand on his chest. "I miss that too."

He kissed me long and deep, his tongue touching mine. He kissed me until I was a drippy, needy mess and then he pulled back, his eyes dark with desire.

"Let's put you to bed."

"Stay with me," I begged.

"Can't," he rasped. "Because I can't keep my hands to myself, and you're still hurt."

Disappointment flashed across my face, but I nodded.

Tempest was already curled up in the center of my bed. We left the bathroom doors open in case she wanted to wander between us during the night.

Declan pulled back the covers and I eased into bed. He covered me and then kissed my forehead, my eyelids, and then my lips. "Can I get you anything else?"

"No, I'm good." I paused.

"What is it?" he asked, taking a seat at the edge of the bed. "What's got you thinking?"

"I'm so happy," I whispered.

"And you're terrified it's all gonna go away?"

I nodded and set my hand on my stomach.

"Hadley, that's not going to happen." He smiled and lifted our hands and brought them to his lips.

Tears filled my eyes.

I sat up and Declan gathered me into his arms. I pressed my forehead to his chest, and clung to him. When my tears had abated, I pulled back and looked at him, sheepish.

"You okay?" He pushed the hair away from my face and tucked a strand behind my ear.

I bit my lip. "No."

"No?"

"I'd be a lot better if you were in bed next to me," I said, looking at him through a sweep of my lashes.

He sighed. "Like I'd ever say no to you. All right, bear snack, I'll sleep in your bed. But if your father catches me in here, we might only have one child because he'll make a gelding out of me."

Sniggering, I shoved the covers down. He turned off the main light and gingerly felt his way to the bed. He climbed in and covered us. Tempest immediately moved up and under.

"Declan?" I murmured, my eyes drifting shut.

"Hmm?"

"How many children do you want?"

"As many as you want."

Smiling, I drifted off to sleep, dreaming of babies with dark hair and blue eyes.

CHAPTER FORTY-ONE

THE RANCH

SALEM

Well, we're dying here.

POET

Yeah, how did the appointment go?

ME

I'm pregnant.

WYN

We know that already. we want all the info.

SALEM

What's the sex?

ME

It's too early to know. But we do know our due date . . .

POET

Tease! Come on

WYN

Tell us

ME

My due date is Christmas Day.

SALEM

Stop it that's too perfect.

POET

omg!!!!

ME

I don't know if it's good. Won't he or she's birthday be overshadowed by Christmas?

SALEM

Nah. Just means double the presents

POET

I'm shopping for Christmas onesies right now. OMG this one has candy canes on it

WYN

I found one that's green with matching striped socks. An elf!

SALEM

and just like that, three aunts were born.

POET

The three wise aunts.

WYN

Hmm. You sure about that?

POET

Fine. One wise aunt and two knuckleheads.

SALEM

better. I can't wait to spend Christmas at the ranch.

I held my breath.

WYN

Absolutely. I'll be in Telluride for the first half of December with the Carringtons. Colorado is just a hop and a skip to Idaho.

POET

Switching gears and looking at plane fare . . .

SALEM

Hey, did you open the rest of your boxes?

ME

I was about to do that.

SALEM

Hurry up.

ME

Do you want me to make a video and film my reaction?

WYN

Could you?

I sighed.

ME

Yes. Hang on.

I was setting up my phone to record when the doorbell rang. Muddy was out running errands, so I got up off the bed and walked downstairs. Tempest followed me.

The bell rang again.

"I'm coming," I yelled.

I got to the door and all but yanked it open.

Shock rippled through my body and my jaw dropped. "*Gianni?* What are you doing here?"

My ex-fiancé stood on the porch, dressed in a pair of dark Japanese denim jeans and a gray wool sweater with product in his luscious, dark hair. "Hey, Hadley."

"How did you know I was here?"

"Nico. He said you went home for a visit."

"Okay, but *what* are you doing here?" I demanded again.

"Can I come in?"

Tempest stepped outside and sniffed Gianni's leg.

"That's a goat," he said.

"I live on a ranch," I clipped. "What do you expect?"

His expression softened. "I don't blame you for being mad at me. But please, Hadley. Give me just a few minutes?"

I was a recovering people pleaser. And though the shock was wearing off at seeing my ex, I would be lying if I said I wasn't curious about why he was on my doorstep.

Without a word, I stepped aside.

He came into the foyer and stopped, looking around in curiosity. Tempest entered behind him and then went to her water and food dish in the corner of the kitchen.

"It's just like you described it," he said.

"Yep."

His expression softened. "I should've come home with you when you asked."

I shrugged. "It doesn't matter now."

"It doesn't?"

"What do you want, Gianni?"

"You. I want *you*." He reached into his pocket and pulled out my engagement ring. "I flew to New York to get this before coming here. I gave it to you when I proposed, and it belongs on your finger."

"How did you know where the ring was?" I asked in confusion.

"Salem texted me that she'd left it on my nightstand."

"Oh. Right."

I looked at the ring again.

"I want you to come home. I want us to be together."

I frowned. "This is my home."

"What about New York? We had a life there."

"No, Gianni, *you* had a life there," I said. "And you walked out on me the minute there was a problem."

He sighed. "You don't know how much I regret that. I was in Italy without you, but everything reminded me of you. I made a list of the wines I knew you'd like, the dishes I couldn't wait to make for you, the sights I want to show you on our honeymoon . . ."

I rubbed my third eye.

We were having this conversation in the middle of the kitchen, and it felt like it was happening to someone else.

"Please give me another chance," he begged.

The front door opened. "Bear snack, sorry I'm late. I stopped by Sweet Teeth and grabbed you some chocolate chip—"

Declan came to a halt when he entered the kitchen and saw me standing with my ex-fiancé.

"Bear snack?" Gianni asked, his gaze bouncing between me and Declan. "What is that, a nickname?"

"Ah, yeah," I said awkwardly.

The two men were sizing each other up, neither one saying anything. They were both nearly the same height, but Declan was more muscular, while Gianni had a leaner build.

I felt the tension between them, but I wasn't sure how to diffuse it.

"Declan, Gianni. Gianni, Declan."

"Declan," Gianni repeated.

"Her boyfriend," Declan stated. "And the father of her child."

I winced.

"Father of her . . ." Gianni looked at me in shock. "You're infertile."

Declan dropped the bakery bag on the kitchen table. "Not anymore."

Gianni's expression tightened. "So let me get this straight. We break up and you come home and jump in the sack with the first guy you see? And now you're knocked up in a couple weeks? Hadley, what the—"

Declan's punch interrupted Gianni's tirade, and the next thing I knew fists were flying.

"Stop!" I yelled. "You can't fight in here! If you break my grandmother's china, she'll kill both of you!"

Neither of them heard me.

Declan had sprung into protective boyfriend mode and Gianni was . . . well, he wasn't going to take a fist to the face and not do anything about it.

I hastily went to the sliding glass door. "Out! Both of you!"

Gianni swung and clocked Declan across the jaw, momentarily stunning him.

Somehow, I managed to coerce them in the direction of the back porch. With fresh mountain air, and no hindrances, they went hard for each other.

I closed the door and watched from behind my hands, closing my eyes whenever one of them got in a particularly nasty punch.

The front door opened, and Muddy called out, "There's an expensive rental car parked outside."

"Gianni," I replied.

Muddy came into the kitchen, her eyes widening when she stood next to me and witnessed the public display of masculinity going on outside.

"And they say nothing happens in Huckleberry Hill," Muddy murmured.

"We have to stop them," I said.

"Why?"

"Well, because . . ."

"Better to let them get it out of their systems," she said. "Declan's defending you. We should let him do it."

Despite the violence, my heart tripped with appreciation at Declan's action.

"So, should we make popcorn or . . ."

"Muddy, you're shameless."

"Are you going to give me the rundown of what happened?"

"Gianni showed up and was in the middle of proposing to me again when Declan walked in."

"He *what?*"

"Yeah." I looked behind me and down at the floor. "I think he might've dropped the ring when Declan socked him in the eye."

I looked outside and saw that the two of them had moved to opposite sides of the porch and were attempting to regain their breath.

"Oh, so Declan started the fight?"

"No, Gianni started the fight when he accused me of running home and jumping in bed with the first guy I saw and getting pregnant."

Muddy raised her brows.

I rolled my eyes. "Fine, so he wasn't wrong."

"And how did Gianni find out you were pregnant? Did you tell him when you refused his proposal?"

"Nope. Declan decided to drop that little piece of news for me," I said. "After he announced that he was my boyfriend."

"Someone was feeling a little territorial."

"Is it wrong that I liked it?" I asked. "Help me find the ring, would you? I think the fight is over."

"Yep, I think you're right."

I found the engagement ring underneath the china hutch. I was just pulling it out and dusting it off when the sliding glass door opened.

Gianni and Declan came inside. Declan's lip was busted and he had a lump on his jaw. But Gianni's nose was crooked and bleeding bad, and one of his eyes was beginning to swell shut.

"Gianni, is it?" Muddy asked.

He nodded.

"I'm Hadley's grandmother," Muddy explained.

"Nice to meet you," he mumbled.

"Can you guys give us a minute?" I asked, looking at Declan and then at Muddy.

"Sure thing, sugar. Come on, Declan. Let's go ice that lip."

Declan walked toward me and stopped. "You okay?" he whispered.

"I should be asking you that," I whispered back.

"I'm fine." He touched my cheek and then kissed my forehead. "Come find me when you're done?"

I nodded.

"Come on, Tempest." Muddy scooped up the goat and the three of them left. The front door shut, leaving me alone with a man I'd once loved. A man who now felt like he belonged to another version of me. A version of me who had lived another life.

A lesser version of me.

I held out the engagement ring to him. "Even if there was no Declan and there was no baby, I still wouldn't go back to New York with you. You told you me you loved me. You told me my infertility was something you could deal with. But then you did the one thing in the world that you can never come back from—you *left* me, Gianni. You left me and you didn't look back and now it's too late. I don't want to be with someone who isn't strong enough to stay with me through thick and thin."

He stared at the ring, and the with a deep, regretful sigh, he took it back. Gianni opened his mouth like he wanted to speak, but at the last moment, he closed his lips.

There wasn't anything more to say.

CHAPTER FORTY-TWO

The Ranch

Declan sat on the front porch of the cabin, nursing a beer. His lip had stopped bleeding, but his jaw was definitely bruised.

"Is he gone?" Declan asked unnecessarily.

I nodded. "He's staying in town for the night though. At the Regal Beagle."

The Regal Beagle had once been an old bar and brothel that serviced the miners of Huckleberry Hill during the silver rush in the late 1800s. It was built up in the Roaring '20s and then boarded up during the Great Depression. It sat there for decades untouched until Huckleberry Hill grew big enough to support a bed and breakfast. The decor was still Victorian grandma-core at its finest, and over the reception desk was a picture of the owner's beagle wearing a crown; hence the name.

"I don't like the bastard," Declan said. "But his eye was swelling shut. Was he safe to drive?"

My lips twitched. "I had Dad drive him."

"Did you now?" Declan's slow grin stretched across his face and then he winced when his lip split open again. "Damn it."

I raised the bakery bag. "Want one?"

He shook his head. "Those are all for you."

"Okay then. I'm going for it." I dove into the bag and pulled a cookie out and bit into it.

"Why didn't you tell him who I was?" Declan asked finally. "For that matter, why didn't you tell him you were pregnant?"

"First of all, you walked in right after he arrived and second, I was trying to avoid something like that," I said, pointing at his lip. "Did you break his nose?"

"Yep. His nose was too perfect to begin with." He paused. "You didn't tell me he was handsome."

"Not *that* handsome." I tried to keep the smile inside. I was starting to really like my new jealous, possessive Declan.

"Seriously, Hadley. Were you going to tell him who I was? Or tell him anything about me if I hadn't shown up?"

"No. I wasn't going to tell him about you or the baby."

"Why the fuck not?"

I looked at him, my brow furrowing. "Because it wasn't about you or the baby. It was about me."

He swallowed. "Go on."

"He wanted me to go back to New York with him. He wanted to pick up where we left off, start all over again or whatever. And I told him that he walked out on me the minute things got tough. He thought he could tell me how much he missed me, and that Italy wasn't the same without me. He thought I still felt the same way about him that I had before. But I don't. I really don't, Declan. I didn't tell him that after I fell in love with you I realized it was never like that with me and him. There's no reason to hurt him like that. What's done is done."

I fell silent and looked at the bakery bag. And then I spoke again. "I think I fell out of love with him the moment he left me. Because I never once begged God or the universe or whatever for him to come back to me. I never wanted him to come here. You have to believe me, Declan. I love *you*. And I love you in a way I never loved Gianni."

"I believe you," he said gruffly. "I just needed to hear it."

I laughed. "If anything, seeing Gianni in person made me realize how much I've moved past it all. Past him, past that life. Past the loss of what could've been."

I looked at his hand. "I want to hold your hand, but your knuckles look swollen."

"They are, but it doesn't matter." He took my hand in his. I made sure to hold it loosely.

"So about you not being possessive or jealous . . ."

He arched a brow. "He had it coming."

"Oh, he definitely did." I gasped. "Shit."

"What?" Declan asked.

"I was in the middle of a conversation with the girls when Gianni showed up. They keep bugging me to open the rest of my boxes."

"Let's go," he said, rising. He opened the cabin door and Tempest trotted out onto the porch.

I picked her up and we walked back to the main house. It was quiet. Dad hadn't returned yet and Muddy had made herself scarce.

We went up to my bedroom and I set Tempest down onto the bed. Declan dragged the few remaining boxes out of my closet and sat on the edge of the mattress.

He handed me his knife and I cut open a box. Shoes. I cut open another. More clothes. The third box . . . jackpot.

I held up a black lace teddy.

"No," Declan said, his eyes darkening.

"Oh, yeah." I peeked into the box. "A whole box of lingerie. Neatly stacked and folded with tissue paper."

Declan groaned. "God, it's been forever since I've been inside you."

"Call it foreplay, Declan," I said with a laugh. I felt around in the box, wondering if there was anything else I hadn't seen yet.

An envelope was at the bottom of the box. I glanced at Declan and opened it and took out a heavy piece of cream stationary.

Dear Hadley,

I love you and hate you at the same time. I know you're happy, and the right choice was to leave New York, but I miss you every day. It's not the same having you across the country, but I get it. My life is here, yours is there. I'll come home for a visit when the distance is too much, and I have to see you.

The girls and I got you every piece of lingerie we saw on your private not-so-private Pinterest board. Seriously, get a stronger password.

Miss you, love you, and if Declan is reading this then tell him I give my blessing.

Love, Salem

P.S. Lingerie is expensive, dude. And if anyone asks, it wasn't me who sold Gianni's clothes at a consignment shop. Also, it wasn't me who signed him up for a gay dating app.

With a laugh, I brought the note to my chest. And then I handed it to Declan. He quickly scanned it and let out a booming laugh.

I heard the sound of the front door open. "Hadley!"

"Crap," I muttered, closing up the box of lingerie. "Quick, get this in the closet."

"We really need to move back into the cabin," Declan said, as he placed his beer bottle on my nightstand. He got up and put the box into the closet.

"Up here!" I called out.

I heard the heavy tromp of my father's footsteps and a moment later my door opened.

"What are you guys doing up here?" he asked.

"Nothing," Declan and I said at the same time.

"Right," Dad drawled.

"Is Gianni still alive?" I asked.

"Yes. Unfortunately," Dad said. He looked at Declan. "You did some serious damage to his pretty-boy face."

"Sure did," Declan agreed.

"Saved me the trouble. Thanks, Declan."

"My pleasure."

"I think we deserve a beer," Dad said.

"One step ahead of you." Declan gestured to the night-stand where his nearly empty beer bottle rested.

"Ah, I better catch up then," Dad said. "It's three p.m. anyway. Perfect time to celebrate."

"Celebrate what?" I asked.

"Declan defending your honor," Dad said. "Among other things."

"What other things?"

"Let's go downstairs," Dad suggested. "Muddy should be back any moment."

Declan and I exchanged a glance. Dad was being unusually cryptic. He left the room, leaving us no choice but to follow. Tempest was the first one out the door.

By the time we made it downstairs, Dad had already grabbed himself a beer and made himself comfortable in the den.

"Sparkling water? Ginger ale?" Declan asked me.

"Water's fine," I said as I took a seat on the couch.

Tempest jumped up into my father's lap and draped herself across him. Declan returned to the den with my water just as the front door opened.

"We're in the den!" Dad called out.

Muddy appeared, her long braid slung over one shoulder. "You didn't say anything yet, did you?"

"I waited for you," Dad said.

"Can I get you a drink?" Declan asked. "We're having beer."

"Beer. This is not a beer conversation. Whiskey." She sat down on the couch next to me. She set her big, brown leather bag on her lap and riffled through it, pulling out a manilla envelope.

"What's that?" I asked.

"Patience," she admonished.

Declan handed her a drink and then sat on the brick bench of the hearth and waited.

"Go ahead," Muddy said to Dad.

"You sure?" he asked.

"I'm sure."

"Okay." Dad smiled. "Well, normally, I'd wait to give you this gift until after you were married." He shot Declan a look.

"Patience," Declan quipped.

"But since these are extenuating circumstances," Dad went on. "We thought it was fitting."

Muddy handed me the envelope. I unsealed it and pulled out a deed. "Is this what I think it is?"

"Yes," Muddy said with a smile.

"What is it?" Declan asked.

I held it out to him, and he took it. He glanced between Dad and Muddy. "You're gifting us land on the ranch?"

"A hundred acres to build your own house and start a life," Dad explained. "You're going to need the space. That cabin isn't big enough for you or your family . . . or your goat."

I let out a surprised laugh. "Oh my God!"

Declan rose from his seat and walked to Dad. Dad moved Tempest to his chair and stood.

"Thank you," Declan said, his tone somber. He looked at Muddy. "Both of you."

"Welcome to the family, son," Dad said.

I watched my boyfriend embrace his future father-in-law and brushed away the tears in my eyes.

Muddy patted my thigh and I all but launched myself at her. "Thank you," I whispered.

"Anything for you, sugar."

I pulled away. "You know what this means, right?"

"What?" Declan asked.

I grinned. "I get more goats!"

CHAPTER FORTY-THREE

Town

"No," Declan said.

I lifted Tempest toward his face. "Please?"

"No," he said again, but his voice lacked any firmness.

"But I bought her a harness. If she were a dog, we'd take her."

"But she's not a dog, and we're not going to be *those* people."

"What people?"

"Those people who have to bring their baby goat wherever they go. We'll have to find goat friendly restaurants. Goat friendly bars."

"We're in Huckleberry Hill," I stated. "Everything is goat friendly."

He sighed and ran a hand through his dark hair.

"Come on, *you know you want to*," I said with a smile.

"Fine," he relented. "We'll take Tempest to the Mushroom Festival."

"Yay! You made us both very happy!"

"Let's get ready and get out of here," he said. "You're feeling okay, right?"

"Hmm. Yeah, I feel fine," I assured him.

"Your side?"

"Tender, but it no longer hurts when I breathe." I looked at him through my lashes. "Good enough to . . . ya know."

"Ya know?" He raised his brows.

"Don't make me say it."

"Say it."

"Good enough to be hogtied and rode hard."

"*Ma'am.*" Declan widened his eyes.

"I'm in love with a cowboy." I shrugged. "May as well take full advantage."

"I know you're recovered, but maybe we should ease into that." He kissed the end of my nose. "Come on, let's go to the festival and talk about this later."

"I don't want to talk about this later. I want to talk about this now. Do I need to stamp my foot and throw a tantrum to get your attention?"

"No, you definitely don't need to throw a tantrum to get my attention. I know where you're at."

"You don't want to touch me anymore, do you?" I asked.

"What? Are you crazy? I'm going out of my mind not touching you," he said.

"So let's remedy that." I pressed my hand to his chest and stepped closer.

He covered my fingers with his. "I just want to make sure you're okay."

"I'm okay. The doctor said everything looks good and as soon as I felt well enough to be intimate, that I could be. Well, I'm ready. I'm so ready I'm about to hump your leg like a dog in heat."

"There's a visual," he whispered huskily.

"Please, Declan," I whined.

"I love it when you beg." He nipped at my lips.

I opened to him, and his tongue swept inside my mouth. His other hand cradled my head, keeping me exactly where he wanted me.

A cell phone rang.

"Ignore it," I begged against his mouth. "Take me to bed."

"If I take you to bed now," he murmured. "We'll miss the festival. And we can't miss the festival."

"Why not?"

"Because."

I frowned. "That's not an answer."

"It's our first year together at the Mushroom Festival. I'm going to be walking a baby goat in a harness."

I smiled. "You really want to go to this festival."

"I really do."

"Why?"

"Why? Because I live here."

"Uh-huh."

"And we're together. I want us to be together and do things in public like a real couple."

"You're adorable."

"I know." He preened.

I reluctantly moved away from him and went to his closet.

He walked to the nightstand and checked his phone. "I think that was the phone call about the brand deal."

"Oh yeah?" I asked.

"Yeah. Finish getting dressed. I'm gonna go handle this. Meet me out here when you're ready."

"Okay."

He kissed me once again and then left the bedroom, shutting the door behind him.

After the spring storm, the weather had finally turned. It

was warm enough for me to wear a sundress but I still needed a light jacket. My favorite was a red and white polka-dot dress with a flouncy skirt and spaghetti straps.

I sat on the edge of the bed and put on a pair of socks and then went into the living room, Tempest trotting out behind me.

Declan had just hung up his phone and he turned to look at me. He whistled in appreciation. Tempest thought that meant she was being summoned and went over to him.

"You're gorgeous."

I did a slow turn for him and then at the last second, flipped up my skirt to show him what he was missing.

"God, woman," he moaned. He walked to the hat rack and put on his cowboy hat. His flannel shirt was rolled up to the elbows and he was wearing a pair of jeans that made me want to bite the meaty part of his butt.

"Stop staring at me like that," he warned.

"Like what?"

"Like you've seen me naked."

I grinned.

Declan put Tempest into her harness and then clipped the leash to it. "This is ridiculous."

"Nothing hotter than a man walking his baby goat," I said. "Stay close to me. I'm worried some other woman will try and kidnap you and take you home."

"I won't leave your side," he promised. "Are Muddy and Connor going to the festival?"

"They're already there," I said. "Are you going to tell me about the phone call?"

He opened the front door and went onto the porch. "I'll tell you on the drive."

"Where's my jean jacket?" I asked, looking around at the cabin—the cabin that had exploded with a bunch of stuff I'd gotten from New York.

"Already in the truck," he said. "I put it in there for you. Along with a water bottle and some snacks."

"Yeah, definitely stay close to me. When other women find out how attentive and amazing you are, I'm going to have to beat them off with a stick."

I slid into my cowboy boots and closed the cabin door behind me.

"Is it wrong that I like you jealous?" he joked.

"I'm not jealous." I tossed my hair over my shoulder. "But I will cut someone if they flirt with you."

He smiled. "No, not jealous at all."

Declan opened the passenger side door of the truck for me, and when I climbed in, he put Tempest on my lap. She immediately moved to the seat between us. Declan closed the door and then walked around the truck and got into the driver's side.

When we'd made it down the long driveway, Declan finally started talking.

"The coffee company is looking to push various roasts into every smokehouse in the country. Wasn't as simple as a photo shoot and a paycheck. They need me to get back on a horse and tour the country and sell the product along the way. They drove a hard bargain and didn't want to take no for an answer. They kept throwing out numbers that were hard to say no to . . ."

"Oh yeah?" I looked at him.

"Yeah." He shrugged. "But when they said it meant I'd have to hit the road again I told them no amount of money was going to pull me away from my family. They finally gave up. They left the door open for me to change my mind though." He took one hand off the steering wheel and reached over and touched my belly. "But there's nothing that can pull me out of retirement."

"You sure?" I asked, biting my lip.

"I don't want to be away from you and I don't need the money. I wasn't entirely honest with you."

Anxiety spiked through my chest. "Oh?"

"I told you I had a nest egg?"

"Yeah."

"It's more than a nest egg, Hadley. I did really well on the rodeo circuit and I didn't blow it on stupid shit. I've made some investments . . ."

"Meaning?"

He looked at me and grinned. "Meaning, I can build you the house of your dreams."

I covered his hand with mine and stroked him. "No regrets then?"

"None."

"Jeez, you're perfect."

He laughed. "I'm glad you think so."

Downtown was already buzzing and Silver Street had been blocked off from parking. We drove down a side street near Sweet Teeth to try and find an alley to park in and saw swarms of people.

"Whoa," Declan said. "You think this is festival traffic or Sweet Teeth traffic?"

"Both? I thought for sure Sweet Teeth would've slowed down at least a little bit since their video, but it's been this way for at least a week."

Declan finally found a spot three blocks away. We got out of the truck and I set Tempest on the ground, ensuring I had a good handle on her leash.

We headed in the direction of downtown, passing neighborhood houses that had been around since the inception of the town. They were painted cheery, bright colors and for the festivities they'd decorated their porches with mushroom paraphernalia. One house had a full-sized stained-glass morel mushroom in the window.

Declan and I walked hand in hand toward the fray. A jam band playing 90s country covers had set up in the middle of the festival. There were booths of all kinds. Arts and crafts, mushroom tonics, foods featuring mushrooms.

My stomach rumbled.

Declan laughed. "I heard that."

I tugged him toward the booth that had meat pies with mushrooms. "I forgot my purse."

"I'm your wallet, Hadley," he said with a chuckle, handing over bills to the cashier.

I gave Tempest's leash to Declan and took the meat pie. I carefully unwrapped the foil and my mouth watered at the smell of spices and a homemade pastry shell.

Declan and I moved off to the side to enjoy the food. I was in the middle of a bite when I heard, "Mia, can I pet the goat?"

"Ask first," a petite brunette said.

A gangly dark-haired boy who couldn't be older than thirteen approached. "Do you mind if I pet your goat?"

"Sure thing," Declan said. "She likes people."

The boy crouched down and held his hand out to Tempest. "This is so cool."

"You've seen a goat before." Mia smiled. "At the Texas State Fair, remember? You even got to milk one."

"Yeah, but I've never seen a goat on a leash," the boy replied with a grin. He shoved his too-long hair out of his eyes.

Tempest leaned against his knee, eager for more attention.

"Where's Colt?" the boy asked. "Scarlett would love to pet a goat."

"He's buying her that stuffed mushroom plush toy. The one she wouldn't let go of. They'll catch up to us in a minute."

She looked at me and smiled. "My toddler was about to have a meltdown. We're not above bribery."

I laughed. "Well, you have to do what you have to do. Where are you guys visiting from?"

"What, you don't think we're locals?" Mia asked with a wry grin.

"Sorry, the slight Southern twang gave it away," I said, handing the half-eaten pie to Declan in offering. He took it and gave me the leash.

"We're from Waco, Texas. But my dad lives in Coeur d'Alene. I heard about the bakery here—what's it called, Sweet Teeth? Yeah, I think that's it. I saw something on social media and we decided to pop over. We had no idea there was a festival going on."

A tall, burly, heavily tattooed man approached, wearing a baby carrier with a toddler perched on his back. She was clutching a fuzzy mushroom toy for all it's worth.

"You caught up to us," Mia said, kissing his cheek. "Silas found a goat to pet."

"A goat on a leash," the man said. "Never seen that before."

"Sorry, I didn't introduce myself," Mia said. "I'm Mia. This is my husband, Colt."

Colt held out his hand to Declan.

"Declan."

"Nice to meet you," Colt said.

"I'm Hadley." I pointed to the goat. "That's Tempest."

"Silas, and Scarlett," Mia said, referencing the children. "So this town is a little treasure."

"It is," I agreed.

"Are you from here?" Colt asked.

"Born and raised," I explained. "My family owns a ranch about fifteen minutes out of town."

"A ranch?" Silas perked up, and he looked at Declan. "Wait, are you a cowboy?"

"Sure am," Declan said with a grin. "I have a motorcycle too."

"No kidding," Colt said. "What do you ride?"

The two of them started comparing their motorcycles and moved toward each other, leaving me to talk to Mia.

"Is there a good real estate agent in town?" she asked, pitching her voice lower.

"Just one," I admitted with a grin. "We don't have the need for a lot of real estate agents. Our town is only about eight hundred people."

"Hmm." Mia looked around. "That might change soon."

"I hope not. I love my small town."

"I get it. Once a place is discovered it gets overrun. I love how small and quaint it is here. Did that sound condescending? I didn't mean for it to come out that way, but my God, it's like a freakin' movie set here."

I smiled. "You weren't condescending in the least. So you're thinking of moving here?"

"Oh, no, not permanently. But maybe a vacation home or something. Plus, it's an easy drive to Coeur d'Alene."

"If you think it's pretty now, you should see it in autumn," I said dreamily. "So, the agent's office is actually at the end of Silver Street."

"We're on Silver Street, right?"

"Right. This is our main street."

"Why isn't it named Main Street?"

I shrugged. "We do things differently in Huckleberry Hill."

"Huckleberry Hill. You've got the charm baked right into this place, don't you?"

I laughed. "We absolutely do."

CHAPTER FORTY-FOUR

Town

Silas reluctantly pulled himself away from Tempest and we said goodbye.

"Nice family," Declan said.

"Very nice," I agreed. "Cute kids, too."

"Our kids are going to be that cute," Declan said as he chucked the foil from the meat pie into a garbage can.

His words, spoken so easily, warmed my insides. I took his hand, and we continued to amble. I admired trinkets I had no use for and said hello to several people I knew.

"Can we stop at Sweet Teeth?" I asked. "I want to say hi to Gracie."

"Sure thing. We have to get in line though. And are you sure your dad and Muddy are here? We haven't seen them yet."

"We'll probably bump into them."

The line to Sweet Teeth snaked out the door, but it was

only ten-people deep. As we were waiting, I saw Dr. Swanson—Jane—walking hand-in-hand with my father.

"Well, look at that," I said, nudging Declan and gesturing with my chin. "I think they've reconciled."

"If you love your father, you won't give him shit about it."

"It's because I love him that I *will* give him shit," I said with a grin. "But not in front of Jane."

Dad saw me and waved. "Hi."

"Hi." I looked at Jane. "How are you?"

"Good," she said. "I hear congratulations are in order."

"Uh, thanks. Dad told you?" I frowned at him. "He said he wasn't going to say anything until I was ready to tell people."

"I didn't tell her," Dad stated in confusion. "I kept your confidence about the news."

"Then how does she know?" I demanded.

"Lucy," Jane said.

"How does Lucy know?" I looked at Declan. "Did *you* tell her?"

"No. I didn't tell her."

Wade approached, holding hands with Chelsea. "It was your ex," Wade said, clearly having overheard the conversation.

"How do you know that?" I asked.

"Before he drove out of town, he stopped into General Merc. Lucy plied him with questions, what with him being a stranger and all busted up. He dumped all over her and then stormed out of the store."

"What, were you there too?" I asked.

"Yeah, actually, I was." Wade looked sheepish. "Congratulations, you guys."

"Thanks," I muttered. "Jane? When did you hear about my news?"

"Yesterday," she admitted. "I was at the diner when Lucy was gabbing with Eloise."

"Who's Eloise?" Declan asked. "I haven't met an Eloise."

"Eloise owns Poofant—the only hair salon in town," I said with a pained expression. "Eloise also can't keep her mouth shut."

"Which means . . ." Wade trailed off.

"Which means?" Chelsea repeated.

"Half the town already knows I'm knocked up with your baby," I said, looking up at Declan.

Dad made a noise of distress. Jane put a hand to his chest. "Easy there."

"I should've killed Gianni when I had the chance," Dad said, his overprotective streak coming out.

"Yeah, you should've," Declan agreed.

"Hey." Dad glared at him. "My daughter wouldn't be in this position if you'd kept the stallion in the barn."

Muddy strode up to us, enjoying an ice cream cone. "It's a party. What did I miss?"

"Hadley's ex-fiancé told Lucy about Hadley being pregnant with Declan's baby. And Lucy told Eloise," Chelsea said. "Right? I got all that right?"

"You got all that right," Jane said. "And Connor and Declan are getting into it because Connor blames Declan for Hadley's situation."

"It's not a *situation*," I muttered. "It's a baby. And we're all happy about it."

"Hey, Hadley!" Mr. Jenkins called out as he was walking by. "Congratulations on the baby!"

"Fuck," Declan muttered.

"Thank you!" I called back. To Declan, I said, "Have you met Mr. Jenkins?"

"No."

"He owns Dusty's," I explained. "And likes to gossip with his customers behind the meat counter."

"Why is it called Dusty's if his name is Jenkins?" Declan asked.

Everyone was quiet as they looked to each other for an explanation.

"No idea," Muddy finally said. "Well, the cat's out of the bag now. There's no keeping this under wraps anymore."

Tempest bleated at Muddy. Muddy looked down at her. "No, you're not getting any of my ice cream."

"Will you hold the leash?" I asked, handing it to Muddy. "The line into the bakery is about to move."

"Got her," Muddy said.

"Can I get anybody anything?" I asked.

They shook their heads.

"We're going to keep exploring," Wade said. "See you guys later."

Chelsea and Wade walked off just as the line moved inside. Gracie and her husband Cole were behind the counter. Her in-laws came out from the kitchen with trays of fresh baked goods.

"Hey guys," Gracie greeted with a bright smile. "Congratulations!"

I held in an internal sigh. "Who told you? Lucy or Eloise?"

"Neither. Amber Winston told me. She was a little snide, though."

"Who's Amber Winston?" Declan asked.

"The resident mean girl of our graduating class," Cole explained. "Congrats, dude."

Declan shook Cole's hand. "Thanks, man."

"We still need to have dinner," Gracie said. "Cole's parents will babysit Bella."

"Their one-year-old," I clarified. "Where is she?"

"Abby's younger sister is babysitting," Cole explained.

I ordered a chocolate milk, much to Declan's amusement, and a couple of pastries to go.

We got our orders and stepped outside the bakery and rejoined the group that was waiting for us.

"I've had enough of the festival," Muddy said, handing the leash to Declan. "I think I'm headed home. I'm that way."

"We'll walk with you," Dad said. "We haven't seen those booths yet."

We said goodbye and then Declan and I ambled the opposite direction. We stopped off in front of the jam band. Declan scooped Tempest into his arms and brought us both to his chest. Even though the song wasn't a slow one, it didn't matter.

With Tempest sandwiched between us, we danced together. He wrapped an arm around me and I pressed my cheek to his chest. I sighed and closed my eyes, breathing in the moment with this gorgeous man that had completely stolen my heart.

When the song ended, he reluctantly let me go and set Tempest down.

"There's a barn dance in the fall," I said, looking up at him. "You wanna go with me?"

"Trying to lock me down months in advance?" Declan teased. "Hell yeah, I'll go with you."

We wandered toward the end of the street and saw the Mountain Mutt Rescue booth with dogs up for adoption.

"Come on!" I squealed.

"Hang on," Declan said with a laugh, tightening his grip on Tempest's leash.

"Hi there," the volunteer greeted with a wide smile. Her blonde ponytail was nearly on top of her head and the name on her blue T-shirt with the rescue's name read Pam.

"Hi," I replied.

"It's been crazy!" Pam said. "We started the day with fifteen dogs. We only have four fur babies left. Let me know if you want to spend any time with them."

"We're just looking," Declan said. "We already have our hands full."

Pam looked at Tempest. "May I?"

"Sure thing," Declan offered.

Pam crouched down to pet Tempest.

I wandered through the tent. The four remaining puppies wagged their tails when they saw me approach. "So sweet," I murmured, wanting to give them all the love in the world.

"They're from the same litter," Pam explained. "Two boys and two girls. Nine-week-old Border Collie Aussie mixes. They need a lot of room to run and they'll do best with folks who understand that they're working dogs. They'll get depressed if they don't have room to roam and things to herd. Two of their siblings and their mama were already adopted."

"Perfect ranch dogs," I said.

"Yes, exactly," Pam agreed.

"Hadley . . ." Declan warned.

Tempest maneuvered around the crouched volunteer and went to investigate the puppies. Four waggly, furry butts signaled that Tempest wasn't a threat to them. One of the puppies rolled over onto its back and showed Tempest its belly.

"I'll take them," I blurted out.

"Great!" the volunteer said as she stood up. "Which one?"

"No, I mean I'll take *all of them*," I said again. I looked at Declan who cracked a smile and stared at me.

She frowned. "I'm not sure—"

"I'm Hadley Powell," I explained. "Connor Powell's daughter. We own Elk Ridge. It's a thousand acres of cattle ranch nestled in the mountains just north of here."

Her expression cleared. "Oh, you're *Hadley!* Congratulations on the baby!"

I paused. "Oh. Uh . . . thanks. So, the puppies?"

"Absolutely. Let me just start the paperwork . . ."

I looked at Declan and grinned. "You might want to go get the truck."

"Yes, dear. Am I taking Tempest with me?"

"Please." I leaned up to kiss his cheek and whispered, "Leave your credit card."

He sighed again. "Yes, dear."

CHAPTER FORTY-FIVE

THE RANCH

"Your father is going to kill me," Declan said, glancing behind him at the puppies in the back seat of the truck.

I reached behind me and pet one of the dogs and it began to nibble my finger. Tempest was back there and it was becoming clear that she thought she was one of the puppies.

"He'll be happy once he gets used to the crazy," I said. "The thing you have to understand about my father is that he says no first, but then he always comes around. It's his way. He's stubborn."

"Huh, like someone else I know."

"Oh stop." I laughed.

We'd made sure the puppies were empty before we put them in the backseat on a towel. By the time we got home, they were all asleep, nestled together in a ball of fur.

"You get to be the one to tell your dad," Declan said as he pulled into the driveway of the main house next to dad's vehicle.

"I'll take care of it," I assured him. I unlatched my seat belt.

"We need to talk about getting you a new car," Declan announced. "I don't like the idea of you driving a farm truck without all the bells and whistles of modern safety."

I sniggered. "*Now* you're being captain safety? Where were you with the condoms?"

"You told me I didn't need them," he said with a gaping mouth.

"I don't think I ever said that *explicitly*. It's hard to remember that night."

"Hard to remember? Seriously?"

"What led up to the conception," I drawled. "We'd had bourbon and I was so down bad for you it was all fuzzy static up there."

"Down bad." He shook his head. "Yeah. You so were."

"So were you," I pointed out.

"Never said otherwise." He leaned over and kissed me. "But also, we never had the conversation after that night either."

"Hmm. As Salem called it, we were raw-doggin' it from the beginning."

"No complaints on my end."

My gaze dropped to his mouth. "Me either."

"Stop stalling. Go tell your dad about the puppies."

"I'm not stalling. You're the one who brought up the new car idea."

"It was on my mind." He shrugged.

I opened the passenger side door and got out.

"Signal when it's safe."

I went up to the front porch and opened the door. Muddy was resting in her chair, crocheting the same project she'd been working on since I'd gotten home.

Dad was on the couch with Jane cuddled up next to him.

"Hey," Dad greeted. "Where's Declan?"

"Out in the truck," I said. "Can you come outside for a second?"

Dad frowned and nodded. "Everything okay?"

"Everything's perfect," I said with a smile. "I have a surprise for you."

"Uh-oh," Muddy said, setting her crocheting aside. "I better come see what it is too."

"Wait for me," Jane added.

The three of them followed me out of the house and to the truck. Declan was still in the driver's seat.

I opened the back door of the truck.

"Puppies?" Dad asked. "You brought home four puppies?"

"Yep," I said. "Declan paid for them."

Dad looked at Declan. "You didn't tell her no?"

"Have you tried telling Hadley no?" Declan defended. "It's impossible."

"How can you say no to puppies?" Jane asked, reaching her hand out and stroking the back of one of them.

"Like this: *no*." Dad attempted to back away.

"Stop being a grump," Muddy said, elbowing him and Jane out of the way. She picked up a puppy and thrust it into her son's arms. "You miss having a dog. Admit it."

"Now you have four," I said with a smile.

"Oh no." Dad shook his head. "They'll stay outside. They're outdoor dogs. Barn dogs. Ranch dogs. Not sleeping-on-the-bed dogs."

One of the puppies let out a whine and Jane picked it up and started crooning at it.

"What kind are they?" Muddy asked as she picked up another one of the puppies.

"Border Collie Aussie mixes," I said. "The volunteer didn't want to let them all go to one home until I explained I lived on a ranch."

Declan climbed out of the truck, gathering Tempest in his arms, leaving me to pick up the last puppy.

"No," Dad said, though his tone lacked conviction. "Absolutely not. We'll keep one of them. Maybe two. The other two can go to the Argentum Ranch. Max has been needing some good herding dogs."

The puppy in my father's arms lifted its head and licked Dad's chin. Dad looked down at it and I watched in real time as my father fell hard and fast for the little beast.

Without a word, he started toward the house.

"Where are you going?" Jane asked.

"Where do you think I'm going?" Dad growled. "I'm finding them a box to sleep in."

Declan pulled his buzzing cell phone out of his shirt pocket and looked at it. He stood and pushed away from the dinner table. "Will you excuse me for a moment? I'll be right back."

"Where are you going?" Muddy asked.

"My rodeo buddy is returning my phone call," Declan explained. To me he said, "The coffee thing again."

I nodded.

He pressed a button and put the cell to his ear and stalked from the house, the front door closing behind him.

"Coffee thing?" Muddy asked. "What does that mean?"

"His best friend is still on the rodeo circuit and he got a brand deal. It's a coffee company and they wanted Declan too, but Declan said no. Now he's telling his friend, Bowman, that he's officially saying no."

"A brand deal," Dad repeated. "He hasn't said anything about that."

"It's a recent development. And he was going to say no all along, so that's probably why he didn't tell you." I stood up and began to gather the dinner plates. "Jane? Are you finished?"

"I am," she said. "Let me help you with these."

"Thanks," I said.

We picked up the dishes and brought them to the sink.

"Why wasn't he going to take the brand deal?" Muddy asked. "It's good money I bet. Probably better than what your father pays him."

"Mom," Dad warned.

"Just stating a fact." Muddy shrugged. "There's no money in being a ranch hand and everybody knows it."

"He has no desire to go back to the rodeo circuit. Aside from potential injuries, he's very happy with his life. And if you must know, Declan's got a nest egg and investments from the rodeo circuit."

"That's good to hear," Dad grumbled. "Because if he thinks he can leave my pregnant daughter—"

"You really think Declan would do that?" I asked, turning and raising an eyebrow.

"Never doubted him for a second," Muddy said with a grin.

"Neither did I," Dad admitted. He stood up. "I'm going to go check on the puppies. Jane, you want to come with me?"

"Sure. Right after I help clean up."

"I'll take care of it," Muddy said. "You go snuggle some puppies."

"They're so sweet," Jane said.

"We still need names for them," Dad said.

"How about Hufflepuff, Ravenclaw, Slytherin, and Gryffindor?" Jane suggested with a smile.

"Those names sound familiar," Dad said. "But I'm drawing a blank."

"They're the Hogwarts houses," I said with a laugh.

"They don't roll off the tongue easily, though," Muddy

said. "Can you imagine yelling, *Hey Ravenclaw stop eating cow shit!*"

"Peter, Susan, Edmund and Lucy?" Jane pivoted. "The Pevensie siblings from *The Lion, The Witch, and the Wardrobe.*"

Dad's face paled and he made a hasty retreat.

Jane frowned. "What did I say?"

"My mother used to read that book to my sister and me when we were kids. The whole series, actually."

"Oh." Jane chewed on her lip. "I didn't know."

"Of course you didn't," Muddy assured her. "You're just bringing a lot of stuff to the surface. Stuff that Connor has never really dealt with."

She rubbed the back of her neck. "Just when I think we're about to make a real stride forward . . ."

"Keep going," Muddy told her. "He needs you. He needs to open up again."

Jane looked at me, and I nodded in agreement. "I think you're wonderful, and you make him smile in a way I haven't seen in a long time. You'll get no argument from me. And you're welcome at all our family dinners."

"Thanks, Hadley." She squeezed my hand. "I better go talk to him."

She went in the direction of my father and disappeared.

Muddy stood up. "She's good for him."

"I think so."

"Have you told Salem about her?" She began loading the plates into the dishwasher.

"No, I haven't. I don't really know what to say."

"How about the truth?"

"Yeah, but this isn't my thing to share, you know?"

Muddy was quiet for a moment and then she said, "She's going to lose her shit when she finds out."

"Yeah, she will," I agreed.

"And you don't want her to kill the messenger, right?"

"She'll kill me anyway. When she finds out I've known for a while. And when she finds out that Jane had dinner here *and* sat at Mom's place setting? Yeah, I do *not* want to be around Mount Saint Salem when that happens."

"You and me both, sugar." She sighed.

A phone chimed.

"Mine," she said. She picked it up from the counter and glanced at it. "Why don't you go find Declan? I can finish this up."

My gaze narrowed. "Who texted you?"

She gently pushed against my hip to get me moving in the direction of the door. "Go."

CHAPTER FORTY-SIX

THE RANCH

I stepped out onto the porch and slid into my most comfortable slippers. My jaw dropped when I saw that the walkway to Declan's cabin was lit with candles in mason jars, lighting my way underneath a starry night sky.

When I arrived at the cabin, I bent down and picked up a pair of candy-cane patterned socks resting on the lowest step.

The next pair of socks had Santa Claus on them. The pair after that had gingerbread men. I followed the trail of socks into the cabin.

"Declan?" I called out.

There was no answer.

I continued to follow the sock trail—all of them were Christmas themed. The path of socks led into the bedroom. The bottom drawer of the dresser was open and a pair was hanging out. And then only one sock with a mistletoe pattern hung out of the top drawer. I had to open it to get to its mate.

Something was inside the sock; an obvious, square-shaped object.

Declan appeared in the doorway and leaned against the doorjamb.

"Where did you come from?" I asked.

He grinned. "I was hiding in the bathroom."

I turned my attention back to the sock. "What's in there?"

"Why don't you find out?"

I picked up the sock and put my hand into it, my fingers encountering a smooth velvet box. I pulled it out and stared at it.

With a deep breath, I opened it.

A gorgeous, traditional diamond solitaire twinkled back at me.

"Declan," I whispered.

"I love you, Hadley." He pushed away from the doorjamb and came to me. His hands cradled my cheeks. "Marry me."

"Yes," I breathed helplessly.

He took the engagement ring from the jewelry box and slid it onto my finger. He then linked our hands and brought them to his chest. "Come to bed with me."

He undressed me slowly, like a present he wanted to cherish forever. He worshipped my body with his tongue and fingers, mindful that I still had some bruising on my side. But he was gentle and unhurried, drawing out my pleasure until I could no longer contain it.

And when he thrust into me, our eyes met and held. He began to move, and something built between us. Something I couldn't deny.

We'd already made a baby together.

I'd fallen in love with him.

But this . . .

This was something different.

Something that had no words, because words weren't enough to describe it. It was the feeling that I was home. That *he* was my home.

Across time.

Across space.

He was the home I'd been searching for and that I'd been blessed to find.

We came together, our simultaneous release powerful. So powerful it brought tears to my eyes.

He kissed the tears as they fell from my cheeks and then he held me close.

We didn't speak for a long time. Our hearts slowed and beat in rhythm, our skin cooled. He pulled the covers up around us.

"Your proposal was perfect," I murmured, brushing a kiss against his jaw.

"I'm glad you thought so. That call from Bowman was to get me away from the dinner table so I could light the candles and make a sock trail. Then I texted Muddy so she'd send you to the cabin."

I chuckled. "Christmas socks."

"Christmas baby."

"It was perfect." I snuggled deeper into him and held out my hand with the engagement ring. "This is stunning. You have good taste."

"It's an antique European diamond, but I had it placed in a modern, yet classic setting."

"When did you do this?" I asked, lifting myself up so I could look at him.

"If I tell you it's going to make me sound insane." He rubbed his jaw, the raspy sound of his whiskers thick against his skin. "The night after we slept together the first time."

"You didn't."

"Told you. I sound insane."

I kissed his nose, his cheeks, and then his lips. "Well, I'm insane about you, too. So I guess it worked out in the end."

"Yep."

I laid back down and closed my eyes. "Tempest is still with the puppies?"

"Yeah. She's going to stay the night with them."

"They've bonded."

I traced a pattern on his chest.

"I called your sister."

"When?" I asked.

"Few days ago. Told her what I was planning."

"Did you, now? The little sneak managed to keep it a secret from me. What did she say?"

"She gave her blessing, but she did warn me not to hurt you or I'd have to answer to her."

I sniggered. "You have to remember she's feral."

"Feral and protective," he said. He ran a hand up and down my back. "We need to pick a wedding date. And I'd like it to be sooner rather than later."

"June 3rd," I said.

"You said that fast." He paused. "That wasn't when you were getting married to the bastard, was it?"

"No," I assured him. I lifted myself up and looked at him. "It's my mother's birthday. I don't know, maybe it's weird. Maybe it'll taint our wedding anniversary, but I thought . . . I don't know. Maybe it'll ease the pain a bit? And it's like she'll be included even though she's not there."

He stroked a thumb across my cheek. "June 3rd is perfect."

I smiled and turned my head to kiss his wrist. "Is there anything you won't give me?"

"Doubt it."

I bit my lip.

"What?" he asked with a grin. "What do you want?"

I rolled on top of him and straddled him. His hands slid up my body and gently caressed my breasts. "I want to have my way with you."

His grin was slow. Hot. Devastating.

"Bear snack, you can have me any way you want me."

EPILOGUE

A couple months later

SALEM

I closed the door to the apartment and raised two brown bags to chest height. "We're celebrating."

Wyn and Poet were both on the couch underneath a shared blanket. Wynn dragged her eyes from the TV to look at me while Poet hit the clicker and paused the screen.

"Celebrating?" Wyn asked with a wide smile. "What are we celebrating?"

"Me." I grinned.

"I thought you were supposed to be out to dinner with your boss," Poet said in confusion. She set the book manuscript she was currently reading aside and thrust the blanket off her. "We didn't expect you home for at least another hour."

I placed the bags down onto the small kitchen table and pulled out to-go containers from the restaurant. "Boss forgot about his daughter's ballet recital, so when his wife called him to ask where he was, he left. He gave me an apology and said I could take all of our food to go. We hadn't even gotten our appetizers when he got the call."

Wyn came and inspected the bag. "What did you order?"

"Burrata. And the bucatini with guanciale."

Wyn moaned. "Gimme."

"Not without Prosecco," I said.

"I'll get it," Poet said as she wandered to the refrigerator.

"Did your boss get a chance to tell you what he wanted to discuss?" Wyn asked. She pulled out the plastic silverware and held it up.

"No, let's use real silverware," I said. "And yes, Jack told me the reason for our meeting."

Poet brought three champagne flutes to the table, along with the bottle. She opened it quickly. The cork popped and she poured out the Prosecco.

She handed us glasses. I held mine up to make a toast, my two best friends waiting eagerly for an explanation.

"He told me he wants me to be the creative director of the Rudolph Lancaster project."

"No!" Wyn gasped.

"Yes!"

Poet clinked her glass against mine. "Congratulations!"

"This is huge!" Wyn said.

I took a sip of Prosecco. "It *is* huge. I can't believe it. Who would've thought speaking without thinking would result in a promotion?"

Rudolph Lancaster was a young, hungry fashion brand that was interested in expanding their clothing line. At the moment they were heavily focused on the nautical, sailing theme in their lineup. Their equestrian and western line was promising, but the marketing firm they'd hired had completely botched their vision and they were looking for a fresh start.

They'd come to us—Beckett and Bastion—for a different direction. I'd sat in on the meeting with Jack Beckett, one of the owners and the Creative Director of the firm. He'd shown Rudolph Lancaster's current marketing plan for the equestrian, western line and before I even realized what I was doing, I'd spoken up and blurted out that nothing about it was authentic.

I'd grown up on a ranch—I knew authentic western styles, and I was in tune with wanting to look good and be comfortable while working a thousand acres of property. They were shocked at first, but after asking me a few questions it was clear I'd piqued their interest.

"Did you call Hadley and tell her the good news?" Poet asked.

I shook my head and popped open one of the to-go containers. "I'll call her after we eat."

The three of us devoured the food.

"No dessert?" Wyn asked with a pout as she finished the last bit of her meal.

Poet pushed up the nose of her dark glasses. "We can walk to the bodega and get some sweet treats."

"Oh, good idea," Wyn said. "What do you want, Salem?"

"Anything chocolate," I replied. "I'll clean up and call Hadley."

A twinge of sadness spread through my chest. Normally, she would've been the first person I called when I had news, good or bad.

But she was at the ranch with her fiancé and they a had baby on the way. And I was in New York living a different life.

We were moving in two opposite directions for the first

time in our lives. It scared me, but I wasn't sure there was anything I could do about it.

Wyn grabbed her phone and her wallet, and she and Poet were out the door. I began to clean up, chucking the empty to-go containers into the garbage and setting the dirty silverware in the sink. I'd wash them later. We didn't have a dishwasher in our pre-war apartment, but that wasn't uncommon in New York.

I was wiping my hands on a dishrag when my cell rang. I dug through my purse, finding it at the bottom.

Hadley's name flashed across the screen and I grinned, pressing answer. "Good timing, twin. I was just about to call you."

"Salem," she said, her tone grave.

My spine snapped straight. "What is it? What's wrong?"

"It's—you've got to come home, Salem. It's Dad. There's been an accident."

Thank you so much for reading! Scan the code to read a snippet between Declan and Hadley!

ADDITIONAL WORKS

Saddles & Spurs Series:

Huckleberry Hill (Book 1)

Lavender Lake (Book 2 - preorder)

The Tarnished Angels Motorcycle Club Series:

Wreck & Ruin (Tarnished Angels Book 1)

Crash & Carnage (Tarnished Angels Book 2)

Madness & Mayhem (Tarnished Angels Book 3)

Thrust & Throttle (Tarnished Angels Book 4)

Venom & Vengeance (Tarnished Angels Book 5)

Fire & Frenzy (Tarnished Angels Book 6)

Leather & Lies (Tarnished Angels Book 7)

Heartbeats & Highways (Tarnished Angels Book 8)

SINS Series:

Sins of a King (Book 1)

Birth of a Queen (Book 2)

Rise of a Dynasty (Book 3)

Dawn of an Empire (Book 4)

Ember (Book 5)

Burn (Book 6)

Ashes (Book 7)

Fall of a Kingdom (Book 8)

Others:

Peasants and Kings

ABOUT THE AUTHOR

Wall Street Journal & USA Today bestselling author Emma Slate writes romance with heart and heat.

Called "the dialogue queen" by her college playwriting professor, Emma writes love stories that range from romance-for-your-pants to action-flicks-for-chicks.

When she isn't writing, she's usually curled up under a heating blanket with a steamy romance novel and her two beagles—unless her outdoorsy husband can convince her to go on a hike.